Unbreak Me

Unbreak Me

◇◇◇◇◇◇

MICHELLE HAZEN

JOVE
NEW YORK

A JOVE BOOK
Published by Berkley
An imprint of Penguin Random House LLC
1745 Broadway, New York, NY 10019

Copyright © 2019 by Michelle Hazen

A JOVE BOOK, BERKLEY, and the BERKLEY & B colophon are registered trademarks of Penguin Random House LLC.

Library of Congress Cataloging-in-Publication Data

Names: Hazen, Michelle, author.
Title: Unbreak me / Michelle Hazen.
Description: First edition. | New York : Jove, 2019.
Identifiers: LCCN 2018043771 | ISBN 9781984803290 (pbk.) |
ISBN 9781984803306 (ebook)
Subjects: | GSAFD: Love stories.
Classification: LCC PS3608.A98884 U53 2019 | DDC 813/.6—dc23
LC record available at https://lccn.loc.gov/2018043771

First Edition: August 2019

Printed in the United States of America
1 3 5 7 9 10 8 6 4 2

Photo of sky by Calin Tatu/Shutterstock
Photo of horses by RapidEye/Getty Images
Cover design by Colleen Reinhart

To New Orleans,
because there's no place else like it on this earth.

Thank you.

One

◇◇◇◇

A perfect barn was like a perfect woman: suspicious.

LJ Delisle didn't have much experience with perfection, which was why he was giving a little side-eye to the stable's immaculate floor. As he explored up the aisle, brass name plaques glinted at him from the stall doors. The horses themselves were glossy and muscular but so manicured there was no sign that they'd ever broken a sweat.

He stopped to pet one's velvety nose. "You been juicin', hmm? Don't lie to me now." The gelding whickered, blowing speckles of snot all over his white job-interview shirt.

LJ chuckled. Well, the horses seemed normal enough, even if the stable was straight out of a magazine shoot. He left his new friend and stuck his head into the tack room. "Anybody here?"

No answer from the racks of saddles.

Probably he was just uncomfortable because this was so different from where he grew up. There was nowhere as beautiful as New Orleans, and few places as screwed up. The crumbling brick sidewalks he loved were edged by jagged potholes and scattered with glass from windows broken by burglars and vandals. The red sizzle of boiling crawfish spiced the air, and humidity squatted heavy over the ever-threatening river. Mud backed up into the streets with every hard rain, a reminder of the sharp edge between civilization and chaos.

To LJ, flaws felt like home.

He continued down the barn aisle, reminding himself not to get his back up when this caliber of facility was exactly what he'd come to Montana to find. Along with a fresh start and a chance to train horses his way. Besides, getting out of the Deep South was just about the only choice for a black man who wanted to break into the exclusive club of the horse-showing circuit.

Now he just needed to find the person who was supposed to be interviewing him and convince them the spritz of horse snot on his shirt only increased his qualifications as a trainer.

He reached the exit on the far side of the barn, and his strides stuttered as he saw the horse outside in the arena.

"Glory hallelujah," he muttered.

The Lawler Ranch quarter horses looked classy in their stalls, but in movement they were the difference between a Dumpster full of sheet music and a song. The stallion outside was all muscle, his tail as dark as the long braid of the woman riding him. He was giving her hell, trying to buck, but instead of fighting him, she funneled all that energy into grace. The horse's hooves floated over the ground as it transitioned to a half pass as seamlessly as an Olympian.

LJ leaned a shoulder against the barn doorframe and watched. It was how people were meant to ride. Not battling for dominance or jerking at the reins. Flowing, all the potential of two beings focused on one goal.

He forgot all about brass nameplates and just soaked it in.

Eventually, the woman dismounted and walked her stallion toward the barn. LJ shook off his daydreaming and stepped back out of sight, trying to buy time. When people met him, their brows usually rose right along with their eyes as they looked up, then up some more. Six and a half feet was too much for most, so he liked to have a smile and a quip at the ready to put them at ease. Except watching her ride had wiped his mind clean of jokes.

She had to be Andra Lawler, the name at the bottom of the emails that had invited him to drive to Lawler Ranch for the "extensive, in-person interview process." Anybody who rode that well must be in charge of hiring the other trainers.

Even off the horse, she drew his eyes. Her walk was all grace and confidence, the stallion following along meekly at her heels. As she got closer, the pale skin and delicate features under the shadow of her hat became clearer. She hadn't seen him yet, but even in relaxation the lines of her face teased at his imagination like a story only half told.

LJ approached the doorway, taking a breath to introduce himself and raising his hand to shake hers.

She crossed the line of shadow cast by the barn and walked straight into his outstretched hand, his fingertips bumping her ribs. Her chin jerked up and a scream ripped out of her, so unexpected and loud that LJ startled, too. The stallion reared, his hooves flashing as the woman flinched away from LJ and into the far greater danger behind her.

LJ grabbed her and yanked her out of the way. The scream cut off into eerie silence, and her muscles tensed under his hands. Goose bumps broke out on the back of his neck, his instincts shrilling all the alarms at how fast this whole situation had gone wrong. Before he could try to diffuse whatever the hell this was, she jerked away from him and fell. Her sunglasses jumped off her nose with the impact of ass on concrete, but instead of reaching for them, she gasped for air and her wide green eyes unfocused. She didn't even seem to register the stallion, who reared again. His hooves pawed the air inches from her unprotected head. Close. Way too damned close.

LJ jumped in front of her and caught the reins, swinging his body in between the frightened horse and the woman on the ground.

"Andra!" a male voice sounded from behind him.

LJ started to look, but then the stallion tried to bolt and the reins burned through his fingers. He blew out a breath and steadied himself, speaking low and sweet to the horse until it quieted, too. As soon as he could, LJ turned to check on the woman. She was still on the ground, hunched convulsively forward with an older man crouched at her side. Solid shoulders filled out his faded shirt even as a potbelly tested the last button above his belt buckle. "Talk to me, sweetheart," he said.

No response.

"Your horse," the man tried. "Andra, your horse!"

"It's okay. I have it under—" LJ stopped as the man flapped a hand at him, not glancing away from Andra.

As soon as he mentioned her responsibilities, she blinked, taking a small breath. Then she shot to her feet, glancing around. She registered the horse first. Then LJ, her lashes widening in the belated reaction to his height he'd been expecting. He didn't have a joke ready this time, either.

He swapped the reins to his left hand and put out his right. "I'm LJ Delisle. And damned sorry I startled you that way."

Her throat worked, her shoulders tense beneath the old T-shirt that said, "Eat. Sleep. Ride." She took his hand, her grip strong and certain despite the sweat dampening her palm. "No, I'm sorry. I didn't expect anybody to be standing there."

"That'd be your cue to explain what in the blazing hell you're doing in my barn, son." The challenge came from the older man's mouth with all the softness of a pistol being cocked. Beside them, the stallion's ears swiveled forward, and he danced at the end of the reins.

LJ snapped up taller, bristling, then slapped on a smile to cover it. It was a fair question, however little he appreciated the other man's wording. "I was about half an hour early for my interview. Nobody answered the door at the house, so I came on up to the barn."

"Interview for what? We're not hiring."

Or maybe they *were* hiring until he scared his future boss flat on her ass. He'd seen a lot of people get leery at the breadth of his shoulders, but her reaction was a long way past normal.

"Dad, were you listening to me last month at all?" Andra's voice was tight. "If we had somebody to get the colts from weaned to saddle broke, Jason and I could train a lot more horses per year. We might even have a shot at matching demand for once." Her father opened his mouth, and she glared at him.

"Uh, I'm happy to wait up at the house until my scheduled time." LJ glanced between father and daughter, then offered the stallion's reins to Andra.

"No, it's okay." She swept her sunglasses off the floor and waved them toward the stallion now standing patiently at his side. "That can count as your first interview question."

A smile tickled his lips. "Hell, if all you needed was to see if I could hold a horse, you might as well start filling out my W-4s."

"That won't be necessary," Mr. Lawler said. "We're not hiring."

Andra scowled at her father, the pallor that followed her attack starting to give way under a flush of anger. "You agreed to let me place the ad."

"I agreed if an appropriate candidate came along . . ." He cleared his throat.

LJ's jaw locked, and this time, he put the reins in Andra's hands without asking permission. "I'll wait at the house," he said to her. "If you want to speak to me about a job, that's where I'll be."

He headed for the exit, his insides all fists and fire. He was all too aware that he'd just turned his back on the owner: an owner who'd decided after his first glance that he wasn't an "appropriate candidate" for employment. His new chance here was cinders, and there was no point even glancing at the beautiful horses he passed.

His friends had warned him how it would be out west, but fool he was, he figured anyplace had to have more opportunity for a black cowboy than southern Louisiana.

"You agreed I could pick someone I was comfortable with," Andra's voice hissed behind him as he tried to shut out the sounds of the argument he was leaving behind.

"Comfortable? He wasn't here five minutes and you were having a panic attack!" Mr. Lawler protested. "I don't care about training more horses per year, Andra. What I care about—" Mr. Lawler's voice was lost in the snap of the breeze as LJ's long legs carried him farther from the barn.

Even if she wanted to give him the job, he'd probably always be in the middle of an argument between her and her father. That wasn't going to earn him the freedom he wanted to try his own, gentler training methods.

LJ hesitated, thinking of Andra's kind hands on that stallion's reins. But then his gaze fell on his old pickup, parked in front of the Lawlers' log-and-river-rock mansion. He'd left his secondhand suit-cases stashed by last night's campsite, but the rust-fringed dent in his driver's-side door told the whole story he was trying to hide. And it wasn't one of years of experience with the caliber of horses who were named in sentences instead of single syllables.

When he graduated college and chose the stables over an office, he knew it'd probably be ten years or more before he was training horses instead of shoveling up after them. Which is why when he'd gotten Andra's email asking him to interview for a trainer position rather than a groom, he should have known it was too good to be true.

"Mr. Delisle!"

Her flat accent mangled his name so badly he almost didn't recognize it. She jogged up to his side.

"I'm sorry," she said. "I asked you all this way, and I do want to interview you. I'm sorry about my dad." She glanced away, a wisp of black hair blowing against her cheek. She was younger than she sounded in her emails. Possibly younger than his own twenty-eight. But at least she hadn't written him off the way her father had.

"I appreciate you wanting to give me a chance, especially after I startled you." That was understating the issue, but he didn't want to embarrass her. If it weren't for the scream, he'd think she'd had some kind of asthma attack, or maybe a seizure, because it'd been so violent. Except there was no denying he'd triggered it. He wouldn't blame her daddy for wanting to get rid of him after that, but the "appropriate candidate" comment still itched under his skin. "Still, I don't think there's any reason to stick around if the owner of the ranch isn't of a mind to get to know me past the obvious."

"Oh, it's not because you're, um . . . African American." She glanced up at him.

He tried to smile, but it felt strained. "You can say black. My people lived on Saint-Domingue before it was Haiti, and we lived in Louisiana before that became America. I'm black Creole from way on back, Ms. Lawler, and proud to claim it."

She blew out a breath. "I'm sorry this has been such a mess. Can we just start over? I'm Andra Lawler." She emphasized the *ahn* sound at the start, and he realized he'd been saying it wrong inside his head. This time she held out her hand to shake his.

He hesitated. This job would mean everything to him. But this ranch might not be big enough for him to avoid her father.

Andra was still holding out her hand, waiting for him, and he couldn't stand to leave her hanging. The horses he'd seen in that stable were worth putting up with her jerk of a father, and Andra really seemed to want him to stay. He tried out a smile. "LJ Delisle, and so happy to meet you." He let the syllables of his family name roll off his tongue so she could hear the *De-lye-el*, the *s* ignored by everyone except well-meaning cowgirls.

She shook his hand, strong as any cowboy. "I thought the initials were only for emails. You go by LJ?"

"The name my mama gave me is a mouthful and a half. Best to stick with plain old LJ." He winked, screwing his proper interview front all to hell. Though it would be completely worth it if he could tease her out of her own stiff formality. "Now how about this extensive interviewing process?"

As soon as she met his gaze, he got lost all over again in that half-told story behind her eyes.

She took a little breath, as if she was the one who needed to prepare herself, and started toward one of the barns. Not, he noted, the one they'd left her father in. As he followed, he caught the sound of

Lady Gaga playing from a tractor shed nearby, drifting out along with the sound of curses in a very female voice.

In this new stable, the horses were younger than the last bunch, but the light in their eyes was the same: quick, bright, curious. Not the dull stare of a horse left in a pasture until its brain went sludgy with stillness. LJ's pulse quickened. Here were animals begging to be given something to do. This job might not be as fresh of a start as he'd hoped for, but the horses at least were everything he'd been dreaming about and then some.

"This is Taz. Her father was the AQHA Farnam Superhorse, and despite our best efforts, she's terrified of lead ropes." Andra threw open a stall door, and the movement held none of the frozen hesitation of that moment when she'd collapsed backward onto the floor. "She's your second interview question."

Two

◇◇◇◇

Andra propped her arms on the stall door and tried to focus on the man working with her horse. She was not in the mood for the level of adulting required to interview a potential employee. Right now, all she wanted was to disappear into her own little cottage and forget who she was.

This morning should have been her chance to convince her dad—and herself—that she could handle a man being on the property. Humiliating herself and nearly getting trampled by her own mount had not been on the agenda.

As she watched, LJ took the lead rope and hid it under a pile of hay. Taz eyed him from across the stall, looking wary, her head ducked low. He leaned against the wall, shoved his hands in his pockets, and started whistling. It took Andra a second to recognize the tune, and she frowned. Rage Against the Machine was an odd choice for soothing an animal.

LJ was an odd choice all around. She was determined to hire the best person for the job, man or woman, but she hadn't expected him to be so . . . big. She'd been the tallest girl in her class at five ten, but he towered over her by more than half a foot. Not the lanky kind of tall, either. Every inch of him was packed with muscle.

Not that it should matter. He didn't seem like a creep, and that smile of his wasn't the least bit threatening. It was mischievous and full of fun, brightening his whole body from his suspiciously clean cowboy hat to the tips of his scratched boots.

She hadn't planned on going toe-to-toe with her overprotective father until after she hired someone. And it especially sucked that she'd had to do it in front of LJ. She should explain, but he probably wouldn't be any happier to learn her dad's objection was because he was the wrong gender instead of the wrong race.

Taz nosed through the hay until she found the lead rope, and then she backed away, ears laid back. LJ didn't react, keeping up his whistling until the filly forgot the rope. Then he took his hands out of his pockets, hid the rope behind his back, and started playing a game with the horse that was somewhere between follow the leader and hide-and-seek. Andra smiled. It was similar to a game she played with her own mare, Gracie. When no one was watching, that was.

Even if he had witnessed one of her freeze-ups, she was glad she'd kept LJ around for the interview. He was the only candidate who'd answered her emailed questions by talking about horses instead of himself. And in those moments when she'd been helpless, locked up tight by a glitch in her own brain, he'd only moved to protect her.

LJ led the way through to the outdoor pen attached to the stall. He laughed as the filly trotted to follow, nosing around to see what he had hidden behind him.

Andra squared her shoulders. It didn't matter what he thought of her, or even if he'd already seen her at her craziest. What mattered was if she could trust him with her babies.

For the next forty minutes, she watched his every movement. She'd found that you could tell a lot about a man by what he thought was wrong with your horses. As far as she could see, LJ couldn't find a thing wrong with hers. He didn't seem to be in a hurry, either. He spent the whole time playing games with Taz, sometimes with the lead rope he was supposed to be training her for, sometimes without. One thing was for sure, though: neither she nor the horse could take their eyes off him.

She cleared her throat. "That's good for today."

"Good" was putting it lightly. Instead of forcing obedience, he'd teased the horse toward a curiosity that soon had it doing exactly what he'd wanted in the first place. She liked his style.

LJ patted the filly one more time and let himself out of the stall, smiling almost shyly. "Tell me you've got another twenty questions as smart as that one, and I'd just about work for free."

Without the fence between them, anxiety tightened her belly, like it did every time a man got within arm's reach of her. Her vision was drawn to the thick knuckles of his work-scarred hands. They were big enough that his fist could cave in most of her face with a single blow.

He frowned. "Are you all right, Ms. Lawler?"

She blinked. She was at home, and safe. Not only that, his talent with horses made it clear she couldn't afford to let her phobias keep holding her back from hiring men.

She planted her feet, the decision already made. "You can call me Andra. How long will it take you to gather your things and move up here? We've got an on-site apartment furnished and ready to go."

This was about her horses, not her. She wouldn't have to see him that often, so it didn't matter if she still wasn't comfortable around men. She faked calm for the benefit of a dozen animals a day—every trainer did.

Doing it for a single human shouldn't be any harder than that.

LJ walked across the stable yard, wondering exactly how much tonight's dinner was going to suck. On a scale of one to aggressive foot fungus, he was guessing maybe an eight.

Jason Lawler walked with him, dead silent, which seemed to be the normal state of being for Andra's brother. He'd met broken trombones with more to say. Of course, LJ had been known to talk the ears off everything from horses to grocery checkers, so he wouldn't have taken Jason's relative quiet too personally if he hadn't been getting the freeze-out from the rest of the family as well.

Daddy Lawler had spent most of the last three days giving LJ heavy-browed sideways looks, always finding tasks to do nearby, as if LJ might shoplift a quarter horse. And Andra, the Lawler whose opinion he cared about most, was straight-up avoiding him.

Since starting here, he'd glimpsed her only a few times: once in the far pasture, jumping ditches on a chestnut gelding. In the main arena, teaching a bay mare to do lead changes. Her back, heading out of the stables every time he headed in.

Her name, on the other hand, followed him everywhere he went. The staff told him Andra wanted to try crossing these bloodlines, Andra taught this horse to pick up its own fallen rein, Andra did the imprint training on this foal and this one and this one . . . and yet she was nowhere to be found when he wanted a rundown on the stock he was supposed to be working with.

The breeze kicked up dust around their boots, and Jason sneezed.

"Bless you," LJ said automatically.

Jason nodded and kept walking. LJ wondered if it was possible to lose brain cells from lack of conversation. He'd been here only three days, and he already missed his gregarious hometown neighborhood.

He dropped his eyes as they got closer to the ranch headquarters with its raw log pillars and river rock accents. Everything was so new here, the paint all fresh and smooth without humidity creeping in under every tiny chip. He rubbed the back of his neck, wishing he'd thought to paint Mama's steps one more time before he left.

He took a breath and tried a new topic on Jason. "You know what would really help me with the colts? Balloons. Or horns, maybe, if you've got them."

The other man gave him a sideways look, incredulous eyes nearly as brilliant a green as his sister's. "You throwing a birthday party or breaking a colt?"

He shrugged one shoulder and grinned. "Hell, why not do both at once? Think we can get cake and ice cream out of it?"

"Wait, how is ice cream going to help with the colts?" Jason just looked confused.

"Uh . . . never mind." LJ braced himself for the dinner ahead, preparing to carry the conversation for an entire family of turnips. Thank God these people's horses had more of a sense of humor than they did, or he'd have gone barking crazy already. At least he'd gotten a couple of smiles out of Andra that first day. Apparently not enough to make her forget their rocky initial meeting, though, or she wouldn't be avoiding him. "So what's the occasion for dinner?"

"No occasion. Meals are provided with your wages. Didn't they tell you when you got hired?" Jason stopped on the porch of the main ranch house and scrubbed his boot through the cleaning brush bolted to the floorboards.

"Might have missed that part." Probably because he'd worked through dinner all three nights. Now that he was finally free to use his own training ideas without his uncle glaring over his shoulder, he couldn't get enough time with the horses.

"Guess that explains why you haven't been showing up. Stacia was starting to take it personally."

"Stacia?" He followed suit on the boot scrubber.

"She's the cook and mechanic."

"Huh. Can't say that's a combination you see every day." He almost made a joke, but with Jason as his only audience, it didn't entirely seem worth the effort.

Jason scratched the back of his neck, glancing off the side of the porch. He lowered his voice. "Stacia's parents have never been great at holding a job. Back in high school, she was always running around here with Andra, soles of her shoes falling half off, jeans all stained up and ripped. Dad started paying her to cook for everybody, then when he found out she knew how to change oil, he paid her more to work on all the ranch trucks."

Jason paused with his hand on the doorknob and smirked.

"You're lucky you didn't hire on a few years ago. We were all eating grilled cheese for a long time. She was faster learning the car stuff, mostly because she figured out there were YouTube videos of everything." He opened the door. "But you didn't hear that from me."

"Understood." LJ came inside, wondering why he hadn't seen the women together, if she had been Andra's best friend since childhood.

Jason led him through a high-ceilinged, rough-beamed foyer and into a dining room sparkling with windows. The space was dominated by a scarred oak slab of a table so battered that it immediately transformed the mansion-sized room into a home.

A woman slid a big pan of meatloaf into the center of the table, curly brown hair swinging around her round face. She turned, and LJ struggled not to stare at her shirt. It was a Harley-Davidson tank that left her toned shoulders bare, the skull picture on the front outlined with a glitter of purple sequins.

"That old flatbed's engine get the best of you yet, Stace? Heard you cursing again today." Jason took off his hat with a smile and dropped it onto one of the hooks lining the wall. LJ hung his battered old cowboy hat on the next peg, glad to have ditched the too-tight job-interview Stetson back at his new apartment.

"No, but that roping horse sure got the best of you when you dropped your loop over your own fat head," Stacia said. "You were hoping nobody saw, weren't you?"

He coughed once into his fist. "Stacia, this is LJ. He's starting our colts."

"Don't change the subject, and don't you dare sit at my table without washing those hands you just coughed into, Jason Lawler." Stacia turned her blue eyes on LJ and smiled. "We're happy to have your help. I know your apartment has a kitchen, but you're always welcome up here. If you can stand the company."

She stuck her tongue out at Jason, who feigned like he was going to wipe his still-unwashed hand on her. She narrowed her eyes and didn't move. LJ had to stifle a laugh as Jason's bluff fell short.

Stacia nodded to the people filing into the room. "Let me introduce you around to everybody else who works here."

LJ shook hands with people for a few minutes, though he'd met most of them here and there around the ranch in the last few days.

Now that they were all in the same room, though, it was hard not to notice this was the Hollywood fantasy version of a ranch staff: all women with a smattering of old men. He and Jason were the only males under fifty in the entire place.

LJ hesitated for an extra second, trying to decide where he was supposed to sit, but the room was rowdy enough that nobody noticed. Apparently not everybody was as quiet and uncomfortable with each other as they were with him.

Jason and Stacia elbowed each other back and forth, their horse-play escalating until they knocked one of their plates askew. Bill Lawler winged a dinner roll at his son from his place at the head of the table, nailing him squarely in the temple.

"Dear Lord, thank you for this food," Bill said, "and for giving my old muscles enough aim that I can still hit my son with it. Amen."

Jason reached for one of the platters, and Stacia smacked his hand.

"What? Dad already said grace."

"It's Sunday."

"It is?" Jason pulled his hand back, glancing toward the door.

LJ kept his hands in his lap, his peripheral vision raking the rest of the table for clues as to what people in Montana did differently on Sunday, if it wasn't praying.

"Andra usually shows up on Sundays. We'll give her another five minutes," Stacia said.

One of the older cowhands piped up, "Hey, you know what else is special about Sundays, Jason? That's the pornless day."

"When you're as awkward with the ladies as Jason is, no day can afford to be a pornless day," said Rachel, a forty-something woman in a Coors Light cap whom he'd met yesterday.

Stacia snickered. "Isn't that God's own truth . . ."

"Last I checked, Curt—" Jason began, but broke off when his sister came into the room. The laughter died away, too. LJ gave Andra a smile to say hi, but she had her eyes down and didn't see.

"Hey, guys. You didn't wait on me, did you?"

"Nah," Rachel lied, and grabbed a dinner roll. Everybody started passing food, but the room stayed quiet as Andra took a seat.

LJ shifted, his chair creaking under his weight.

"Hey, Andra," Stacia said. "The flatbed I was working on today—that old Dodge? When you rev it, it sounds almost like that band you used to blast my ears out with."

Andra blinked, pausing in the middle of dishing up some green beans. "Um, Nightwish? Wait, or do you mean Black Sabbath?"

"Black Sabbath." Stacia smiled. "Remember, you used to say you were going to walk down the aisle to one of their songs, even after I swore I wouldn't be your maid of honor if you did. You said your wedding was going to have the biggest dress and the loudest music in the whole damn county."

A slight smile touched Andra's face, and her eyes flickered to Stacia as she passed the green beans down the table. "I can't believe you remembered all that. It's been so long."

"Hard to forget. My ears have never recovered."

Andra took a breath like she might say something else, then hesitated and fell silent. LJ fidgeted with his fork. For having been Stacia's friend since high school, Andra seemed pretty shy around the other girl. He dug up a chuckle just to break the tension of the moment. "I wouldn't have minded seeing that. White wedding dress or black?"

Everyone stared at him, and Bill glared.

"Uh, I don't know." Andra poked at her green beans. "Hadn't thought about it in years."

Ouch. He'd stepped into something there that he hadn't meant to. Maybe she'd had a broken engagement or something. "So, uh, did anybody see that last Cubs game?"

No one answered.

LJ concentrated on dishing up his plate, stealing glances at everyone as he tried to puzzle out the shift in the mood of the room. The dirty jokes had ended as soon as Andra showed up, and it wasn't only him she was avoiding looking at—it was everyone.

He snuck another look at Andra, her dark head bent toward her food. He was the new guy, so of course he was going to be a little left out at first. But this was her home, and he was here only because she'd stood up for him. She shouldn't be uncomfortable or isolated here.

He couldn't stand the idea that she might feel alone.

Three

✦✦✦✦

Boots thumped from outside on Andra's porch. She blew a hair out of her face and straightened from her downward-dog stretch. After all the upheaval in her normal routine this week, afternoon yoga sounded perfect. Unfortunately, all it had done was remind her how sore she was from getting bucked off during that morning's training session.

The footsteps were even heavier than her dad's. They stomped like somebody was trying to make a lot of noise or kick something off their shoes. Must be Jason, then. Her cottage was a good half-mile walk over a hill from the ranch. Of the two people who ever made that trek, her brother was the most likely to kick his dirt off on her porch instead of in the yard. Andra rolled her eyes and stepped off her yoga mat, headed for the door even before the knock sounded. It was lower down than usual and muffled, as if Jason were knocking with his boot.

She opened the door, and the frown froze on her face as LJ's shoulders filled the doorframe.

He was holding . . . a cake?

"Um, hi," she managed.

She reached behind her back to undo the knot that pulled her T-shirt tight against her chest, shaking the baggy hem so it would fall to cover some of her leggings. What was he doing here? Oh crap, she'd promised to talk to him about the horses.

"Look, I'm sorry. I know I said I'd come talk to you a couple days ago, but then Socks kicked one of the grooms, and Mary Kay lost a shoe, and I completely forgot." She hadn't forgotten, so much as she was . . . working up to it. Giving him a few days of seeing her around the ranch when she was in control of herself, before she got close enough she'd have to see his opinion of her in his eyes.

He shrugged, careful not to tip the tall cake off its platter. "I think we got off on the wrong foot the day we met, and our do-over didn't really stick."

Oh God. Apparently, he wasn't tiptoeing around anything today.

LJ grinned—a playful, twinkly-eyed one that made him look like he was just having more fun than everyone else. "Besides, nobody's afraid of a guy with a cake."

A smile tugged at the edges of her mouth. "I've never heard that."

"No? It's completely true. Not to mention, bringing a cake is the best excuse to eat some. I mean, it's yours. You don't have to share. Of course, if you don't, you may want to pass a tissue or two my way, is all I'm saying." He widened his eyes mournfully.

She glanced at the cake, the white icing whipped into gorgeous swirls. "Did Stacia make that? She used to be terrible at baking." She gripped the edge of the door a little tighter. Maybe her friend had been practicing. It wasn't like she knew what Stacia was up to these days.

"I'm a little offended. A man doesn't bring a borrowed cake for an apology." He lifted the platter and gave it a waggle. "We've got lemon velvet with French buttercream here. You oughta get it out of the heat soon, though. The sun melted the frosting some on the way over. It's a hike to get up over here, you know it?"

Oops, he was feeling around for an invitation. Duh, and she was still standing in her door like some kind of freak. "Um, come in." The least she could do was feed him some cake and try to act like a normal person. She stepped aside and racked her brain for small talk that didn't involve anything on four hooves. "You know, I can't quite place your accent. You said you were from Louisiana, but I've met lots of people from there at rodeos, and they didn't sound quite like you."

"Well, you can tell I'm from the South because I interrupted your workout with dessert." He tipped his head toward the yoga mat she'd left by the couch. She smiled, and his grin brightened a couple more watts. "Seriously, though, I think I've got a little bayou country from my days on my uncle's horse ranch, cut with the rhythm of the Lower Ninth, maybe some southern drawl creeping in from the Mississippi border. And New Orleans has a sound all its own, always has." Between one word and the next, his words straightened to all square corners instead of luscious curves. "Then again, if my mother is listening, I sound strictly like the Yankee university she helped pay for."

"Your mom doesn't like your accent?" Andra frowned. "Doesn't she have one?"

"Mama thought I wouldn't get a decent job unless I talked like a white banker from Wisconsin." He shrugged.

Her eyes widened. "That's not fair. Why should you have to fake an accent to get a job?"

"That's the way the world works. People have ideas about what intelligence should sound like, and I don't expect I'm going to change all of them on my own." He winked. "I tutored English composition for work study all through college, so I can play the game. I have to admit, though, sometimes it's nice to sound like home."

Andra laughed, a little self-consciously. "I don't think I even realized we had an accent up north until you imitated it."

"Oh, it's an accent all right, sweetheart. And you've got it thick as anything."

Heat crept into her skin at the endearment, though she didn't get the feeling he was really flirting with her. She glanced away, the afterimage of him seared on her lids. His deep-brown eyes were a couple of shades darker than his skin, and they always seemed to be laughing. He was handsome, with high cheekbones and sensual lips. The kind of man she would have looked twice at, once.

He was also the first non-Lawler man she'd had in her house since it was built.

Andra shook herself. Normal people did not make their guests spend the entire visit standing in the foyer. As she led him farther inside, their shapes were reflected in the French doors separating the living area from her bedroom, their distressed white paint framing glistening glass panes. She'd rescued the doors from her mom's room before they tore down the old house, and Dad hung them on a barn door rail for her so they slid aside, taking up less space.

"The kitchen's right here." She gestured, then dropped her hand quickly. Her whole house was basically two rooms plus a bath, and he wasn't blind. She didn't need to map out the refrigerator and sink for his comprehension.

He gave a low whistle. "My sweet God. My mama would kill for this kitchen. Do you mind if I take a picture for her?"

"Uh, sure. If you want to. Here, I'll take that." She lifted the cake from his hands. For its size, it was surprisingly light, as if it were whipped from sugared air with a touch of cream. She set it on the table while LJ took out his phone and snapped a picture of her open barn-wood shelves stacked with white dishes, and the riverstone-pebbled wall behind the sink.

He grinned as he shook his head and tapped out a quick text to go with the pictures. "My little cake is just about embarrassed to be seen in a place this nice."

He leaned back against her counter, crossing his feet at the ankles as he texted, and she bit the inside of her lip. Originally, she'd painted this room white so it would look bright and cheery, but it had always seemed blank instead. LJ's smile belonged in her homey little kitchen in a way she never had.

Andra blinked and looked away. "I'll get some silverware." She rattled through one drawer, and the one below it, but neither held a cake knife or a pie server. Instead, she settled on a couple of forks and a butcher knife. By the time she was finished, LJ had already lifted plates off her shelves and set them on her round café table.

"This place looks pretty new." He ripped two paper towels off the roll and tucked one under the edge of each plate for a napkin. "You lived here long?"

"A few years." She sat down. Wait, was that too weird? She didn't have anything else to keep her hands busy, but he was still bustling around her kitchen as if she were the visitor. "My family helped me build it after college." She managed a smile. "After the dorms and a couple of years of apartments, I was ready for my own space instead of moving back into Dad's house."

LJ went back to the front door and took off his hat, hanging it on a hook next to her jacket before toeing off his boots.

"Oh, you don't have to do that. These floors have seen plenty of boots."

He shrugged, padding back to the kitchen in his socks. He hooked a foot around a chair leg and pulled it out, relaxing into the seat. She didn't often see him without his hat, and her gaze kept flicking back to him. His hair was buzzed so close it was barely more than a shadow of black, leaving nothing to detract from the distracting line of his jaw. And his lips.

"You built this?" His brows bounced up, and he glanced around the great room, scanning the lines a little more analytically this time. "I'm going to pretend like I'm not impressed right now."

"Oh, we hired out some of the plumbing and all the electric. Curt helped a lot. He's one of the grooms. You've probably met him. And an architect fixed up my basic plans." She shrugged. "I still drove plenty of nails, though." Not that it mattered. What did she care if he thought she was the kind of girl who sat back and waited for other people to build her house?

LJ picked up the knife to cut the cake, saying something she didn't catch. The blade looked impossibly long and sharp in his huge hand. Her fingers clenched in her lap, and she deliberately looked at the clean white of the cabinets below the sink.

Relax. There's a whole room here, not just a knife.

LJ glanced over, then reversed his grip, handing the knife handle-first across the table to her. "Must have left my manners at home to-day, helping myself to your cake in your house." He smiled. "Lemon velvet's my favorite, is all. If I get grabby, feel free to slap my hands."

Andra took the knife. The metal reflected her image back at her, including her "May The HORSE Be With You" T-shirt. The one with the hay-colored stain at the shoulder. Yeah, she was so prepared for guests.

Suddenly, the thought of another hour of pretending they weren't both thinking about it seemed overwhelming.

"It was a panic attack." She laid down the knife and met his gaze without flinching. "I'm sure you've figured that out by now."

He nodded. "Was it because I startled you, coming out of the shadows like that?"

Something about the fact that he wasn't squirming in his seat made it easier to talk about. "I was assaulted in college, and ever since . . . I get those occasionally."

His eyes unfocused for a bare instant, and he swallowed.

She turned the cake platter, trying to decide how many pieces to divide it into and also giving him a minute to process. Somebody would have mentioned it in front of him eventually, and now they could move past it. "I love what you've done with Taz, by the way. I saw her following you all over the ranch yesterday. Has she gotten any better about being near lariats?"

LJ didn't seem to hear her. He picked up his fork and turned it in his hands. Then he tapped the end twice on the table and set it down. When his eyes came back up, they were dark, almost angry. Andra drew back from the table, her breath snagging at his reaction before she realized it probably wasn't her he was upset at.

LJ gave her a smile, but it was a crutch's awkward hobble compared to the smooth spread of his usual one. "I . . . wish that hadn't happened to you."

The words were so halting that it took her a second to process what he'd said. When she did, it was like every rib in her chest eased a little more open. Nobody had ever said that. Their eyes had said it, their pitying, twisted expressions, but those words seemed off-limits for reasons she could never have explained. "Yeah." She half laughed. "Me too."

"Thank you for trusting me enough to be honest." His eyes didn't fidget away from hers, and she nodded, a feeling expanding in the air between them. Something big, too big for strangers. Whatever it was, it didn't throw LJ off his stride. He got up from the table. "You want milk with your cake? It's better with milk."

"Sure," she said without thinking. She hadn't talked about this stuff for so long, because no matter who it was, saying anything about her attack killed the conversation and the mood. But LJ seemed to be able to take in the enormity of it all and still look her in the face. Then again, her brother had told her he was just as easy with the horses. Nothing shook LJ up, and he was always willing to make up a new technique on the spot if his old one wasn't working. Few trainers were humble enough to be that flexible.

He flicked open the fridge. "Grocery day, huh?"

"What?"

He arched an eyebrow. "You have orange juice, half a pack of American cheese, and . . ." He peeked in the fridge again. "A pickle. *One* pickle."

"There's plenty of food in the freezer." She glanced away. She hadn't promised him dinner, so what business was it of his what she kept on hand?

He opened her freezer, then quickly snapped it back shut, turning wide eyes toward her. "Do you realize you have a microwavable Salisbury steak in there?"

"No." Who knew what was in there? Some kind of steak seemed a likely option, though.

"Stacia made rack of lamb last night." He crossed his arms. "With plum sauce. From scratch. Pretty sure that means you ain't got any excuse to be choking down microwave dinners."

Andra frowned. "Eating at the main house is like having lunch in a junior high cafeteria. I can barely hear myself think."

He snickered.

"What?" She half smiled, even though she wasn't sure what they were laughing at. It was just nice he was teasing her instead of getting all awkward and stiff, the way most people did when they found out about the attack.

"The cafeteria comparison is kind of fair considering there was a food fight last night. One that ended with a tater tot in your daddy's hair and a scowl on his face that I think rated at least a six on the Richter scale."

"Tater tots with a rack of lamb and plum sauce?" She wrinkled her nose. "Really?"

"I thought it was weird, too. That's not a Montana thing?"

She laughed. "Maybe more like a Stacia thing. She always traded for everybody's tater tots back when we were in school."

"That explains it. Turns out tots aren't half-bad in plum sauce, if you go for the crispy ones." He pulled his phone out of his pocket. "I'm sorry, but I have to do this."

Four

◇◇◇◇

"Uh, you do?" Andra frowned. "You have to do what exactly?"

He opened the fridge and dropped to a knee in front of it, holding up his phone to click a picture before he swiveled and took a shot of the door, too.

Her eyes widened, then she jumped forward to swipe a moldy, half-used cube of butter out of the door rack. She threw it in the trash with enough force to make the can rattle.

"My mama's not going to believe this is the fridge of a grown-ass woman." He stood up, already texting away.

"You cannot text your mother pictures of my refrigerator!" Andra made a grab for the phone, and he shot it high over his head where she couldn't reach, clicking once with his thumb.

"Too late, already done." He stuffed the phone into his pocket, went back to the table, and cut a huge wedge of cake without bothering to divide up the rest.

"Isn't there some kind of release form you have to sign to take pictures of someone's private business?"

He licked frosting off the knife blade, eyes dancing. "Maybe business a little privater than half of a pack of American cheese."

She gaped at him.

"I know, I know." He rolled his eyes. "More private, not privater."

She snatched the knife from him, taking it to the sink to cover her stunned blush. "How am I supposed to cut a piece for myself when you already licked the knife?" she muttered.

She couldn't believe he'd made an actual joke. To *her*. And it had been a borderline dirty joke, at that. Everyone in this county had followed the trial of her assailant, and no one had so much as given her a sideways smirk since the day she moved home from college. People were too uncomfortable now to ever have fun with her. Gossip, however, was a whole different animal. She knew behind closed doors, they whispered and speculated, and more than one of them thought she was at fault for what had happened to her. But in public? No one had dared make an off-color comment to her in over five years. It was ridiculous: like they thought the attack had damaged her sense of humor or something.

"This is only an appetizer," he said, as he cut the cake. "Trust me, we don't have time for a full serving right now. Wait for it . . ." Even before he'd fully lifted his hand to point to his pocket, it chimed with a new text message. Followed by another and another, the first chime not even finishing before the next started. "Told you so."

He grabbed a plate with his right hand and raised the cake platter with his left, jogging it just right to get the loose piece of cake to tumble out onto the plate, landing frosting-side down and cracking his perfectly fluffy sunshine-yellow cake layers apart.

She came back to cut her own piece, but he nudged her aside to snatch up a fork and stab it into the cake. "Grab your shoes. We've got to go." He shoved the bite in his mouth and rolled his eyes in dramatic ecstasy. "Hot damn, I'm good." He snatched another piece up on the fork. "One for the road?" He held it up, and the cake was in her mouth before she was certain how it'd happened.

And then smooth vanilla melted on her tongue and lemon struck the perfect sting to balance it, her mouth watering even as she chewed. "Oh my God."

LJ laughed. "I'm going to take that as a compliment." He flashed to the front door and stomped into his boots. Then he ruined the whole effort of taking them off by coming back across the kitchen and stealing another "bite" that was nearly half the slice.

"Hey, leave some for me!" Andra grabbed the fork out of his hand, laughing when he coughed on his enormous mouthful. She got herself a little more frosting this time, but as she was going back in for more, LJ stole her fork and tossed it in the sink with a ring of metal against porcelain. His phone chimed again.

"See?" he said, as if that were the closing statement to an argument they hadn't actually been having. "Gotta go." He grabbed her hand.

She threw a longing look back at the cake even as he towed her across the kitchen. "Where?"

LJ dropped his hat onto his head as she stuffed her feet into her boots. He opened the door and spun her out through it without ever releasing her.

He's holding my hand.

Okay, but was he holding her hand or "holding" her hand? Before she could sort it out, LJ let her go, hopping off the porch without touching a single step. "Wanna take the palomino express or stick to the boot train?" He motioned to the pasture next to the house, where her horse, Gracie, had paused in her grazing to watch them cross the yard.

"Depends. Where are we going, exactly?"

His pocket chimed again. "Yeah, no time to mess with horses."

He turned his back on the paddock. LJ strode up the hill, and Andra had to break into a jog for a second to catch up with his long legs. The grass rattled beneath their feet, already starting to dry to brown under the relentless bake of the summer sun.

"What's the deal with keeping that mare here instead of the main stables, anyway?" he asked. "You move her just for the commute? She's pretty flashy to play glorified taxicab." He allowed a glance over his shoulder, and he sped up again when his pocket chimed.

Gracie was her best friend, but that wasn't the kind of thing an equine professional was supposed to say. Andra lifted her chin. "Her

name is Allure's Graceling Queen. She's mine, but she's also one of
the ranch's retired champions. So many of our other projects need
riding time that if I didn't ride her to work and back, I'd hardly ever
get on her."

"Pretty name."

She let a little bit of a smile curve her mouth. "I named her after
a book. It was about a girl with the gift of being able to win any
fight."

"She can't be more than eight." He turned off instead of taking
the worn furrow in the grass that headed toward the barn. "Little
young to be out to pasture, huh?"

"She won Hi-Point All-Around Champion at Congress last year."
Andra lifted her chin a touch. "Not too many mountains to climb
after that."

He stopped on the long covered porch of the staff housing building. Each apartment opened onto the porch, and he stood one door
up from Stacia's. Andra glanced over at that door and then behind
her, uncertain what was down here that he wanted to show her.

LJ stared at her. "You own the Hi-Point All-Around Champion?
As in, you didn't only train her—she belongs to you. No co-owners
or anything."

"Nope," Andra said, distracted by the growl of her stomach. The
bright taste of lemon had awakened her whole mouth, and she suddenly realized she was *hungry*.

He snorted and opened the door. "Great. Can I borrow your Fer-
rari next time I need to make a run to town?"

His teasing distracted her so she was inside with her eyes adjust-
ing to the lower light before she thought to pause. "Wait, is this your
apartment?" She'd asked Jason to get LJ settled on-site, so she knew
he lived in one of the units. Why would he bring her to his place?

"Home sweet home." LJ laughed as if it were a joke.

Andra tugged at the end of her ponytail, thinking about how long
it'd been since she'd been in a man's apartment. The walls in the employee housing were so thin Curt couldn't watch *Jeopardy!* without

Stacia calling out the answers. They were far from alone, and even if they had been, she had the feeling LJ wasn't the type to try anything. She kind of liked the way he joked with her. The way the news of her past had made him sad, but he'd still treated her like any other woman.

"Here you go." LJ interrupted her thoughts by dropping a paper grocery sack in her arms.

She caught the sides and frowned down into it before sending a quizzical look at her companion. He was already crouched in front of the refrigerator, pulling things off shelves and out of drawers, muttering to himself.

He stood up and dumped a load of vegetables into her sack. Kicking the fridge closed, he opened a cupboard. Jason's apartment always reeked of sweat and muddy boots, but LJ's smelled like oranges and oven-warmed vanilla.

Andra set the sack down on the tiny rectangular table pushed up against the wall. It wobbled when she bumped it, one leg a hair shorter than the others.

"Okay." She shook her head. "Seriously, what does your phone ringing have to do with why we are so urgently raiding your vegetable drawer?"

"Because cake isn't a square meal, and I can't in good conscience leave you alone to starve on pickles and orange juice. The vegetables are for spaghetti." He went back to the cupboard and pulled out a box of pasta, flipping it to her without looking to see if she was ready.

She caught it with both hands and paused for a second before she packed it in the grocery sack.

"As for my phone ringing itself hoarse, I bet you homemade hush puppies against your palomino that all those texts were from my mama, promising to whoop my ass if I didn't make sure you were fed." He went back to the fridge for a package of Italian sausage. "She'll probably insist I teach you how to cook, too, so you don't have to eat anything labeled 'Salisbury steak' ever again." He patted her shoulder on his way to the table, as if she might be as distressed as he was by the concept. Spices spilled out of an overloaded rack on the counter, and he plucked several jars from among them.

"LJ, you don't have to teach me to cook. I'm too busy to bother most of the time, but I can make anything I want to." Which was entirely true, as long as what she wanted was mac and cheese or scrambled eggs.

"Take it as my apology for scaring you the first time we met." He turned around, standing closer to her than anybody ever did. And yet his eyes were so warm and earnest that she forgot to move away. "I'm from the Lower Ninth Ward. We don't turn our back on folks who've hit hard times."

Andra inhaled, putting it together all in a rush. His résumé said he was from New Orleans. Had he been there during the floods? She'd been a teenager when Hurricane Katrina came through, and he was maybe a few years older than her own twenty-seven. That place he'd mentioned—the Lower Ninth. It tickled a faint memory in her. Maybe she'd read about it somewhere, but it didn't seem polite to ask.

Instead she cleared her throat and said, "Spaghetti, huh? Shouldn't you make something southern? Gumbo or grits, maybe?"

"My mama loves all food equally." LJ smiled. "But I thought I'd save the sashimi lesson for later."

"Sash-who-what?"

He rolled his eyes and picked up the grocery bag. "Come on, Andie-girl. Your kitchen's better than mine, and we obviously have a lot of work to do."

Five

◇◇◇◇

The sand in the arena smelled scorched, the summer sun cooking every bit of moisture out of the ground and the people who walked upon it. But Andra wasn't paying any attention to the sweat sticking her shirt to her back, or the four-year-old gelding she rode. In fact, she finally gave up and stopped, because she was laughing too hard to properly cue the animal.

LJ trotted a buckskin filly along the outside of the arena fence, saddlebags rattling and warbling a terrifyingly electronic version of "Ice Ice Baby." He batted his eyelashes at Andra as he brought his horse to a stop. "What? You know Mary Kay doesn't appreciate it when you laugh at her."

"Oh, I'm not laughing at *her*." Andra tried to bite back her smile, side-passing her gelding away as the horse fought the bit, trying to push his head over the fence. "What's going on with your, ah, music box saddle?"

He reached back and jiggled the noisy saddlebags, Mary Kay startling and throwing her head before he calmed her once again. Then "Ice Ice Baby" was overlaid by a meeping version of Beethoven's "Für Elise." The horse stopped, flicking her ears back to listen.

"Cell phones." LJ grinned. "They're all set to go off at different times. Can't sell your babies to some cowboy who's gonna get dumped on his behind the first time his girlfriend texts him while he's out riding."

She laughed. "Good point."

She'd seen a few people get thrown because their cell phones rang, but she rarely saw anybody taking the initiative to get colts used to different types of ringing sounds. She liked the thoughtful way LJ approached horses. A few days ago, she'd caught him setting a saddle backward on a yearling. He claimed that animals always thought the saddle felt funny at first, and this way when he turned it forward again, it fit so much better the horse accepted it at once. His gentle, creative training tactics were exactly what she'd been wanting for her ranch's stock.

"What?" he said, and she realized she'd been staring.

She shook her head. "Nothing. I was just thinking it's weird seeing you on top of a horse instead of next to one. That's good, though. We hired you specifically because Jason doesn't have the patience for the groundwork the colts need, and I don't have the time."

He whistled through his teeth, patting Mary Kay's neck. "Hear that, girl? The lady is surprised I can ride." He shook his head. "I'd be offended if I didn't think it was so funny that you hired me without seeing me on a horse, after all your talk about the 'extensive interviewing process.'"

She wrinkled her nose at him, caught off guard by how easily he slipped into her flat accent. "Shut up."

He laughed. "Careful. The Politeness Police are going to come for you any second, sirens blaring."

"I'm not that polite."

"Sure you're not. And I'm not really all that tall," he drawled.

She rolled her eyes and snorted. After a week of cooking lessons, she was getting used to his teasing. "You know, since you can apparently sit a horse, I should mention we have a rodeo coming up."

"Thought this was a fancy show barn." He did jazz hands, scaring Mary Kay and having to take a second to settle her. "Rodeo's allowed, too?"

"Better be, or we might have a hard time selling all the roping horses Jason insists on training. This is only our tiny local competition, though. Good for business, but better for fun." She raised her eyebrows. "If you're nice, I might even lend you a horse. You rope much?"

LJ smirked. "I'm not going to get much roping done from the back of a stick horse, and something tells me that's all my behavior's going to win me."

"You might be right about that." She smiled and nudged her gelding with her heels, moving into a smooth sitting trot. "Think about it. You've got a week and a half."

"Hey, you busy this afternoon?"

She stopped and took a second to school her horse on turning on his haunches.

When she was finished, she looked up. LJ was still waiting, apparently too much of a trainer himself to get offended at being prioritized behind a learning moment for a horse. "Am I busy? Always. But I could probably juggle some things. Do you need help with one of the foals?"

"Nah." He took off his hat and swiped a sleeve across his sweaty forehead. "I'm headed into town to get some groceries. You ought to come along."

Shadows chased across the ground between them as the breeze pushed thin clouds in front of the sun. The scent of toasted almonds drifted toward her, and she inhaled, wondering if it was LJ. He always seemed to smell like something delicious.

"Have I been eating too much of your food during our cooking lessons this week?" She shifted in her saddle. "I could give you some money to cover it."

He rested a wrist over his saddle horn, the corner of his mouth pulling up into a crooked smile. "You? Eating too much? Even on the pitiful salary you pay me, I think I can afford two extra bites and a dinner roll per day."

"Your salary is twelve percent above industry standard!"

"Sure, but I'm thirty percent better than industry standard." He grinned. Mary Kay shied at a bee flying by. He turned her in a circle, her hooves kicking up dust.

Andra rolled her eyes behind her sunglasses, though she couldn't help a smile. LJ was rarely serious for longer than two minutes at a stretch, but she liked that he wasn't all kid gloves and dark, pitying looks when she was around.

"Anyway, I don't need you to come to the grocery store to bankroll your cooking lessons. I need you to come because I'm still weeping inside over the state of the avocado you tried to feed me the other day. Somebody's got to teach you to properly choose produce."

"Maybe I was trying to get rid of a bad avocado." She lifted a brow. "Ever think of that, Mr. Thirty Percent Better Than Everyone Else?"

He smirked. "I love it when you give the finger to the Politeness Police, Andie-girl. I'll pick you up at four."

Fluorescent lights buzzed overhead, forcing their presence into every corner of the grocery store.

"Easy with your fruit testing there. That's a peach, not a tractor tire." LJ nabbed the now-dented peach from Andra with a wince.

"If you're going to keep making fun of my produce-choosing skills, you should realize we're standing in an entire room of things I can throw at you. Did I mention I was a pitcher in college?"

He smothered his smile. She got a cute little spark in her eye when he teased her. Loosened her right up, which she definitely needed considering how tense she'd gotten when he drove them past city limits today.

"Nope." He took her hand, undeterred, and folded a fresh peach into it. "Gentle now. You want a little give but nothing too squishy."

"What do you mean, nope?" She ripped a plastic bag off the roll. "Does that mean the peach is a yes or no, Bossy?"

"It's a yes. Now pick me four more." He nodded toward the display and took the bag so her hands were free. "The nope was to you being a pitcher in college. 4-H is my bet. FFA, maybe. Honor roll, definitely. Softball, no way you had time. Not the way you sit a horse."

She glared at him, and he snickered. One point for him, none for her. Girl had a half-decent poker face, but he was learning to read her okay. Especially that little smile tugging at the corners of her mouth that the scowl couldn't quite cover.

When he was a kid and first visiting the ranch, his uncle had told him, "Horses do all their talking with their ears. So they look at humans and think, 'They ain't got nothing to say.' But humans speak with their faces, and horses can't move their faces. So humans look at horses and think, 'They ain't got nothing to say.'"

Andra's face usually stayed as smooth and beautiful as any marble-hewed Michelangelo. She did all her talking with her back. Iron stiff, or easy and supple, going with the flow the way she did when riding one of her beloved horses. Right now, her back was still about two jokes away from relaxed. What was it about going to town that set her off?

The grocery store manager peeked at him from across the display, pretending to rearrange the already-stocked Fuji apples. LJ gave him a pointedly wide smile and tipped his hat, glad he'd traded out for his clean Stetson before he left the ranch.

"I'm going to grab some walnuts," he told Andra, setting the bag in their cart.

An apple leaped out of the store manager's hand and dropped to the floor, rolling bruisingly away. Normally, LJ would have chased it down for the man, but he wasn't quite in the mood.

His mood wasn't improved any when the manager abandoned the apple in favor of following him to the bulk bins, lurking practically in his hip pocket as LJ filled a bag with walnuts. There went the idea that the manager was interested only in the novelty of an out-of-towner hanging around the daughter of local ranching royalty. Nope, this guy thought he was protecting his inventory.

LJ's plastic bag ripped and he retrieved a new one, careful not to use too much force as he transferred the walnuts over. Sometimes he wished people would outright call him a thief. An insult was a hell of a lot easier to respond to than a sideways look, or a clerk who always just so happened to be in the same aisle as you.

He took a breath and unlocked his jaw. "Nice weather we're having, huh? Supposed to rain later this week."

The manager's eyes widened, as if he hadn't expected him to speak. Or maybe he'd screwed up his enunciation. He'd been letting it slip too often lately, when he was alone with Andra. Girl must have a thing for accents, because the steel melted out of her spine when he let his out to play.

"Um, is that so? What day?"

"Tomorrow. It's already clouding up out there." Actually, it'd still been hot enough to melt the tar on the pavement when he escorted Andra inside, but he needed something to say.

The manager nodded, relaxing a little.

LJ went back to Andra, double-checking her peach selection.

"Not bad. You want to get some ground beef? Highest fat they'll sell you. We'll need it for gravy. I'll nab us some dried mustard and herbs, and we'll be out of here."

Before he'd even finished talking, she was pushing the cart toward the meat section. "I'm on it."

LJ took a second look at her when she failed to tease him about needing more seasonings. She never missed an opportunity to tell him his spice collection was ridiculous.

Her lashes were down and her shoulders up, eyes skittering away from the other shoppers, especially the one pink-cardiganed matron who kept staring their way.

He ground his back teeth and headed for the fresh herbs. He should have known better, taken a few weeks to get people used to him before he showed up with a white rancher's daughter. Hell, he did know better, but that didn't make it less ridiculous. He wasn't going to hide his friends just to keep the town gossips quiet.

He rushed them through checkout, even letting Andra pay for a small portion of the groceries because he didn't dare argue with her and give the grocery checker a reason to claim domestic disturbance.

Once the groceries and Andra were safely loaded into his truck, he blew out a long breath. "I'm sorry about that." He forced a chuckle. "I think I might be the first black guy this county has seen outside a TV screen. I didn't mean to embarrass you."

She tucked her hands between her knees, pressing her palms together and staring out the side window. "They weren't looking at you, LJ."

His shoulders hunched tighter, because white people always rushed to make excuses. As if racism wasn't a thing anymore, because in their world, it wasn't. So they gave everybody else the benefit of the doubt, like they didn't even realize that meant they were doing the opposite to you.

"Yeah, Andra. They were." It came out harsher than he'd meant it to, so he swallowed and said, "It's fine. I knew when I moved to Montana that I was in for some wide eyes."

It was even worse back home, though. The store manager still tracked him from aisle to aisle even though he'd never stolen in his life. The Lower Ninth hadn't had its own grocery store since Hurricane Katrina. Everybody knew exactly where he came from as soon as he unfolded his little wheeled cart, and they always expected him to lift a few items to make up for the bus fare on the three different route changes he had to wait through to get to the nearest store. Only in the middle of winter was it cold enough he could make it home before the milk started to turn.

It was the stares, even more than the weight of the groceries, that made him insist his mama let him do the shopping.

How was she getting by now? Before he left, a store had finally moved into the Lower Ninth—not a supermarket, but a corner store opened with the life savings of a guy LJ had bussed tables with back in high school. He'd bought everything he could there but still had to trek to town for the meat and milk. Mama had the cart, and the neighbors had promised to pitch in, but it was a lot of weight for her.

Even when he'd bought his truck and moved out to his uncle's ranch, he'd done the shopping for her every weekend.

He tossed his hat on the seat between them, trying to shake off his mood. It was going to be different up here. It had to be.

"I'm sorry," Andra said. "I didn't mean to say . . . Anyway, they do it to me, too. If it makes you feel any better."

"Yeah, not so much." LJ started the truck, forcing a chuckle because it was that or break something, and breaking perfectly good things was a rich man's habit. Even if people snuck an extra look at her from time to time, they didn't follow her around, waiting for her to slide merchandise into her pockets.

"I think today was worse because I was with a man. That's top-shelf gossip around here."

His foot stomped too heavy on the accelerator, but all he said was "Small towns are the same everywhere, huh? It's just like that where I come from."

"New Orleans is hardly a small town."

"New Orleans is a whole heap of small towns piled up together," he said, happy to change the subject. "Hell, when I was little and stepped out of line, ladies three blocks away would whup my butt and then send me home to tell my mama what I'd done. It wasn't until I went to school that I realized not everybody in the world knew my name by looking at my face."

"Yeah, well, they know my face around here, too." Andra laughed, and it was every bit as sour as his had been. "It happened five years ago, but the trial was big news, so my picture was all over the papers for a long time after I was kidnapped. Nobody looked at me the same afterward. And they never stop fucking *staring*." The last word hissed out viciously, and if LJ could have thought straight in that moment, he might have been surprised at her swearing.

But he couldn't think. Couldn't drive.

"Kidnapped" meant a hell of a lot more things than "assaulted."

LJ pulled over. There was a gas station at the side of the road, so he parked next to a pump. He should say something to her, something comforting between two people who had been gawked at by strangers because of things they couldn't change.

But he failed her. All he could do was mumble "Got to get gas" and hope she didn't notice he was at three-quarters of a tank when he bailed out of the truck. He crammed the pump nozzle in and gripped the trigger until every finger joint ached. Otherwise he'd punch the truck, and he didn't want her to see another man letting anger flame into violence.

He couldn't tell if it was the gas pumping or his own blood thundering through his head, but he couldn't hear a thing.

Kidnapped. How long had she been trapped in that nightmare before someone came after her?

Andra pulled her knees up to her chest, watching LJ through the window. He put away the gas pump, started toward the driver's-side door, and then doubled back and paced another lap behind the truck. His thick shoulders hunched, every muscle fiber cranked taut. A flicker of movement caught her eye, and she turned to see the gas station clerk watching through the station's window, her thin arms folded tightly over her uniform shirt.

Andra didn't blame the girl. Right now, LJ was six feet five inches of simmering energy, and nothing about him looked safe. After a week of cooking lessons, though, she was learning to read him. When he went silent and inwardly drawn, it was because he was too angry to trust himself to speak, but not at her. When she'd first confessed she'd been attacked, he'd gotten very, very quiet. She understood that kind of anger: the sort you could never quite swallow.

It was nice to not be the only one feeling it, for once.

LJ got into the truck. His hands were so careful as they gripped the steering wheel that it was obvious he was capable of breaking it.

Andra rested her chin atop her bent knees, wincing. "You okay?"

His chin twitched sideways in half a head shake that never made it back the other way. His palm tapped the wheel once, twice. She tensed as she waited for the third tap. It never came, and he didn't turn on the truck.

"Please, just . . . tell me how you got away. How it ended. Otherwise, I'm not real sure I'm ever going to sleep again."

Andra didn't talk about the things Gavin had done to her in that room. Not to her family or therapists. Not to anybody but the cops and the courts. But she'd googled LJ's home neighborhood a few days ago, and the first pictures that had come up were of terrified people clinging to their roofs during Hurricane Katrina, just to stay above the floodwaters. He understood what it meant to be trapped. And she wanted him to know that whatever else Gavin had done to her, he hadn't won.

"I worked out the screws holding the headboard on. With my fingernails."

LJ looked over and blinked, his eyes nearly black, and she could tell he didn't understand.

"When he left the morning after he took me, I was afraid he was never going to let me go—" She broke off, ducking her chin against her knees.

The hopelessness of that realization wasn't something she cared to remember, even now.

"Anyway, the foot of the bed was tied to the radiator because the first time he left the room, I tried to drag the bed over to the window. And I was cuffed around one post of the headboard. So I worked out the screws on that side and slid the cuffs off." She flicked her fingers, feeling the strong nails where there'd once been only bloody nubs and that stiff, painful ridge of not-quite-nail underneath that wasn't thick enough to budge a screw. "It took me four hours."

Two hundred and forty of the longest minutes of her whole life. Holding her breath, listening for sounds that he'd returned and it was too late to escape. Andra dropped her feet to the floor of the truck and folded her hands in her lap. Her spine sat in an exactly straight line along the back of the seat.

"He'd wedged the door shut from the outside, and I don't know where he put my clothes—" She broke off. LJ didn't need to know that part. "I had to go out the window. It was a small one; I almost didn't fit."

"Good God," he said. "If you hadn't made it—"

"I know. But I thought if one person saw me like that, it'd be over." Gavin had said even if she told anybody, it would be her word against his and no one would listen. But if she had a witness, he couldn't drag her back even if he caught her. You couldn't get undressed wearing handcuffs, so if you were naked, everyone knew you'd been naked when you were cuffed. Anyone who saw her would know the whole story in a glance. Andra's hands lifted to pull at her hair, and when she realized what she was doing, she dropped them back into her lap. She was in a truck five years later. There was nothing in this moment to be upset about.

"What do you mean?" LJ said, his voice strained as if it was having a hard time making it out of his throat. "Did someone see you, and . . . it wasn't?"

"Nobody saw me. The street was empty. When I screamed for help, it sounded so weird I kept having to fight the urge to lower my voice."

That was the part that always came back in her nightmares. The hard jab of gravel under her bare feet. The tiny spots of blood her fingers left on people's doors, and the way the handcuffs rattled when she lifted her hands to pound on the first house, then the next, and the next.

She would take all of that haunting her dreams if it meant she never had to relive what came before it. Even so, there was a certain feeling that came with the dream, and it got darker with every house she ran to. In the dreams, the street had no end.

"I went to three houses before anyone came out."

LJ took his hands off the steering wheel and put them in his lap. The first few times he'd come to give her cooking lessons, she couldn't take her eyes off those hands. They were too big. He could circle her entire arm with his fingers and snap the bone as easily as he cracked the joint of a chicken. And yet, as he listened, those hands trembled more than hers.

"No one answered? What the hell kind of town—what the hell kind of people . . ."

Andra reached over and laid a hand on his arm, his skin blazing hot beneath her palm. She let go almost as soon as she realized what she'd done.

"It was the middle of the day. Everybody was gone at work." She knew that now, but when she knocked on that first door, she hadn't been thinking so clearly. It felt like the whole world had emptied out, and no one was left to care what happened to her. "Someone did come," she hastened to add. "She heard me pounding on her neighbor's door. She had to lean on a cane, but she dropped it to—" She'd dropped it to wrap her cardigan around Andra's shoulders.

Andra swallowed. She should have gone back and thanked her. When the woman came to testify in court, Andra couldn't even look her in the eye.

She cleared her throat, the quiet in the cab crushing her. Her stomach flipped over. She shouldn't have told him the whole story. She should have stopped with the window, because what could he say after all that? And they had to drive all the way home still, with her story suffocating the air between them.

"The police came, and then my family. I'd been missing for nineteen hours, but Gavin had taken my phone and texted my roommate, so no one even knew I was gone." She lifted her chin, determined to make him understand the story had a happy ending. "He said no one would believe me, but they did. It was close for a minute, because people saw me staggering around at the party like I was drunk, because of whatever he put in my drink. He said I was just tipsy and said yes but then took it back. But it was hard to explain the cuffs, the way I had to escape out a window. He was convicted and actually got jail time. My lawyer said I was lucky, because that almost never happens in ra—" She swallowed. "But I had a witness. I had evidence. And I went through the hell of testifying so other girls would be safe."

LJ turned and started digging behind the seat. She scooted forward to give him more room, even though she wasn't sure what he was doing. After a second, he produced a screwdriver and leaned over to tuck it into the purse at her feet.

He straightened, and his deep-brown eyes met hers. Andra jerked, she was so surprised. People didn't look at her when she told that story. They looked down, and they shook their heads with pursed lips. They wrote what she said into their reports. But they never looked her in the eye.

"If you ever come to my door," LJ said, "I'll answer."

Six

◇◇◇◇

LJ was getting mighty comfortable in Andra's ranch-style kitchen. She had a big island that was perfect for chopping and a slick little kitchen faucet that came right off and turned into its own sink sprayer. He'd been worried she might not want to have him around as much, after their trip to the grocery store had taken such a somber turn. But instead she'd gulped down a deep breath and invited him up to make soup.

He couldn't help but match her courage after that, so he took his own deep breath, shook off his sadness to tease a fresh smile out of her, and just like that they were friends again. Maybe even a little more than they had been before.

Today, the pot on her stove was billowing steam, condensation beading on the kitchen wall. LJ wiped sweat off his forehead and started to unbutton his shirt so it wouldn't cling to his skin.

Andra smacked him with the dish towel. "Keep your clothes on, Delisle. And don't think I'm going to burn the crap out of myself on these peaches just so I can 'learn' or whatever nonsense you come up with."

"It's hot!" he protested, fighting back a smile at Andra's haughty scowl. Unable to resist, he slid a chair across the kitchen to her. "Sit down if you're gonna swoon."

She snorted, picking up a spoon to stir the peaches in the boiling water. "Yankee girls don't swoon, Casanova. And you've got a pretty high opinion of your abs."

"I better. You have any idea how many sit-ups it takes to get abs like these?" He crowded her out of the way and stole the spoon, his shirt still hanging open as he fished peaches out of the pot and dropped them into the waiting bowl of ice water. "Not too long, now. You want them to blanch, not cook."

"I'm going to *blanch* you if you keep hip-checking me out of the way all the time." Andra planted her hands on her hips. "Whatever happened to a simple 'excuse me'?"

"Well, *excuse me* if you were boiling my damned peaches to death." He didn't even try to keep the laughter out of his voice. Pretty well his favorite thing in the world was getting Andra to threaten him with violence. Freud would likely have a heyday with that, Jung even more so. He just couldn't help it. Watching her get all puffed up and indignant and not a whit afraid of him did his soul some kind of good.

They'd never discussed what she'd told him about her kidnapping the other day after their grocery store run. And he'd never asked about all the parts she hadn't told him.

He'd thought about it, all right. All through that sleepless night of staring at his darkened phone on the nightstand. Answers were only a quick Google search away, but he kept thinking about the news helicopters circling overhead while he and his neighbors were still stuck on his roof, waiting for rescue. People were entitled to privacy in their pain.

And Andra was entitled to people looking at her without seeing the story behind that court trial. Now that he'd seen the shadow of horror in that woman's face in the grocery store, he saw the echo of it in everyone who looked at Andra, even on her own ranch. Stacia didn't look away as quickly as Andra's brother did, but her gaze was even heavier with regret. And Bill . . . now that LJ knew her attack wasn't a simple mugging, the weight in her dad's shoulders made a lot more sense. As did the fact that he hadn't been keen to hire a young, intimidatingly tall man to work close by his beautiful daughter.

"Now pull them out of the water," LJ said. "Easy does it. If you prepared them right, the skins should just fall right off."

"If I burn myself, you better believe you're doing the rest."

"Quit your crying. Aren't cowgirls supposed to be tough? The peaches are in *ice* water, so they'll be plenty cool enough now." He gave her ponytail a gentle tug. She tensed, but not much, and she kept right on skinning peaches for their cobbler. Warmth melted through him that had nothing to do with the steam off the stove. Encouraged, he let his hand drift down to rest on her shoulder.

"What are you doing now?" She asked it on a sigh, as if he were a puppy whose antics she tolerated with much complaining and maybe a little bit of affection.

"Using your shoulder to prop up my hand—what does it look like? Trust me, if you had to haul around the weight of these great big arms all day, you'd get tired, too."

"Think it might be your ego that's tipping the scale, friend." Her voice was light, but her eyes strayed from the peaches toward the open front of his shirt.

He just smiled, one thumb idly rubbing her shoulder as he watched her work. He missed hugs, but he didn't want to push his luck. In the South, every woman for seven states around was a hugger, and most of the men, too. Did Andra miss hugs? He worried that she might.

This Sunday's meal at the main house hadn't been any less awkward than the last couple. She'd come late to dinner, left early, and barely said a word in between, even when Stacia and Rachel started snarking at each other and it escalated into settling a bet with a leg-wrestling match in the living room. Stacia'd won a week's worth of gas for her motorcycle with a neat little leverage trick she wasn't about to explain to Rachel.

Among her boisterous family, Andra still existed in a bubble of silence no one seemed to know how to cross.

She finished with the peaches and hip-checked him right out of their cozy little moment. LJ laughed. "What's wrong with a simple 'excuse me'?"

"I'll find my manners about the time you put some clothes on." The comment was offhand, but he smirked when her gaze snagged on his abs for an extra moment. She coughed, reddening, and spun on her bare feet to get a mixing bowl off her open barn-wood shelves.

LJ frowned and glanced away from them. They looked nice enough, but nobody who'd ever fought paint prices and paycheck cycles to keep a house sealed from the weather would think that rain-grayed wood was a natural choice for decorating.

"Tell me what to mix up." She gestured him toward the cutting board. "I'm tired of doing all the grunt work around here."

His eyebrows shot up, but he smoothed his face before she could turn around and notice.

"All right." He stepped up next to her, studying her out of the corner of his eye. She watched his hands too close when he held a knife, so he'd quickly gotten into the habit of delegating all the chopping to her. This time, when he pulled a paring knife out of the butcher block, she only smiled and tipped a sideways look in his direction.

"Did you see that last spin I got out of Socks today?" she asked. "Haunches never budged."

"I did notice that, actually." He divided each peach into sections, handling them gently so they wouldn't bruise. He had to fight back a smile every time the knife moved and her eyes didn't follow it. "It was a beautiful thing. Absolutely beautiful."

Seven

◇◇◇◇

Dust hung in the popcorn-scented air, the dirt by the fence malty with spilled beer. By the rodeo grandstands, the women's going-to-town-day perfume was too thick to breathe. LJ had moved down the rail until he was closer to the bull chutes, where all he had to contend with was the grass-green tang of manure.

He'd been busy all morning, warming up his lariat and other people's horses, polishing hooves, and spraying ShowSheen on every animal in sight until both trailers full of Lawler horses were shiny enough to star in a shampoo commercial.

Now he was taking a break. Ever since Andra had stepped out of the trailer's tack room, dressed to perform, he'd felt a little like a drunk man playing sober. He needed a second alone to reassure himself that he knew how to walk the line.

Gone were her ragged jeans and baggy T-shirts with horsey sayings on the front. Instead she wore a shimmering, champagne-hued silk shirt that drifted all soft and flimsy over the curves of her breasts, nipping in at her waist before it gave way to a set of black chaps tailored to the flare of her hips. Golden letters down one leg said, "Miss Rodeo Wild Falls 2008." But it wasn't the clothes, or the lipstick making her lush mouth look even more kissable than normal. It wasn't even the spill of black curls that bounced saucily against the small of her back. It was the way her spine stood tall, her muscles coiled with excitement, not nerves.

Andra was always beautiful, but with the kind of confidence that practically invited you to stare?

She was stunning.

He'd been gritting his teeth all day against the other cowboys whistling at her, but as long as she was safely on her mare's back, Andra just laughed and waved at them. Under that tiara-spangled Stetson, she was a whole new woman. One he wanted and didn't recognize all at once.

Right now, she and her father were circling their horses in the narrow on-deck area behind the roping chute. The team in line before them shot out into the arena, hot on the heels of a sprinting calf, but he didn't even follow long enough to see if they caught the head.

"You stare any harder, your eyes are going to fall out of your head." Stacia took a swig out of a bottle of Coors Light, then propped her crossed arms one fence rail lower than his.

"You know drinking cheap beer gives you hairy palms, right?" LJ pulled his gaze away from the warm-up area.

Stacia smirked. "Not so fast as other things do." She poked him with one sharp elbow. "Congratulations, by the way."

"Second place." He hadn't competed in steer wrestling in a long time. A week wasn't long enough to bring him up to speed, even for local rodeo standards. He winked. "I didn't write home about it, but I did send a text message."

She snorted and took another swig of beer, the sequins on her shirt catching the sun and daggering light straight into his eyes. Today, it was a longhorn bull stitched onto her tank top. "I don't care if you got eighth as long as you came in ahead of Curt. Now I can remind him all year long that he's getting old, and I can get more work out of him."

"Hey, if you were using me for your own ends, you oughta cut me in. It's only right."

She pursed her lips. "Hmm, what do you need? Considering his time came in two slots behind yours, I bet I can razz him into doing most of your chores."

"Let me save it up for a hangover day."

Stacia tipped her beer to him. "Smart man."

LJ looked out into the arena, tucking his smile down deep where she wouldn't notice it. He'd been working on making friends around the ranch for weeks without any luck. When they all gathered to watch baseball games on Curt's flat screen, he heard the cheering and laughter from farther down the row of employee housing, and he'd usually head up to Andra's so he didn't have to think about why no one had asked him along.

Today was the first day they'd seemed to loosen up around him. Something about dusting Curt off after he rolled in the dirt with a calf, fixing a busted clip on Annie's rein right before she needed to do a hot lap with a flag. Here, they were all behind the grandstands together.

He shrugged his shirt a little straighter on his shoulders. He'd said goodbye to all his friends back home in exchange for the chance at a different life out west. Still, the ranch would feel a lot more like home if people were comfortable enough to give him a hard time. If he knew he could have a barbecue and anybody but Andra would show up.

The crowd tittered with laughter at a joke that came through the speakers, and Stacia rolled her eyes. "What do you think of this announcer?"

"He's . . . different. Reminds me of a guy in a lawn chair on your front porch, telling stories about everybody he's known for way too long."

"Nailed it." Stacia laughed. "Lucky for you, you're an out-of-towner so it's all new. The rest of us have heard the same stories every year since we were trying to ride a sheep in exchange for a half-melted Popsicle."

LJ's smile had a hard time making it up to full size. "Yeah. Lucky me."

"I can't believe he's held off until this late in the day to tell his favorite one about Andra. Usually he tells it twice before I hit the bottom of my first beer."

"Yeah?" He tipped his head toward her, trying not to catch the glare off her sequined tank top. "Which one's that?"

"You'll see."

Despite Stacia's certainty, it took another five riders before the announcer got to the Andra story, and LJ was ready to excuse himself to get back to work when he finally heard her name.

"We've got a real treat for you folks today . . . " The announcer chuckled, his voice wincingly loud out of the speaker above LJ's head. *"The first member of our next roping team is our former Miss Teen Rodeo Wild Falls and also former Miss Rodeo Wild Falls: the lovely Cassandra Lawler."*

"Wait. I bet it's coming now," Stacia said.

Andra trotted her palomino into the arena, waving to the crowd.

"I have to tell you folks, I still remember the day when this little lady nearly forfeited her chance at the Miss Teen Rodeo Wild Falls crown. She got in . . . well, we'll call it a bit of a disagreement with one of the other contestants about the girl's enthusiastic use of spurs."

Andra glanced up at the announcer's booth and shook her head. Bill rode into the ring, calling something to his daughter and chuckling when she stuck her tongue out at him. LJ leaned in closer to the fence, watching her face while he listened.

"Little Cassie Lawler, all of sixteen fiery years old, dropped her saddle right in the dirt. She got rid of her bridle, vaulted back onto her horse, and rode the whole horsemanship pattern at liberty." The announcer chuckled. *"The judges didn't know what to think. First, they disqualified her. After some discussion, though, they decided the greater display of horsemanship outweighed the points she lost on congeniality, and she went home with the crown."*

Whistles erupted from the crowd, and LJ laughed. "Of course she did."

Stacia propped one of her motorcycle-booted feet on the bottom rail. "Girl could always ride. She and Jason used to push each other to do all kinds of crazy stuff—racing all over the ranch blindfolded, seeing who could jump the highest fence bareback. Might as well have been competing for who could break the most bones, because that's how it ended up. But he stopped challenging her after she came home from college, and she never calls him out anymore."

"Jason? Really? He seems kind of quiet."

"Yeah, with most people, but not with Andra and me." She tapped her bottle against the fence. "I guess they're both quiet these days. As teenagers, they were a little nuts, but it was kind of fun to referee their bets."

He glanced down at her, not sure what to make of the tone of her voice. "Do you ride?"

"Sure, who doesn't?" She smiled up at him. "I prefer something with a bit of a growl to its RPMs, though. Horses are too much trouble when you can swap out for an engine that comes standard equipped with common sense."

"Today, we get the pleasure of a father and daughter team, with Bill Lawler himself shooting for the heels. And if that old salt misses them, I give every single one of you permission to stand up and boo as loud as you can." The announcer laughed straight into the microphone. *"Aren't you ready yet, Bill?"* he asked as the ranch owner and his daughter got their lariats adjusted, swinging them to test the length. *"Do you need a minute to do some of that New Age yoga?"*

Stacia shook her head. "God, he's embarrassing. We're never going to get a decent-sized rodeo around here with that yahoo running the show."

LJ snickered. "I think he's kind of funny."

She blinked. "Really? After the way he introduced you?"

His fingers tapped restlessly against the fence. When he rode into the arena, the announcer had informed everyone he was the first "Negro" cowboy to grace the Wild Falls Rodeo. His back had gone stiff so fast his horse had spooked. But he was trying not to lose his temper every time somebody said something ignorant.

He attempted to keep his face blank and only glanced over at

Stacia. "Considering the next time he talked about me, he called me 'African American' three times in one sentence, I figured somebody had a little chat with him."

She took a drink of her beer. "No idea what you mean."

He shifted his weight, his elbows grinding into the fence as his arms tightened. She meant well. Funny how that didn't help when all he wanted was to be introduced by his name and home state, like all the other cowboys.

LJ swallowed and tried to shake it off. Getting mad was only going to make him stand out even more. He looked over at the roping chutes, his eyes searching for black hair and a golden shimmering shirt.

Stacia said something else, but he missed it as Andra backed Gracie into the corner of the starting box, the mare's hindquarters tucked tight against the pads on the fence. Bill's Roman-nosed sorrel fidgeted, his hooves dancing in place. In contrast, Andra's palomino mare stood alert, her ears pricked straight forward and all the motion in the world poised in her stillness. Andra swapped glances with her dad and then nodded to the guy operating the calf chute.

The calf leaped free, and Gracie bolted out of the starting box, her huge strides spraying arena dirt out behind her. LJ shifted to his other foot, and that fast, it was over.

Andra's loop dropped over the calf's head, Gracie whipped left in midstride, and Bill's lariat was already sailing through the air as Andra turned the calf just so. His rope snapped taut on both the calf's rear legs before LJ could complete a blink.

Then Andra and Bill slowed down a touch, both taking an extra second to adjust their horses to gently catch the calf between the tension of their two ropes without yanking.

"*Holy jumping jalapeño!*" the announcer yelped. "*I think we've got ourselves a new arena record! I should have known, folks. I should have known that you do not dare a Lawler unless you are ready to come in last. Well, I still remember the time Bill and I were boys and we both had our eye on the same girl for the senior prom.*

I bet she's in the crowd tonight. Can anybody see Sheila Peterson? Sheila Peterson, friends, she—oh, there she is! Just as pretty as high school, folks, and she welcomed her first grandchild into the world last week."

"The time, Russ! Tell us the time already," Stacia hollered. She dropped her forehead against the fence. "I'm sorry, LJ. You're probably mentally packing the U-Haul to move away from this little hick town, aren't you?"

He chuckled and pushed off the fence, one eye on the exit gate closest to where Andra was gathering her rope up. "I'm already cooking up the start to the stories he'll be telling about me in a year or two. If I get too wild, I might have to take that favor you owe me in the form of a bond out of the county jail in the morning. For now, though, I'd better get ready to beat Curt in tie-down roping."

"Beat Jason, too, and I'll go raise some hell along with you," she called after him.

He tipped his hat to her, his eyes already wandering toward the arena. Andra rode toward the exit, her hat brim angled down but not quite hiding the smile tugging at her lips. He wanted to pull her off that gorgeous mare into a hug and tease her until he kicked that smile all the way loose. What he *should* do was go and get his borrowed horse ready.

She wasn't his girlfriend. She didn't seem like she was in a place for a serious relationship, and she wasn't the kind of woman he felt "just casual" about. Besides, he was still the out-of-towner trying to earn his way into the inner circle of the Lawler Ranch. But if there was one thing he'd learned from growing up in the cliquish neighborhoods of New Orleans, it was that you don't start to belong without acting like you already do.

LJ headed for the arena.

Energy sizzled up through Andra's legs and burst out through her mare's jigging trot as they left the rodeo arena. A dozen horses of all different colors waited while their riders unrolled cuffed chaps and adjusted their saddles, or stacked their lariats over and over again, trying to get the loops to lie smoothly.

In the chaos of the waiting area, Andra caught sight of a pale gray hat and the slash of a familiar, brilliant smile beneath it. Gracie's nose turned that way before Andra fully made the decision.

"Hey, hey, Rodeo Queen." LJ grinned. "What was that pretty little rope trick you just pulled?"

She rolled her eyes. "I knew once you saw these freaking glitter chaps, you'd never stop calling me that. I was nineteen, and I loved dressing up and fast horses, all right? Besides, Dad thought it would be good advertising for the ranch."

"Uh-huh. And what was the excuse for the teen tiara?" He arched an eyebrow, struggling to hold back a smile.

"Same thing. Only three years more naive."

LJ lost the battle against his smile. "I bet." He came closer and laid a hand on Gracie's neck. The horse blew out a breath and finally stopped dancing. "How about that time, huh? You and your daddy make a hell of a team."

He smelled like baked potatoes and melted butter, a strangely sweet combination that had her leaning a little closer before she stopped herself.

"Dad and I have worked a couple of steers together." She tipped her chin at him. "What horse did Jason give you for tie-down roping?"

"King Al, I think he called him."

"King's Smoky Allure?" Andra frowned. What was her brother thinking? That gelding wasn't ready yet, even for a local rodeo. He kept going sideways instead of backing up to keep the rope taut when the cowboy jumped off to tie the calf. "Never mind that. Take my horse." She swung down, her leg narrowly missing a cowboy who rode by while still buttoning his shirt, his reins hanging loose over his horse's neck.

"You sure?" LJ blinked. "Figured I'd have to sign over the title to my truck and my mama's house for enough collateral to touch an animal that well-bred."

"Al's nice enough, but Gracie will do everything but put your boots on for you. Which might be good, since you were working with the colts when you should have been practicing. Besides, I think she likes you." Andra passed over the reins to her mare, who had her head contentedly drooping while LJ scratched underneath her bridle straps. "Do you want me to swap out her saddle real quick?"

"Oh, I think I can manage a saddle switch without any help." He winked and flexed his arm until his biceps strained the cotton of his shirt. "But if you're worried, you can take a feel, make sure you think I can handle that pony of yours."

She shoved him away, snickering. "You never miss an opportunity to show off those arms, do you?"

"Of course I don't. You know how many push-ups I had to do for these biceps? Besides, they always make you smile . . ." His dark eyes twinkled, and he held his arm up farther as she tried to smother a laugh. She knew better. The more she giggled, the more he hammed it up. Sure enough, he picked up one of her hands, rubbing it dramatically up and down his arm. "Oh yeah, give it a feel. You still worried I can't lift that bitty little saddle?"

A throat cleared. Loudly.

Andra's grin began to fade as soon as she turned to see her dad standing next to his horse with every muscle in his face locked tight.

"LJ. I believe you have work to see to elsewhere."

LJ straightened up. "Mr. Lawler, we were just—"

"*Now.*"

Andra's stomach dropped, an instinctive reaction to that voice she'd heard every time she'd been in trouble since she was born.

LJ's hands clenched on Gracie's reins. "Sir, I don't mean any disrespect, but your daughter and I were only joking around. If she were uncomfortable, she'd have told me to knock it off."

Her eyes widened. She had thought her dad was mad that LJ was chatting instead of working, but obviously this was something more.

"I require my employees to follow my directions." Dad planted his boots a little wider. "You want to keep this job past today, son, you won't make me tell you again."

"If it had to do with the job, I'd already be gone. But if it has to do with Andra, that's her call." He looked to her.

She forced a smile, trying not to glance around to see who was watching. "It's okay, LJ, really. Just go get ready." This wasn't his problem, and the longer he stood here, the worse it made the mottled heat that burned up her neck and toward her cheeks.

He jerked a nod—to her, not her father—and walked away, his strides stiff and so long her horse had to break into a trot to catch up.

As soon as he was out of earshot, Andra spun around. "What the hell was that, Dad? He was kidding—he didn't mean anything by it."

"Don't be naive, Andra," he snapped. "He meant every filthy word." Behind him, his gelding stomped a foot. Dad took a step closer, lowering his voice enough that the clinking spurs and conversation of the waiting area kept their conversation private. "This is exactly why I didn't want to hire a young man onto the ranch. They look at you and start wanting all sorts of things you can't give them."

"You were worried I was giving him the wrong idea." Her jaw dropped and cold slammed through her whole body. "You know, damn you, you *know* I refused to dance with Gavin at that party. Did you think I was being a tease then, too?"

He wouldn't be the first to say it. After a whole childhood of jeans and riding boots, she used to love dressing up. The night of the party her dress had an asymmetrical hem slashed across the muscles of her thighs, paired with sky-high stilettos. When she told Gavin she didn't want to dance, he gave her this incredulous up-and-down look like yes was the only answer she was allowed to give. So she told him off, in front of all his friends.

Saliva pooled thickly in her mouth. She remembered putting aside her second beer later that night without finishing it, because she felt a little woozy. She remembered looking for her friend, because she wanted to go home. She remembered waking up cuffed to a bed in Gavin's tiny rented house.

Fingers bit into Andra's upper arms, and her head whirled, her lungs tightening to stone in her chest.

Oh no. Not here.

Her father's voice broke through as he shook her, and she realized vaguely that it had been there all along, even though she had no idea what he'd been saying. "Don't you say that, Cassandra Lawler. Don't you ever even *think* that. You've never done anything wrong. Not then, not now. I'm—" His voice went gruff, and he had to cough to go on. "I'm the worst father in the state if that's what I made you think."

She pulled in a breath, and relief washed through her. If she could breathe, she wasn't having an attack. She focused on his mossy-green eyes, the color closer to hazel than the brighter shade she and her mother had shared.

"I want you to feel safe in your home," Dad murmured. "That's all. I knew that man would start wanting more, and as soon as he did, it would remind you of all this stuff you might not be ready for." His thumbs brushed over her arms. "After what you've been through, I want you to know it's okay if you're never ready. You'll always have a home here, and family, and you'll never be alone, okay?"

She stood there, his words getting louder and louder in her ears until they were practically screaming at her. She shook off his hands and grabbed the reins of his horse, leading the gelding out of the crowd without a backward glance because she knew her father would follow. She dodged around a cowboy tightening his cinch, heat burning in two points on her cheekbones as she kept her eyes forward. Whatever the crowd heard, it didn't matter. Every person in this town knew how messed up she was and every disgusting detail of why because the trial transcripts were public documents.

Everything that had been done to her body was public property.

She rounded a fence to a quieter corner of the fairgrounds and stopped. Her dad's gelding almost stepped on her, then backed up quickly, snorting. She dropped his reins and let the well-trained horse stand as she whirled to face her dad. "I'm *always* alone." She narrowed her eyes at him, her vision tunneling to the single point of his pale, round face. "Haven't you noticed? When I'm riding, when I'm eating. Every moment of my damned existence, I'm alone."

He blinked. "We . . . I thought you wanted it that way."

She looked away toward the arena. Why wouldn't they think that? That is what she'd wanted, at first. Peace and quiet with no scouring eyes. No expectations that she'd start to smile and laugh the way she used to, or show up to ride in a tutu covered with Stacia's sequins because she was so tired of living in dirt-streaked jeans.

Expectations she couldn't fulfill, because she couldn't even meet a man for a job interview without ending up in the fetal position.

"You're right," she whispered, and her voice cracked. She knew she was messed up. She'd known it for years. It just hurt so much more coming from the man who had scorched her hair trying to help her learn to use a curling iron. She lifted her head. "Maybe I'm *not* capable of having a relationship. But that's never going to change if you scare off any man who comes within a mile of me. That's my choice, Dad." She took a step forward. "*Mine*. And nobody's going to take it from me."

"Of course not," he said hoarsely. His eyes started to shine, and he blinked quickly.

Andra swallowed. She'd never seen her father cry, not even at her mom's funeral, but she'd heard him. That first night after her family drove two hours to bring her home, arriving at the hospital after she had already finished the horror of the rape kit. When she was safe in her childhood bedroom, she'd heard her father crying down the hall, well after midnight. She'd heard him again when she moved back after college graduation. That was the first reason she began to think of building her own place, but it was far from the only reason.

"Sweetheart, if you think you want to try dating again, that's good, but . . ." He took off his hat and scrubbed a hand across his head before putting it back on. "Are you sure he's the guy you want to start with?"

Her chin snapped up and her teeth ground together. "Is this because he's black?"

"It doesn't have a thing to do with his color, Cassie." He used her childhood nickname, as if he were too rattled to remember it had changed. "But he was raised in the city, and differently from you. If you want to find a partner, it should be somebody you have more in common with."

She planted her hands on her hips. "So it's because he's black." She stalked a couple of steps away, then spun back around, glaring at him. "Seriously?"

Dad frowned. "Don't take that tone with me. Your generation likes to talk as if seeing any difference between two people makes you a bigot. But race is a lot more than color. It's the way they treat women, what they think is important. The way they talk and act. You hardly know a thing about this man. You think you're going to fit in with his family? And don't forget he came up here for a job first. Dating your employees gets . . . complicated."

"Well, you know what's simple?" she snapped, her voice growing stronger with every word. "I want my life back. I don't want to just make it through one day at a time, counting myself as lucky if I don't have a panic attack. I want to build a life I'm proud of, and I'm the best judge of how to do that, not you."

He clenched his jaw. "Okay. I am proud of you, sweetheart, whether you want to believe it or not. But don't bite off more than you can chew just to spite your dad."

She stiffened. Slowly, from her stomach to her lungs, her shoulders to her neck, until her whole body felt brittle. He'd said it with so much love in his voice that she couldn't even argue with him. What if he was right, and she would never be normal again?

"Okay," she mumbled. "I better get going." She kept her head down as she strode away, not even sure where she was headed.

Was that what her dad really thought of her? Was that what *LJ* thought of her?

Eight

◇◇◇◇

When all the other staff started drawing straws for who would go to the bar and who would take the horses home, Andra volunteered to drive the first trailer. Stacia barely argued with her, and no one looked surprised that she'd rather go home alone instead of celebrating that she had helped break the record time for team roping.

In contrast, when LJ volunteered to drive the second trailer, everyone was surprised but her, and Curt ribbed him until LJ's silence shut him down. She thought it meant he wanted a chance to talk to her privately, but apparently not. He didn't say a word to her as they packed up, or even after they got back to the ranch and they were alone.

One of the horses stamped a hoof, breaking the quiet of the barn. A stall door creaked. Andra snuck another glance down the aisle at LJ as she scooped up the pile of leg wraps to put them away. When she came back out, he was dusting hay off his hands and walking toward the mare waiting in the crossties. She kept her eyes on the ground as she passed, heading out front to move the trucks.

She backed the first trailer into its storage spot, and then the second. She was unhooking the last safety chain when LJ's footsteps rustled in the dirt behind her.

She sucked in a breath. Maybe she should apologize for giving him the wrong idea. But she wasn't sure if he was actually interested in her or if her father was reading too much into it. She had thought Dad didn't want to hire a man because she was still skittish around young—and especially muscular—members of the opposite sex. Instead, it turned out Dad thought she was too stupid to realize the effect she had on guys, and too traumatized to do anything about it. Her skin burned all over again as she thought about it.

Slowly, she turned to face the man she had thought was becoming her friend.

His jaw tightened as his eyes flicked between hers. "Look, I, ah . . ." His Adam's apple bobbed. "If I stepped over the line with you today or embarrassed you in front of your dad, I didn't mean to. You know that, right?"

She sucked in a quick breath. "You didn't. *You* didn't do anything wrong, LJ. I shouldn't have . . . I mean—" She couldn't finish. Not only because it was humiliating to say she hadn't meant to lead him on, but because her stomach felt all mixed up, like maybe it wasn't the truth. If he'd wanted to spend time with her as more than a friend . . . it felt wrong to like that thought so much. She wasn't ready for more, so it was hypocritical of her to long for it.

Maybe her father was right and she had been hinting toward that with LJ, however subconsciously. But he was her employee, and she'd gotten him in trouble. She should be more professional, not burden him with all her mixed-up feelings and problems.

"Thanks . . . for all your hard work today."

His eyes narrowed at her almost imperceptible pause, but then he nodded. "Okay. Congratulations on breaking that record, by the way." He barely waited for her weak smile before he headed for his own apartment, his strides long and stiff. He was still upset, and she had no idea how to fix it.

Andra went back to the barn and gathered up Gracie, blinking back tears. Her mood was too heavy for her to climb up onto the tall palomino, so she clung to the mare's lead rope and started the long walk back to her own house.

Earlier, she'd watched LJ in the calf-roping event, peeking around the far corner of the grandstands so neither he nor her father would see her do it. She'd embarrassed him enough already, her dad blowing up at him just because he was friends with her.

She could tell by LJ's quick, tight movements that he was angry as he stuck the pigging string between his teeth and backed Gracie into the starting box. But he didn't over-spur Andra's horse, and when he flipped the calf onto its side, he set the 250-pound animal down so lightly she didn't even hear the thud. Once he had the calf tied and the buzzer marked his impressive time, he didn't celebrate. He just walked back to Gracie and vaulted back on without touching a stirrup, the move as effortless as if he were pulling on his pants.

She hated that she was the reason his ever-present grin had disappeared, even for the space of a single afternoon.

Now Andra stopped in front of her house, staring at the darkened windows. The only sound for miles was the wind scouring the grass, the chirp of crickets from beneath her porch steps. She turned abruptly, pressing her cheek against her horse's warm neck. Gracie whickered, but she didn't have arms to hug her or a voice to comfort her. She was Andra's best friend, and she was only a fucking horse.

Somehow, this had become her life. Home every night to empty, silent rooms, and every time she laughed, somebody looked surprised. This morning, her old Rodeo Queen chaps had felt like a costume borrowed from the personality she used to have. She'd walked out of the trailer, and the cowboys' whistles had reminded her of the days when she blushed and preened under their attention instead of cringing. Revisiting her old self for a morning had felt utterly foreign.

Was Dad right? Was this all she would be capable of now? Was this who she *was* now?

Gracie backed away and trotted off a few steps before turning back with her ears pricked, offering her favorite game: the equine variation of tag. When Andra didn't chase her, she walked closer, then trotted away again, her head high and hopeful.

"Not right now, girl." Andra took her horse to the paddock and hugged her tight before she took off the halter. The empty windows of her waiting house taunted her until she turned back toward the ranch, and she started to run.

She had no idea what this person she had become was capable of, but she was sure of one thing: tonight, she wasn't going to plod quietly back to her cell.

Nine

◇◇◇◇

LJ slung his shirt onto the floor of the bathroom and yanked off one boot, letting it fall with a clunk. Movement flickered in the mirror over the sink, but he didn't turn his head to look at himself. Instead, he ripped off the other boot and half threw it, the leather skidding across wood-grained laminate and flipping out into the hall.

All he had here was an old Billy Cook saddle, clothes, and a saxophone. He could quit in the morning. Hell, he could drive out tonight if he wanted. LJ flipped his belt buckle open, the worn edges of the silver reminding him of his uncle. He'd been running that ranch north of New Orleans for nearly twenty years, though the owner barely paid him enough to keep his fridge full. LJ always had a job there, as long as he didn't mind muscling horses into obedience to keep up with the grueling training schedule the owner insisted on. Unfortunately, he minded. One whole hell of a lot.

LJ, honey, the world isn't going to bend for you.

His mama was right. It would be the same anywhere he went, and all his mad was going to do was slow down the process. People needed a chance to get to know you, to let your actions argue them out of whatever they decided when they took their first look at you. Besides, he would always be too tall to slide under the radar, a little too broad in the shoulders to set people at ease.

He bent down to turn on the shower, and the gush of water against porcelain nearly drowned out the knock at his door.

The faucet squeaked as he cranked it back off. Must be an emergency with one of the horses. Andra hadn't seemed in much of a hurry to talk to him earlier, and with everyone gone to the bar, he was pretty sure they were the only ones left on the property.

After the scene earlier, he doubted she was here because she wanted some company for dinner. His abs flexed, anger burning deep in his gut like a fire that never went out. He shoved it a little further back.

LJ was already reaching for the doorknob when he realized he had forgotten his shirt. Another knock rattled the door, even harder than the first. Shit, the horse must be in bad shape. He opened the door.

Andra moved so quickly he got only a flash of mussed black curls before her fingers slipped cold over his cheeks, her lips hot against his.

His heart jumped, thumping into an erratic rhythm. Her hands clung to his jaw, and his slid into the soft strands of her hair, stroking them between his fingers as he bent lower to her level. She smelled like leather and horses, wind and salt and a sweet wisp of one of those things women put in their hair. She all but devoured him, fierce and frantic. He held steady for her, drinking in every touch of her lips and waiting for her to ease into sync with him. Shock still echoed in the back of his mind, but he wasn't about to let her go.

Her little gasp of a breath broke against his lips as she sagged into him, his dangling belt buckle catching on the loop of her jeans.

LJ's hands slid down to the curve of her back, and he pulled away just enough to see the tears flooding down her cheeks, and the streaks of mascara that only emphasized the wildness of her green eyes.

"I don't want to be broken," she gasped.

His fingers tightened, the shimmery fabric of her blouse warm from her skin, her waist impossibly tiny against his broad palms. Something had happened to her tonight, something bad. He didn't know what, and he didn't know how that added up to the whirlwind of a kiss she'd planted on him. All that mattered now was getting her safe. He guided her away from the door, tipping his head toward his kitchen. "Come inside. I'll make you a sandwich."

She stepped back, swiping at her face with shaking hands. He toed the door closed and buckled his belt, tugging his jeans a little straighter because that kiss alone had brought him halfway to standing. But every other thought in his crowded head got kicked to the curb at the sight of her distress.

Her sniff was loud in his small apartment, and he flicked on the kitchen light so it would seem more welcoming.

"I'm sorry," she blurted out. "I shouldn't have done that. I don't even know why I came here."

He frowned, leading the way into the kitchen. "You can always come over here. Don't have to have a reason."

"I know you were upset earlier, and I didn't even ask what was wrong." She sucked in another sniffling breath. "It's okay if you're pissed at me. I didn't realize—and then I thought maybe—" She dropped her hands, as if to keep them from wiping at the tears that still hadn't stopped. "I need . . . I really need someone to talk to right now."

He pulled out a chair for her and brushed her arm with just his fingertips, guiding her toward it. He kept his voice gentle, the hint of gravel at the bottom of it nothing he could control. "Don't you worry about me; I'll be just fine. Why don't you sit down and tell me what brings you to my door, needing an ear?"

She dropped into the chair with a hard exhale. "My dad."

LJ crossed the kitchen and ripped off a paper towel for her, anger threatening deep in his gut as he handed it over. His tone dropped half an octave when he answered. "Yeah, don't apologize for him. It ain't no thing." He straightened, the skin tight across his cheekbones. "Men never want their white daughters taking up with black dudes, especially not when they're the hired help. That's older than this country."

He could still feel the give of her lips pressing into his, the way her hands clung to his cheeks. He hated that he had anything to do with the tears staining her face. Earlier, he'd thought she was embarrassed because they'd been caught in a situation that looked flirtier than what it was. Shit, all he had wanted was to make her smile.

The anger twisted, writhing higher until he had to move. He got out a frying pan and dropped butter into it, tilting the pan so it would start to run as it heated.

"That's not why he was mad," she said. She paused to blow her nose, and as he processed her words, his grip froze with the pan still tipped to the right.

She hadn't denied that there was something between them. She'd flown through his door tonight and kissed him, and he had not the first damned clue what that all meant.

The butter began to melt and slide, pooling into the far edge of the pan and filling the kitchen with its warmth and aroma.

"Dad doesn't care that you're black. But he's not making any sense. It's almost like he hates you, and he's making up reasons why."

He snorted. "Sure. He has a weird feeling about me, like I might be trouble. That's how it works. Nobody thinks they're racist, Andra. They just think some people can't be trusted, especially not with their daughters."

She paused, the paper towel wadded in front of her. "I just can't imagine my *dad* . . . But maybe you're right. He kept saying how different you were from me, and he doesn't even know you." She shoved the paper towel away. "That's not all of it, though. He thinks we have nothing in common, but mainly he thinks I'm not capable of having a relationship. And that by spending time with you, I'm leading you on."

Heat roared through LJ's ears. He flipped off the burner and set the pan aside, going back to the table.

He pulled out a chair across from Andra, his jaw muscles locked tight as he propped his elbows on his knees so he'd be closer to her height. Then he looked up at her. "Two things."

She nodded, eyes on the wadded paper towel she was shredding in her lap.

"First, there ain't any 'leading on' between me and you. Ever."

Her gaze jerked up to his, and he watched it flicker toward his bare shoulders and back to his face.

"I got no expectations, and we're both free to do anything we please. Anything that feels good to us, you got that? You wanna come to my door and kiss me into next week, you do that. If I want to make you a sandwich in my apartment after your father made it damn sure clear he didn't want us alone together? I'm gonna do that, too." Louisiana tasted thick in his throat as he spoke, but he didn't try to clean up his roots. He wanted her to hear the truth of him, and he couldn't do that with any fake university accent. "'Leading on' is for assholes who think the world owes them something."

The corner of her mouth turned up. It wobbled a little, but it was kissing cousins with a smile, and he'd take that. Hell yes, he'd take that.

"What's the second thing?" she asked, her voice still more hesitant than he'd like.

LJ made himself calm and neutral, the way he had to for the colts. And then he asked, "What do *you* think about what your dad said?"

"He's right." Her eyes started to water again. "I don't want him to be, but he is. I never meant to be a hermit, LJ."

His eyes narrowed, but he nodded. She ate dinner with him almost every night, but he'd bulldozed his way into her house and into those cooking lessons. As far as he'd seen, it was the only time she spoke to another person about something that wasn't a horse. So as much as it grated on him, he didn't argue with her assessment of herself. He just let her talk.

"After the attack, there was the trial. I went back to college, because I wasn't about to let that jerk chase me away." She looked away, moving his salt shaker so it was lined up next to the pepper. "Everybody knew what had happened."

He was all the wrong sizes. His throat too small to breathe

through, his shoulders too big to stay still. His hands clamped use-
lessly together, dangling between his knees. He ignored all the jigsaw
pieces of himself and listened.

"When they looked at me, it seemed like the filth of what had
happened was all over me." Her voice rasped against the silence in
his kitchen. "I had to say, out loud in court, what Gavin did."

He shook his head, his gut twisting acidly. It wasn't right, to make
somebody speak to strangers about something so private. Where was
the justice in that?

Chair legs squeaked over laminate flooring as he pushed to his
feet. He couldn't change what had happened, but he needed to do
something for her. Besides, he had faced enough hard days with an
empty belly to know it was better if you didn't have to.

"I'm sorry," Andra said. "You probably don't want to hear about
all this."

He flicked on the burner again. "You talk," he said. "I'll cook." He
looked back and caught her eyes from across the kitchen. "Okay?"

Her head tipped slightly to the side, like a surprised nod. "Yeah."
She took a breath. "Okay."

He ripped off a paper towel, wiped out the pan, and then put in
fresh butter to melt while he took down some sourdough bread.

"I didn't drop out. I kept going to class, all the way through graduation."

"Good." From the fridge, he chose cheddar and his tiny, prized
chunk of parmesan and knocked the door closed with his elbow.
"Glad you didn't let that bastard ruin a degree you earned." He
dropped the cheese in front of her and retrieved a grater and a plate.
"Can I put you to work?"

"Oh, yeah, of course." She pulled the grater toward her. "My senior year was hell, and I spent a lot of it in courtrooms. When that
was over, I came back to the ranch, and I just wanted everyone to
stop looking at me. My family didn't know how to talk to me anymore, and conversation was weird, stilted, when I was around. So I
took my share of the past profits from the business and built my

cottage. I wanted to be left alone for a minute—that was all. Around that time, Dad gave me Gracie, and I threw myself into training her."

"He gave you that horse?" LJ flicked a glance at her before he dropped a piece of bread on top of the melting butter.

Andra smiled. "I know, right? A palomino quarter horse with top-notch bloodlines and four white socks isn't something a good businessman can spare to put in his daughter's stocking at Christmas." She started grating cheese, her eyes dry now that she had something to do with her hands. "It helped, though. The first time I got back on a horse was the first time my body felt right again. It was good to come home, but I've spent too much time just making it through the day, you know?"

"Yeah," LJ said. "I do know."

After Katrina, it was all about getting people off the rooftops. Then being able to find a bottle of water for Mama when she was thirsty. A hose to rinse the mud off his only set of clothes. He went to college a few years late, partly because there was nowhere to graduate from high school in the year after the flood. And partly because he couldn't concentrate on solving for x when what he needed to solve was how to build a roof that kept the rain out with no money and even fewer skills. But he didn't say any of that, because Andra needed to talk tonight, not listen.

"I thought I was doing okay," she said, frowning down at the plate as she grated even faster. "And then today, it was so obvious . . . this isn't the life I want. I love the horses, but all I think about is who has a sore foot and the point rankings our animals are pulling in the show circuit. I don't want that to be all I am."

He flipped the bread to its other side and came over to where she'd grated nearly all his cheese. "Can I borrow a little of that, do you think?"

She sat back, blushing. "Sorry. Think I got carried away."

"With the cheese, or with me?" He winked.

She groaned, dropping her face into her hands. "You're never going to let me live this down, are you?"

"Depends." He sprinkled the cheese onto the toasted bread, flipped off the burner, and put a lid on the pan. "You give me a second kiss to think about, and I might just forget to tease you about the first one."

He turned around and leaned his hips back against the counter, crossing his arms. He hadn't wanted to leave her to get a fresh shirt, but when she peeked over her hands at him and her gaze dipped to his abs, he was very happy he hadn't gotten dressed.

He tipped his chin up, just enough to catch her attention. "I'll forget it," he said quietly. "If you want me to."

She blew out a breath, her hands dropping. "I—"

He waited, his heart thumping so loud he was afraid he wouldn't be able to hear her over the drum of it.

"I wanted to see if I could feel anything." She glanced at him and then away. "It felt good." Her voice trembled. "But I just . . . I don't know if I want any part of all that, ever again."

He nodded. "Fair enough." That's exactly where he'd thought she was at until she'd up and kissed him. But she hadn't asked him to forget about it, and he'd told her where he stood—and that she could stand anywhere she pleased when it came to him. Too bad her daddy didn't agree.

LJ lifted the lid off the pan, scooped her sandwich onto a plate, and cut it once diagonally, the cheddar and parmesan melting out the sides.

He took it to the table and slid it in front of her with an easy smile. "For now, how about you just eat your sandwich, Rodeo Queen?"

Ten

◇◇◇◇

Andra pushed up the sleeves of her sweater, once red but now faded to a rusty pink. She tucked an unraveling thread back into the cuff before she pulled the cutting board across the table and took a mushroom out of the bowl. After three days of rain, her whole house smelled of sagebrush and wet, dark soil, even though she'd showered and changed into clean clothes when she got home. LJ looked like he'd changed, too, but his jeans were wet up to the knees from walking through the tall grass to get over here. His shirt was dry, though, a soft cotton Henley that clung to his shoulders before falling loosely over the curve of his lower back.

She let herself look an extra minute because she was sitting at the table and he was facing away from her, working over two different skillets on the stove. The thickness of his shoulders did something deep inside her, and she wasn't entirely sure what to call it. She imagined running her hands over his back, fitting her palms into the curve of his spine above the waistband of his jeans. Thanks to the night she'd surprised him at home, she knew how he looked without a shirt. Now she couldn't stop imagining how it would feel to do more than look.

The thought of touching him was like the longing for a fluffy blanket on a frosty night, but it had a zing of danger, too, like a beautiful horse you knew was too wild to ride. She didn't know what the hell to do with feelings that argued with each other that way.

She shivered and tucked one of her legs up under her on the chair, tugging the hem of her sweater out to cover more of her. LJ set down the spatula and crossed to the thermostat in the living room, bumping it up a couple of notches.

"I'm fine—don't waste electricity," she said. "I'm already wearing a sweater in June, for crying out loud."

"How am I supposed to concentrate on cooking with your teeth chattering away over there?" He looked beside the couch, and then he opened the closet. "You've been getting soaked to the skin all day going from the indoor arena to the barns. A sweater isn't going to cut it. Where are your throw blankets?"

"Don't have any."

His hand started to rise to the phone in his back pocket, and she threw a mushroom, nailing him above one hip bone. "Don't even think about it." She got up and grabbed her barn jacket from the hook by the door, spreading it over her legs when she sat back down. "There, happy?" He laughed, and his camera phone clicked. "Damn it, LJ! Don't you and your mama ever get tired of laughing at me? I have plenty of blankets. For my bed. Which is where people use blankets."

Her scowl was only halfhearted. It was hard to be mad at a guy who texted his mother daily, even if they seemed to think she was some kind of barbarian for being clueless about words like "braise" and "poach," as if they came up so often in conversation.

"We're not laughing at you," he protested, though the twitching of his lips gave him away as he typed out his text message. "This is for your own good. Once she sees what you're using for a throw blanket, she'll have one knitted up for you by Monday morning." He put his phone away, picked up the mushroom she'd thrown, and went back to the vegetables he was sautéing. "If we get another three days of rain, you might be grateful by then."

Three days of rain. Which meant it had been three days since the rodeo, three days since she'd kissed him, and he hadn't made a single move. In fact, he hadn't changed toward her at all. He was casual, playful, his jokes were dirty as ever, and his hands never strayed past a quick tug to the end of her braid or a brush across her shoulders, whether they were in the barn or in the privacy of her house.

She propped her chin on her hand. She'd spent every one of those days thinking the word "relationship" into tatters, along with everything that might mean, and she still didn't know if the life she wanted for herself would ever include a man. What she did know was that she wanted to explore the curves of LJ's shoulders. Unfortunately, she wasn't sure that's what *he* wanted. Maybe he just liked having company at dinnertime. She couldn't imagine him eating ready-made meals at the main house, with the way his hands were so quick and competent on a skillet handle or a whisk, fitting each tool as if they were made for that purpose alone.

Outside, the rain picked up, the steady drum on the roof getting louder.

She dropped her hand onto the table. "LJ?"

He picked up the skillet and gave it a flick so all the bell pepper slices leaped up and flipped themselves over. "Mm-hmm?"

"What did you think when I kissed you?"

He shouted with laughter. "Probably exactly what you'd expect a man to be thinking just then, Andie-girl."

She scowled at his back. "I'm serious."

"Me too." He switched to the other skillet, turning the zucchini slices for their stir-fry. "I was halfway through my first glory hallelujah when I realized you were crying, and that pretty much cured me of the idea that the kissing had anything to do with me."

Of course it'd had to do with him. She'd been lonely, and his house was the only place she'd thought to go. She sat back, the wooden chair creaking. But then, she hadn't really hung out with other men since she'd been kidnapped. If her dad weren't so overprotective and the ranch were overrun with eligible bachelors, maybe she would have been kissing them instead.

Her throat clamped closed at the idea. Strange mouths, strange men. She'd take her empty house a thousand times over that. Of course, they wouldn't be strange if she spent as much time with them as she did with LJ. But which of the men in town would she even ask out? She knew all of them, and she wouldn't want to share the tiny space of her kitchen with a single one of them.

"C'mere," LJ said, cocking his head to beckon her over since both his hands were occupied.

Andra's heart crashed up into her ribs. She pulled the jacket off her lap and set it aside with shaking hands. The few steps across the kitchen to his side might as well have been miles, and for the first time in weeks, she felt how intimate it was to be alone with him in this house. Her gaze jumped from his relaxed face to his hands, busy with the skillet and spatula, trying to guess his intent.

Maybe he would turn and kiss her, as confident as he always was. When she'd kissed him, it had been fast and hard, her thoughts whirling, so she hadn't had time to catalog all the things she'd been wondering about ever since. His lips looked sensual, soft. She wanted to know if they'd feel different if she were gentle, exploring his shape instead of crushing him to her. What it would be like to have his chest touching hers.

She swallowed. She never would have had the courage to kiss him the first time if she'd had this much time to think it over.

"The thing with cooking vegetables," LJ said, "is that they're all different. They all have a temperature that will ruin them, and right below is the sweet spot, only enough heat to get a perfect caramelization."

She blinked and startled color rose to her cheeks. This was about cooking? Quickly, she looked at the skillet, hoping she hadn't done anything to give away what she'd been thinking. "Is that why you're doing them in different skillets?"

"That, and you don't have a wok, sad as that is. Anyway, if you do it in the right order in a wok, you can get them to all finish at the same time. Since you're a beginner, though, I thought it'd be best to master one at a time." He handed her the spatula and started discussing the differences between the needs of zucchini and those of bell peppers.

He smelled like pine trees and rain. Andra stared down at the stove, trying to focus. That was not remarkable. Everything smelled like pine trees and rain this week. It was more like something about being caught between the heat of his skin and the heat of the stove, where olive oil and bright-red bell peppers sizzled. That damn rain-water scent on the smooth skin of his chest that she could picture all too clearly despite his shirt.

"Okay, but how can you tell when they're ready?" she asked.

"Bite 'em." He grinned and snagged a bell pepper out of the skil-let, white teeth flashing as he popped it into his mouth. "But if you aren't so brave and dashing as me, or if your tongue burns easy, poke 'em with a fork."

He got one out of the drawer and folded it into her fingers, guid-ing her hand as they tested one of the pieces of the bell pepper. His hand was huge, each finger so much wider than hers, and not at all hesitant about holding her. Her heart beat so fast, spots danced in front of her eyes.

"You should feel the tension of a little resistance," he said, "but softness, too."

She nodded, backing up as she tried to ignore the tingles rippling up her inner thighs. "Right, yup. Got it."

He let her go, cocking an eyebrow at her expression. "You feeling okay? You're looking a little flushed, as my mama might say."

She leaned against the refrigerator where it stuck out from the counter, and closed her eyes. She was not imagining the double meaning to his every word. Nobody's mind was lower in the gutter than LJ's. He was flirting with her, had probably always *been* flirting with her, according to her father. It was just a different brand of flirting than she knew what to do with. All possibility, no pressure. And he was certainly doing it on purpose. The man missed nothing. Not the tiniest flick of a horse's ears, not the morning he brought her

coffee because her belt had missed one loop on her jeans and he figured that meant she'd been in a rush that day.

What bothered her was how *easy* it was. He'd invited himself into
her kitchen and her life from virtually his first day on the ranch.

"You took this job for the horses, right?" Her voice came out a
little faint, and she opened her eyes to see him frown at her.

"I certainly didn't take it for the pension plan."

She bit her lip, hesitating. Watching her, his expression changed.

"Ah." He laughed. "Don't flatter yourself, darlin'. You were
something else, riding that fancy stallion like you both belonged in
the Olympics. But it was Taz who ran away with my heart that first
day. That and all this." He nodded toward the window. "Big sky full
of second chances."

Her stomach twisted, uncertain whether she was relieved or offended he hadn't taken the job because he wanted to pursue her. Then
the second part of his statement caught her, and her eyes narrowed.

"Do you need a second chance?" she asked slowly.

"Doesn't everybody?" He flicked off both burners and stepped
close to her all in one smooth movement. One hand landed on the
refrigerator, above her head; one on the counter, next to her hip. He
was near enough to let her feel his body heat, but not caging her in.
She could step out from under his arm easily, and with a surge of her
pulse, she almost wished she couldn't. LJ stood so close his body was
her entire world. Cozy but thrilling. She wanted him pressed against
her so she could drown in that bizarre reaction, breathe it in and
glory in it.

He ducked his head, his drawl a lower pitch than usual. "What's
on your mind, beautiful?"

She could only blink, as if steam were effervescing out of the air
between them and she couldn't quite see.

"You keep asking all these questions." He licked his bottom lip,
a quick slick of tongue over that *mouth* of his. "Why don't you ask
me what you're really wanting to know?"

"The cooking lessons." Her mouth was so dry she had to swallow before she could continue. "Was that flirting? Is that why you offered in the first place?"

His hand dropped, the inside of his wrist warming her shoulder as he opened the fridge. Taking her other shoulder, he spun her around. "See that?"

She stared, puzzled. Milk, orange juice. Cheese and eggs and containers of leftovers and some lettuce that was starting to go off.

"That's what a fridge is supposed to look like." He let the door fall closed. "I like you."

She didn't move. He was right behind her, the closed fridge giving them no excuse to keep looking in its direction. They were too close for anything except hugging, her bottom so near the front of his jeans that she couldn't even shift her weight without touching him. This was the point where she should pull away.

He tapped one finger against the fridge door. "I would have done that much even for somebody I didn't like. As for the rest?" His knuckles skimmed down the back of her arm so lightly that the rough yarn of her sweater woke up her entire body, her skin rippling with goose bumps. "Now, that might be flirting."

"Might be?" she asked breathlessly.

His breath stirred her hair, as if he'd bent a little closer. "Depends on if you want it to be."

She knew the exact instant he backed away. It could have been the faint change in temperature, or the creak of the floor, or something else an instant before those things registered. She inhaled.

"Until then, no." LJ put a new pot on the stove. "It's not flirting."

He must have cranked up the thermostat too much, because beneath her clothes, she was sweating. She turned to stare at him, fighting the urge to gulp air. He knew, damn him. He'd known exactly what his nearness was doing to her. "If that wasn't flirting, what the hell was it?"

He flipped a dish towel to hang over his shoulder, but the laugh she expected never came. "Hope," he said.

Eleven

◇◇◇◇

LJ climbed the stairs in the Lawler house slowly, the stir-fry he'd made with Andra sitting heavy in his stomach. He should have made this visit the day after the rodeo. Hell, a real man would have done it after their first cooking lesson, when he made spaghetti and Andra made him forget that anything in the world mattered beyond getting her to smile. The steps seemed to waver under his feet, and deep down, he knew exactly why he hadn't done this sooner.

The top of the stairs led to a long hallway, the golden pinewood floors softened by a scattering of Navajo rugs. When Stacia had answered the door to the main house, she'd told him Bill Lawler's study was the fourth door on the left. She'd also said she'd have a whiskey waiting in the kitchen for him when he was done. And some towels to mop up the blood.

LJ stopped, his shoulders twitching under the too-crisp fabric of his fresh shirt. Stacia's teasing hadn't exactly eased his nerves. He'd come here to make a good impression, and he knew what a long shot that was. What a long shot he was.

Every place he'd ever been, people's eyes had made assumptions about him. Teachers thought he'd be disruptive and probably slow. Coaches thought because he was tall, he'd like basketball. Cops thought he was either coming from making trouble or headed to make some more. He'd left New Orleans for a better job, sure, but Montana was also supposed to be his chance at fresh eyes.

His chance to meet people who'd see how curious and willing his horses were, instead of frowning like his uncle and saying his way took too long. People whose hands wouldn't tighten on their purse straps when they saw him, their eyes dropping to the sidewalk too fast to catch his friendly smile.

He hadn't expected the change to happen overnight, though, and he hadn't won himself any ground by arguing with Bill at the rodeo. He already had an uphill climb to endure with whatever conclusions Bill had drawn about LJ: whether they were because of the color of his skin or the fact that the older man's head barely came up to his shoulder and Bill was used to being the top dog on his own ranch. Or maybe because he was a man in his twenties, like Andra's attacker must have been.

The problem was that when somebody treated him differently, he could never be entirely sure what part of him it was they didn't like, so it always ended up feeling like all of him.

LJ started down the hallway. His mama hadn't raised a coward, even if his toes fidgeted with every step.

When Andra said her father thought she was leading LJ on, the old anger had boiled in his chest, and he hadn't cared about his new start. He cared that *she* believed he had something different to offer. But if he didn't convince her father of the same, he wouldn't be around long enough to see if he could prove her right. And back home, he was going nowhere.

LJ stopped in front of the fourth room on the left, his hands flexing at his sides. He balled one into a fist and used it to knock on the door.

A low chuckle sounded from beyond. "Stacia, if you tempt me with one more piece of that blueberry pie, the only horse that'll be able to carry me is a Clydesdale."

LJ opened the door. "Not Stacia." He stood tall, trying not to think about the price of the thick rug he stood on. "I was hoping you might have a minute free so we could talk."

Bill Lawler stared at him from over the top of plastic drugstore reading glasses. Slowly, he swung his chair away from the desktop monitor so he faced the door. "Why don't you have a seat." He pulled off his glasses and tossed them onto the desk.

Bookcases lined the room, most of them stuffed with old ledger books, vet manuals, and trophies. So many of the latter they were crammed in by layers instead of displayed one by one. Atop each one, golden horses gleamed tauntingly.

To get into another stable with a record like the Lawlers boasted, he might be looking at ten years of lunging horses for minimum wage before he could do any real training. God, he didn't want to go home—back to holding manure rakes at the City Park stables and busboy tubs at night.

LJ crossed the room, ducking as he passed beneath a low-hanging chandelier of elk antlers. The big leather chair huffed beneath his weight when he sat down. This whole house felt solid, safe from howling hurricane winds and softened with country touches, like horses were a way of life for everyone. Not just for the people who could afford the City Park stable fees.

He took off his hat, exposing the close-cropped hair he'd freshly buzzed before he came over. He'd bought a set of clippers before he moved up here, knowing there wouldn't be a barber for miles that would know what to do with his hair.

LJ turned his hat in his hands, then settled on putting it in the chair next to his. "We got off on the wrong foot the other day, but I wanted you to know I didn't mean any disrespect toward you or your daughter. I was just—" He searched for how to explain the reasoning behind his particular brand of lowbrow humor when it came to Andra. "I think people are too careful around her sometimes. I think it makes her feel uncomfortable." But no, that wasn't quite right. "Or left out, or something."

LJ tried not to wince at his fumbling. His debate coach from college would be so depressed by his performance right now. When he was debating anything he cared about, he got too impassioned and forgot to use his prepared points or to school his accent.

Bill's chair creaked as he leaned back. "I doubt the lack of flirting around the stable yard is what makes her uncomfortable."

"*I* don't make her uncomfortable." Shit, why had he said it that way? "Sir," he tacked on. "She likes me."

Bill's bushy eyebrows shot up.

"I mean, what I meant to say was we've become friends. That's all." As true as they were, the words tasted like a lie. That hadn't been all they were since way before she'd kissed him. He wanted to know her, and it was a weird, mixed-up wanting that wasn't exactly about sex or romance or even friendship. It was more he wished she were permanent, like family. Wanting her in his bed was only a part of that huge, wordless dream.

LJ waited, inhaling a breath that smelled smooth like leather polish. The familiar scent should have put him at ease, but instead he started to sweat in the hollows where his arms were pressed against his sides.

Bill leaned forward again, picking up his reading glasses and folding them, then tapping one end on the desk. "LJ," he said. "Do you think you're the first man who's stepped onto this ranch and fallen boots over Stetson for my daughter?"

LJ's muscles clamped hot over his bones. "No, Mr. Lawler. I do not." He doubted he was even the fortieth man to look at Andra and decide he never wanted to look away. But he came here tonight because she'd looked back. With dilated green eyes and her chest heaving for air beneath that old pink sweater as she asked him if he was flirting, her gaze unable to tear itself away from his mouth even as she said it.

"In college, Andra was . . ." Bill started, his body going tense. He glanced toward the bookshelves and cleared his throat.

"I know, sir."

"You do?"

"She told me." LJ shook his head. If he was going to have any chance at winning this man's respect, he needed to stick to the truth. "Some, anyway."

Bill's chin ticked up. "I expect you read the old articles about it."

"I didn't."

They stared at each other. Hazel-green eyes to brown, and LJ would have ripped out his own lungs before he'd have blinked.

Bill finally nodded. "Okay. Either way, you know my daughter needs to be able to relax when she's home at the ranch. What she doesn't need is a bunch of cowboys sniffing after her, hoping to coax her into bed."

"With all due respect, what your daughter needs is not for everybody to treat men like something so terrible she stiffens up every time she sees one. All you're showing her is that she should be afraid."

Bill's nostrils flared, and he dropped his reading glasses. "And I suppose you're suddenly the expert on what she needs."

"It's not like that." LJ shot up rifle-straight in his seat. "Sir, all I want is to do my job." One more breath to keep his voice precise and even. "And a chance to prove that your daughter is always safe with me."

Bill's fists clenched so fast the paper of his desk blotter crumpled and tore partially free. "Safe? The first time I caught you alone with her, she wasn't even breathing, she was so scared. She hadn't had one of those attacks in months until you came around. You have no clue what you're sticking your nose into."

Bill glowered across the desk.

"Do you think I'm stupid?" he went on. "I see how you look at this ranch." His eyes narrowed, the creases beside them fanning out to show all the years he'd spent riding under the brutal Montana sun. "You come here and see a beautiful young girl—vulnerable, lonely. And you think you can charm your way into a permanent position on a ranch you could never afford in two lifetimes."

The air in LJ's lungs scorched his cells, boiled up his throat. He'd never given Bill a single reason to think he was using Andra to secure his job here. If anything, spending time with her had endangered his position. But this wasn't about logic. This was about an overprotective daddy who had hardly spoken to a black man before and decided after one glance that he wanted better for his little girl.

LJ's hands locked on to the armrests of his chair. He could snap the thick wood beneath this leather and toss it to the ground, flip the heavy mahogany desk onto its side with only one hand. Let this self-righteous asshole know exactly how dangerous he could be.

Which would also prove to him exactly how much he couldn't be trusted. "I would never—"

"Prove it." Bill's eye twitched as he sat back in his desk chair. "You want this job? On your own damned merit?"

LJ stuffed his festering anger down deep and nodded.

"You can keep working here, or you can try and date my daughter. Not both." Bill's hazel-green eyes went hard. "If what you want is a career here, then you earn it honestly, by showing me with hard work and years of loyalty that you're an asset to the ranch. And if you want my daughter, you get your own job and support yourself without her family money paying your bills."

LJ couldn't even blink. The closest show barn of this caliber was hundreds of miles away, not that it mattered. The Lawlers were the only ones in the business willing to pay a novice trainer enough that he could send anything home to help his mama with the bills. He would know: he'd spent three years before this working on his uncle's ranch and searching for a better job anywhere in the country.

The hard truth was that horses were a rich man's hobby, and he'd never be a rich man.

LJ tried not to picture his mama's expression when he had to come crawling home because he got fired. She had no problem railing at him about burning the soup or getting up late for school, but when he really disappointed her, she went quiet. Like she was confused because she truly believed in him. When he failed, his steel-willed mama lost her stride a little bit.

But this wasn't an ultimatum; it was a trap. If he kept working on the ranch, Bill would fire him either for getting too close to Andra or for the first tiny mistake he made. And if he chose her and quit, he'd have to go so far away he couldn't afford to travel back to see her.

"I understand," LJ said. And he did. He grabbed his hat and left the office with his head high and straight.

He understood that nothing he said and nothing he did would change what the man behind that desk thought of him. And it made him want to burn the entire world down, with himself howling in the center of all of it.

Twelve

◇◇◇◇

Andra pulled her feet up onto the narrow bench in the dressing room and hugged her knees to her chest. She glared at the clothes crowding the hooks on the wall and falling onto the floor of the tiny department-store cubicle. This was ridiculous.

No, riffling through her own closet this morning had been ridiculous. She'd never noticed before that every shirt she owned had either a horse printed on it or a horse-related stain somewhere. Or both. Mostly both.

The sun hadn't even risen when she realized she couldn't stand to wear a single thing she owned. Had she always looked this sloppy? She used to have a whole section of her closet for fun and flattering non-work-related clothes. Now she had a single dress, which she pretty much only wore for funerals.

Grabbing her keys, she'd texted her dad that she was taking the day off and headed for her truck. She was in the mood to feel pretty, damn it, and how could she do that while wearing a shirt marked with green horse slobber?

This morning, it'd made sense. Now she was staring at a lot of shirts in styles that hadn't even existed the last time she went shopping, while her mind chased its own tail in a dozen different circles.

She yanked out her phone, but her list of frequently called numbers was painfully short. She wasn't talking to her dad or brother about this, no way, and Stacia would think she was insane. All the other numbers were for ranch employees, and for once, her problem had nothing to do with a horse.

She chose a name, hit "Call," and squeezed her eyes shut.

"'Lo?" LJ answered, managing to make the single syllable sound warm as the southern sun.

"I need you to do that thing where you make everything seem simple."

He laughed. Was it a little strained, or was that her projecting her own mood? "Ah, I don't know if I'm so good at that today."

She hesitated. "Is everything okay?"

"Sure, sure," he said quickly. "I was wondering if you were playing hooky or if you were gone for, uh, something else." He cleared his throat. "Doesn't matter. Tell me what's complicated, and I'll do my best."

"The day of the rodeo was the first time I'd put on makeup since I got kidnapped."

Wow, it sounded even crazier when she said it out loud. She covered her eyes with her hand and blurted it all out.

"I thought I was living my life, and suddenly I realized I let *him* change me, everything about me. Five years after it happened, and he's controlling the way I look every day. How screwed up is that? I actually felt good at the rodeo, you know?" She took a breath. "So I went shopping. Except now everything that looks good shows off my body, and it's like, why do I want to feel beautiful? Isn't that an excuse for wanting to appeal to men? And I don't *want* them to look at me, so why am I going to all this effort? But should I have to look and feel crappy just because I don't want to date? So now I'm stuck because I have no idea what the right answer is."

Her eyes popped open. Of course she had just word-vomited all of that on the one guy she might kind of want to flirt with. Except she wasn't sure of that, either. She wanted to touch *him*, yeah. She just wasn't sure she could handle it if he touched her, and she was well aware of how unfair and insane that was.

"Is that all?" he asked after a pause.

"All?" she squeaked. "Are you kidding me right now? I've been locked in a dressing room for over an hour. The employees are probably going to call the cops on me."

"Hell, girl . . ." He chuckled. "It ain't no crime to look beautiful. Doesn't have to mean anything."

A laugh jumped out of her. She pressed a hand to her chest as the tension started to ease.

"Buy yourself something nice," he said. "Anything I need to do for you at the ranch so you don't have to hurry back?"

"No, that's okay. I'll see you at dinner. I had an idea for tonight, so don't bring anything over." She let her head fall back against the wall. "LJ?"

"Mm-hmm?" A horse whinnied in the background, and she could picture LJ so clearly, an arm propped on a stall door, looking as perfectly at home in her barn as he always did in her kitchen.

"Thank you," she whispered.

"Ain't no thing at all. Have a good time."

She dropped the phone to her lap, blowing out a long breath. The screen returned to her favorites list, and she found herself staring at Stacia's name. It used to be they could tell each other anything. After her kidnapping, she hadn't wanted to drag Stacia down into the depression she faced or talk about what had happened, but it had been years now. Was she going to keep letting that one thing define all her choices, from T-shirts to which person she called when she was upset?

She lifted her phone again and chose a different name.

"Andra? What's, uh . . . what's going on?" The tone of Stacia's voice was a perfect measure of how long it had been since she last called.

"Hey, I ditched work today to go clothes shopping, and to be honest, I think I suck at it. Would you . . . Do you want to come meet me?"

"Did you get bucked off on your head?" Stacia snorted. "I buy motorcycle shirts online and hand-sew my own sequins because the

world is too brain-dead to realize that some girls like a little glitter
along with their RPMs. What about that makes you think I'm qual-
ified to be your fashion adviser?"

She should make a joke. A normal person would make a joke.

Andra closed her eyes and whispered, "Because you're my friend."
Even as she said it, she hoped like hell it was still true.

"Okay, your funeral," Stacia said. "Where are you at? And hey, if
Bill busts my ass for not getting the oil changed in the Chevy today,
I'm totally telling him it was your idea."

LJ shot a look toward Andra's door, jumpy as hell that Bill would
choose tonight to visit his daughter. But after her frantic call this
afternoon, he wasn't about to abandon her to a dinner alone.

"And then Stacia told the clerk where she could stick her push-up
bra, which is how we got kicked out of T.J. Maxx." Andra hip-
checked him out of the way of the silverware drawer, and a smile
tugged at the corner of his mouth.

He turned away from the door. "I thought you said it was a JC
Penney."

"No, they didn't kick us out of the JC Penney. They asked us to
keep the volume down, which might as well have been the same
thing." She whirled past him on the way to the stove.

Even though he knew she was about to scratch the nonstick coat-
ing on her pot with that metal spoon, he didn't say a word. He was
enjoying her mood way too much to puncture it. He crossed his arms
over his chest. "Only one day of shopping with your bestie and
you're giving me a run for my money on who the motormouth is
around here."

She snorted, stirring the tomato sauce. "Maybe I've been waiting
for you to stop jabbering all the time so I could get a story in edge-
wise, hmm?"

"Hey, if you don't like the conversation, you can always kick me
out and invite your friend over, subject her to whatever experiment
it is you have going there." He struggled to keep a straight face so

she'd rise to the bait. Sure enough, she planted one hand on a curvy hip and glared at him.

Stacia should take her shopping every day if it gave her this kind of spark. It wasn't the better-fitting, dark-wash jeans, or even the subtle drape of the silky deep-green shirt that hugged Andra's waist and didn't drown her breasts in extra fabric. It was the shine in her eyes, the way every smile didn't seem to have to fight its way onto her lips.

"Are you ready to hear the theory behind my magic, or are you going to keep making fun of me?"

"Oh, I'm ready for the magic to show up. I just kinda doubt it's going to happen with your tin-can sauce there."

She pointed the spoon at him. "Watch it, Delisle. Anyway, you said the secret to your mama's spaghetti sauce was Italian sausage, lots of garlic, and a little bit of brown sugar."

That and newly roasted tomatoes, fresh herbs, and about eight more spices, but if he didn't want that spoon upside the head, he probably shouldn't point it out. "Uh-huh."

"I figured I could make it a ton quicker with canned sauce as long as I used fresh garlic, and I remembered I had big, soft cloves of garlic in a restaurant once . . ." She paused dramatically, her smile tugging a matching one onto his face. Until she picked up an unpeeled bunch of garlic and tossed it in the pot of boiling water.

"Oh!" He reached out to stop her, but it was too late.

"What?"

"I, ah . . . I guess I thought that water was for the pasta." He tried not to look at the waterlogged garlic.

"It is." She grinned. "Once the garlic is soft enough to put in the sauce, we'll reuse the water and have garlic-flavored noodles." She tipped her chin up. "Admit it, LJ."

He must not have covered his horror at her culinary butchery well enough. "Admit what?"

"My spaghetti is going to be better than your mama's."

"No way."

She advanced on him, pointing with the spoon. "Say, 'Cassandra

Lawler, you have won, and I'm going to text my mama right now to tell her we've been out-spaghettied.'"

He raised his hands. "Girl, you're talking crazy."

She clucked her tongue and went back to the stove. "Kicking your ass is what I'm doing." She stirred the sauce.

"Don't say that out loud. My ancestors can hear you, and they're flipping over in their tombs."

She banged the spoon against the edge of the pot. "Hear that, Delisles? That's the sound of your family reputation biting the dust. Right here, right now." She reached out with the same spoon and prodded her garlic experiment to check it.

He groaned as he came up behind her to steal the spoon. "I can't stand it. You're boiling garlic with the skins on, girl! Boiling it!"

"Damn right I am." She did a little shimmy. "Take that, old fogy Delisles."

"Haven't you heard of New Orleans voodoo?"

"I'll voodoo your—"

He laughed, cupping a hand over her mouth. "Don't say it! Talking like that, you'll raise the spirits right up and—" All her weight dropped, and he broke off, catching her by instinct as she fell.

Thirteen

◇◇◇◇

LJ's first clue to what had happened was the choking gasp that fell from Andra's lips. He lowered them both to the kitchen floor, her tensed body half in his lap.

"Shit. I'm sorry, that was stupid as hell. I didn't mean to scare you." Why had he put his hand over her mouth? There were about a hundred different ways she might have ended up cuffed to a bed, and at least fifty of them started with somebody coming up behind her and covering her mouth. "Shh," he murmured, stroking his hands slowly down her arms. "You're okay. You're safe."

Last time this happened, she was rigid as a bridge beam. This time, she trembled so hard she was almost convulsing. It was so erratic that at first he didn't realize the fluttering movements of her hands were pushing at him. She was trying to get *away* from him.

He let her go, flinching back. She curled against the cabinets, the ends of her hair catching a stray wisp of onion skin from the floor. Her arms locked against her chest, her lips starting to tinge with blue as her mouth gaped open and she tried to pull in air her lungs wouldn't accept. She was going to suffocate right there while he watched.

"Andra? What do I do?" he begged.

Her eyes widened a little more, like his panic was contagious.

If he called her dad to pull her out of this, he'd kick LJ off the ranch, maybe worse. *Think, damn it.* "Hey, you left the burner on," he attempted, remembering how her father had reminded her of her loose horse to pull her out of her other attack.

Andra didn't answer, her lips twitching in airless gulps.

He reached to comfort her, and when she flinched, he bunched his hands into fists and shoved them against his thighs. "You've got to breathe, sweetheart. One breath, please. Just one."

She started to tremble again, her cheeks stark white and shading to gray. She was looking right at him. Jesus, she knew who he was, she knew where she was, and she was still terrified. Her father had been right to try to keep him away. It wasn't her memories that had frightened her. It was him.

Nausea roiled in his stomach, and he had to swallow saliva back to keep from throwing up.

He rolled up onto his knees before her. "Please," he whispered, his voice as gentle as he knew how to make it. "Please be okay. I need you to be okay."

Her little gasps were getting weaker. Even if he called her dad right now, Bill could never get here in time. Could a panic attack actually kill you? Why the hell hadn't he researched that when he had all the time in the world? Back when she was still breathing.

Why didn't she scream? Throw something at him? Shit, *he* wanted to scream. Anything but this terrible, breath-held howl of silence.

LJ grabbed her by both arms. "Hit me."

Not a blink. Not even a flinch this time.

On the stove, the garlic water boiled over with a hiss of steam. He shook Andra, his knuckles smacking into the cabinet behind her. "Hit me, damn it!" he shouted.

She moved. Finally, finally she moved, her hand twitching against his chest as she pushed at him.

"Come on, you can do better than that." He crowded right up into her face. "Come on, punch me. Hurt me. Make me leave you the fuck alone."

She turned her face away and shoved, the strength coming back into her arms.

"Harder!" he shouted.

This time he got a fist. As he was drawing in a breath to yell at her again, another hit landed, and then she was screaming, coming at him with both hands at once. The punches slammed into his chest, his arms, battered into the thin skin over his ribs, each impact like an exhalation of relief. He'd never felt anything so glorious.

And then they stopped. She blinked at him, her gaze focusing on his, with her fist still upraised.

"Andra?"

Her eyes filled with tears, and it took everything he had left not to reach for her. Instead, he scooted back, giving her the space she'd fought for, that she so obviously needed. His touch only made everything worse.

A sob caught in her throat, and she moved, so much faster now that she was in his lap before he realized what she intended to do. Her arms clutched tight around his back.

"I'm sorry," she whispered. "LJ, I'm so sorry."

He didn't have a prayer of resisting this time. He was holding her before he could debate leaving versus staying or even taking the pot off the stove.

They locked into each other, her tears wet against his neck, her breath huffing warm down the collar of his shirt. His ribs ached with the ferocity of her grip. He had no idea why she wanted to touch him now, when he was the one who had scared her nearly to death a moment ago. But then he didn't care, because she was in his arms and she was okay.

He stroked a shaking hand down her tangled hair. He hadn't been this crazy for a girl once in his whole life, and he couldn't even get through cooking dinner without slamming her into a panic attack. Her father had warned him he would do this to her, and he wanted her so much that he didn't listen. He never fucking listened. He just did what he wanted and damn the consequences, like his mama had always said. But this time he was hurting someone other than himself.

This time, he'd hurt Andra.

Andra pulled away first. LJ held her so gently, she thought he'd probably stay on the floor for the rest of his life if she asked him to, but his legs had to be falling asleep, and she needed a tissue. She rolled to the side, her butt hitting the hardwood floor next to his, and she let her head sag back against the counter. One second. She'd rest for one second, and then she'd get up.

The floor creaked beside her, and she cracked one swollen eyelid to see LJ stand and turn off the stove. Her nose was too clogged to smell, but she had probably burned something. So much for showing him up at cooking. So much for buying new clothes that made her feel like her younger, more confident self. It was distinctly the same old self slumped against this cabinet like a used dishrag.

A roll of toilet paper appeared in front of her, and she took it.

LJ lowered himself back to the floor, and their shoulders touched, creating a warm spot that counteracted the chill of the floor. "Can I ask you a question you're not going to want to answer?"

She laughed. Sharper and louder than his question probably warranted, because how fucked up was this day? How much more blatant could the evidence be that her past still owned her present? That it always, always would.

"Knock yourself out." She ripped off some toilet paper to blow her nose. The sound was rude and disgusting, but the sexy ship had sailed about half an hour ago.

He flipped around to face her, pulling his knees up and gripping one thick wrist in his opposite hand. His eyes were darkly circled and the tiniest bit red. "This is probably the last thing you want to talk about, but I was wondering how many different things trigger those."

She shook her head, pulling her knees up to match his so she wouldn't feel so limp. "They just happen, LJ."

"I scared you. Both times." His eyes flicked away, and when they came back, there was a light in them that was almost pleading. "But I thought if you knew of other things that caused them, too, or if we could nail down a pattern, maybe we could shake you loose of it."

She raised her eyebrows. "What, like I'm one of your colts and you just need to blow an air horn a couple of dozen times until I'm used to it?"

His shoulders hunched and he dropped his knees, sitting cross-legged instead. "I don't know. There's got to be something we can do, right? They're not . . . permanent."

"I'm not a stupid animal, LJ." Her hands fisted around the tissue, and she gritted her teeth. She shouldn't be yelling at him after what she had put him through, but seriously? "I can think through my own fear. I do it a thousand times every freaking day, okay? But this?" She threw an arm out. "My brain, my body, my *everything* locks down. I can't control it, and it's like I woke up in that room all over again and everything I took for granted about life was gone." She shut her mouth. Fast, hard, because he didn't need to share that moment with her. No one did.

She shoved to her feet.

The kitchen was a wreck. Of course it was. She had been totally butchering dinner, but she'd been in too good of a mood to care if her experiment failed. She grabbed the pot with the shreds of garlic floating in it and dumped the contents into the sink. A cloud of steam billowed up from the water and fogged the window above it, blurring the sunset light in the meadow grass out front.

"You want me to go?" His voice was quiet, and he was still on the floor.

She dropped the pot in the sink and gripped the edge of the counter, letting her head fall. "No. I'm sorry, LJ. None of this is your fault, and I'm sorry you keep ending up in the middle of it."

"The hell it isn't." He shook his head. "I'm the trigger. That's what you don't want to say." He jerked to his feet and headed for the door.

"Even just the sound of metal creaking will do it," she said, and he stopped. "Smells, dozens of them. I don't even know what they all are. One specific brand of laundry detergent, spilled beer." She swallowed. "It's not being scared so much as being startled that triggers it. When I don't know it's coming."

He was still looking toward the exit, so she reached for his arm, wanting him to stay but not wanting to beg. His muscles flexed under her hand.

"It wasn't only that, Andra. You looked at me and you *knew* me." His voice went hoarse. "And you were still afraid."

Her hand fell away as he turned and paced two steps, scrubbing both hands over his close-cropped hair.

She needed to say something, do something, so that this moment wouldn't be the end of whatever this thing was between them. "I can't help it," she whispered. "It's not your fault. It just happens."

"It doesn't. Not according to your daddy. Not until I started shoving my way into your life because I didn't want to wait until you invited me. *Damn* it." He laced his fingers behind his head and stared up at the ceiling, one of his knuckles popping when it clenched too hard.

He was so wound up it made Andra's heart pound to take a step closer, but she did it anyway. She was taking a chance she knew him well enough that what she was about to do might be the right thing instead of exactly the wrong one. She hated to see him upset, but at the same time . . . it was for her. And that simple thought melted her entirely.

She ducked inside his bent elbow and pushed up onto her toes, laying a kiss on his cheek.

He blinked and dropped his hands. "What was that for?"

"For caring," she said softly. "And for not waiting for an invitation."

The wound in his deep-brown eyes was one she had no idea how to heal, because it ripped deeper with every word out of her mouth. "I care a hell of a lot more than you think, Andra." He stared straight over her head, toward the exit, but he didn't move. "I hate that I'm making everything harder on you just by being here."

"You're not. You're making it . . ." She touched his side, and when he didn't pull away, she stepped closer, warmth spreading through her at the intensity of his reaction. "Different. Good different."

"Didn't look like good from here." He blew out a breath. "Fuck, those things scare me. You know it?"

"I know." After a second, she let her hands settle on his waist. When that seemed okay, she slid them around to the curve of his lower back, the muscles to either side of his spine filling her palms. "I'm sor—"

"Don't apologize. Just let me hold on to you for a second, okay?" His arms came around her, and he rested his chin on top of her head. "I don't want your daddy to be right about me, Andie-girl." The words were so low they were no more than a rumble in the places where his neck touched her forehead.

"I don't want him to be right about me, either," she whispered back. And she didn't let go.

Fourteen

◇◇◇◇

A crisp wind blew rain in across the hills, but birdsong still drifted in through the stable windows, like Montana birds were too tough to pack it in for the weather. LJ patted the silky neck of the colt he'd just finished riding, and grinned. He could understand those birds. The air was so clean up this close to the mountains, he never wanted to go inside, either.

His phone shrilled from his pocket, and Snap jerked away from him, burning the reins across his palm. Sucking in a breath, LJ winced and let the phone ring as the colt paused, stiff-legged and wild-eyed. It was going to take more than two rings to get past that reaction, but he didn't dare wait more than three.

He answered the phone. "Hel—"

"LJ Delisle, what are you doing that's so important you can't answer the phone when your mama calls?"

"Juggling colts, that's all." He cleared his throat and focused on dropping his accent as he led Snap up the barn aisle. Mama had stretched her every penny when he was in college so she could send him money to supplement his scholarships and meager work-study paychecks. The least he could do was show her she'd gotten something for her investment. "How are you?"

"Well, I'm fixing to mail you some things this week. Some green tea—I know you hate it, but it's good for the antioxidants—some fish fry in case you're getting low, and a new Tai Chi video I love. Don't you dare lie about doing it this time, either. It's good for your joints, and you'll thank me when you're old. Oh, and Andra's afghan. I hope she's not one of those prissy types that needs a blanket to be all one color, now. It costs the earth for a ball of yarn these days, so I had to make do with what I had lying about the house. How's that girl coming along in the kitchen?"

He smiled and used one hand to slip the bridle off Snap's ears. "I must be better at teaching horses than humans. She tried to boil garlic last week. Didn't peel it or noth—anything. She threw the whole bunch in the pot, skins and all."

"She didn't!" Mama clucked her tongue.

When he took off the bridle, Snap threw his head, so LJ pinched the phone between his shoulder and ear so he could repeat the process a few more times, waiting for the horse to calm. "I can't get Camellia Brand beans up here, but if you mailed me some, Andra might be able to manage red beans and rice. She's about a year off from being ready for gumbo."

Mama sighed. "Folks always act like making a simple roux for gumbo is some kind of voodoo magic. Pure foolishness. How's your job? Are you getting along okay with your boss? They're his horses, LJ, and you know that means you got to do things his way."

"He mostly stays out of my way when it comes to the training." On the fourth try, Snap released the bit without a fuss. LJ swapped bridle for halter and patted the horse, thinking of the whack his uncle would have given the colt for throwing his head. "You should see the stock they have up here, Mama. Did I tell you Andra loaned me her horse for the rodeo? King Cash and Allure bloodlines, and she didn't bat an eyelash. She's got that mare tuned up something beautiful, I tell you."

She laughed. "You never met a horse you didn't like, even if it was cross-eyed, knock-kneed, and mean as a stepped-on snake. And what do you mean, 'when it comes to the training'? Are you butting heads with the owner on something else?"

LJ gritted his teeth. He should have chosen his words more carefully. "He, ah . . . he's not so hot on the idea of me hanging around his daughter."

"Lyndon Johnson, tell me you're not risking your good job over some pretty girl."

He swallowed a groan as he clipped Snap into the crossties. "Mama, please don't call me that."

"I'll call you that as many times as I have to so you can remember the great man I named you for. I guarantee President Johnson didn't get to the White House without learning to pick his battles."

"Actually, he ramrodded through anything he wanted, from civil rights bills to the Vietnam War. It's part of what—"

"I am not done speaking. I know you think you don't need to take orders from any living soul, son, but until you can pay your own paycheck, you got to swallow down that pride of yours and behave."

LJ jerked the cinch loose and hauled the saddle off the colt's back. "I'm only giving her cooking lessons."

She snorted. "You think he don't know what two young folks get up to, alone in a kitchen? Mind your manners and stay away from that girl if that's what your boss wants. You wanna be exercising horses for a hundred dollars a week and arguing with your uncle over the right way to do every blessed thing? Well, then keep it up."

"You *told* me to teach her to cook!" LJ's voice spiked enough that Snap balked, throwing his head and yanking on the crossties.

"Don't you raise your voice at me, young man. When you've lived twenty more years and raised a child of your own, you can tell me my business. Until then, you close your mouth and listen to somebody who knows better than you do. You hearing me?"

"Yes, ma'am," he mumbled, kicking the tack room door out of his way and hoisting the saddle up onto a rack. The phone slipped from between his ear and his shoulder, and he caught it before it fell.

"Now I'll send up those red beans quick so you'll have 'em, then mail the blanket slow and cheap, but I don't—" She broke off with a little gasp, and then there was silence on the line.

"Mama? Mama, are you okay?"

He left the tack room and paced down the barn aisle. She still didn't answer. He exploded out into the sun with long strides, as if that would put him any closer to Louisiana than he'd been inside.

"Mama?!"

"I'm fine. Stop shouting in my ear." Her voice wasn't right. Not weak, but . . .

"What are you doing home?" It was too early for her to be off work yet, even with the later time zone there. "Why aren't you at work?"

"I took the day off. Now tell me more about—"

"What do you mean, you took the day off? What for? Are you feeling all right?"

"Don't you interrupt your elders, LJ. I have been working since before you took your first breath, and if I want to take a day off, that's my business. When you've lived twenty more years and raised a child of your own, maybe then I'll need you to tell me how I should spend my time. Until then, you mind your own affairs, you understand me?"

"Yes, ma'am," he said automatically, but he didn't remember to blink until his eyes started to burn from the glare of the sun. Was she sick? It could be simply a cold, or she could be headed into another flare-up. "Are you having an okay time getting the groceries?" he ventured. "No problem getting them home on your own?"

"I'm just fine. Don't you worry none about me." She dropped her voice. "Son, I'm proud of you, being neighborly and looking after that girl. But if her daddy's your boss, you have to do what he says. It's just that your heart's too big and so's your temper. I know you don't want to hear your conscience telling you the truth, but you're grown now. It's your job to start listening."

He squeezed his eyes shut, the beginnings of a headache throbbing behind his temples. "Yes, ma'am."

"Now, I'll mail your package later this week, so keep an eye out. I love you, son. Mind your—"

"Mind my manners, I know. I love you, too, Mama." He hesitated, searching for another question that might give him a better idea of whether she was sick, but she'd already hung up.

He tapped the phone against his lips, squeezing it too tightly. If she was headed into another one of her lows, she'd have to tell him because he'd need to take some time off to help out. He was probably worrying for nothing, when he should be focused on his career.

It wasn't only this job he was looking at losing. The horse-showing world was small and gossipy, not to mention whiter than a snowstorm. If Bill Lawler talked his reputation down, he'd have a hard time getting any job in the equine world that paid better than working a drive-through window. His mama was right. The smarter thing would be to do as he was told instead of pretending there would be no consequences for pursuing what he wanted.

Andra had said he was making things better for her, not worse. She was the one whose opinion mattered. And yet if her dad knew he was still spending time alone with Andra, he'd lose everything. His chance with her, his chance at a new life. Any possibility that he *was* actually helping, like she'd claimed.

"What, so you think you can take up the whole barn aisle, not leave anything for the rest of us?"

The sound of Andra's voice felt like the whole world tapping him on the shoulder. His pulse jumped, and he cleared his throat before he turned around, the lightness of her tone tugging up the corner of his lips. "I wouldn't dare. Not if it meant taking on your fists again."

"What do you mean, again?" Andra scoffed, lifting Snap's cross-ties so she could lead a bay gelding underneath to the next set. "It's not like I beat you up every time you take the crossties closest to the tack room. Though maybe I should."

Screw her dad. Andra sounded happy. When he'd first started working here, she'd never sounded like anything, because she'd hardly spoken.

LJ stuffed his phone into his pocket and raised his eyebrows. "I was talking about what you did to me last night." He started unbuttoning his shirt.

Andra stopped with her hand on the crossties. "Uh . . . LJ?"

He sauntered closer, enjoying the way her eyes followed every button. He spread the two sides of his shirt open, and his smirk widened into a grin. "See that?"

"Oh my God. I *didn't*."

"You sure enough did. Look." He took her hand, fitting her knuckles to the bruise on his ribs. "Fits like Cinderelly's shoe. This beauty's going to go every shade of purple before it fades, I can tell. I'm impressed."

Her gelding flicked an ear, and LJ looked up to see Jason. Andra's brother stood alongside a buckskin mare, his brow furrowed as his eyes bounced back and forth between LJ's bare chest and Andra.

LJ took a step back, clearing his throat as he began to button his shirt. Yeah, if this little scene got back to Bill, he'd be on the curb by morning, his bags hitting the pavement beside him. Especially if Jason caught a glimpse of that bruise.

"Uh, what are you guys doing?" Jason asked.

"Buttoned my shirt wrong this morning." LJ smiled tightly. "Andra was kind enough to point it out."

Andra's head jerked toward him, but she didn't call him on the lie.

"Okay," Jason said, his brow creasing deeper. He didn't move.

LJ raised his eyebrows, taking a step forward. "You need some help with that mare? She sure was giving you hell earlier."

Jason set his jaw. "She's fine."

"Well, I'd better get to work. More than enough colts around here to keep me busy." LJ popped the quick releases on Snap's crossties, dropping the ropes so the clips banged against the stall doors on either side of the aisle.

It took every bit of self-control he had not to knock Jason's shoulder out of his way when he stalked by. He didn't look at the other man, because he hated that fucking expression. He'd seen it last week, too, when he got pulled over taking one of the ranch trucks to get an oil change. The local sheriff didn't happen to think anybody who looked like him could afford something that shiny. It only got worse when the man approached the truck, his hand drifting to the butt of his service pistol as he took LJ's measure.

He'd spent his whole life trying to be a person who didn't trigger that suspicion.

Seeing it in Jason's green eyes, so like his sister's, was nearly unbearable.

Fifteen

◇◇◇

Andra was blowing on a molten-hot bite of Salisbury steak when her cell phone rang. She flinched, the cardboard tray holding her dinner folded, and the meat slithered out onto the tile with a wet plop. "Ugh!" She dropped the tray on her kitchen island, sucked the fork clean before tossing it into the sink, and picked up her phone.

"Hello?"

"Hey there, Rodeo Queen." LJ's deep voice rumbled through the phone. "You up for dinner tonight?"

Her breath hitched in her throat. "Um, yes?"

The day after her last panic attack, he'd said he was going up to the main house to eat with the crew. The second day, she'd waited for him to come up until nearly midnight, and then had a Pop-Tart for dinner. The third day, she'd waited until nine before she ate without him. Today, she'd pulled something out of the freezer by six thirty, her mood so heavy the microwave had to beep three times before she remembered to lift her hand and open the door.

LJ was too nice to tell her he'd rather not spend his suppertime with somebody who could freak out at any second, but she figured the fact that he was staying away said plenty. And then the phone rang. Now she didn't know what to think. Where had he been the last three days?

"Good, good," he said. "Hey, I finally made you something from back home, but nothing southern cooks up quick, so it's been on the stove since morning. Any chance of you coming down to my place to eat tonight?"

Her gaze cut over to the soggy brown disc of meat on her floor. "Of course, yeah. What time?"

"Whenever you feel like wandering my way. Door'll be open."

She hung up, staring at her phone. He'd sounded as relaxed as he always did. It was hard not to think of the arguments she'd been having with him in her head for the past few days, about why he seemed to have quit their cooking lessons over something she couldn't help.

When she saw him in person, she wasn't certain she'd have the guts to say any of the things she'd been thinking. Or even if she should. A normal person wouldn't have been hurt just because their friend decided to eat dinner elsewhere for a few days. But then, she wanted him to be more than her friend. She just wasn't sure how *much* more.

The Salisbury steak succumbed to paper towels and some cleaning spray. Even in the garbage can, the gravy smelled so bad she took the trash out before she left. She'd been eating them for years and never remembered hating the scent before. Maybe the generic brand she'd bought this time had changed its recipe or something.

She hopped on Gracie bareback for the short ride so she wouldn't have to take the trip over the hill alone. As they descended toward the ranch, the sun drooped low against the flank of the pine-fringed hills, sending golden light across the pastures that did nothing to warm the chill beneath her ribs.

At the main ranch, she found a paddock full of geldings to put the mare in, threw her a flake of hay, and walked toward the employee apartments. She knocked on LJ's door, her hand jittering so the sound came out more urgent than she'd intended.

He answered with one corner of his mouth lifting into a smile. "What you knocking for? Afraid I was naked?"

She snorted, feeling almost normal again as she came inside. "Why wouldn't I be? You can hardly ever keep a shirt on."

"My mama always complained about the same thing when I was a kid." He shoved his hands in his pockets. "Make yourself at home. Sorry it isn't much down here. I figured it would be less obvious than me walking over there lugging a pot of beans."

"Obvious?"

LJ glanced away. " 'Dangerous' is what I meant to say. Carrying a hot pot of red beans over that hill with my big, clumsy feet."

She bit the inside of her lip. There was definitely something going on with him, but she wasn't sure she was brave enough to face whatever it was. Especially if it might mean the end of their dinners together. She sat down in one of his straight-backed chairs. "It's fine. I'm just glad you called."

Her gaze jumped toward the floor, focusing on the clean-swept boards. Out loud, it sounded way too accusing, and she'd decided on the way down she didn't want to make a big deal out of those three days.

"I told you I'd be having dinner at the main house for a while."

Had he said that? She couldn't remember whether he'd said it was for one night or whether he hadn't specified. But then, he didn't have to answer to her. He could eat his dinner anywhere he wanted.

He kicked his boot against the floor. "Not sure why I bothered. Didn't help."

"Help what?"

His jaw flexed, the two muscles in it hard and separate for an instant. Then he smiled, though the lines of it didn't sit just right. "I thought I'd try my hand at charming your daddy." LJ's cheekbones were high and beautiful and almost distracting enough she didn't see how fast his smile faded this time. "I don't like the way he looks at me." He glanced at the stove. "I wanted that part of my life behind me, but I'm still the same person. Guess I shouldn't be surprised some people are always going to think I'm a thug, no matter what I do."

She crossed the kitchen, stopping when she realized his hands were caged in his pockets, not gesturing along with his voice or dancing across pots full of food. The oddness of it knocked her words a little off-balance, so all she could think to say was "LJ, no!"

He laughed. Just one choking note of it, and then he turned away, one hand coming free of his pocket to scrub at his face. "Shouldn't have picked tonight to make red beans."

"What?" That fucking word again. She was so sick of saying that word, of the squirmy question mark it carried with its single, stupid syllable. LJ's back was right in front of her, his white T-shirt stretched over his shoulders and hanging thin over his lean waist. Close enough to touch, if she dared. And he was hurting. She could hear it, but she couldn't decipher what he was trying not to say.

She laid a hand on his back. "LJ." Suddenly it seemed so wrong that she still didn't know what the initials stood for. "Tell me what's wrong."

He turned just enough so her hand slipped around to his side, and he caught it with his own, drawing it up his chest so he was holding her palm over his heart. It pulled her so close she could either tense and stand a breath apart from him or let her whole body brush the backside of his. She melted that last step closer. The toe of her cowboy boots brushed the heel of his, her breasts pressed into his back.

"I wanted him to think I was good enough."

She caught her breath. LJ's confession was so quiet she wasn't totally sure she'd heard him right. "What are you talking about? You're good at *everything*. Training, cooking, keeping all the employees from fighting with each other. Not to mention you were the one who caught that billing glitch with our account at the feed store last week. Just because my dad is grouchy, don't think that means anything."

He squeezed her hand and let go, turning toward the stove. "It ain't no thing. Hey, you hungry?"

She dropped her hand back to her side, still warm where his body had been touching hers seconds ago. But his tone made it clear he didn't want to pursue the topic. "Yeah. Can I help with dinner?"

"Not much left to do. Sorry I cooked without you. You have to take your time to soften up a pot of beans. Even then, they need to simmer nice and hot for a long time, until all the flavors start to borrow from each other a little bit." He flashed her a quick smile, then bent to grab a pot. His other hand dipped into a drawer for a spoon as he dropped the pot on a burner, flicked the lid off onto the counter, and opened a cupboard. "Guess I forgot to start the rice."

LJ never forgot anything in the kitchen. His was an orchestra performance, every piece perfectly timed, and no matter how much she teased him or messed up or got in his way, no piece ever fell out of that pitch-perfect timing.

Her boots punched the floor as she slipped around in front of him. "No."

He frowned, catching her long braid and pulling it forward over her shoulder. "Careful. Burner's on. No what, girl?"

"No, you don't get off that easy." She narrowed her eyes. "What's wrong? If it's my dad you're worried about, never mind him. He's got a rock for a personality and a bronze sword in the part of his brain that was supposed to help him adapt to the modern world." She reached for him, his waist hard with muscle beneath his shirt. She tried to ignore that as she gave him a little shake. "You didn't call me for days, and now you're smiling all funny. We're friends, right?"

He tugged her braid, his lips finding their smile again. "Yeah. We're friends." When he released her hair, his knuckles whispered over the highest curve of her breast. Her heart dropped a thousand feet in a second and then surged back upward, hammering toward his touch, but it was already over.

She stood between him and the stove, her palms cupping his hips over his battered belt, as close as they'd been that night when he'd caged her against the refrigerator and told her he wasn't flirting—he was hoping.

"This is flirting," she whispered. "That is, if you want it to be."

"Andra . . ." He swooped down to her level, his lips trembling a breath away from hers before they touched, a quick and desperate brush that spoke of nearly failed restraint. She pushed up onto her toes and met him more firmly.

His arms slid around her back and lifted her into his solid chest. This time, he kissed her deep and slow, exploring her mouth in ways that left nothing private and nothing to be embarrassed about.

When he paused, tipping his forehead against hers, she realized her feet were dangling off the ground. Nothing about bearing her weight changed the way he stood.

"You sure know how to cheer a man up." He chuckled breathlessly, and she smiled, feeling so light that she wondered whether it was *his* smile on her face, the one lit one hundred fifty watts brighter than the rest of the world.

He hugged her into him, his big hand sprawling over her back before he bent to set her on her feet, smoothing her braid forward again so it was away from the flames.

"See what happens when I make you New Orleans food?" He grinned and turned off the stove. "You get just like us. All grabby and wanting to take your clothes off."

She tried to scowl at him, but her mouth wouldn't cooperate. "I'm not stripping yet, Delisle."

He laughed. "Finally saying my name right, too. Telling you, it's all in the red beans."

When he touched her shirt, she glanced down, wide-eyed, but all he did was gently rebutton the part of her collar that had come undone in the passion of their kiss.

She let her hands rest on his waist the way they wanted to. "Is that why you haven't made me any southern food until now? Worried it'd make me all crazy like you?"

"Yup." He ducked his head and kissed the end of her nose. "All crazy." He stepped back enough so she could see his face, but not far enough she had to drop her hands. When their eyes met, his smile wavered a little. "It's harder than I thought, you know? Smelling home. Not being there."

"You miss it?" she whispered. Sometimes she missed home, and she still lived here. But it would never be the same as she remembered it from when she was young.

"All the time, baby girl." He chuckled, the rumble deep in his chest only making it halfway to a real sound. "No way not to. That place is me. Sometimes I think I'm a fool for thinking I could leave."

Her fingers tightened, and she consciously relaxed them, not wanting to hold him too tight. Instead, she smiled. "So New Orleans is all dirty jokes and crazy-good food and happy horses?"

He laughed, the corners of his eyes crinkling in a pleased way that made her feel better. "It has plenty of dirty jokes, Andie-girl, though not everybody's are as good as mine. And most of the food is even better than what I can make. In New Orleans, food isn't something you eat and forget. It's the way you live. Your time, your air. Your memories." He paused, his belt soft and flexible under her palms. The leather was as warm as his skin. "As for horses, nah. I pushed a shovel in the City Park stables for a while, but they have all the trainers they need. New Orleans isn't a place for horses. Too many tourists. Too many houses. Too many everythings except dollars." He grinned. "Besides, in that city, they prefer mules, and we know how mule people are."

She gasped theatrically, widening her eyes. "Not mule people."

"Well," he hedged. "They got pretty good mules." He dipped his head to take a tiny kiss, and it was so casual she wondered if this was their new normal. If kisses were like his touches, his smiles . . . if they were just part of what it was to be close to him. She wanted to be special to him, as stupid and selfish as it sounded even to think it. She wanted to know him more deeply than anyone else did, to make him smile the biggest. But she had no idea how to even start.

"LJ, what does your name mean?" she whispered, strangely afraid he wouldn't tell her.

He looked away and scrubbed a hand over his head, but then he smiled. "Aw, sweetheart, I gotta make a whole lot of love to you before you'll forget to go running when I tell you that sad piece of business."

She blinked. They still needed to make the rice. He'd said as much earlier. She turned away and grabbed a measuring cup. "How much water is it for rice again? Is the ratio two to one or three to one?" This was why she'd never make him smile as easily as other girls probably could. She was barely learning to laugh again herself, and she hated that there were so many things that still made her uncomfortable.

"Andra." He stepped up behind her and tipped her chin back toward him. She unwound when she met his eyes. They were soft, concerned. They were so beautifully *LJ*. "That's better," he murmured. "All I meant was, I need to find a way to make you like me so much you don't mind my stodgy old name. Let me see if I can show you, huh?"

She had to swallow to get a word out of her dry throat. "Okay." Her vision whitened at the edges. What was he going to do? She sucked in her stomach, waiting for his fingers to grasp the button on her jeans.

When he touched her hair, she felt the tingles melt from her scalp all the way down her back. She squeezed her eyes shut, but it didn't slow the strobe of lights.

His forehead touched the back of her head, his fingers swimming up the coils of her braid as his breath warmed the nape of her neck. She couldn't think. Everything in her mind was slow and thick and lovely. A small click of plastic broke the silence of the kitchen when the bottom of her measuring cup sagged to the counter.

"Lyndon," he breathed, and then he moved, his chin touching the other side of her braid and sending thrilling light shows of sensation up into her scalp. "Johnson."

She dropped the measuring cup. She couldn't tell by the sound whether it landed on the counter or the floor, but she needed to hang on to something. She reached back for his hands, and they found hers without her having to turn or even open her eyes. Their fingers curled together, and the oddness of the angle didn't make a bit of difference. His lips touched a kiss in front of her ear, and she thought he might be smiling.

"Thirty-sixth president of the United States."

She turned around, taking a deep breath that smelled spicy and savory all at once. "You're named after a president?"

He dipped a nod. "Sure am. He came to the Lower Ninth after Hurricane Betsy to see what he could do for folks there. My mama wasn't even born yet, but our family didn't forget that. She wanted a great son, so she named him after a 'great man.'" His face twisted like he'd stepped on a nail.

"LJ? What's wrong?"

He dropped his head, closing his eyes. "I think she's sick, Andie-girl. I think she doesn't want me to have to come home, so she's not saying, but I got a bad feeling."

She caught his hands again, bringing them up to cradle them against her chest the way he had hers earlier. "Do you—could you be wrong? Have you asked her?"

He shook his head. "Can't make things right," he said in a gruff voice. "Not even for myself, and I know that's all she wants."

Her forehead furrowed. "Is that what you really think? Is that why you left?"

"I left because everybody there thinks that way." His eyes came back open. "They think things are against them, that they're never going to change. Ain't saying they're wrong, but I don't want to live like that. I want to think I have a chance at something new." He glanced away. "But I miss it. I don't have any kin here. Y'all still have porches up here, but nobody sits on them. Hardly even play since I moved."

"Play?" She squeezed his fingers, eager like every detail he shared brought them a little closer. Made him more hers, somehow. "You mean an instrument? Are you in a band?"

He focused on her, a smile tugging at his mouth. "See, back home, that's not even a question. Everybody plays something. And a band . . . I play with three or four, depending on who has a gig. Jump in on a second line or a funeral when somebody I knew died or they could use a sax player." He shrugged. "Whenever I needed an extra buck, I'd take the hike down to Royal Street and play a sidewalk set.

Everybody did. Here, I think if I started playing music on the street, I'd get arrested or something."

She winced. "Wild Falls isn't known for its culture, I guess." She wanted to know what a second line was, but she didn't want to let him distract her from what was important. She took a step back. "Do you want to call your mom? We can make dinner later. I don't want you to be worried about her."

He hooked a finger into her belt loop and tugged her back over to him. "You don't know my mama." He wrapped his arms over her shoulders and rested his chin on top of her head. "Do you want to know what she'd say if I called?"

She nodded, the point of his chin biting into her head. Her stomach rumbled, and she hoped he didn't hear it.

"'Son,'" he said, lifting his tone to a fond falsetto, "'when you've lived twenty more years and raised your own child, then maybe you can go demanding to know things that aren't any of your affair. Until then, I can look after my own self and so can you.'"

Andra smiled. "I think I like her. I bet she'd scare the hell out of me."

"She'd probably make you a pie. You'd be fine." He kissed the top of her head. "Sorry. Here I am talking away and starving you. She'd whup my ass for that. You're probably three days underfed as it is." He turned away and started assembling dishes. "Kept thinking you'd come up to the main house for supper, but you never did."

"I like it better when it's just us."

He smiled, not looking up from what he was doing. "Me too, Andie-girl. Me too."

Sixteen

◇◇◇◇

Usually after they did the dishes, LJ walked home. But this time, it was Andra's turn, and she didn't leave. Instead, she kept pointing to things around his apartment, asking where he got this thing or that, the story behind the few small objects he'd brought with him. Reading the backs of his western novels, smiling at his Miles Davis and Rage Against the Machine CDs, and teasing him about his outdated stereo. He talked until he thought for sure he'd lose his voice, telling some true stories and some outlandish ones, and some that were a bit of both.

When she smiled, it made him feel good. He couldn't stand to send her home when he knew all it would take was one call from his mama or one knock on his door from Andra's father, and he might never get to see her again. As far as Bill knew, LJ had chosen to keep the job and walk away from the woman. His boss had no idea how impossible that choice would prove to be for LJ. Give up himself, his life, his dream. Or give *her* up.

How could he, when he couldn't even look away from her face?

Andra was different tonight. Bolder. He couldn't tell if it was because they hadn't seen each other much this week or because he'd kissed her. He was afraid it might be because she'd seen through the cracks of him to some of the damage he usually kept hidden. He tried to be the one who always had a grin and a joke, because so many people had it worse than he did. But with Andra, maybe it helped her to know she wasn't the only one with too much darkness in her rearview mirror.

When they ended up in his bedroom, he wasn't sure what to think. He watched her out of the corner of his eye, wishing he had a nicer place to bring her to. He'd bought a longer bed because the old one left his feet hanging over the edge, but the new one barely left walking space in the small room. Plus, it was sitting right on the floor like it belonged to one of those drug dealers who always bought a king-sized pillow top from their first haul of little plastic bags, forgetting all about the frame that was supposed to go with it. On the far side of the hastily made blankets was his secondhand saxophone case, its edges glaringly frayed.

"Sorry about this," he muttered. "I'm saving up for a bed frame." She frowned. "Furniture is supposed to be included with the apartments. You should have told us the bed wasn't big enough."

"I can buy my own bed."

A little bit of the old stiff went back into her spine at his tone, and LJ wished he had kept his mouth shut.

Pride is a rich man's vice, his mama's voice reminded him.

Andra turned away, probably searching for something else to ask for a story about, but all that was left was his closet. His handful of shirts hung to one side, leaving nothing but a vacant rod above the bright-blue cracked paint of the last object he ever wanted her to see.

She paused, and he ground down on his back teeth. She was so careful of everyone normally, she might not even ask, but she'd know it meant something.

Of course she would—it was half a fucking door. Who the hell kept that in their closet? He glanced away, his leg muscles twitching.

"You don't have to tell me about it," she said quietly.

This girl. Jesus, this girl.

He stepped up behind her and ran his knuckles down her shoulder blades, so she knew he was there, before he dropped his head to her shoulder and buried his face in her hair. His arms wrapped around her waist, and for a second, he was breathing in frothing floodwater, debris slamming into his ankles as he pulled her higher on the roof, toward safety. He blinked and loosened his grip so he wouldn't hurt her.

"It was my door."

Water damage blistered the bright-blue paint, and spots of old mold still dirtied the finish. A rusted doorknob sprouted from one side, the wood broken on the other where it had been wrenched off its hinges. He'd chainsawed off the bottom half to make it smaller to store, leaving just the spray-painted X and the numbers.

"What do the numbers mean?" Her arms covered his, her hands cupped protectively. How long had it been since somebody tried to shield him? His own mother had given that up about the time he grew taller than she was, when he was ten.

LJ pulled his back straight again, but he didn't let her go. "The one on top is the date the rescuers cleared the house and who cleared it. The one on the bottom is how many bodies they found."

"*Bodies?*"

He stared over her head at the numbers. "Some of our neighbors came over to wait out the storm, because my mama's gumbo is the best for miles around, and she'd made a whole mess of it. When the levee broke, water came into the house so fast we lost Ron Gravier while trying to get up to the attic and out onto the roof. Then it was just me, up there with the women and children. I was only a teenager, but I was the biggest and the strongest by a long shot. I grabbed them, was pushing them higher on the roof when the Graviers' house came off its foundation next door and came crashing down into ours. When it hit us, half of them went in the water. I was pulling them out, throwing them back up onto the roof, and there was another jolt and Mama went in. It was raining so hard, and the wind—"

He stopped, because there was nothing to say about wind like that. It pushed so hard, there was no standing against it.

"It was the loudest thing I ever heard. All I could think was to hold on to Mama with one hand and the roof with the other. I forgot about the kids." His voice went hoarse, and he coughed to clear his throat.

He released Andra, afraid he might hold her too tight.

"We got Letty out of the water, but by then, CPR couldn't bring her back. Or maybe I wasn't doing it right, because I just did what I'd seen on the poster in the gym. Mama never said anything, but I know if she had the strength, she would have hung on to those kids." He nodded to the door. "That number two. It's for Ron and Letty Gravier. We lost Aimee Mitchell off the roof, too, but I don't know what happened to her body." He hadn't seen her in the water, hadn't seen her ever again. "The number should be three."

Andra turned around, her eyes dark in a way he hadn't seen in anyone who wasn't there during Katrina. He set his jaw, but she didn't speak. Just lifted his hands and kissed his fists. The right and then the left.

"Tell me how you got out," she said.

He looked down. "Lots of boats got busted up in the storm, so it took a long time to get some together to rescue all the folks who were trapped. Took days before they got to my house. The news helicopters kept circling, filming us, but they didn't help."

Andra's shoulders clenched. "*God.* You think when you go through something so terrible, that if one person could see, they'd help. Of course they would." She shook her head. "I'm so sorry."

He shrugged. "Those news crews had cameras, not ropes, and there was nowhere to land. There was plenty of bad in those days. Not enough cops, too many freaked-out soldiers, everything all messed up. But it was volunteers who came and got us off that roof, volunteers who helped us clean up the debris once they pumped the water out. I don't ever forget that." He sat down on his bed, the mattress creaking, and he stared at that old half door. "I always meant to frame it. It's— hell, it's my whole life, right there. But somehow it never made it out of the closet."

She sat down next to him. "Did you ever talk to a therapist, after?"

"No time, no money. For a long time, I was busy trying to get a roof built over our heads again. And by then . . . Lots of people talk about Katrina, everything it messed up, everything it took. I didn't want to think about it."

"Funny how the not thinking about it doesn't make it go away." She looked down at her jean-clad knees, the right one brushing his.

"No. It don't." He slung an arm around her shoulder, and she looked up at him. She put a hand on the bed, pushing herself up enough to kiss his cheek. Her small lips—it was such a tiny gesture, but it knotted his throat all up. He had to clear it twice. "What was that for?"

"Because of course you'd try to save everyone."

He shook his head, thinking of all the days of digging through rubble, looking for trapped survivors. Splinters all through his raw hands and no way to get gloves or tweezers. Wading through half-submerged streets, the bullet wound in his leg weeping blood under filthy bandages. The air so hot the dirty water started to feel good. "Didn't do no good. After Katrina, it was too late to really save anybody."

Her hand traveled up from the bed onto his thigh. "Maybe. But you didn't give up on them. Just like you didn't give up on me."

It was hard to think with her hand so close to his fly, but he managed a laugh out of a dry throat. "You did boil garlic with the skins on. But I think I can make a cook out of you yet."

"That's not what I meant," she whispered, and kissed him.

This time, her tongue took the lead, sliding slow and uncertain along the edge of his. He fought back a groan of pure longing. As soon as she moved, he missed her touch. His hands curled around the warm sides of her waist, holding her steady on the wobbly edge of the mattress.

She felt so good everywhere that at first he didn't notice the slight tugs at his collar were her fingers, unbuttoning his shirt. As soon as her fingertips took their first, soft taste of his skin, he stalled.

She was undressing him. *Andra* was in his bed and she wasn't afraid. She wanted him naked, and she maybe even wanted him to touch her, and just . . . him. She'd chosen *him*.

He gasped raggedly. "Wait."

He caught her hand and held on to it so she couldn't think he was rejecting her. This had to be the first time in years she'd put that hand under a man's shirt.

"I need a minute." His cock swelled with every one of his heartbeats. The head was so sensitive, he was afraid if he even adjusted himself, he'd explode.

"LJ?" Her voice shook.

He kissed her knuckles without opening his eyes. "Ah, sweet girl . . . The things you make me feel, I—" Earlier, her eyes had widened at even the words "make love," but that's the only thing he could think to do right now. He was bursting with it, emotion exploding out of every pore in his skin. He wanted to surround her in pleasure, kissing her with his entire body. But Andra wasn't ready, and he knew it. Especially not with him half out of his mind with longing.

He was so damned afraid he wasn't good for her, and that her daddy knew it and would fire his ass. That his mama would get sick and he'd have to go back home. He didn't want to go back, and he was afraid to leave Andra. He was even more afraid that he *should*.

He cupped her face in his trembling hands, sliding them down her neck, her shoulders. "Listen, Andie-girl. I need to—I want to—"

She bit her lip, and in her hazy green eyes was all the desire and trepidation that told him he was absolutely right.

"Let me show you," he whispered.

He shot off the bed, and even the change in position was enough to make his dick throb. He adjusted himself gingerly as he crossed to his saxophone case, opened it, and popped the reed into his mouth. He rolled the reed around, wishing he could taste her instead. He wanted to listen to her gasp as his lips explored her skin. Even if it wasn't today, they would get there eventually. She had to know there was no one who would cherish her body more carefully than he would.

She shifted on the edge of the bed when he came back with his instrument, her cheeks flushed. She still looked confused, maybe the tiniest bit hurt. He tucked the reed into his cheek and ran his knuckles from her cheekbone down to her jaw. "I want to make love to you."

She licked her lips, but he wasn't imagining the jump in her pulse that beat so openly in her throat.

"I know we need to take it slow. That there are things that might remind you of something bad, when it's supposed to be nothing but good." He touched her chin, lifting it enough that he could leave the softest of kisses on her lips. "So listen instead, because music is always pure. Always safe, the way you are with me, okay?"

Her face changed, warmth spreading through the stiffness of her cheeks. "LJ . . ."

He smiled and closed his eyes, because the way she said his name was a whole different kind of music, and it might be he loved it even more than jazz.

He fitted the reed to his saxophone, stood, and lifted it to his lips. He started low, with the barest hint of sound, like fingers whispering up bare legs. A tease with a vow all wrapped up inside of it.

The first note he gave his whole lungs to was the fullest of his life. It vibrated from his chest all the way down to his toes. He'd half planned to start with one of the jazz standards, but that wasn't what came out. Instead, it was the rush of watching a beautiful stranger riding a beautiful horse. The twinkle of her green eyes the first time he made her smile. The relief after her second panic attack when she crawled into his lap for comfort.

The notes softened, winding low and sweet and slow. When he opened his eyes, she was smiling. Her arms were hugged around her knees as she sat, totally comfortable on his bed, her belly warmed with his food.

The music looped, deepened, as he imagined how it would be the first time she let him take off her clothes. His lids drooped as he played through how it would feel to have her trust, warm along with her skin. Her thighs opening for him, relaxed and easy.

When he opened his eyes this time, they found hers and held as the tide of the music rushed faster, each return swelling to match the desperation of what he felt. How there could never be enough: enough time, enough pleasure. Enough of her.

He dropped to one knee before her, his fingers flying and lungs burning as he promised himself to her, one note after another in the truest language his tongue had ever known. And when the air ran out, his forehead dropped to her knee, his shoulders heaving as he gasped. Her fingers wound over the sweat-slicked skin at the back of his neck, and she held him. So tightly, her hands desperate, like she wanted to sing back to him but didn't know the tune.

That night, Andra never went home.

Seventeen

◇◇◇◇

Andra ducked her head, blushing as LJ opened his door with one hand, the other skimming the small of her back as he let her out.

"I don't understand why you won't let me make you breakfast," he said.

"I'm okay. And I still have to shower and change, so I'm running late as it is."

He ducked his head, nibbling kisses along her neck until she giggled. "Smell plenty good to me." She swatted halfheartedly at him, and he stole another kiss anyway. "I'll leave the door unlocked. Whenever you get hungry for lunch, let yourself in and heat up some of the red beans and rice. They only get better the longer the spices soak in."

She groaned. "There's no way they can get better. I think I ate four bowls of them last night. Probably won't need to eat again for weeks."

"You're just catching up for all those Salisbury steak years." She glanced away, and his eyes narrowed on her face. "What's that look for?"

"Um . . ."

"You didn't." He straightened to his full six feet and five inches. "Tell me you did not eat Salisbury steak on my watch."

"You were at the ranch house! What was I supposed to do?"

He shook his head. "You're breaking my heart, Rodeo Queen. Cracking it into little bitty pieces."

She grabbed the front of his shirt and hauled him down to her level, loving that he could smile and kiss her all at the same time.

She meant to say something smart-ass, but by the time she got done kissing him, she couldn't remember what it had been. "Bye," she said instead.

His grin brightened another twenty watts. "Bye," he drawled.

He closed the door, and then Andra heard the smacking of exaggerated kissy sounds. "Damn, you two are nauseating," Stacia said, dropping a tube of sunscreen to the side of her chair on the porch and rising to her feet.

Andra stopped, an itchy flush rising under her clothes. She wanted to dance, to fidget, to brag or laugh out loud. She had no idea what to say.

Stacia laughed. "Yeah, you ought to be blushing, leaving that flashy palomino of yours parked in our corral all night for everybody to see."

Andra rolled her eyes and tried to rein in the smile that wanted to stretch across her face. It had been too many years since they'd talked about boys. She half wanted to, but it felt weird to share details as an adult. She started walking instead, her strides long and self-conscious. Dew dampened the leather of her boots as she kicked through the chilly grass.

Stacia jogged to catch up, following even when Andra started heading up the hill away from the stable. "Personally, I don't know how you lasted this long. That body and those manners wrapped up in a southern accent? I had at least four Jane Austen love affairs with him in my head the first week he was here."

"Jane Austen?" Andra wrinkled her nose. "What do you mean?"

Stacia bumped her shoulder. "Lots of talking and longing looks across the drawing room. It's the way he treats you like you're a lady, you know? And then he smiles, and my fantasy goes straight from the ballroom to hard-core tack room fucking." She stopped, her blue eyes going round. "Please tell me you're getting hard-core tack room fucking."

"Uh, not exactly."

Stacia fell silent for a few steps, and Andra's shoulders clenched more with every one. This is why she'd started avoiding her friend after the attack. As well-meaning as Stacia was, Andra didn't want to talk about her issues with sex. Though last night, she'd slept in LJ's bed. The whole night had passed softly, with her twined in his sheets and his bare, muscular arms, without the hint of a panic attack. She hadn't even been nervous.

Andra bit her lip against a grin she didn't want to explain.

"I should have guessed you were staying over when I heard that gorgeous saxophone solo last night," Stacia said. "I mean, I've heard him practicing through the wall before, but the other nights, I didn't have to change my panties afterward." Andra choked on a laugh, and Stacia bumped her shoulder again, encouraged. "Is that a yes? Did he woo you with his great, big . . . saxophone?"

This time Andra couldn't hold back the laugh. "You're ridiculous. And how are you two not best friends? You'd think your minds would have bumped into each other by now, wandering around in the gutter all the time."

Stacia hooked a thumb back toward the house. "I've got to get breakfast on, so I should run. But if you want to talk more about crushes and boys, well . . ." She grinned. "Then call your brother. He's got more X chromosome than I do any day of the week."

Andra rolled her eyes, laughing. "Duly noted."

"On the other hand, if you want to share any juicy tidbits about how that man uses his saxophone . . ." Stacia walked backward down the hill, her sequins glittering in the light of the rising sun. "Then call me immediately."

LJ's rocking chair creaked lazily, Andra's squeaking a faster rhythm next to him. The last rays of the day's sun baked the browning grass in her front yard, bees humming along over the tops of the scattered wildflowers.

"So . . ." She peeked over at him with a tiny smile, the cute one she used when she was about to give him hell. "Is this it?"

"It?" He worked up an imperious glare. "What else could you possibly need than a pretty afternoon and a porch to enjoy it from?"

She tucked her hands under her legs, pushing off the floorboards with one toe to keep herself rocking. "No, it's nice, the whole porch-sitting thing. I haven't done much of it even though I bought the chairs. I just wasn't sure if maybe there was more to it."

He wasn't about to admit it, but he didn't feel as content on the porch up here as he did at home. The view was incredible, steeply pitched hills with the velvety texture of closely packed trees leading up to distant mountains. Horses grazed in Andra's paddock like a painting of the life he'd been dreaming for himself since he got his first cowboy hat from the dollar store.

But the contentment of it was ruined by the knowledge that he was exposed to the whole horizon line, so all Bill had to do was walk up over the hill, and LJ would lose his job, his future, and any chance he had at being close to Andra. His chest was as tight as an over-wound clock. The way she'd looked at him since last night . . . if he had to leave the ranch, would she try to see him again? It was the kind of thing he knew better than to hope for. It seemed like when you reached that high, life always found a way to slap you back down.

He coughed into his fist, hoping it would make his voice sound more normal. "Well, it helps when there are neighbors around on their porches to visit with or a little music to play." His phone beeped and he jumped, coming to his feet as he dug it out of his pocket.

"Everything okay?" Andra asked, her hand freezing halfway to her glass of lemonade.

He barely heard her over the pounding of his heart. The text was from his friend Ty, but it was only asking for his help with some building-permit paperwork. Nothing about Mama. He picked up his glass and swallowed half of it down without even tasting the sweet burn of the citrus he'd spent half an hour perfecting.

"LJ?" She touched his wrist, her brows knit low now. "Is it your mom? How's she doing?"

He shook his head. "Wasn't her. She missed work again yesterday. I called there looking for her, they said she took the day sick, and when I called home, she wouldn't answer. Had to get a friend to go check on her. She was sleeping, and she still won't admit she's getting sick again."

The creaking of Andra's rocker paused, the bees in the yard louder in the silence. "Can I ask what her diagnosis is? I mean, if you don't mind talking about it?"

"Lupus." He shoved a knuckle across his lower lip. "It's an autoimmune thing. Like AIDS, but backward, because your body attacks everything: germs, its own self." He tried to smile. "Figures. My mama never did know how to stop fighting, even when it was time to rest. The lupus comes and goes, and when she gets sick with anything else, it makes it flare up. Sometimes she's fine, and sometimes she has spells where she's so weak, it's all she can do to lift her hand with nothing in it."

Sympathy drew deep lines at the corners of Andra's eyes. "It must have been hard on her, being a single mom with that to deal with."

"She went to work every day, even if she could barely walk across a room without resting." LJ shook his head. "Wouldn't let me quit school to help with the bills, so I had to do what I could with afterschool jobs, getting off shift at midnight and running my ass all the way home so I wouldn't miss curfew. She got a lot worse after Katrina, though. I don't know if it was being wet for so long, or not getting enough to eat in the Superdome, or the damn formaldehyde leaking out of the walls of our FEMA trailer." He scrubbed both his hands over his head, leaning his elbows forward onto his knees. "Probably all of that and more. Seems like everybody was sicker after Katrina."

She glanced down. "Is there any treatment for lupus?"

"Pills. Doesn't fix it." He shrugged. "I wanted to move away after college, but she was never well enough to be alone until recently. She's been so healthy this past year, and I thought—" He sat back in his chair. "I don't know what I thought. That I was selfish and I wanted a life of my own, I guess." The wind picked up, rustling through the grass, and even that sound was different from home. He liked it, even as nostalgia echoed riverboat foghorns in the back of his mind.

"Are you going to have to go back?" She wasn't looking at him. Her long lashes were swept down, muscle knotted tightly around every vertebra in her spine. He reached over and smoothed his palm down her back, aching in all the space between his ears that he'd forced into silence.

He knew the answer to her question.

But he also knew that the touch of his fingers could ease the tension in her muscles. He wanted her brilliant-green eyes to look his way and brighten with the laughter he could always tease out of her.

He didn't want to admit his life in Montana had been a pipe dream, one a part of him had always known couldn't last.

Eighteen

◇◇◇◇

When they'd first come out onto the porch, Andra had been starving. Now she was just nauseated. Her stomach twisted so tightly she couldn't quite sit up straight, even with LJ's hand soothing its way down her back, rubbing the knots out of muscles she hadn't even known she was clenching.

LJ had been different lately, more and more sadness creeping in around the edges of his brilliant smile. He talked about his home more often, and it was becoming clear the greater part of him was still anchored there. She bit the inside of her lip. His fingers danced lightly down her back, but her body was a wad of old bolts, all rusted together.

She couldn't imagine knowing your parent needed your help and being so far away. She couldn't imagine what would ever hold him here if his mama asked him to go.

"Hey, come over here," LJ murmured. She moved almost too quickly, glad he was missing her touch, too. He guided her into his lap, and his arms wrapped around her, his chest so wide there was plenty of room for her to curl in beneath his chin. "Didn't mean to let my mood get you down, Andie-girl," he murmured.

She shook her head, her hair catching on the button of his shirt. "Wasn't your fault."

The warmth of his skin melted through her, starting in all the places where they touched and sighing its way in further, her muscles relaxing as if under a deep massage. The way she felt when LJ touched her . . . it wasn't a feeling she could remember from any other time in her life. Not even in middle school, when simply holding hands could leave her breathless and giggling into the phone to Stacia long after she was supposed to be asleep.

If he left, would anything make her feel this way again?

The three days when she'd had dinner alone loomed in her memory, and she tilted her head up, hoping he would see the invitation.

He smiled when their eyes met, his finger grazing her chin to lift it the last little bit he needed. His soft lips held hers, the scratch of the stubble beyond them harsh when she deepened the kiss. Her hand cupped his throat, and his pulse sped up, beating more urgently against her palm.

A moan rose in Andra's chest, and she pressed closer, her free hand pulling the hem of his shirt out of his pants so she could feel his skin. It was impossibly smooth, the muscles flexing beneath in immediate reaction to her touch. For a moment, she hesitated, remembering how he'd stopped her the last time she'd gone for the buttons on his shirt. But this time his hands were rough on her waist, hugging her into him so tightly it was almost hard to move, and she wanted more than this.

Her teeth grazed his bottom lip as she shoved his shirt out of the way, her palms making it as high as the thick pads of his pecs. He half growled and shifted beneath her. "Andra, you—"

She didn't let him finish, her tongue bolder than it had ever been. Every space between their bodies was a nagging reminder of what it was like when her house was empty of the lilt of his drawl, and she hated it.

She stepped off his lap and grabbed his shirt in both fists, hauling him up after her. She stumbled but he caught her, ending their kiss with a ragged gulp of air. His brown eyes were hazy with need. She pulled him inside, the front door banging back against the wall and ricocheting closed. His weight shifted toward the couch, but she took his hand in hers and slid the old multipaned doors aside on their tracks.

"I, uh—" he said.

It was the first time he'd been past those doors into her bedroom, and she kept toward the center of the room so he wouldn't hit his head on the ceiling that sloped down to either side. He looked huge in here, so tall in her nook of a bedroom, but somehow familiar, too. The way he'd looked at home in her kitchen the first time he'd stepped through the door.

When she made it to the foot of the bed, she spun around, her heart pounding so hard the movement made her head swim.

"I want to . . ." She squeezed his hand. "I want to feel you." She lost her nerve to look into his eyes and focused on his buttons instead, popping them open from the bottom as if he'd be less likely to stop her there than if she dared to begin at the top.

His lips brushed her bent forehead. "You can do anything you want to when it comes to me, sweet girl."

She exhaled in a little cry of inarticulate air and pushed up onto her toes, kissing him hard and fast with no plan at all. It meant so much to be wanted so completely, even when her hands were more unpracticed and clumsy than sensual.

LJ's palms cupped her waist and slid around the small of her back, thumbs rubbing slow and steady.

His shirt came all the way open under her urgent tugs. She dropped to stand flat-footed and watch as she pushed the fabric up and over the muscles of his shoulders. Her hand was starkly pale, fingers trembling as she traced a path down the ripples of his abs to the button on his jeans. Her throat pinched closed as she took hold of the fastening with both hands. Somehow, she felt if she could be naked next to him, it would soothe the sprinting fear. As close as they were right now, something in her was still screaming that he might leave and once he was gone, there were no guarantees she'd ever hear his voice again.

And even as wanting him wrung her mouth dry, she knew there

was a good chance that pulling down his zipper would throw her into an attack she had no chance of stopping.

"You scared?" LJ's hands covered hers where they had been frozen on his button for three long breaths. His thumb tucked inside the curl of her bloodless fingers, fitting just right into the hollow at the center of her palm. "Most girls are," he said conversationally. "'LJ, it's so big and hard,'" he added in a southern falsetto. "'Ain't no earthly way it's gonna fit in there. Couldn't you make it a little smaller now?'"

She choked on the laugh that caught her by surprise, lifting her head to find his eyes warm and his smirk a little crooked. "Aren't you ever serious? I'm trying to seduce you here."

"Oh, I'm plenty serious. And you're plenty seducing me." His smile deepened. "Weren't we just talking about how scary big you made my dick?" His thumb stayed cuddled inside her palm as he took his other hand and gave his fly a sharp pat. "Behave yourself, now. Don't frighten the lady off."

Her gaze wavered on his, her giggle fading away too fast. "I want to," she said. "But I also don't want to have a stupid panic attack right now."

He winked. "If you do, I promise we can make out when you're done."

She burst out laughing again. "LJ, you're shameless."

"Horny," he corrected. "'Horny' is the word you're looking for, darlin'. Here, we'll do it together. You want the high road or the low road?"

She caught her breath, heat pooling between her legs even though she wasn't sure what he meant. She wanted every kind of road, as long as he was offering it to her in that voice. "Low road." Whatever that was, it sounded dirtier, and for the first time in years, Andra thought she might like dirty.

"We southern boys are great fans of the low road." LJ flicked his button open and slid down his zipper. Maybe the high road was over the pants, and the low road was under. She hoped so.

Through the opening in his jeans peeked blue boxer briefs: tight
for riding, cheap cotton worn thin over the bulge beneath that made
all his jokes about size seem like maybe not jokes at all. His thumb
smoothed its way out of her palm and over her knuckles as he eased
both their hands into his pants. His hand supported hers, warm and
undemanding even as he dropped his head back and groaned.

"Love that low road."

She giggled breathlessly, her fingers relaxing enough to curl around
him. His cock flexed and hardened into her grip, and she realized she
was still breathing—no attack in sight. She laughed again.

"Not the response I was going for there, sweetheart," he rasped.

She didn't respond to his joke, because she couldn't unglue her
eyes from the thick ridge beneath her hand. She inched upward, feeling the line that marked the head of his cock through the cotton. He
sucked in a breath and let go of her hand, giving her all the freedom
she wanted to explore on her own.

"Can I?"

He nodded quickly, and she dipped past the elastic of his boxers,
the heat of his erection searing against her hand. The skin was so
much silkier than the rest of his body, and her heart fisted. She'd
forgotten that: how penises felt.

Andra shoved the breath out of her lungs and reached for LJ with
her free hand, his side hard and comforting. His cock jumped eagerly
in her hand, and she closed her thumb around it, happy that he liked
the contact as much as she did. His hips curled, rocking himself a
little bit deeper into her fist as a matching thrill of arousal rose in her.
He wrapped his arms over her shoulders as his cheek came down to
rest against her temple. Stray hairs tickled her cheek, stirred by his
fast breathing. A subtle tension radiated out from his body despite
his relaxed stance.

"Feels good," he murmured.

Slowly, the tingles in the rest of her body centered on her hand,
that drugging ease he always brought seeping into her in waves. Oxygen filled her lungs, washed the fear out of her. His erection wasn't

any different than the rest of him. A little too hard, a little too big, and comfortingly familiar in a way it shouldn't have been, considering how recently they'd met.

She began to explore in earnest, testing his response to a firm grip, a soft slide of her palm. Listening to his breathing change when she stroked the pad of one finger over his tip. He dropped his forehead to the top of her head and swallowed audibly.

"Does the low road have a low road?" Andra asked. "Like a basement road, maybe."

He chuckled, the sound as deep and fathomless as the pulse of a bass drum. "You tell me."

She slipped her other hand into his pants and pushed them down. The muscular curve of his ass branded her palms on their way by, and as soon as he was busy kicking out of his boots, that's where her hands returned.

He was naked.

She knew it, but it took her eyes a little longer to take in the full reality of it. Her gaze fell from his collarbone to his arms to his slim hips and that lean V-cut that led straight to his erection. The strength of his body was written in every line of him, blaringly impossible to ignore without the buffer of clothes. It should have scared her.

She brushed her knuckles down his abs, watching them shiver under her touch. LJ had the power to force anything he wanted, but he had always let her lead, everywhere they'd ever been together.

"Please kiss me," he whispered hoarsely, his arousal swelling even as he said the words.

She slid her hands around his back and did. His dick hard against her belly, her lips slow and deliberate. Not rushing because she was afraid he'd say no or accidentally clashing teeth because she didn't remember exactly how kisses were supposed to go. Just melting open to make room for his tongue to stroke hers, the sensation of it trickling down through her chest and prickling along her inner thighs. Her body felt languid, soft. Sensitive to every ripple of his muscle pressed against her clothes.

His hand sank into her hair as he groaned against her lips, then took her mouth even more deeply. His hips twitched forward, rubbing his arousal against her belly. An arrow of heat streaked up inside her, and long-unused muscles squeezed wantonly. A sense of hollowness began to grow in her, and her inner muscles flexed again. Andra gasped, writhing against him.

"God," he growled, deep and low. "You can't do that, darlin'. Or you need to never stop doing it. One or the other."

Every one of his heartbeats was clear in his erection now, pulsing against her stomach. Her hands reluctantly left his skin, rising to her own buttons.

LJ stepped back, and her hands froze before she realized he was doing exactly what she had done—pulling away so his eyes could feast as much as his hands had. And then she remembered seeing his whole glorious body unveiled. If she looked half that beautiful to him, she wanted to watch his expression when he saw her for the first time.

Andra lifted her gaze to his face. He lagged for a second before his own eyes came up to meet hers. She smiled. "It's okay," she said. "You can watch."

He swallowed. "Best news I've had all year." He bobbed his eyebrows. "Need any help? Buttons are feisty little things, but I've pretty much got a handle on them. Happy to show you, if you want."

Her smile grew at the familiar rhythm his drawl settled into when he was trying to tease a laugh out of her. She liked that it didn't change, even when he was stark naked in her bedroom. Her hands moved swiftly down the buttons, the shirt falling open to reveal a black sports bra. The button on her jeans didn't bother her the way his had, because she was watching LJ's face. His jaw ticked tighter, then tighter still.

She pulled her zipper down and stepped out of her jeans. Her sports bra was more of a wrestling match. LJ rescued her halfway through, pulling it up over her head and freeing her arms. It seemed symbolic to undress for him, and she'd wanted to do it herself, but she couldn't remember why once his long fingers slipped into the sides of her panties, because that felt even better.

That hollow feeling throbbed sharply as he pulled her underwear down her legs, and she found herself hoping his hands would retrace their route back upward.

Instead, he stood, cupping her face in his hands. His kiss was warm and rough, and frustrating as all hell because she wanted more than that now. At least until his chest bumped hers and her nipples hardened immediately, the sensation painfully bright without her bra.

"Lay with me," she whispered, walking backward to her bed. When the cool wood of her footboard hit her thighs, she edged around to the side, sitting and scooting backward so she could lie down. LJ's eyes devoured every part of her, even as his hands stayed well away from all the flesh she'd bared for him.

But that wasn't what she wanted.

She wanted to rub herself over every inch of his body, to soak up the slow, deep magic of him so she could live on the memory of that alone. Just in case.

Andra beckoned him closer. He shook his head slowly, his eyes smiling even as he dropped a knee onto her bed and eased down next to her. His hand cupped her shoulder and stroked down her side. Past the dip of her waist and the flare of her hip, that gnawing tension at the center of her winding tighter as his hand passed by all too far away.

"Don't pinch me," he said.

Now it was her turn to shake her head, jostling her foggy brain to try to decode his words. "What?"

His palm stopped at her knee and rose again, spreading warmth over her skin as it circled around to cup her bare bottom. "If this is a dirty dream I'm having about you . . ." He grinned. "Forgive me, but I don't want to wake up."

"I might want to have it more than one night, though." She scooted closer until his cock rested exactly against the part of her that needed friction the most. She let out a small sigh. "Can you make that happen?"

"Going to town tomorrow to fill the whole pickup with sleeping pills," he vowed. "We can dream straight through till Christmas."

She tipped her hips forward a little, her nipples kissing his chest as she leaned in, swimming in the scent of him. Today, it was fresh-baked bread and green pasture grass. The aching between her legs was only getting worse. She'd wanted to hold him, kiss him, and now she wasn't sure that would be enough. She rocked against him once more, and LJ groaned. He gripped her ass, sending tingles all the way up to her scalp, and then he thrust against her.

"Oh God," she gasped, parting her legs and hooking one around the back of his. He shifted, nuzzling himself in more firmly against her swollen clit and bucking his hips in small, sharp movements that had her eyes rolling back under fluttering lids.

She hadn't thought she'd ever want to have sex again. Her mind shied away from the idea whenever she considered it, but having him right here, his dick hard and ready . . . she couldn't think about anything but how good it would feel to clasp it inside of her. To let him rub over every too-sensitive nerve ending that was begging to be touched right now. She huddled into his chest, gasping against the heat of his skin.

"Does that feel good, sweetheart?" he murmured against her hair, rocking more gently now in a way that teased her with knowing how forceful he could be, and exactly how much she wanted him to be.

She nodded so fast her head clipped his chin, and he laughed. His hand slid from her bottom down the back of her leg, dipping a little closer to the center of her.

"I can make it feel better," he whispered. "If you want me to."

She meant to answer, but the sound came out as a whimper. She strained toward his fingers. It was impossible to feel self-conscious when she was being pulled apart with wanting a million things she didn't have. One thing.

His fingertips found where she was slick and wet. She gulped air, and he drew her closer into his chest and touched her. One finger, sliding over wet skin and then up higher, opening her until his cock could sit right against her clit. Her leg muscles clenched and her toes curled, and she bit down on nothing, her teeth grinding together.

"LJ, oh God, I need to—" She pressed against him again, but it was sharp and too sensitive and she was so empty, her muscles squeezing inside as if they were waiting for him.

She pushed him away and he let her go immediately, his head coming up as she scrabbled across the bed to the nightstand. She yanked the drawer out, grabbing a box that Stacia had stuffed into her shopping bag the day they'd bought her new clothes. She dropped it twice trying to get a condom out, and then LJ took it from her, ducking his head to see her eyes.

"Andra, girl, are you sure about this?"

"I need you," she gasped. "God, I didn't think I'd ever feel like this, and I can't even think, and I need you *right* now."

His eyes darkened nearly to black, and he kissed her so hard she tipped over onto her back. He followed her down, his lips ravishing hers in a way that let her know he'd been holding back before. Way, way back.

Distantly, she heard the rip of foil, and then his hands spread her thighs open. She whimpered, curling toward his hands to steal a little more of his delicious warmth, that crazy, amazing feeling only he could give her. The blunt head of his cock nudged her, and he stopped kissing her for half a second, then his tongue delved deep. She moaned into his mouth as he took his dick in one hand, circling her entrance in the most maddening of teases as he wet the condom he wore.

He gasped something, and she gripped the base of his neck, pulling him back to her mouth. He groaned and pushed into her. She was so wet, and the tip slipped right in, but then he was too thick, and pain jolted when her body tried to stretch to fit him.

Pain. The battering of a pubic bone grinding against her own, every impact like a punch as a dick scraped raw and dry inside of her. Blink. The dusty ceiling of Gavin's room and that one thread of a spiderweb hanging in the corner, taunting her, because she wasn't free to stand up and knock it down.

Andra opened her mouth to scream, and every tendon inside her locked, the air in her lungs hardening into stone in an instant.

Nineteen

◇◇◇◇

Andra's vision flashed between her ceiling and the web-strewn ceiling of a rental house far away. She couldn't leave this place. Couldn't move, could never leave. Fingernails raked down the insides of her lungs, ripping delicate tissue and leaving fire in their wake. On top of her, LJ froze.

Her eyes stayed fixed on the ceiling, but in her peripheral vision, she saw his head lift as if to see her expression. As soon as he did, he pulled out. "Andra. Andie-girl, stay with me, now."

His hands cupped her face, and they were every bit as warm as they had been seconds ago, but nothing could touch her now. Terror roared through her, and her body revolted. Every beat of her heart stretched it to bursting, and it couldn't hold out.

"Look at me," LJ demanded, tilting her face away from the ceiling and toward his face. Brown eyes waited for her, held hers. "You're all right," he promised. "I am never going to hurt you, girl. Not ever."

She believed him. She knew she was in her cottage now, not that old rented house where Gavin had chained her down like an animal. But it didn't change anything, because her body was broken, and it was suffocating her. LJ was going to watch her die.

She could still feel the cuffs on her wrists, the burn of worn flesh against uncaring metal. She couldn't get away. Couldn't breathe. Her vision started to gray around the edges, and Andra knew it was about to happen.

She couldn't die here.

She exploded off the bed, hitting the floor. Her chin burned where it scraped the carpet, but she didn't care. She flung herself across the room and landed in a heap at the base of the window. She watched her hands clawing at the windowsill before she remembered the latch was up higher.

"Andra, what are you doing? Where are you going? I'm leaving," he said, his voice receding. "I'm all the way out in the hallway now, okay? You don't have to run from me. I'm going."

Her arm was so heavy, but she couldn't die here. Couldn't make him watch. She shoved her arm up high enough to get the latch, pushing it open and then throwing the window up.

Air poured in, and her hands gripped the sill. She was free. She was out. She choked down one breath, then two. Outside, it was twilight, wind riffling through the open grass. There was no pavement. No street. No silent doors waiting in judgment of her. She sagged, her forehead hitting the cool paint of the sill.

"LJ," she tried to say. She had to wet her lips and swallow, her throat sandpaper dry, before she could try again. "LJ."

The yarn that settled over her back was thick and soft. It must be the blanket his mother had made and mailed to her. The way it curled around her reminded her of the cardigan the old woman had hung on her shoulders that day.

LJ tucked the blanket more securely around her, his hands never touching her skin. She turned, her limbs so heavy that even that small movement was an effort.

"Okay now?" His voice was quiet, but his eyes echoed with hurt. She lifted a hand to his face, and he flinched away.

"LJ . . ."

"Why?" he demanded. "Why'd you tell me you wanted me if you were scared?"

She let her hand drop. "I wasn't." She needed water if she was going to talk. Water and about three days of sleep.

"What did I do wrong, then?" His voice almost broke, and tears rose to sting at the edges of her lashes. "Too fast? Too rough?"

She shook her head. "It wasn't you."

"It was me."

LJ jerked to his feet, grabbing his boxer briefs and hauling them on.

"It *is* me, Andra." He whipped on his jeans. "It's me doing that to you, every f—" His jaw flexed. "Every time, it's been me who left you cowering on the floor, and I don't know how to be any different. I . . ." He stopped with his shirt hanging from his hands. "I don't know how to hide how much I want you."

"I want you, too," she whispered, her fingers tightening on the edges of the blanket.

"No," he said. "You don't."

He pulled on his shirt, staring at the floor. Her shoulders shrank, the chill in her skin creeping down into her chest.

"LJ, I told you, the attacks have nothing to do with you." She shook her head. "They just happen and I'm sorry, but I can't stop them. I thought you understood that."

He crammed buttons into holes so fast that threads popped audibly. "I'm not dumb enough to think that happens to you when you're out working the horses or shopping with Stacia." He shrugged to straighten the shirt on his shoulders and stomped into his boots. When he looked up at her, his eyes were like two holes punched into the dirt. "It keeps happening because I scare you. Because something I do reminds you of him. I'm not going to keep doing that to you, Andra." He headed for the door.

She leaped to follow him, leaving the blanket in a pile below the window. Adrenaline pushed all the fatigue out of her limbs as she sprinted across the room and caught his shoulder before he crossed into the living room. "LJ, don't." She pulled until he turned to face her. "I don't know what else to say to make you believe me, but you have to. All I wanted was to be close to you. I screwed it up, and I didn't have a single choice in the matter, okay? Are you seriously going to make it worse by walking out on me right now?" She dropped her hand, hugging her arms over her chest. She wished she wouldn't have left the blanket behind.

LJ shook his head. "You didn't screw it up. I did."

"That's what I keep telling *you*!" She shoved him, somehow gratified when he fell back a step. "You said there were no expectations between us. You said whatever we wanted, we could try, no problem. Was all that bullshit? Because I didn't lie to you, LJ. I freaking *told* you I didn't think I'd ever want to have sex again, and suddenly I did, and I would be so happy about that right now if I hadn't ruined it by acting like a total freak."

His eyes darkened. "You're not a freak."

She snapped a hand out at his clothes. "Right. You're just leaving because you remembered you left the stove on, right?"

He gritted his teeth, then he dropped his head and blew out a breath. "Shit."

He reached for her and folded her into his arms. The goose bumps from cold faded away from her skin, but she still stood a little stiffly, not sure whether they were done fighting.

"I'm sorry. I feel bad, and then I don't always say the right thing . . . I just . . ." He kissed the top of her head, like it might make up for the words he never finished, but she was already tensed against them.

"You just what?"

"Do you think you'll ever stop feeling *him*?" he whispered. "When I touch you? Because I want to make you feel good, but knowing that any second, it might remind you of something terrible . . . it makes me want to cut off my own hands."

Andra closed her eyes. "I'm sorry."

"Don't be sorry, sweet girl. Please don't."

She hugged him tighter, but somehow it didn't help at all. Her house was so quiet it suffocated any word she might have offered.

There was nothing to say anyway. Nothing but lies or a truth that would have him heading for the door all over again.

He kissed her forehead. "I have to go."

She blinked rapidly and stepped back. "Yeah, okay." She kept her voice steady, turning to get her clothes so he wouldn't see the tears in her eyes before she could fight them back.

He caught her from behind and hugged her again, warmth bleeding through his clothes. "Not like that, Andie-girl. I'm nasty company right now—that's all. Why don't you come down for breakfast? We'll talk, and I'll load you up on French toast and grits."

She touched his arms where they were wrapped over her chest. "Okay."

"Okay." He let her go, but there was no creak of footsteps announcing his exit.

She didn't turn around. She didn't have anything left, not tonight.

Finally, the floorboards creaked. Hesitant and slow. Out of her room and through the living room. The front door opened and paused again. When it closed behind him, she thought she'd be relieved.

She wasn't.

Twenty

◇◇◇◇

LJ cracked an egg into the bowl with one hand, whisking with the other until the eggs frothed. He dropped the shell into the trash and poured just a hint of cream in with the eggs, then a droplet of vanilla extract and a scattering of cinnamon. After a pause, he added more vanilla, because he was pretty sure Andra would like it that way.

His eyes were grainy with fatigue, and he hoped Andra had slept better than he had. He wished there were a way he could have stayed last night, just to be certain she was okay. But that was the whole problem: if he was there, she was worse, not better. She probably never had panic attacks when she was alone. He stared down into the eggs, his jaw aching before he realized he was grinding his teeth.

He straightened and reached for the bread. Food. It was the one pure way he could care for her. The one thing he was sure not to fuck up.

The clock on the microwave informed him it was still too early to expect her. Way too early to worry she wouldn't come. He took out a box of cornflakes, then a bag of oatmeal, and hesitated. Mama traded off which one she used to coat her French toast, but right now he couldn't think of which Andra might like best. Hearty and savory or light and crisp.

He checked the clock again, but it was still too early. Not so early in New Orleans, though, and talking to his mother might keep him from going flat crazy while he waited to see how Andra was this morning. If she was nervous about seeing him, too. Or if she was maybe angry with him, even though she'd said she wasn't last night. She'd chased after him when he'd first started to leave. That had to be a good sign. Or at least not a bad sign.

He snatched up the phone and dialed. Mama would love it if he called to ask her opinion about French toast, anyway. Except instead of a ring, a recorded message kicked on, informing him that the number was out of service. What? He checked his screen, but that was definitely her number.

He'd been sending half his paycheck home every two weeks. That should have been more than enough to cover the phone bill. He paced across the kitchen, wiping down already clean counters as he shot glances at his phone. With him this far away, Mama would turn off the water before she'd let the phone lapse. There had to be some kind of emergency. Something wrong with the house, or maybe her job.

He dropped the rag and dialed the restaurant where Mama worked. Hedda picked up, rattling off her standard greeting even though it wasn't business hours yet.

"Hi, Hedda. It's LJ."

"LJ, baby!" she squealed. "How's your new job? They feeding you okay up there? Can you even get grits that far north?"

"Mostly just instant," he admitted. "Hey, is Mama around? I had a question for her."

There was a pause, and he checked the screen to be sure the call hadn't dropped.

"Baby, you know your mama's out on leave, don't you?" Hedda asked slowly. "I figured you set some help up for her, because she said she didn't need me to stop by, bring any food or anything."

"How long?" He gripped the edge of the counter.

"A week, maybe two. Let me check the calendar." A pan clanged, and then pages rustled. "Last Tuesday was the last time she came in.

LJ, haven't you talked to her? I can send Antoine over there before we open if you're worried."

"Can you? And have him call me when he gets there. She must have, uh, turned her ringer off or something." If he told Hedda the account was turned off, she'd take money out of the register to pay it herself. The IRS had fined her nearly out of existence on that last audit, because she took money out whenever her friends needed it and usually didn't remember to add it back in when she did her taxes. "I'm coming home. Have Antoine tell Mama I'll be there as soon as I can."

He threw the eggs down the garbage disposal just as a knock came at his door.

Andra.

Fuck.

He shot out into the living room and wrenched the door open. She stood there with her arms crossed over her chest, and his head was so messed up, he couldn't even decipher the look on her face. She'd come after all. She wasn't so mad that she didn't show up.

Five minutes ago, that would have made him happy enough to sing, but right now he could barely see straight. He let her in and dashed back to the bedroom with the dawn light streaking across the floor. "I'm sorry the food isn't ready. There's bread for toast, though, and leftover pot roast in the fridge. It's no kind of breakfast, I know, but it'll get you started, anyway." He pulled a suitcase off the top shelf of his closet in an avalanche of other stuff, then opened a drawer in his dresser and grabbed everything in it.

"You're leaving."

He glanced back, and she stood in the doorway of his bedroom, looking terribly small. Exactly the way she had last night when he left her. He stopped, a pair of boxers dripping off the top of the pile he held. They fell across the toe of his boot. "I'm sorry, Andra. I know I said we'd talk this morning, but I've got to go." All the time he was messing with French toast recipes, he should have been think-ing of what to say. Because here was his chance to set things right, and he had no idea how to do it. Instead, he clutched at what he did know. "My mama's sick." His insides wrenched, because saying the words aloud made them feel way too real.

"Um, okay."

He dumped the boxers into the suitcase and ripped open another drawer, that odd jangling feeling returning to his head. "I tried to call her this morning, but her phone was disconnected." The next drawer banged out so hard it came off the rails. He had to take a second to thread it back in, hoping he hadn't broken the dresser. God knew he didn't have the money to spare right now. "I called the restaurant, and they said she's been out sick for almost two weeks." He punched down the mound of jeans, trying to make them fit inside the suitcase.

"Two *weeks*?" Andra's voice sounded worried now, and only then did he realize she hadn't believed him before.

He swallowed. "My mama will go to work even when she's too weak to cook. They'll let her man the cash register, because she can set up on a stool and hold herself steady on the counter, even when her ankles swell all the way to her knees." He looked up at Andra, at her wide green eyes, and his stomach twisted. He should be reassuring her, not dumping his problems on her, but the more he thought about his mama sick and alone, the more frantic he got. "She's not even going to work right now. I have to go home."

She was already nodding as she stepped forward. "Right, of course. Can I help you pack? What do you need?"

"Everything. Your daddy's going to kill me. Probably he'll throw away anything I leave, with me taking off without giving notice. Oh! Mary Kay was favoring her back left leg yesterday. I couldn't find anything, but I thought I'd check it again this morning and see if she shook it off. And there's a rail loose in the big arena. Two posts down from the gate. I meant to fix it this week, but Curt's going to have to do it. Hold off on training Taz with the rest of the group I got ready for you. She's still iffy about ropes, and I've got an idea I want to try on her, if your daddy will give me another chance after this." He spotted a stray boot and threw it in on top of the jeans.

"I'm not going to let him fire you." Andra grabbed a crumpled tote bag off the closet floor and started folding shirts into it. "If your mom's sick, you have to go. Leave anything you want to. It'll be here when you get back, and it won't fit on the plane anyway."

"I'm taking my truck."

She stopped moving, and he ducked around her to strip shirts off hangers, wadding them into the empty corners of his suitcase.

"What for?" Her voice was so small he almost didn't catch it.

"The buses barely run to the Lower Ninth, and ambulances are even slower. We don't have a hospital nearby since Katrina. If Mama needs help, I won't be able to get it for her without my truck." He slammed his suitcase shut and ripped the zipper closed.

"That'll take days to get home. I'll drive your truck down, and you can fly. You'll get there faster. I mean, if she needs you right now . . ."

"Can't afford gas and a plane ticket, too." Not to mention they'd need every penny for medication and supplies if she was sick again. He grabbed his suitcase and the tote Andra had packed, then hefted his saxophone case and headed for the door. That'd have to be enough. He'd do without everything else. "I've got a friend looking in on her for now. He's supposed to call me as soon as he gets over there." He nodded toward the kitchen. "Will you turn off the coffee-pot, please? Pour it out so it doesn't mold."

She rushed to do it, and he'd tossed his stuff in the bed of his Datsun and was halfway to the barn by the time she caught up. "LJ, what do you need your saddle for? You said you didn't have a horse to ride back in the city."

He ground his teeth, striding down the dark barn aisle. He'd for-gotten to hit the lights, and the sun was barely up. She was right; he was wasting time. He almost left it, but no. "It's my saddle," he mut-tered. He never went anywhere without it. Even the thought felt wrong.

Andra stopped. "LJ, if you want to leave, just say it, okay? You don't have to lie."

He came back out of the tack room, and the betrayal in her face nearly sent him to his knees. He dumped the saddle on the nearest bale of hay and crossed to her, pulling her into his arms. He was too desperate to be gentle, and his chest ached as he squeezed her as tight as he'd allow himself.

"Not lying," he said gruffly. He wished to God he were. "Listen, I'll call you as soon as I can, okay?" He bent to look her in the face, searching those gorgeous green eyes. Jesus, no wonder she thought he was a liar, running out on her right in the middle of everything that had happened last night. "I'm sorry, Andra. So damn sorry, and I wish I could tell you when I'll be back, but I never know how long her spells will last. One way or another, I'll come back and we'll talk all this out—I promise."

Now he felt like a liar.

All last night, he'd been awake, wondering if she'd be better off without him, and it wasn't until this morning that he knew his mama needed him. Besides, there was always the chance this would be the flare-up that never released its grip. He hadn't been there for months, and there was no way to know if Mama had been eating right, or remembering her meds when she was working long shifts. The woman would probably drop dead before she'd call and pull him away from the job she'd been so proud of.

Andra's eyes started to shine with tears, and he turned away and grabbed his saddle. If he made her cry, he couldn't take it. Not right now. And every minute he stood here was a mile closer he could have been to New Orleans.

When he made it to his truck, he turned back to say goodbye, and she wasn't there. He stood, shifting his weight from boot to boot. But he didn't have enough words to fix everything he'd done wrong, and there was no time to make it up to her, either.

God, he was a failure. His mama was lying sick and alone, thousands of miles away, and he'd left the woman he loved crying over him in a damned barn. Not to mention he was about to wave goodbye to the career he'd hoped all his life for, because no way did he have enough time to go to the house and plead for time off from Bill, who was itching to fire his ass anyway.

LJ threw himself into the truck and cranked the ignition. He'd call and beg every kind of forgiveness later, but for now, his family needed him.

Twenty-one

◇◇◇◇

"Asafetida." Andra wasn't sure if it was her voice that sounded funny or the word itself. Tapping the little plastic spice container with one fingernail, she said it again. "Asafetida." She bent a little more forward, the beer bottle in her hand clinking against the counter. LJ's spices were a foreign language, smells and shapes and colors gathered into shakers with labels she wasn't sure how to pronounce.

She ran her finger down a container of coriander, so softly that she could feel the seam where the plastic had been melded together. She wished she could feel LJ's fingerprints on it, too. Before she had cleaned his apartment, she should have thought of all the marks of him she was wiping away. Andra wondered if his fingerprints were still on her skin. After six days of sweat and showers, probably not. If the FBI dusted for signs of his presence, they would be all over this apartment and her cottage, too, but she would be clean. It didn't seem right, didn't seem possible that he could have disappeared from her life so completely.

Tipping the bottle against her lips, she took a drink, wincing at the burn of the carbonation in the beer. It had been years since she'd had a drink. She'd barely made it through the neck of the small bottle, and already her head felt light, the lines of everything in LJ's apartment a little more vivid than they had been. Until she'd cleaned out his fridge, she hadn't realized LJ even liked beer. He'd never drunk one in front of her, but there were two beers on the shelf of his fridge, the other four to the six-pack missing. He must think she was terribly fragile, that he couldn't even have a beer when she was around. The thought had made her angry, and she'd cracked one open for herself.

She'd had enough of the past dictating her present. It had driven LJ all the way across the country from her. She knew he would have gone whenever his mom needed him, even if they weren't fighting. But that would have felt more temporary, the space between them shrunk to nothing by teasing text messages and calls full of laughter. Not this gaping, silent lack in all the moments that used to be filled up with his gregarious presence.

She circled the kitchen, trailing her fingers over things as if her fingerprints might make up for the lack of his. The wobbly table didn't wobble anymore. He'd fixed it at some point. But of course he had: LJ fixed things. That was who he was.

It was why he couldn't stand thinking he was causing her panic attacks, but it wasn't him at all. She felt safer here, among the few things he'd left behind, than she did anywhere else on her own ranch. Of course, he couldn't know the truth of that, because he wouldn't even answer her calls. It was sex she was messed up about, not him, even if she couldn't make him understand the distinction.

She'd listened to his voicemail message enough times it was stuck in her head. It started with a chuckle, as if just by calling, you were part of a joke he was sharing only with you.

Y'all probably called this number by mistake, but just in case your taste in friends is really this bad, leave a little ditty at the beep, and I'll call y'all back.

She loved the slow wrap of syllables around the word "y'all." He'd never said that word to her, but there it was in his voicemail. Twice. Maybe it was one he used all the time, and she hadn't known him long enough to notice.

Maybe there were a lot of things she hadn't noticed about him. The LJ she knew would never have ignored her calls—not for anything.

That had never changed until her messed-up reactions had ruined their first time in bed together. No matter when his mother's health improved, she suspected he wasn't coming back, because he probably thought it was better for Andra that way.

She tipped the bottle up and swallowed over and over again until it was empty.

The floor tilted under her feet as she walked to the door, and she had to catch herself against the wall. Either that beer was especially potent or what little tolerance she'd had in college was long gone, but the buzz felt surprisingly nice. It had been beer in a red Solo cup that Gavin had slipped the drugs into, but it was about damn time she stopped blaming every bottle of the stuff for the sins of that single long-ago beverage.

The beer was the first step: peeking inside the door to her past when for so long, she'd kept it bolted shut. She wanted to throw that door open now, rip it off its hinges, and burn it to cinders, like a smoke signal that would call to LJ to tell him it was okay to come back.

Andra let herself out of his apartment and started the long journey up to her cottage. Why the hell had she built it so far from the rest of the ranch, anyway? It was so deathly quiet up there. She used to want to be left alone, but now . . . she wasn't so sure anymore.

She mounted her porch steps and opened the door. Pausing for a second, she studied the clean white surface. If she were to paint an X across it, and her own numbers, would it help? The date she'd escaped. One man. Nineteen hours. Zero bodies. That zero should count for something. At the least, it was kinder than what LJ had been through.

Andra walked into her empty house with the couch on one side, the kitchen on the other.

Sex.

It was the root of all the problems in her life. But how could she work on getting more comfortable with it when he was all the way down in Louisiana? There was absolutely no way she was going to download one of those hookup apps and let some stranger put his hands all over her. Of course, at least with a stranger, she wouldn't care if she disappointed him.

Andra's eyes narrowed. Maybe there was something she could do without getting anyone else involved. She crossed the room to her couch and grabbed her laptop off a side table. When she opened it, it glowed to life on a page of equine nutritional supplements. She called up a new tab and typed "sex toys" into the search bar. Her eyebrows shot up at the images that appeared. "Wow, okay," she mumbled, and tried a different search term.

She'd never owned a sex toy herself—she hadn't missed sex after Gavin, and she hadn't had a lot of experience before him. It wasn't until she met LJ that she even remembered what it felt like to get that little tingle, that warmth that tugged and asked for more. There were a lot of things she never thought she'd want until she met him.

The new site loaded with a whole page full of pictures of dildos. She clicked on one and stared. There it was: the one thing that had ruined her life for the last five years. From the first moment her body had been violated, her personality had started twisting itself into knots she had no idea how to unravel.

The plastic penises didn't look intimidating at all right now. But then, they didn't look like much fun, either, and that's what people bought the synthetic versions for.

The urge to call LJ flitted through her head. Surely he would answer, the way he had when she'd called him from the dressing room. He was busy a lot of the time when she called, but when it was important, it was like he always knew to pick up. But what would she say to him? "Hey, I'm trying to get over my penis phobia because I happen to want yours. But when it's not attached to you, it looks kind of weird." No man wanted to hear about that.

She returned to the main page, scanning all the different choices. A catch took hold in her throat as she tried to figure out what size would be most effective. How many times would she need to deliberately trigger the panic before it lost its grip on her?

She'd had hundreds of those attacks, and the feeling of impending death never got any less real. But if she could make it past the fear, maybe it was peaceful beyond that. Free of loneliness and disappointment.

Just free.

She scrolled down so fast the pictures began to blur, until she stopped on one of the largest dildos. It was the most realistic looking, and every rib in her chest drew tight and brittle as she stared at it. Well, good. It was fear she was looking for, fear she needed to batter herself with until she could finally stop caring.

The little arrow hovered over the "Buy" button while her vision wavered around the edges, tears blurring the screen. Maybe she should pay extra to ship it faster, to start this miserable process sooner and just get it over with.

The arrow began to shake, and she took her fingers off the track-pad. She snapped the laptop closed and shoved it off her lap. It hit the edge of the couch cushion and flipped onto the rug.

Nothing about this felt right, and she couldn't do it. She wouldn't.

Andra curled around herself like her belly was an open wound, and began to cry.

The window had been dark for hours when she finally quieted, her eyes so swollen she couldn't have seen even if there had been light. She sniffled, the arm of the couch wet beneath her face. It was late, and she was exhausted. She hauled herself upright and shuffled across the house to the shower, turning on only a single light as she went. She shed her clothes mechanically and stepped under the spray, the *shh* of the warm water soothing her aching head. Her mouth was scratchy with thirst, but she wasn't hungry even though she hadn't eaten dinner.

Why hadn't she eaten? Why didn't she ever fucking eat unless LJ was there to cook? She didn't need to lose weight, didn't need to shape her body to anyone's pleasure. Her best friend was a cook, for Christ's sake, and even Wild Falls had restaurants. It was like some part of her didn't think she deserved food.

She swallowed past her tattered throat and remembered how hard it had been to look at herself in the mirror at all those department stores. She kept trying to hide her body under fabric but from who? From what?

Gingerly, she reached down and touched her belly. It was a little concave, the skin velvety and dotted with water droplets. She lifted her hand and laid it over one breast. She didn't touch herself except when she was washing up, and her nipple felt odd against her hand.

It shouldn't, though, should it? It was hers. It was her.

Her lip trembled and she cupped her breast, cradling the weight in her palm as the water slipped over her shoulders, surrounding her in warmth. This was how LJ touched her, no matter if it was her back, her elbow, her knee. Even her hair. His hands were always smiling, and he was never careless in how he put them on her.

She wished she could touch herself with the same respect.

That website should have been exciting, maybe even a little arousing. She could have been clicking through to the most interesting toys instead of choosing the one that scared her the most. She'd been approaching the purchase as if it were a vaccination instead of a joy. Planning on using it roughly, a punishment against a body whose reactions kept betraying her. Everything about that suddenly struck her as wrong.

When her wrists had been bound to Gavin's headboard, her body had felt like a cage she couldn't rip her way out of, but it wasn't a cage or a burden. It had carried her. Through nineteen terrible hours, and out the window. Her fingers had worked those screws free, even after her fingernails had broken and bled.

She let her hands cradle the muscles of her arms. They'd lowered her from Gavin's window. Her legs had caught her and propelled her away. She'd rescued herself when no one else had.

Andra closed her eyes and stroked her palms down herself, the way she would the coat of a foal newly into the world. Her skin was soft, vulnerable. Unbidden, love rose in her: natural and quavering, the way it did for every innocent foal.

For years, sex had become this dark, looming threat, and then an unreachable fairy tale that was easy for everybody else. But it shouldn't be any of those things. Shouldn't be about power or guilt or just suffering through in the hopes of eventually reaching normalcy. It was supposed to be about respect and nurturing and pleasure. Exactly the way she'd felt when LJ played his saxophone. He'd made love to her without a single touch.

Tipping her head against the wall, she listened to the patter of droplets against the tub, falling like a quiet rain. Her hands slipped over her hips, nerve endings beginning to tingle as they recognized a touch gentler than what they were used to. Her thighs were more sensitive the closer she traveled to the insides. She'd forgotten that, and now it seemed like a secret path she was learning to follow again.

There were places on her body that naturally felt pleasure more easily than others. It was the exact place, actually, where she'd clasp her legs around a man. Something deep within her squeezed at the thought of LJ's slim hips nestled between her legs. But even without him, this felt . . . good.

She trailed her fingers up the inside of her thigh, coming to rest at their juncture. There was a flinching in her, like that was something off-limits.

"No more punishment," she murmured. "You never did anything wrong." She cupped her hand over her center and rested it there, waiting to feel safe with herself.

It happened gradually, her breaths winding in and out until she realized the tension in her had been replaced with the slightest of tingles. It was the same rush that had opened in her when she'd pulled LJ's naked chest close to hers. Except this time, she wasn't afraid it was the only time she'd ever get to feel it. It was built into her body—the ability to feel pleasure.

It didn't have to be given or taken away by a man. It was her right, and it was as natural as birth and death.

She shifted her hand, chasing the elusive feeling, and a different kind of tension drew up in her. Her body preparing for and *wanting* more. A smile broke across her face at feeling the change so easily, when for so long it had seemed impossible.

When it came, her orgasm rose in her like joy. The waves of it expanded, sparkling all the way down to her toes, out to her fingertips. Washing through her until she was all new.

It belonged to her: her body, her pleasure, her strength. And now that she knew it, no one in the world could take it away.

Twenty-two

◇◇◇◇

Andra turned off the shower and wrapped herself in a soft towel.

She had thought if everything had started with a penis, maybe it could end there, too. But maybe it had never been about that at all. The attacks could happen in a grocery store as easily as in the bedroom, so it wasn't entirely about sex—it was the helplessness that terrified her more than anything. She couldn't unknow how easily someone could take all her power away from her. There was only one way to fight that, and it was the exact opposite of the way she'd been living for the last five years.

Until she was staring down that website with tears in her eyes, she hadn't realized how many ways she'd been punishing herself for the attack, even though she'd never consciously believed it was her fault. She'd been existing in a kind of withdrawn penance for long enough. She wanted a life, and now she knew for sure that she wanted LJ to be a part of it. With his gentle hands and sunny smile, and the sparkle he woke up in the center of her chest.

The next step in taking charge of her life, and in truly caring for herself, was to go after him.

She turned on the lights and started moving through her house, gathering her belongings. She was in a hurry, but she didn't rush. Instead, she took the time to reconnect with her body after all the years it had felt like an alien thing. Appreciating how easily her arms lifted weight and how smoothly her legs carried her anywhere she wanted to go. She was still whole, though she hadn't felt it in a long time.

When she passed her laptop, she picked it up and bookmarked the website so she could check out the sex toys another time. When she opened it again, she'd be looking to see what she might enjoy, rather than trying to trigger fear until she was numb to it.

It took her until nearly four in the morning to pack everything she might need, since she didn't know how long she'd be gone. She carried her two suitcases to the door, flicking off lights with her elbow as she went. The last one was the kitchen, and she stared into the cheery white space with its river-rock-pebbled backsplash and open, honest shelves. It wasn't the house that was wrong. It was the way she'd been living in it. When she got back, she'd do better.

Andra left her suitcases on the porch and walked to the paddock. She ducked, her loose hair catching on the rough wooden rails of the fence as she climbed between the two lowest ones.

Two horses stirred in the paddock. The old gelding came to investigate, but Gracie pushed him aside, vying for her owner's attention. The palomino nosed at Andra's pockets, looking for treats, but Andra was wearing her good jeans and didn't have any.

"Hey, girl," she whispered, running her hands over the mare's soft nose, her fuzzy ears. She smoothed a bit of cream-colored mane back to the right side, and her swollen eyes started to sting with fresh tears. "I won't be gone long, okay?" But that sounded like the same lie LJ had told her. "Actually, I might be gone for a while. But I'll miss you every day." Gracie nudged her in the belly, her ears pricking forward. Andra stepped in and wrapped her arms around the horse's neck, laying her cheek against her warm coat. She tried to swallow and her face crumpled, the first tear streaking into her horse's mane. Gracie had been the only one close to her for years. Silent and knowing, spunky enough to keep her mind busy when she couldn't bear to think. The mare had grown up with her, in a way.

Gracie tossed her head, whickering softly. Andra stepped back, wiping at her eyes.

"I'll make Stacia bring you loads of carrots, okay? And Jason will ride you. Give him as hard of a time as you want."

She walked away fast before she could change her mind, hitch up a trailer, and try to convince LJ to house the horse in his backyard down in New Orleans. Gracie broke into a trot, following her all the way to the fence, then popping her head over the top and whinnying loud enough to be heard at the main house. Andra picked up her suitcases and tried not to look back, even when Gracie's hoofbeats pounded along the fence, stopped, then galloped back the other way.

Her truck was back at the ranch, so she carried her suitcases all the way over the hill, the sounds of Gracie's distress following her the whole way.

She loaded her luggage and left Jason a note, then crept past Stacia's apartment to let herself into LJ's. All she took was his old half door with the spray-painted marks. Once it was wrapped in a sheet, she propped it in her passenger seat.

She didn't know whether he wanted to see her, and if he came back here, she didn't want it to be just for the door.

He'd been understanding at first, and so patient, but the look in his eyes had been the same every time she'd had one of her panic attacks. They made him feel like a villain, and it was no wonder he didn't want to be with a woman whose trauma stuck him in that role.

She hoped if she reclaimed control over her life, the attacks would lose their grip on her and that wouldn't be a problem anymore. His mom's health, though . . . She had the sinking feeling that wasn't going to be a short-term issue. He might have to move back to New Orleans permanently. Could they handle long distance when everything else was so shaky?

She shook off the questions. He was the only thing in her life that felt right. She needed to see him again, and then everything would be fine. Somehow.

Andra checked the gas gauge before she shut her truck door. She wanted to put a few hundred miles behind her before she stopped. It would be faster to fly, but from how LJ talked about New Orleans, she'd need her truck to get around. If things went well and she was there for more than a few days, she didn't want to have to rent a car.

She went back to the apartments, her steps slowing because this goodbye wasn't going to be any easier than the last one.

Stacia's door was unlocked. No burglar had ever ventured this far onto ranch property, and even if one did, the horses were worth more than anything in the houses.

"Jason, if that isn't you, somebody's about to get a load of buckshot in the backside!" Stacia warned.

"It's me," Andra whispered. "Don't shoot." She poked her head around the bedroom doorframe, her eyes already adjusted to the dark. "Hate to tell you, but that's a revolver, not a shotgun."

"Trust me, it'll still hurt." Stacia put the gun down and flopped back in bed, pulling a pillow over her face. "Ugh."

"Are you sleeping with my brother?" Andra came to perch on the side of her bed, starting to smile. He and Stacia had been sort of bicker-flirting as long as she could remember, but after Jason came back from college and they didn't start dating, she had figured that was as far as it was going to go.

"I'm not sleeping with anyone right now, because I'm *not* sleeping, because I hate you," Stacia grumbled into the pillow.

"Listen, Stace . . ." Now that she was here, her practiced speech was starting to stick in her throat. "I'm sorry. For being a terrible friend for the last few years, and for not braving the main house often enough to eat your amazing food."

Stacia pulled the pillow off her face, a wad of brown hair almost obscuring the killing glare in the one blue eye peeking through. "You woke me up in the ass crack of the night to tell me you're a bad friend? Fuck, Andra, I didn't need a demonstration."

"It's not just for that." Her fingers twisted in her lap. "I'm leaving."

Stacia blew her hair out of her eyes, focusing. "You're going after him?"

"I am." It was strange how the words settled down into her. And they felt better the longer she thought about them. The feeling so distracted her that she didn't realize at first that Stacia was taking a long time to respond.

Her friend reached out and grabbed her wrist. "Look, you know I like LJ. He's a good man, and that's so far out of style these days they don't even have an emoji for it. But he's been gone for almost a week, and he hasn't called once, so . . ."

"We didn't leave on the best of terms." Andra glanced down. "It wasn't anything either of us could help. I need to get out of here for a while, you know? He's told me so much about New Orleans that I kind of want to see it anyway. And I think in person, it might be easier to talk this through. I know him, Stacia. He's not mad. He's hurting, and I need to make him better."

Stacia sat up and pulled her into a hug. "You take care of you, Andra. If that means going to New Orleans, I'll buy the gas myself, but make sure you're doing it for the right reasons."

"I'm so glad to have you back," Andra murmured into her tangled hair. "I didn't want to drag you into my shit, but I missed you the whole time."

Stacia pulled back and pinched her arm. "Well, knock it off now."

Andra burst out laughing, rubbing the sore spot. "Thanks a lot."

"Promise you'll call me if it doesn't work out, okay? I'll fly down there, and we'll see if we can't show Bourbon Street how much damage a couple of country girls can do." Stacia sighed. "I bet they have loads of sequins there."

"Loads." Andra stood up. "I'll bring you back some if you promise to spoil Gracie for me while I'm gone. And guilt-trip Jason into exercising her."

Stacia lay back, waving a tired hand. "No problem. That brother of yours will do anything for a blow job."

"Ew. Talk about an image for my nightmares."

"Got to keep you awake behind the wheel." Stacia pulled the pillow back over her face. "Drive safe."

Once outside, Andra started the truck and drove to her next stop. Last one before she hit the road. She braced herself.

The main house was unlocked, too. But she was apparently terrible at sneaking in, because her father met her before she was halfway to the second floor. He was bare chested, the pooch of his belly extending a little past his belt. His hair was smashed flat in the back from his pillow.

"Andra, what's wrong?"

She shook her head. "Everything's okay, or it will be. I'm going to New Orleans—I need to see LJ. I just wanted to say goodbye before I left."

"What do you need to see him for? I thought you two got over your little flirt after the rodeo, but then he up and left with no notice and suddenly you were moping like you were engaged or something." He scrubbed a hand over his face. "What's all this about, Andra?"

She gritted her teeth. "He's given you no reason to talk about him that way."

"No? Because before he came around, I didn't have employees and daughters running off left and right." He scowled. "You think I haven't noticed how you've been all week? You never even dated him, and he's making you miserable. He's not like you, Andra, and he's not from here. In the end, that's going to bring you nothing but hurt."

She didn't bother arguing their relationship status with her father. She just stood, two stairs below him, and crossed her arms. "Do you remember me, Dad?"

"What?" His brow creased, the bags under his eyes deep in the light from the hallway above them.

"Because I don't. I remember sneaking out to the barn and getting drunk with Stacia, and buying three dresses for every high school dance because I could never pick just one and you didn't mind. But me . . . how I felt inside my own head? It's just gone." She pressed her lips together. "It wasn't until LJ came here and shook everything up that I started to remember how it was to *like* being me."

The furrow in his brow deepened.

"More than that," she went on before he could start. "More than anything to do with me, he's a good man." Her throat went tight, trembling with everything those words meant to her. They were the two best men she'd ever known, and she had no idea how to bridge the gap between them. They were so utterly different and so completely the same. "I wish you could see that, too, because I love you and—" Her voice broke.

Dad was down both stairs between them in a flash, his solid arms wrapped around her back and the smell of Old Spice and horses warm in her nose.

"Don't cry. Don't cry now, sweetie."

The sob tromped its way up her throat before she could stop it, and her shoulders shook. She couldn't do this right now. She needed to get in the truck and make her own future, but her dad's arms felt so safe and it had been a long, long day.

She pulled back and swallowed. "I didn't come here to fight." Her spine drew up tall when she asked it to, her body strong despite her lack of sleep. "I just wanted to say goodbye. I'll call, but I'm not sure when I'll be back." She pressed a quick kiss to his cheek. "I need to start running toward something, Daddy," she whispered. "Not away."

She turned and dashed down the stairs.

"Andra."

She almost didn't stop, but she'd been listening to that voice for too many years not to. She turned back with her hand already on the doorknob.

Dad cleared his throat and paused, like he was weighing his words. "He hasn't lived here that long, honey. There are probably a lot of things about him you don't know about. And okay, maybe you've got a crush on him, but—are you sure it's a good idea to just go showing up down there?"

She pressed her lips together so they wouldn't wobble. "No, I'm not sure. But I'm going to find out."

"You're a fool, LJ Delisle."

LJ nudged the water glass a little closer to the bed, the ever-present knot in his stomach loosening at the evidence that Mama was feeling well enough to lecture him. "Your pills are right here, but I'll wake you up for your next dose, and I'll make fresh applesauce with bananas for lunch. Dropped a little bit of basil in your water so you can't taste the tap. You want to hit the bathroom before you go to sleep?"

Mama glared at him, the creases alongside her eyes deeper than he remembered. "You drove all the way across the country to make me applesauce? I can make my own dang applesauce. And everybody else's, too, for twenty-eight long years so you could have choices in front of you instead of somebody's dirty dishes."

He winked. "Not a problem. I did the dishes earlier, so there's not a dirty one left."

"Don't you sass me, LJ," she warned. Her throat shook as she held back a cough, or maybe a laugh. He was hoping for the second.

He leaned down and kissed her cheek. "I have choices," he said. "And one of them is to come back and see my mama whenever I please. Don't fuss yourself too much. I haven't been fired yet."

That might not be entirely true, since Bill had never answered the voicemail he'd left explaining the situation, but there was no reason to tell Mama that. Jobs were easy enough to find if you weren't particular about what you did or how much you got paid to do it. He'd always found them, even when there wasn't a plug in the city feeding electricity, and you couldn't drive through the streets without plowing your bumper into a sandbar or a house.

"When's your lady coming down?" She reached for a tissue on the bedside table and blew her nose. His fingers clenched in his lap when he saw how thin her arms had gotten. When he took her to the doctor after he'd gotten home, she didn't even make it over the hundred-pound mark.

"Andra had to work." He glanced away. "Besides, you told me to stay away from her. I didn't think you'd want her to visit."

"I tell you to do lots of things." She sank back into her pile of worn-out pillows. "I sure didn't think you'd choose now to lose your contrary streak and start listening to your poor old mama." She was trying to glare, but her eyelids loosened anyway, drooping shut against her will. LJ brushed her cheek with the backs of his fingers. It was still soft, not the papery brittleness he associated with the elderly. She wasn't old enough to be so sick, but maybe when you had as much personality as she did, you could pack eighty years into forty-five.

LJ watched her slip into sleep, a smile tipping up his lips. It was good to be home.

Almost too good.

He closed the door to her room and headed through the kitchen. New Orleans fit like an old boot, clasping the lumps and calluses of your foot so easily you forgot you were wearing it until you stepped into the shower and remembered you hadn't meant to wear it quite so long.

When he woke up this morning, he hadn't jumped out of bed, eager to get to the barn. Instead, he'd lain there, his sheets wet with summer sweat, irritated at the second-rate air conditioner that had been all they could afford when they'd rebuilt the house. Mentally, he had counted the bills left in his wallet and wondered if there was anything he could pawn to get a leg up on a new AC unit. If there were any odd jobs he could do to pay it off before the buyback slip expired. Trying to make those numbers work out just pissed him off, so after he fixed Mama's breakfast, he played his sax on the porch for an hour, letting the music wash all the mad out of his veins.

Of course, the sound brought Ty out of his house with a guitar. They ended up jamming until Ty was late for his shift and noon had come and gone without a thing done. Then he had to feed Mama scraps of two nights' worth of leftovers before he hoofed it down to the brand-new corner store the Lower Ninth had gotten before he left. It was crowded, and still small and understocked compared to the Rouses that reigned over the whiter neighborhoods.

He'd prayed for years for a grocery store for his home. Now that it was here, every shelf in every aisle made him grit his teeth at the thought of what still wasn't there. When he got home, he put a smile back on his face and helped his mama to bathe, the need for which had made her cranky enough to snap at him before she drifted off to sleep.

All of that meant when he opened the front door and pushed out into the thick evening air, he'd barely had a chance to think about Andra all day. He dropped into the old porch swing, the chain creaking under his weight. The air felt swampy in his lungs after the crisp-paper dryness of a Montana summer. But it was warmer, too, like a home-cooked meal that'd be too spicy for anybody who wasn't raised at your same table.

He hadn't called Andra the whole way out here. His Datsun had coughed and protested through the miles, keeping him busy with worrying about a breakdown he couldn't afford. Every time he'd fallen asleep in the metal coffin of the truck bed, his mind had felt sludgy—too dark to try to pour through a phone line. As much as he ached to hear her voice, he didn't know what to say.

There was no excuse for how he'd ruined their first time together. He hadn't made her feel safe with him, and even thinking of that made him sick with remorse. And then he'd had to run out the next morning before he could even feed her breakfast. It was the worst kind of timing, and yet his guilt mixed nauseatingly with undeniable relief. If Mama hadn't gotten sick, there would have been no way to hide the fact that the more he wanted Andra, the more it scared her. He had no answers, and he couldn't shake the feeling that he was a coward for leaving, even if he hadn't had any other choice.

All those thoughts just fed his superstitious dread. Every time his wheels had gone still long enough to pump gas or grab a sandwich, he'd had flashes of his mama dying before he could get home. Now that he was back in New Orleans, Montana seemed like a kid's cowboy fantasy of a different life.

And that's all it had been. He'd always known that someday, his mama would no longer be able to work and he'd have to support both of them. He'd known that until you made a name for yourself, the show industry paid only starvation wages. But he'd been stubborn and ignored those realities as surely as he'd ignored Bill Lawler's ultimatum. In the end, all that dreaming didn't do a thing. He grew up in the streets of New Orleans, and that was where he was always going to end up, working a job that filled his stomach but not his heart.

The porch swing creaked as he waved away a mosquito, focusing for the first time on the street he stared out at. The freshly painted red stairs up to the Robinsons' porch looked good but almost garishly cheerful next to the flaking trim that was waiting on next month's paycheck. The drooping sun struck a green glow among the lush weeds of the lot next door, the Graviers' vacant foundation peeking up like bleached gray bones begging to be buried.

LJ closed his eyes, and this time it wasn't his mama's slack face that appeared behind them. It was Andra's fingernails, scraping at the paint of her windowsill before she found the latch and threw the window open. How her naked back had heaved as she sucked in the air that was clean of his scent, safe from memories he couldn't shield her from.

She was probably relieved she didn't have to see him after that. He sure didn't feel like the same man who'd sat a saddle on so many of her family's horses. And even when he'd been that man, he hadn't been different enough from her bad memories to make new ones with her.

His hand tightened on the swing's armrest, a splinter of the weathered wood driving deep into his palm. It was no wonder. To teach her how to feel safe again, she needed something better than a man who lost his temper at grocery store inventory and an air conditioner that wasn't even broken yet. Her father, his mama, his own instincts: they'd all been telling him the same thing, and it was about damn time he started listening. Probably Andra would be a lot better off if she never heard from him again.

Twenty-three

◇◇◇◇

Andra threw her truck into reverse, backed up four inches, cranked the wheel, and crept forward five. She reversed again by centimeters, wincing as she watched the bumper of the Honda behind her, half expecting a crash to announce she'd gotten too close.

She'd meant to make a quick stop to eat before she got to LJ's house so he wouldn't feel obligated to feed her. Except she'd had to drive nearly a mile away from the restaurant before she found a spot along the street big enough to wedge her truck into.

Most of the streets in New Orleans were smaller than the narrowest alley in Montana and lined on both sides by cars parked so close together they must have been swung into place by a crane. But as soon as she'd gotten out to hike to the restaurant, the scent hit her.

Lemon cake. Bright and citrusy, wafting on a wave of Madagascar vanilla that smelled like LJ's kitchen. She smiled.

The post-lunch walk back from the restaurant was lovely, the brutal heat made lighter by the weave of arching branches shading the whole street. As she passed the trunk of a tree, the sidewalk climbed and cracked over the top of huge roots. When it dipped back down the other side, it turned from cement to ancient bricks that disappeared under a blanket of moss, only to have their crumbling red edges froth back to the surface again. How many layers of sidewalks were there under this one, gripped in the claws of the tree roots or blotted out by modern gray concrete?

This whole city felt like it had been around for ages, generations of kids and grandparents tripping over these same sidewalks. Maybe if she stayed in this place long enough, where the past and present mixed together in such a glorious mess, she'd start to get some perspective on her own life.

She finally edged herself out of the parking spot and whooped in triumph, smacking her hand into the steering wheel. "Take that, New Orleans! Country mouse can drive!" A horn blared behind her, and she jumped and hit the gas. Her front tire dropped, her teeth snapping together with the impact. She stomped on the brakes, and the horn behind her screamed again. "Shit." Gingerly, she drove out of the pothole, listening for the flap-flap-flap of a flattened tire. It held steady, though, and she made the next turn.

It was probably good she had to focus on negotiating traffic, because it would give her less time to think. In the two and a half days it took her to cross the country, she'd had way too much of that. And way too much time to guess at what LJ was thinking. He'd finally called yesterday, but she had been pumping gas. When she'd hopped back in and seen his name on the screen, she hadn't dared to hit the "Call Back" button. They hadn't been together that long, had never even been on an actual date, and a thousand unanswerable questions about their future were already rattling around in her head.

He'd said if she ever knocked on his door, he'd answer. If she could just see his face, she was sure they could work everything out. And she thought maybe he needed to see her here, outside the safe shell of the family ranch, to believe they might have something real.

She already felt more real. She'd stayed in whatever motel appealed to her for the night, and chatted with strangers she met at stops along the road, even men. She should have taken a trip years ago. It was weirdly freeing to be alone in a place where no one knew her history. She could be anyone.

She took one more turn and then hit a bridge, the sound of her tires buzzing into an even hum as she crossed a canal. Her window hissed down, and thick, humid air draped her face. This was it. The Lower Ninth Ward: LJ's home, which she'd heard so much about. She just hoped there was a parking spot somewhere that was her size.

As soon as she turned onto the first street, Andra's smile faded. The rest of the town was packed to the last inch with brightly painted houses, tiny cars, and enormous trees. But here there was nothing but space. She slowed down, her head swiveling.

The lots were like a mouthful of broken teeth: the houses dotted here and there just served to draw attention to the gaping holes where others should have been. In places, there were only porch stairs left, their steps leading up to nothingness.

When LJ had talked about home, he'd never said anything about this.

A young mother pushing a stroller turned to scowl at Andra's truck, and she realized she was staring. She shook her head and replaced her foot on the gas. Her phone announced that she'd reached her destination, but no house waited at the end of the concrete walk. Andra double-checked the number on the address she'd pulled off LJ's résumé, and peered out her side window. Bushes grew up out of the windows of the nearest house, and the numbers were long gone. The next one looked inhabited, but she gaped in horror at the faded spray paint of the X by the front door. Squinting at those numbers, she forgot to look for the ones that denoted the address.

She couldn't imagine living in a house with the number of her lost loved ones painted across the front. She threw a glance into the passenger seat, where LJ's old door still rested. It looked conspicuous, even wrapped in a sheet.

The house across the street had another X on it, bricks showing through the fading paint. What had the rescuers been thinking, vandalizing homes that way? You couldn't paint over brick. They must have thought no one would ever live in them again.

Andra pulled over, her hands shaking. She deliberately relaxed her muscles, fighting the edge of panic chilling her skin. It had happened twice on the drive down. In a dingy restaurant that smelled of spilled beer, and once when she'd glimpsed a man in a gas station with a profile just like Gavin's. But each time she'd fought through it and kept herself from totally losing control. The trip was her choice. Somehow, knowing that she was taking charge helped battle the attacks every time they threatened to take over.

She took a long, slow breath and looked around. The damage from the flood was bad, but it was over a decade old. That crisis was long past. Still, as distracted as she was by wreckage and the idea of seeing LJ again, she'd be lucky if she didn't run over somebody's dog by accident. The neighborhood wasn't that big. She could walk to LJ's and get her truck after she found her destination.

Besides, there was plenty of parking here. There were hardly any houses, and even fewer cars. She hadn't seen a single bus stop, so no wonder LJ was so insistent that he bring his truck. She hopped out and checked the map on her phone for where to go. A couple of boys rode by on bikes. One offered a shy smile, and the other quickly glanced away. She returned the smile, only then realizing she hadn't seen another white person since she'd crossed the bridge.

It wasn't something she normally thought about, the race of the people around her. Then again, Montana wasn't the most diverse place: other than a handful of Latinos, there weren't many other ethnicities to speak of. Suddenly, she felt clumsy, conspicuous, as if she were being tested.

She ran her hands down her arms, cupping her palms over the bare skin. This morning when she woke up, she'd put on a sleeveless eyelet-lace blouse with a high mandarin collar and delicate, feminine edging. Beneath her jeans, sweat was already starting to collect behind her knees, but at least that was a little less skin showing to mark her as a visitor in this place. She ran her thumb over the bend of her elbow and then started down the street with a long, determined stride.

This was LJ's home. However foreign it felt, she would be okay here.

Music played from nearby, something jazzy and full of brass, but without a drum. A whiff of smoky mesquite wood and barbecued meat drifted out of a grill set beside someone's porch steps. She inhaled, her eyelids drooping, but then the ground dropped out from underneath her.

She stumbled, going ankle-deep in a gritty puddle in the bottom of a pothole. She pulled her cowboy boot out, shaking off the water. Sandals were going on the shopping list, stat. These boots were stifling, the soles transferring the heat of the pavement upward until her feet might as well have been resting in a roasting pan.

The music was coming from this street: a small porch seething with bodies and the flash of sunlight off brass instruments. She passed another vacant lot, trying not to be rude as she peeked toward the musicians, searching for house numbers.

Then the sax threaded up through the center of the song, and she stopped as if the sidewalk had grabbed her boots. It wasn't the song he'd played for her, but all the other music was sharp corners, where LJ's saxophone was smooth curves.

She could hear him, but she couldn't see him. The house itself was narrow as a hallway, painted a bright purple no one would dare in Montana. Every bit of shade from the covered porch was filled with black men holding musical instruments she mostly couldn't name. Trumpets, maybe horns? A handheld keyboard with a tube hanging off it that was tucked into its player's mouth. Two guys lounged on the porch swing, the sousaphone player squished in behind it. There was only one woman, her fingers cradling her instrument with the same loving reverence LJ always used for his saxophone.

Andra finally spotted LJ tucked into the center of the crowd. He was the tallest, with droplets of sweat beading his bare, rippling back muscles as he curled forward into his instrument. The keyboardist glanced at her but kept playing. Up close, their crazy collection of instruments was so battered that the brass held the texture of wadded paper, smoothed back not quite flat.

A shorter man on the porch steps cocked his chin at her, resting his guitar in his lap. "You looking for somebody?"

She resisted the urge to cross her arms and tried for a smile that looked friendly, but hopefully not encouraging of the flirtation in his. "Found him, actually."

The music stopped and LJ spun around. She lifted a hand to shield her eyes from the sun, a self-conscious prickling running down from her scalp.

He blinked, and she waited for that huge, bright smile, but instead he said, "Andra! Hey, uh . . . wow." He set his saxophone on the porch swing. She took a step closer to the house, but instead of coming down to meet her, he opened the front door and reached inside.

Guitar Guy grinned. "LJ, I should have known that was your cowgirl when I saw her walking down the street so fast. She's got the boots and everything."

LJ came back out of the house with a short-sleeved button-down shirt and pulled it on over his bare chest as he stepped over Guitar Guy's seat on the stairs. A scrap of candy wrapper drifted down the cracked sidewalk between his house and the street, and he swooped it up, stuffing it into the chest pocket of his shirt.

Now he smiled. His eyes first, then his high cheekbones, then that huge grin spreading across his face like the sunrise. "What are you doing here, Andie-girl?" he murmured, pulling her into his chest. His arms held more tension than usual, and he hugged her almost too tight.

Over his shoulder, his friends watched, and she closed her eyes. Sweat slicked the skin of his back, and his shirt was clammy against her palms as the sun beat down on them. She'd imagined this moment a lot of times, but never with the dry ache of her tongue begging for a drink of water. She wanted to tell him so many things: that she missed him, that she wanted to help with his mom, that her body didn't feel like her enemy anymore. But all those things sounded stupid to say in front of his friends, and he let her go before she could think of a safer topic.

"Get you in out of the sun, girl," Guitar Guy said. "All that white-ass skin, you're gonna burn."

"Ty," a female voice whispered. "Shut *up*."

Andra's hair clung to the back of her neck, the black strands seeming to soak up all the sun, cooking her scalp. She could barely think. "No, he's right." She gathered her hair up, holding it in a messy handful and waving her other hand to cool the molten-hot pulse at her throat.

She glanced up, and the other girl waved from the far side of the porch, yellow nail polish flashing on a light-brown hand. She gave Andra a shy smile, the yellow lettering on her *Star Wars* T-shirt perfectly matching her nails. Andra grinned back, relief making it come out a little too enthusiastic.

LJ ushered her toward the shade of the porch, using his bare foot to nudge a stick out of the sidewalk and back onto the lawn. The loose basketball shorts he wore didn't match the shirt that hung so nicely from his shoulders.

Ty gave her an easy smile and swung his legs out of the way so she could climb the stairs.

"Guys, this is Andra. Andra, this is Tash, Ty's sister." LJ went on to introduce the five guys on the porch, reeling off names that the heat sapped out of her muzzy head as soon as he spoke them. "Are you hungry? My mama's asleep, but I could come up with a little something."

"Yes," she said automatically, her stomach tightening with a little groan. "Or wait, no. I had lunch on the way here."

Ty laughed, strumming a random chord on his guitar. "Silly girl. Never say you ain't hungry if a Delisle's doing the cooking."

LJ opened the front door for her. "Here, why don't you go inside and cool off? See you in a second."

"Sure, okay." She bit the inside of her lip, then forced another smile for everyone as she went inside. She'd missed the sound of his voice so much, had actually been looking forward to how much richer it might be when he was home and relaxed. Instead his inflections were northern-university flat and precise.

The door closed, leaving her alone in a small kitchen with barn-red cabinets and an upright piano tucked into the corner across from the oven. Chicago Cubs pennants hung from two of the walls, and a fan on the table blew tepid air across her skin, only making her sweat more.

Outside, a low male voice said, "Damn, LJ. No wonder you weren't in a hurry to come home."

Laughter broke out. "Is that how the girls look up in Montana? Because I could get on up there and ride some horses. How hard can it be? I'll ride them horses all night long."

There was the sound of a smack and more laughter.

"Y'all get on out of here before you scare her off," LJ said, his accent rolling low and sweet through his words again. She closed her eyes and just listened.

"Yeah, I had my money on you being back before Halloween, but now I'm gonna bump it out to Mardi Gras."

Her forehead creased. Had he told them he was moving to Montana for only a few months, or were they making assumptions?

"Has Mama D met her?" a baritone voice asked. "She's been talking to my mom for weeks, telling her all about LJ's girl, saying maybe he was going to give her some grandbabies. Bet you didn't tell her you were just messing around with a white girl up there."

Andra flinched, her hands curling into fists, her arms feeling intensely bare.

"Don't be a jerk, Reggie." Tash's voice sounded even smaller in the silence. "Just because she's not from the Lower Ninth don't mean he can't be serious about her. Maybe he wants somebody he has more in common with."

A loud snort. "Right. Because since he went to college, he's too good for the ladies round here? Maybe you ought to have more respect for *your*self, Tash."

"Hey!" LJ's voice snapped out. "You watch who the fuck you're talking to right now."

"Hey, hey, hey . . ." That sounded like Ty, though the tones were more placating than they'd been earlier. "LJ! Come on, man."

Andra whirled to face the door. Oh God, please don't let her have caused an argument between him and his friends. Her pulse raced, but she gritted her teeth against a sudden light-headedness. She was safe here. Even if there was a fight, even if people got angry, she could hold her own. She clenched her hands just to feel the strength in them.

"You want to mind your business? Or do you want to tell me mine?" She almost didn't recognize LJ's voice. She'd never heard it sound so vicious before.

There was a loud burst of breath, like the air had gotten knocked out of someone.

"LJ, ease up, man. Your woman's waiting inside, huh?" Ty said.

"What the fuck ever," the baritone growled, and the porch creaked.

"You listen, and you listen good," LJ said, and no one interrupted him. "That's my girl in there, and if any of y'all have a goddamn thought in your head about her, you better think it so quiet I *never* hear you."

There was no response.

"Damn, Reggie," somebody muttered. "Are you fucking crazy, man? You want to start shit with *LJ*?"

After that, there was nothing for a few minutes. Just the squeak of porch steps, the snap of instrument cases, and the scuff of shoes over concrete.

"I wasn't saying . . ." Tash's voice trailed off, and then she tried again. "LJ, I only meant you had stuff in common with her because you like horses and farms and stuff. Not that you were acting like . . ."

"It's fine."

It was so quiet she thought they were all gone, then Ty said, "Fuck 'em, man. Some people are gonna think what they're gonna think. You can't—"

She fled. Because she knew he was coming in soon, and she didn't want him to know she'd been listening. And she didn't want to hear him upset because of her.

It was an old style of house: narrow with no hallway but with each room opening into the next. There were only two doors leading into the kitchen, one closed and one open to show a sink crowded with toiletries. She went through that one, slamming the door behind her and then groping for a light switch. It was lower and farther across the wall than she'd expected, and when the light finally came on, it was with the scrape of a loud fan. A washer and a dryer sat opposite a bathtub, their bases obscured by a heap of sheets and towels. An odd, sharp scent hung in the air, and she was excruciatingly aware she was in someone else's home—the private space where they ate and slept and washed their clothes. She turned on the tap, splashed water over her overheated face, and cupped some over the sticky back of her neck.

Somehow, she'd considered only LJ's response. She hadn't even imagined she'd be so out of place in his neighborhood, among his friends. And he'd defended her, but his welcome had been . . . off. Not as enthusiastic as he normally was.

She should have expected that, considering she was here without an invitation, during a time when he needed to be focused on his family.

Andra shut off the tap and stared down into the sink. Had coming after him been a giant mistake?

Twenty-four

◇◇◇◇

LJ glared at his best friend. Blood rushed down his arms and into his fists, the muscles in his arms twitching with energy. "Don't push me right now, Ty."

"Look, Reggie's a dumbshit, but he was just saying what everybody else is thinking." Tyrone barely topped five foot seven, but he stared stonily up through nearly a foot of height difference separating his face from LJ's. He was the only guy in the whole neighborhood who'd ever put LJ on the ground, and no one forgot it. "If you're serious about that girl, okay. I'm happy for you, but a lot of folks aren't going to be, and you can't expect them to be."

"Go." He could barely get the word out from between his teeth.

Ty shook his head. "Whatever, man." He picked up his guitar by the neck and sauntered out onto the street.

LJ whirled and grabbed the door handle. It took him a second to relax his grip so he wouldn't shove it open hard enough to rip the screws out of the hinges. There was no sign of Andra in the kitchen, but water ran behind the bathroom door. He bent down and straightened the heap of his shoes by the door, lining them up in neat pairs.

Yesterday, he'd finally scraped up the courage to call her. No Delisle was a coward, and he knew if he wasn't sure what to say to her, she'd be even more lost. He was the one who always broke the ice between them, and whenever he did, her rare smiles usually followed. But that time, all he got was her voicemail. It was clipped and distant and sounded nothing like her.

You've reached Cassandra Lawler with Lawler Performance Quarter Horses. Leave a message after the tone.

For as many times as her number had come up in his missed calls list, she'd never left a voicemail. He joked and rambled on hers but ended up hitting the "Delete" key when asked if he was satisfied with his message.

LJ threw a quick glance at the closed bathroom door and then picked up the chair with the ripped cushion, sticking it behind the table, where it wouldn't be so clear it didn't match the other. He swept crumbs off the table and into his palm.

A door clicked quietly open behind him, and he turned to meet her.

Andra's hair drifted in a wild mass of black, the humidity lifting its normal waves into the bounce and sway of fat curls that begged to hide his fingers. Her denim-clad legs went on for miles, and her cowboy boots made him ache for the open fields of Montana.

She took a small step forward, hugging her elbows. She was moving differently. It didn't feel like he'd been gone long enough for so much to have changed.

"I didn't mean to cause trouble," she said. "I should have called and asked if I could visit."

"'Course not." He pulled a chair out from the table for her. "You're always welcome—you know that. I just would have cleaned up a little if I knew you were coming. You hungry?"

She sat down. "Thirsty, mostly."

"Right, of course. New Orleans in August is nasty." He hunted through the cupboard until he came up with a cup that wasn't plastic. A quick towel swipe had it shining even more, and he took the time to get a few ice cubes from the freezer. "You want sweet tea or water?"

She smiled. "Better do water. I'm half-diabetic already from all the sweet tea I drank at lunch."

"Oh, right. I forget you don't have the stomach for sweet tea." As he filled the glass, he watched her out of the corner of his eye, trying to pinpoint what had changed about the way she moved. She still crossed her arms over her chest, but it almost looked . . . softer? Comforting instead of defensive, maybe.

A strange sound from outside caught his attention. He put the glass in front of her before he crossed the room and peered out the window. His hands curled into fists when he saw the news van setting up a camera tripod in front of the Graviers' empty lot next door.

"What's wrong?" Andra's chair scraped back, and she came up beside him. "Are those reporters? What's going on?"

"Hurricane hit Florida this week. Anytime there's a big one or an anniversary of Katrina, they come crawling all over the place. The Lower Ninth was right at one of the levee breaks where the water flooded in, and a lot of folks around here couldn't afford to rebuild. If they want to get dramatic shots to remind everybody how bad it was, they come here." He looked away, because he didn't want to see her pity. It felt even itchier than that of strangers. "Give me one second, okay?"

He kicked into a pair of sandals and went outside.

"Excuse me," he called, crossing his grass to a cameraman setting up the tripod. "You can't film here. This is private property."

"I'm sorry," the cameraman said, glancing over his shoulder. "I, ah . . ."

Fingers tapped his shoulder. A woman with smoothly styled hair and a pantsuit gave him a sympathetic smile, the politeness tempered with sadness, like they were both attending the same funeral. LJ fought back the fury trying to creep up his throat. It was his home, damn it, not a graveyard.

"I'm so sorry to bother you. Is this your place?" the anchorwoman asked. "We're doing a special on the progress of the rebuilding effort after Katrina. Would you like to be interviewed?"

Of course he didn't want to be interviewed. He was wearing fucking basketball shorts with his summer church shirt thrown on over them. He'd been doing dishes before his friends came over, not dressing up to be on TV. Which was probably exactly what they wanted to show on their little too-bad-so-sad program about poverty after Katrina.

"No," he said, to both questions. "But I'm watching this place for the owner, and the family doesn't want it filmed."

It might as well be true. The Graviers hadn't come back after the evacuation. He'd gathered some warped and muddy photo albums for them out of the wreckage of their house, but they'd never called, and a "For Sale" sign never went up. He still had the albums somewhere back in the shed. They'd never said as much, but he was pretty sure they didn't want to watch the news and accidentally see the place their daddy and little girl had died.

"All right," the reporter said. "Of course not. Here, take my card. Let me know if you or anybody you know would care to be interviewed. It can be a good way to get increased funding for the rebuilding effort."

He took the card and jerked a nod. He knew that, and he wasn't too proud to play the game. The reason his new house had framed up the fastest on the block wasn't because his fifteen-year-old self had been so good with a hammer. It was because he'd found out where the volunteers were staying, and he'd been down there every morning, smiling his face off, telling jokes, and making friends.

But right now, he wasn't in the mood. He turned, acutely aware of his plastic sandals next to her designer heels, and went back home.

Andra was waiting right inside the door. "Is everything okay?"

"Yeah." He closed the door, shrugging the tension out of his shoulders. "They always want to film there, because the porch steps are a couple higher than everywhere else and they stick up good above the weeds. I kept it trimmed down when I was living here, but Mama can't get the pull start on the Weed Eater to go. Arms too short." He poked Andra's arm, working up a smile. "Like you." He glanced back at the table and her empty water glass. "Hey, you doing okay with the heat?"

She winced, putting a hand to her flushed forehead. "I'm really gross and sweaty right now, sorry. Not used to humidity, I guess."

"No, no problem." He refilled her glass and turned the fan so it pointed at her chair. "Sorry the AC's already at the max. Want some more ice?"

"LJ . . ." She touched his arm, the muscles tight under her hand. "Hey, look at me."

He didn't want to.

If he did, she'd see he didn't want her here. In his mama's house, which was half the size of Andra's cottage. In his neighborhood, which news vans were filming so the whole country could shake their heads pityingly. Here, with his friends smirking at him for bringing home a white girl.

She deserved better than all that.

"I'm sorry. I wasn't expecting you, that's all."

"I know," she whispered, her fingers curling on his arm. "Listen, LJ—"

"Tash?" his mama called through her bedroom door. "Honey, is that you?"

Andra's eyes widened. He covered her hand quickly with his. "It's okay," he whispered. "She's been dying to meet you. This is going to make her whole day." At least he hoped so. His mama had been so weird about Andra, and he wasn't sure how to make that fit with knowing she'd been bragging about his girlfriend to Reggie's mama. He dropped his voice even further. "Look, if she's grouchy, don't take it personally. She hates not being able to do everything herself."

Andra shook her head. "It's fine, LJ. Don't worry about it."

He let her go, because they didn't have time for everything unsaid between them, and even if they did, he wouldn't know where to start. Instead, he headed for the bedroom and closed the door behind him, for whatever good it would do. This house had been in their family for three generations, but when they rebuilt, they hadn't had any extra money for interior insulation. Now you could hear somebody brushing their teeth from across the house.

Mama pushed herself up against the pillows, even that small movement making her gasp for breath.

"Hey, did we wake you?" She'd been sleeping so deeply lately, he hadn't worried about playing music on the porch.

She frowned at him. "Why didn't you come get me if we had company?"

He smiled. "Speaking of, guess who's here, Mama?"

Her whole face lit up, the way he hadn't seen it since the first moment he walked through the door with his suitcase. "Did she come?" She reached up and started patting at her hair, which was so thin now that bare patches shone through on her scalp, though still not a thread of gray showed in the black. "LJ, go get my church jacket from the closet. The pink one, with the big buttons."

"Um, to wear with your nightgown?"

She glared. "Lyndon Johnson, if I wanted sass, I would certainly let you know."

"Yes, Mama." He went to the closet and shucked through hangers, finally finding the padded shoulders of her church jacket in the back. She hadn't been well enough to attend the one Sunday he'd been here, but it still alarmed him to see how far back the jacket had migrated. She must not have been up to the two-block walk for weeks.

He carried the jacket over to the bed and helped her thread her arms into it.

"Mama, uh . . ." He didn't dare tell her to be nice, and he couldn't think of a subtle way to ask her not to interrogate Andra.

"Don't mumble, LJ. It makes you look uneducated. Now go and get my makeup bag out of the bathroom, and my hand mirror."

He frowned. "She knows you just woke up. She doesn't expect you to be wearing makeup."

"Lyndon John—" She swayed, bracing her hands in her lap, and didn't finish.

He caught her shoulder. "You okay? Do you want me to help you to the bathroom?"

She reached for a tissue and blew her nose. "I'm fine. Now get my makeup bag. The green one with flowers on it."

He decided to close his mouth rather than say he hardly needed a description. She'd had the same makeup bag since he was a toddler. It smelled like powder and waxy lipstick, and the lining was stained with little bits of color where various things had come open or spilled over the years. "Okay, Mama."

"And put on a pair of pants, LJ. You look like a hobo."

He smiled. It was comforting when she had enough energy to boss him around.

Andra was waiting right outside the door, her hair freshly smoothed. His smile broadened. She raised her eyebrows and mouthed, *"Makeup?"*

He rolled his eyes and held up a finger for her to wait as he disappeared into the bathroom. Considering how he'd left things between them, he couldn't believe she was in his home, about to meet his mama. He didn't know whether he was the luckiest man in the world or the most cursed, because if he couldn't fix things with her, he was going to have to let her go all over again.

There was a choking sound from inside the bedroom, then a light thump. Oh God.

LJ dropped the makeup bag and sprinted back to the bedroom, but Andra had beat him there. She was on her knees next to the bed, holding the trash can as his mother threw up into it. "Mama!"

More vomit splashed into the can, and he grimaced. Gasping, Mama caught her weight on the edge of the bed. Andra set down the trash can and grabbed a clean washcloth from the side table, offering it to her. Mama clutched it in one shaking hand and wiped her mouth. "Excuse me. This flu is terrible. Can't seem to shake it, and in the middle of summer, too."

"I'm so sorry," Andra murmured. "I didn't mean to barge in. I just heard . . . I can go."

Something inside him changed shape, watching the two women in his life in the same room, Andra awkward but so compassionate at the same time. Without even an introduction, she'd rushed in to help, like his family was hers.

His mother looked up, her brown eyes shiny with tears as they pored over every inch of Andra's face. She pulled Andra into a tight hug. "Aren't you the sweetest thing? Of course you are. Of course you would be." And then she started to cry. "Oh, thank God."

"Mama?" His voice cracked.

Andra stroked his mother's thin back, and he remembered her own mother had died when she was a child. She hadn't had a properly maternal hug in over a decade. LJ's hands hung at his sides, his heart thumping hugely. This was a gift he would never have asked for, one so big and expensive that all he could do was turn it over and over, waiting for someone to laugh and take it away from him.

"You go on now, LJ," Mama said, and sniffed. "She's finally here. Give us girls a chance to talk."

Twenty-five

◇◇◇◇

"There you are." Andra closed the front door behind her, stepping out into the muggy night. "You want me to turn a light on?"

"Nah. You can see the stars better this way." LJ smiled up at her from his seat on the concrete steps, patting the space next to him. She took a spot two steps down from him, tipping her head against his knees as she looked up at the sky.

There were more stars in Montana, but the ones in the South seemed more content. Her eyes traced over every pinprick of light, something in the air on the porch seeming to suspend the clock so she could sit there forever with no time passing. She exhaled.

There were so many things unsaid between them, but if time didn't exist, neither did panic attacks. Or the two thousand miles stretching between her home and his. Or everything his friends had said about her this morning.

LJ brushed her hair back, tickling her earlobe. "These still working okay after the afternoon you had? Want me to drive you in to see the doc?"

She laughed. "I can see where you inherited your reserved nature. Rose is a talker, isn't she? I think she pointed out every single nail you put into this house."

"Did she throw up again?"

"One more time. But she kept some crackers down. She's sleeping now."

"Thanks for being so patient with her. I, ah—" He scratched the back of his head. "It means a lot."

"Are you kidding? She told me stories about you all day. I loved it."

He looked down, a smile playing around his mouth. "Shit. You were probably heading to your truck to make a getaway, huh?"

"Actually, I probably should get it. I parked it a few blocks away."

"It's parked around the side of the house. I took your keys off the table and got it earlier. I don't want you walking around alone at night."

"Uh, okay." She sat up and frowned at him. "I walk around at night all the time."

He glanced away. "Yeah, but it's different in the city. Give it a couple of days, until people know your face and word gets around that you're staying with me. Then you'll be fine to go anywhere you want, at least in this neighborhood."

She glanced out at the dark street, scooting a little closer to his legs. It seemed much less peaceful than it had a minute ago.

"So did Mama tell you all about how I won the second-grade spelling bee with the word 'promiscuous'? That's her favorite story."

"She did, actually. Among other things." Andra nudged his legs. "You never told me you got shot."

"That makes it sound worse than it was. It felt more like a bad rope burn, actually. Want to see?" He pulled up his basketball shorts, revealing a line of scar across the outside of his thigh as thick as her thumb. She must have been terribly distracted to have missed that on the one day they'd been naked together in her room.

She trailed her fingers along it, wincing. "She said you were rescuing trapped people out of flooded houses when it happened, but I didn't understand how guns got involved."

"When we chopped into the attic, the guy thought we were looters and started shooting." LJ shrugged. "Things were crazy, and it was an accident. He was pulling people out right alongside me the next day." LJ pointed to the east. "He lives about five streets that way."

Andra closed her eyes and laid her forehead on his knee, her hand cupped over the scar. She couldn't even fathom forgiving someone for shooting her. Much less trusting them to help her chop through roofs while she was standing on a bandaged leg. And yet, because it was LJ, it made perfect sense.

She wanted to wrap her arms around him and hold him so tight all the good in him would start to seep into her, too. But touch alone couldn't close all the gaps between their two lives.

"You know, I got a scar up a little higher, if you want to rub that one, too," LJ drawled.

A smile tugged at her lips and she sat up. "You're terrible, you know that?"

"I know it." He grinned, leaning back with his elbows propped on the porch edge. "Mama's been trying my whole life to return me to the stork, but he wouldn't take me back without a receipt."

"That's not what she told me. She said you were lost for two months, and she just about went crazy trying to find you." Andra shook her head. "How is that even possible?"

LJ hitched a slow roll of his shoulder. "No way to charge a phone, even if you didn't lose it in the flood. If somebody wasn't right in front of your face, there was no way of knowing if they were alive or dead. It took them three days to rescue us off the roof, because there were so many other people to get to first, and not enough Coast Guard helicopters."

Her eyes widened as she tried to imagine the hopelessness of being stuck for that long, not knowing what would happen.

"Once they got us, I wanted to help. It was supposed to be too dangerous to go back out there, but hell, I had just *been* out there, and I knew folks were stuck with no medicine, no water. Most people were in pretty bad shape, but I had a strong back, even at fifteen. I got Mama to the Superdome, where there were supposed to be doctors and things, and I snuck off with some guys who had a fishing boat. A few days later, we'd hauled out everybody we could find, and we were trolling around looking for more. The cops caught us. They thought we were looking for something to steal and made us evacuate with everybody else."

He tipped his head back, looking up at the stars.

"When I got back to the Superdome, Mama was gone. They weren't keeping track of who died or who left—they were just sticking people on any plane that would fly. I was big, and I didn't have any ID on me, but somebody finally figured out I was underage. They shipped me straight off to foster care.

"Mama's phone got lost in the flood, and when her number started working again, it went to somebody else. I knew the number to the ranch my uncle managed, but their phone lines were down for weeks, and turned out they'd evacuated with the stock anyway. Without an address to write each other . . . it's a big world, turns out." His knee started to bounce a little, but he didn't look away from the sky.

Goose bumps raked across her skin. "It's so scary that you can just lose somebody."

He smiled and stroked her arm with the back of one finger. "It was a good thing. Nothing else would have made Mama learn about the internet."

She laughed. "You give a whole new meaning to 'glass half-full,' LJ Delisle."

"That was the problem—the Delisle. Mama called social services in every state, but somebody spelled my last name wrong in the database, and of course she didn't have a single picture of me left after the flood. The woman called the president of the United States." He grinned. "He didn't answer, I guess, but a White House intern talked her through setting up a MySpace profile, and she found me in five minutes. She was all the way up in New Jersey, and I had landed in Texas. When she flew down to get me, that was the only time in my life I saw her cry." He glanced over, bumping her side with his knee. "Until today."

Andra took a deep breath, so many things swirling through her chest that she wasn't sure how to talk to him about them all. "She says she's dying, LJ."

She bit her lip as she remembered what Rose had told her as soon as they were alone.

My son is a good man, but he feels everything too deep, and he can't stand it if he can't fix every last problem he sees. You're the only girl he ever talked about who wanted to take care of him, not the other way around. And I'm so glad God set you down here before He took me.

LJ shrugged twitchily, leaning forward to rest his forearms on his knees. "The doctor says it might feel like she's dying, but as long as she takes her meds and doesn't overwork herself, she can live almost as long as anybody else. It depends on what complications come out of the lupus."

Andra let out a quiet breath. All day, she'd barely been able to look at Rose without thinking of how much it had hurt to lose her mom. She didn't want that for LJ. "She's amazing, you know? You're lucky to have her."

The corner of his mouth tipped up. "Don't I know it."

She watched him as she turned over what his mother had said. She didn't want him to be attracted to her only because he wanted to fix her. She kept thinking of his words in her kitchen.

I would have done that much even for somebody I didn't like.

Of course he would have tried to help her with her cooking and her attacks. He would have been her friend, because he was everyone's friend. But she wanted to believe there was more between them than that.

Into the silence, she said, "Why didn't you call?"

His hands clenched together, hanging between his knees. "I didn't know how to be the man you needed. Didn't know what to say."

A thousand rebuttals ran through her mind, but the honesty in his deep voice held her paralyzed. She understood the helplessness of that feeling too well to argue the point.

When LJ spoke again, his words were rough with strain. "I know it ain't right, but I can't stand the idea of letting you go so you can look for somebody better."

"I don't know what I need," she said, her voice breaking. "But if it's not you, I don't want it."

Being with him should have fixed her panic attacks. She was more comfortable with him than with any other person on earth. She *trusted* him, all the way down into her bones. But they could never have a normal relationship with her brain exploding into fear at unpredictable moments and ruining everything. She couldn't expect him to stay with her when her reactions made him feel like a criminal.

It was an impossible contradiction, but the panic attacks weren't even the only problem anymore. She'd seen for herself how her presence divided his group of friends and set them against each other. Having her in his life made everything harder, and it was the last thing she would have wanted for him.

His hands gripped each other until she heard one of the knuckles pop. "What are we going to do?" he whispered.

And all she could do was shake her head.

Twenty-six

◇◇◇◇

Andra slipped a little farther down in the passenger seat, the sun baking through the back window of LJ's pickup as she waited for him. She trailed her finger along a tear in the upholstery, wondering when it had happened. She had so many years of stories to catch up on, and the more she wrangled out of Rose and Ty, the hungrier she got for the few things LJ would share with her. She was afraid the reason he always put her off with a joke was because his past was so starkly different from hers. His present, too.

For a week he'd been sleeping on the kitchen floor while she slept in his bed. She wanted to try to find the same pleasure with him that she'd finally managed to unlock on her own, but he didn't seem ready to risk it. They'd never talked about what had happened before he left, when they'd tried to have sex. They hadn't had time to talk about much of anything, actually.

LJ was gone most of every day, stringing together odd jobs and day laborer positions to make ends meet since Rose couldn't work. Andra had assured him over and over again that she didn't mind taking care of his mom when he was out. She'd hoped it would give her time to try to fit in with his family and friends, but at least so far, that wasn't really happening. Ty and Tash seemed to like her, but Reggie and his other friends weren't warming up. Andra was worried a lot of LJ's neighbors weren't comfortable coming over now that she was staying there. Even when they'd made gumbo for the whole neighborhood on Saturday, the pot was still half-full at the end of the day. LJ got all fidgety about how to fit the big pot into the fridge, as if gumbo left-overs weren't something he'd ever had to deal with before.

Sometimes she felt like a foreigner, and never more than when his friends came over to jam with him. All she could do was sit and lis-ten, when everyone else knew every word to every song.

Her hands smoothed down her little black skirt. When he offered to take her out tonight, the flood of relief nearly left her dizzy. She knew she was awkward. Too quiet beside everyone else's laughter and easy chatter. Tonight was her chance to try to show him she could fit in down here, in his world that was so different from her ranch. She had to, because she refused to make his life any more difficult than she already had.

The driver's-side door opened, he slung his saxophone case in toward her lap, and then he jumped back with an inarticulate sound, dropping the case on his gear shifter.

She caught it before it slid down to the floor, and smiled. "Hi."

He scrubbed a hand over his hair, blinking. "What are you doing hiding in my truck? I almost hit you in the face with my saxophone!"

"Closer to the stomach, actually." She put the case down between her feet. "I know you said to meet you in town in four hours, but I wanted to come along." She smiled brightly, determined to show she could be as much fun as his friends. "Besides, Mona came early to hang out with Rose, so I wanted to give them some time alone." Rose's friend rarely spoke to her directly, but there was always a tension in the room when she was over.

"How'd you know when I was leaving, anyway? You could have cooked yourself like a loaf of bread in here."

"I rolled the windows down. Also, you check in at Ty's every time you leave to see if he's got a lead on any short-term work. You always say it'll take five minutes, and it usually takes twenty or thirty."

He chuckled and got in. "Plead the fifth on that one."

She tugged at the hem of her skirt. "So where are we going?"

He was dressed for the heat, but nicer than usual, in black shorts and a short-sleeved white button-down that set off his gorgeously rich skin tone. He had a newsboy cap on instead of his usual Stetson, and it made his face a whole different kind of handsome. She liked both.

He started the truck and flipped the AC vents to face her. "Well, I have to rustle up some money so I can actually take you out, but you can probably explore around the French Quarter while I'm doing that."

She pulled her seat belt across her lap. "Doesn't it kind of ruin the point if you blow a bunch of money on a date, then I never get to see you because you have to earn it again? Why don't you let me pay tonight? I have a pretty decent job, you know."

His palm tapped the steering wheel. "Look, I know you can pay your way." His Adam's apple bobbed as he turned toward her. "Let me show you I can pay mine."

She sat back in her seat, thinking about the way he was always juggling dishes at mealtime, making sure she got the plate that didn't have a chip out of it. It wasn't important to her, but it was to him. "Okay. Yeah, of course."

He jerked a nod and started to back out.

"So . . . when you say 'rustle,' do you mean you're going to rob a train, or are you going to get in line again or something?"

He tapped the brakes and stared at her. Blinked. "Oh, do you mean a second line?"

She nodded. "Right. Second line. Isn't that what you said you were doing a couple of days ago?"

He threw his head back and laughed, the sound deep and sexy enough to distract her from the fact that he was laughing at her. "Girl, a second line isn't about actually standing *in line*."

"Okay." She gave his knee a little push, embarrassed but also pleased she'd gotten him to tease her again, a change from his strained thank-yous for her help when he left to find work each morning. "So stop being smug and tell me what it is."

"It's sort of like a marching band, but wilder. Less uniforms, more dancing. It started out as a funeral thing." He put the truck in gear and pulled out into the wide, empty street. "You'd hire some musicians to lead the walk to the cemetery. After that, it would move to a bar, and people would tell stories and laugh and get drunk. So on the way between the cemetery and the bar, you needed the music to cheer people back up again, remind them they were alive. People had so much fun we started doing second lines for everything. We protest with music; we celebrate with it; we grieve with it. It's our language."

He shifted in his seat and smiled.

"Music runs in the family. First bunch of Delisles came from Saint-Domingue to Louisiana, running from all the violence of the revolution that changed the name of the island to Haiti. Best job for a free man of color back then was a musician for parties and such."

"Of course it's in your blood." Andra smiled. "And a second line sounds exactly like the kind of thing you'd do. Go dancing and playing music through the streets, making folks forget they were supposed to be sad."

"Oh! You said 'folks.'" He grinned and squeezed her knee. "You're going to sound like a regular southern belle by the time you go on home."

She turned to look out the window, hoping he wouldn't pursue the topic. They hadn't talked about when she should go back, and she didn't want to, because she didn't like any of the answers.

She'd barely been a block from LJ's house in the week she'd been here. Except for walking down to the corner store now and then, where the music was always loud and unfamiliar and the conversations sputtered out when she walked in the door. She thought he might have stalled about taking her out because he thought New Orleans was too different from the mountains and open skies of Montana for her to enjoy it.

"I like it here, you know," she ventured. He glanced over at her and away, so quick she knew she'd been right that it was something he needed to hear. "How it's filled to bursting with color and history and sound. How every third person on the street has an instrument case and how everything I eat is delicious. The whole city smells like you."

He laughed. "You saying I smell like mule shit and river water?"

"No." She poked him in the side. "Shut up. It's more like you always smell like you've been cooking something amazing, and it's always different. Spicy crawfish, cracked wheat bread, grilled corn on the cob." She shrugged and looked out the window. "It's nice."

A woman watering her plants nodded as they drove past. Andra blinked and turned her head for a second look, because she thought the woman had been white. It was too late to make sure she'd seen right, though, because LJ was already turning the corner.

This was a new street she hadn't seen before, but there were just as many weed-choked vacant lots as on his street. One held only a sun-faded old sign with a church logo that said, "With God's grace, we will rebuild." A little farther down, there was a foundation with the floor still intact. Linoleum gave way to a square of bathroom tile with no walls to guard it from the weather.

Andra's fingers started to hurt, and she loosened them where they were clenched too tightly in her lap. LJ took a right, and a second later they rumbled over a bridge and crossed back into the main city. The houses grew bigger and closer together, porches shrinking to painted concrete stoops, with colorful doors and shutters fronted by lines of tightly parked cars.

"Can I ask you a horrible question?" she said quietly.

He glanced over, then returned his attention to traffic. "You can ask me anything you want to, Andie-girl. You know that."

She hadn't meant to bring it up, but it had been nagging at her mind every time she went outside, and she couldn't keep it in anymore. She took a breath. "Did you ever think it might be easier to get past everything that happened during Katrina if you moved? Even just to a different part of town?"

He tapped his palm on the steering wheel, but otherwise there was no indication he'd heard her. His face looked the way it had

when she'd brought him his old, spray-painted half door: as if he didn't quite know if he was happy or sad.

The Datsun engine went quiet, then loud again as he shifted gears, and his dark eyes flicked to the side mirror.

"Stubborn part of me says no." He leaned back into the seat until it creaked, draping his wrist over the steering wheel. "That place is my family. My big family, you know? They all raised me up. And the Lower Ninth needs people who remember what it was, or it really will be lost. The city wanted to give up and turn the whole thing into a park, you know."

He frowned at the knot of traffic at the next light and whipped a quick turn down a side street, bombing down a couple of blocks until he found a one-way with the right direction of arrow. The tires stuttered and bumped over rough pavement, and Andra grabbed the door handle to brace herself when he wove around one of the bigger potholes.

"I never wanted to give up on New Orleans. But then I left, didn't I?" His sensual lips pulled tight into a grimace of a smile. "It's been a long time, but sometimes it still hurts looking down the street. The Graviers' house is gone. Aimee's house is falling down. There are people from Alabama living in LaToya's place. Most folks never came back. They just washed on down the river to someplace where the water didn't run so high."

He stopped in the middle of the block to let a kid on a tricycle pedal across the street.

"I almost don't want to say this, you know?" He let out a breath of a laugh, rubbing at his lower lip. "But it was easier in Montana." He put the truck back in gear and hit the gas. "*I* was easier. I didn't spend so much time filling out paperwork: trying to get insurance to pay, trying to get Road Home money to come through, doing everybody's Make It Right applications, wrestling building permits."

She frowned. "What do you mean? Your house has been done for years, hasn't it?"

His shoulders hunched, and he glanced out the side window.

"Everybody knows I went away to college. Some of the older folks around here can't read too good, and the schools in the Lower Ninth didn't reopen for two years after Katrina, so the rest of us were a little behind, too. Those insurance companies want to keep their money and say no, your papers weren't right. They don't help you out none."

He swapped hands on the steering wheel, lifting two fingers to wave at a guy crossing the street with a cello-sized music case in a trailer behind his bike. The biker grinned back, and she couldn't tell if they knew each other or were just being friendly.

LJ looked over at her. "You asking about moving away from memories for me or you?"

She let out a breath and watched as they passed by a watermelon-pink house. "I don't know. I think I might be easier away from home, too. Like everybody knowing what happened to me locked me into being that girl."

"Did it, though? When I moved there, you didn't talk to anybody. You just rode. Now I hear you laughing from the barn, and I don't know if you're messing with one of the ranch hands or Stacia or Jason. They look at you different, too, at Sunday dinner. Brighter. I think they're starting to see you the way I see you."

She peeked over at him. "Oh yeah? And how's that?"

His eyes flickered away from the road and stroked down over her bare legs. "Well, maybe not *all* the ways I see you." He smiled, and a wave of tingles sparkled through her.

The street they were on ended, and LJ dodged through several turns at odd angles before they found another continuous street. The houses were getting taller now, porches stacked two stories high and bordered with cast-iron frames dripping with flowers, like arbors frozen in black-painted metal.

"Katrina wasn't the only storm, you know. Sure not the only time we've almost lost the city. Look at this." He spun the wheel and rocketed down a block, dodging the increasing flocks of pedestrians, then turned again and slowed down, leaning into the wheel so he could point up through the top of the windshield. "See that building?

It used to be all tile on the roof, because some governor from Spain required it after everything burned down a couple times in the 1700s. Then in the next hurricane, those tiles all went flying off, breaking people's windows and heads and things."

Andra cringed. "Oh God, I didn't even think of that. They're as bad as bullets, aren't they?"

"Bigger and heavier than bullets." He pointed to the left side. "See the watermarks on that brick? That place is two hundred years old, and I promise you those marks are older than Katrina. We've had floods and fires, yellow fever and locusts. Might as well be a paragraph out of the Bible." He shook his head. "But we're still here. Nobody with the spirit of this place in them ever quits. We just turn a funeral into a second line, dancing away from the graveyard. All the time knowing it ain't our last trip."

She shook her head, trying to imagine rebuilding a house you expected to flood, just because it was near the place and the people you loved the most. And suddenly it seemed like the most human thing she had ever heard.

LJ whipped the truck into a tiny parking spot along the curb. Once they were stopped, he reached out and touched her hand with the backs of his knuckles, sweeping his thumb over her wrist.

"It's why I get mad at these reporters for coming around, taking pictures of what's still broken, when they weren't here for all the fixing. You got to stick around with the ugly if you want it to make you strong."

Andra's shoulders tensed. "I don't know about that. I tried. I stayed in Bozeman after I was attacked, all the way until the trial was finished, and it didn't help a thing." Maybe he could draw strength from living here amid the reminders of the past, but it didn't seem to work that way for her. "It's been *five* stupid years now, and I'm still so messed up, you're sleeping on the floor in the kitchen because you're afraid you'll jar me into a panic attack just by rolling over the wrong way."

"More like I'm afraid Mama would find a shotgun if she caught us in bed together before I put a ring on your finger."

"Don't try and put it on her, LJ. She asked me yesterday if you were in the doghouse for something and that's why I won't 'let' you share the bedroom. You don't even have a couch to sleep on, for crying out loud."

"We've never had a couch. Who would want to stay inside when you've got a perfectly good porch to sit on?"

The weak attempt at humor sagged in the air between them. Andra stared out the side window, the beautiful historic street starting to blur with tears. "It's bullshit," she muttered. "All those 'time heals' platitudes. History fades, but it doesn't disappear, and I don't know if it ever stops hurting." She turned and narrowed her eyes at him. "You didn't stay, either, LJ. Not in the end."

"No, you're right—I didn't." He rubbed his hands down his thighs, glancing at the rusting cast-iron swirls of the balcony they were parked next to. "It's hard to love something so much and see it hurting when you can't fix it. After a while, it starts to eat you alive inside." He met her eyes. "Maybe that's why I left."

Her shoulders drooped, and she wondered if he was talking about leaving New Orleans or Montana.

She blew out a breath. "I'm sorry. I shouldn't have snapped at you. I'm sick of feeling like we're walking on eggshells around each other. I came here because I wanted to fix things with you, and I just . . . I don't know where to start."

He caught her hand. "Hey. We ain't broken. The way I feel about you—" He shook his head, dark eyes soft on her face. "There's nothing you need to fix about that."

Her skin tingled as if there were some kind of magic in the way he was looking at her. In having a beautiful man like him say those words to her and mean them.

"Maybe not about that," she whispered. "But what about everything else?" Like the pile of quilts in the corner of his mama's kitchen that he spread out to sleep on every night. Or the suitcase in his room where she kept her clothes, because she was going to have to zip it closed and go back home soon. The pot of gumbo, unfinished because some of his friends didn't feel comfortable coming over when she was there.

LJ glanced away and coughed, like his throat was tight. "Andra . . ." He dipped his head and kissed her hand. "Let me take you out, okay? Show you a good time in my city." He flashed her a smile so charming it hurt to look at him, because she knew how hard he was trying to be just that. "Forget those eggshells we been tiptoeing on and just be easy with each other again." The confidence in his smile cranked up another notch, but his thumb was sweeping a little too fast over the back of her hand, like it was stealing the last taste it was likely to get. "Can we do that?"

"Yes," she promised, and prayed she wasn't lying. "Of course we can."

Andra fell in love with the city all over again with every scrollwork balcony and mule-drawn carriage they passed, but LJ seemed determined to seduce her even further. For his first offering, he bought puffy French doughnuts he called beignets, dusted with a weightless cloud of powdered sugar. She enjoyed the way his tongue wrapped around the word almost as much as the pastries themselves. From there, he walked her past a sunny square full of artists' stalls to Royal Street. It was blocked off from cars to leave room for musicians to play and tourists to dance, drink, or stroll past the broad windows of bright shops.

They passed a gallery filled with paintings of haunting, skeletal silhouettes of trees, then one featuring photos of naked women, their skin painted with tigers or tree frogs. Drums beat from down the street, and when LJ took out his saxophone and began to play, it curled around the whole tableau like a perfectly fitted embrace.

She'd never tried playing music in the street before, and at first she wasn't sure what to do with herself. She felt out of place, sitting beside LJ's open saxophone case as tourists tossed small bills and sometimes change into it on their way past. But then a young girl wearing an out-of-season bunch of Mardi Gras beads stopped to dance, and an older couple paused as well, tapping their feet as they listened. A guy with some form of trumpet came and played alongside LJ for a while.

Between every song, LJ stopped to wave and tease other musicians he knew, joke with the tourists and tell them crazy stories, getting more outrageous every time he won a smile from her. He introduced Andra as his muse, his trophy wife, a mermaid he'd hauled out of the Mississippi and washed off with a garden hose. She told them he was secretly her bodyguard, a vampire, a famous musician whose name she was sworn not to tell.

When anyone started to dance, LJ's song changed. It swooped to fit the beat of their feet, the shake of their hips, and then it urged them faster, more upbeat, until they always ended up laughing and more out of breath than he was. He thanked everyone who came by, but never glanced at his saxophone case, even when the tens and twenties started to outnumber the ones and fives. Whenever the wind blew a bill away, she chased it down, but he never budged, seemingly happy to let the world give and take away at will.

When he finally stopped to take a break and a sip of water, the shadows slung long and low between the buildings and she was more relaxed than she'd been in days. She stretched her legs out in front of her, leaning her head against the bricks at her back, and smiled. "I always thought the saxophone was supposed to sound sad. The blues and all that."

"You want sad?" He arched his eyebrows at her, then swept his arm out at their current audience: three teenagers and a pair of tattooed girls with their hands locked so closely together that it looked like they were made as a set. "Let the record show the lady asked for sad."

The girl with the scorpion tattoo on her neck laughed. "Don't do it, LJ! Have mercy!"

Andra shook her head. She hadn't even realized he knew these girls, too, but of course he did. Every time they left the house, people would stop to hug him and ask, "How's your mama and them?" Since he was an only child, she wasn't sure what "them" they were asking about, but they all asked it just the same. He was so popular, she wouldn't have been surprised if the statue in the square was of him, too.

She could picture how it would look: him curled forward into his saxophone so every muscle stood out, his eyes closed as he poured his heart into the music. Watching him play made her miss her horses so bad it ached all the way into her teeth. With reins in her hands and a thousand-pound animal between her knees, she was poised and confident, focused and utterly free. She knew what needed to be done, and she knew *she* was the best person to do it.

And just like with her and a horse, LJ's gift needed its match, too: the music and an audience. It wasn't for the attention, though he seemed to thrive on it. It was the way he saw the tiniest hints of emotion on their faces and translated them into his songs until each listener's expression blossomed into something different. It was the near-supernatural push and pull between him and dozens of strangers.

She couldn't imagine how he'd survived through the months in Montana, only practicing alone in his apartment with no band, no spectators. It twisted her stomach to think of it. She could no longer imagine her life without LJ in it, but the longer she was here, the more she realized how much of him had been missing when they lived in Montana.

She wanted him to have everything he loved. Horses and music and his family and friends. The boisterous, aged streets of New Orleans and the open range. She wanted to be one of those essential pieces of his life. But that was a fantasy, wasn't it? A world made out of contrasting puzzle pieces that didn't fit together.

He loved her; she knew that. But he was *LJ*. He loved so many things, and he couldn't have them all. In the end, what would prove to be the most essential?

She hugged herself tightly, her thoughts pressing in until she felt all but invisible in the crowded street.

LJ nudged her, waiting until she looked up. He grinned at her, so comfortable in his own skin. Everything she wasn't. "This next song goes out to my lady."

That tugged a smile to her lips, and their eyes met for a long moment, as if he were hungry for the reassurance of her approval and he didn't want to waste an instant of it. And then he dipped his head and began to play.

It started easily enough. Smooth, like everything he did. As the notes grew, it wasn't the kind of sadness that felt like weight. It was the kind that wound between your cells and made you want to beg for more. And when the song crested, tears came to her eyes as she began to grasp that the beauty of the sound held loss inside of it. It was love, ending. As all things did. All things would.

The feeling expanded, threatening to burst all the boundaries of her. She had to look away from LJ's face, from his sculpted cheekbones and downswept lashes, but her gaze only collided with that of a gallery owner across the street. The woman leaned against the doorway of her shop, tears sparkling in her eyes just like Andra's. She couldn't help but wonder who the woman had lost. Who she was worried about losing.

The song finished, the last note starting robust and boisterous and teasing out into a wisp of sound her ears couldn't quite hold on to. She sniffed quickly, her throat bound up dry and tight.

LJ spread his arms, letting his saxophone dangle from its harness. "All right, now, who needs a hug?" His face cracked into its huge grin. Scorpion-Tattoo Girl laughed, swiping at her eyes as she pretended to scratch her nose.

Andra pushed off the ground and wrapped her arms around him, holding on a little harder than she probably should. His arm was warm against her back after the wall she'd been resting against, and his saxophone bumped against her shoulder. "I don't think I've ever heard that song before, anywhere. What's it called?"

"'Montana,'" he said.

There were so many things that could mean, and she wasn't sure she could face any of them. Especially not with the music tugging her emotions so close to the surface, like a single layer of skin was all that caged them inside. He squeezed her a little tighter into his chest and bent to her ear. "Don't be sad, Andie-girl. Not tonight. There's hours yet before we got to go back, and I'm in the mood to take my girl dancing."

"It's been years." She bit the inside of her lip. "I'm not sure I even remember how."

"I'll remember for both of us," he said, his face lighting up so she forgot the entire street of tourists around them. "Trust me."

And she did.

Twenty-seven

◇◇◇◇

Andra scooped a load of freshly washed sheets into the dryer, then braced her hands against the machine and stretched with a satisfied wince, her legs still sore from dancing. It had been an unforgettable night, hours disappearing in a whirl of colored lights and LJ's smile, the sound of his voice into a microphone when the band at the club had invited him up on stage to sing one with them. But he'd still slept in the kitchen, and when she'd woken this morning, he was already off on a job. Moving furniture, according to the note tucked under the pot of freshly brewed coffee.

She searched the unfamiliar knobs on his dryer for the correct setting. He was so different here. She couldn't deny she was developing a whole new crush on this New Orleans version of LJ, who was as gentle with his elderly neighbors as he'd been with her young horses. Who was every bit as comfortable on a stage as he was in her kitchen, and who could pour his whole complicated soul out through the notes of a song.

In the next room, the front door creaked as it opened, and Andra's heart leaped into her throat. That door had been locked.

LJ had warned her about crime in the neighborhood, but he'd made it sound like everyone knew him and would leave his house alone. She couldn't cower in here, not with his mother lying in the other room, utterly helpless against an intruder.

She dropped the sheets and glanced around the bathroom for a weapon. The plunger. A bottle of shampoo. Nothing in here was going to do her a bit of good.

Slow footsteps crossed the kitchen, and a cupboard opened. Okay, no kind of burglar robbed the kitchen cabinets, and they hadn't forced the door, so they must have had a key. She peeked out into the other room, releasing a breath when she recognized Reggie's mother, Mona.

Mona took a plastic Saints cup out of the cupboard—one of the ones LJ was always nudging to the back. She glanced over at Andra, then continued on to the refrigerator. Her yellow sundress all but glowed against her luminous brown skin.

"Oh, hi. Rose is asleep. We didn't know you were coming over," Andra offered.

"You want some sweet tea?"

Andra shifted her weight, uncomfortable at being treated like a visitor in the house she'd been cooking, cleaning, and living in for days now. "Sure. That would be nice." She needed to do her best to be polite. Rose's best friend was so distant toward her that even offering tea was an improvement, even if it felt a little passive-aggressive.

Mona dropped ice into the Saints cup and topped it off with the tea pitcher LJ refilled every evening. She placed it on the farthest side of the table from Andra, who glanced at it, wondering where she was expected to sit. The floor creaked under Mona's feet as she went back for a pale-blue tumbler, then returned to the fridge to fill it.

"Rose usually wakes up a little more in the afternoons," Andra said.

"That's okay. I didn't come for her." Mona sat and adjusted the fan before she put Andra's sweet tea on the opposite side of the table. "Come here and sit on down." She nodded to the other chair and waited for Andra to settle in. She smiled. "Rose has a lot of nice things to say about you."

Andra's fingers twitched on her chilled cup. Maybe she hadn't been doing such a terrible job of fitting in after all. "Rose is great," she rushed to say. "I've been enjoying spending time with her." Saying it out loud made it sound false somehow. Her toes squirmed under the table, and she ducked her head.

"Are you having a nice visit?"

The fan blew strands of hair ticklingly across her nose, and she pushed them back. "Yes, of course. Well, I mean, it could be under better circumstances." She forced a tiny smile, trying to ignore the part of her that was waiting for Mona to turn cold again. "But however it happened, I know LJ was a little homesick, so it's nice for him to have a few days back here."

"Louisiana sure is a long way to drive for a man you haven't been dating more than a few months."

She set her drink back on the table and lifted her eyes to Mona's. Andra had been training horses long enough to know when someone was testing her. "It's not so far to drive for someone you care about. I wanted to meet his mom anyway. And see his home."

A smile played around Mona's mouth, deepening creases around her lips that showed she'd had many years of smiles before this one. "I didn't expect you to notice that. Rose said you were quick, though, and as sentimental as she can be, she's rarely wrong."

Andra's back stiffened. She didn't want to sit here and be insulted, but she also didn't want to make an enemy of Rose's friend. "To notice what?"

"That this will always be his home."

Her belly flinched at the words, but she only sat up taller.

Mona looked down and straightened the place mat, brushed away a few crumbs. "Rose and I have been friends for thirty-some years, did she tell you that? We were schoolgirls together, in the days when bussing was an idea everybody thought would pass."

Bussing? She almost asked before she realized Mona meant the desegregation of schools.

"The day she found out she was carrying LJ, she was in my

bathroom over on Deslonde." Mona tipped her head to indicate the direction.

Andra smiled stiffly, though she wasn't sure it was the proper response.

"Things were all mixed up for Rose back then, but we couldn't have known what a blessing he would turn out to be. He's helped my son out of a tight spot or two, I don't mind telling you. LJ's driven nails in half the roofs on this street, and after Katrina, he kept the weeds and critters out of the vacant lots around our houses. It took alligators and wild dogs moving in before the city sent people out to do the same for everybody else."

Andra's stomach was too knotted to handle the overly sweet tea, but she tried to keep a pleasant look on her face anyway. Somehow stories about LJ sounded accusing coming from this woman. "He's just the same on the ranch in Montana. Always the first to fix a broken fence or make sure we've ordered new feed before the old sacks run out, even though it's not his job. He even bought a heating pad for our foreman's stiff back and left it in his apartment so he wouldn't have to say thank you and get all embarrassed."

Mona didn't smile back. "I imagine that ranch of yours is pretty big, hmm? Lots of employees?"

Maybe she should talk it up so his neighbors could be proud of the job he'd gotten. Or downplay the success of the ranch so they didn't think she was some kind of spoiled rich girl who'd never done a day's work. "We have a few."

"Well, the Lower Ninth only has one LJ Delisle." Mona looked up, and if her eyes had been cruel, Andra could have argued with her. But instead they were a little tired, and Andra couldn't find a word to say. Mona reached across the table and touched her hand. "I know you like him. Everybody likes LJ. I know he's got a whole lot of cowboy notions clouding up his head, but you said it yourself. This is his home."

"You want me to tell him to stay here when I go back—is that it?" She pulled her hand back. "You may have known him since he was a child, but he's a grown man now. That's his decision."

"It is." Mona sipped her iced tea. "But you have a choice to make, too. Rose is over the moon that you're here, because she's afraid to die and leave her son alone in this world. She thinks you're a smart girl. Kind."

Andra gritted her teeth. "And you obviously think she's wrong."

"No," Mona said. "Rose is most generally right. But a girlfriend won't be enough once he loses his mama. He needs his home, his friends. And the Lower Ninth isn't just a bunch of houses, not the way some towns are. He's part of this place, of what it was before Katrina and whatever it's going to be from now on." Her brown eyes deepened, sympathy with a touch of sadness. "And I think you and I both know he won't have any trouble attracting a woman here."

The knot in her stomach slammed up into her throat. Mona might as well have ripped open Andra's clothes to expose her laundry-day bra. And yet she couldn't argue, because every word Mona had said cut with the too-sharp edge of perfect truth.

It hadn't been that long ago that she'd spent every night alone in her house. Alone because she was too broken to expect anyone to live in the darkness of her life with her. She wasn't that person now, and as her laughter had returned, so had her strength. She deserved more than an empty house, and these days she was strong enough to fight for it.

She leaned across the table, nailing Mona with a steady gaze. "I don't just 'like' LJ, and I'm not down here playing games. I'm in love with him."

Mona nodded, but she didn't look surprised, or any less resigned. "Take it from a mother. The hardest thing about loving somebody is doing what's best for them."

Twenty-eight

◇◇◇◇

The streetlights were starting to come on by the time LJ blasted into his mama's house. His shoulders twitched with the effort it took to close the door quietly behind him.

Andra sat at the piano, her head down though she wasn't playing. He passed her and threw a wad of cash on the table. Fourteen damned hours, and that wasn't near enough money for the shit he'd had to put up with. Permanent jobs paid better than this by-the-day crap, but he had a job back in Montana. He didn't need one here. Unfortunately, the little money he'd saved for a bed frame in Montana had gone into his gas tank, and his last paycheck had gone toward getting Mama's bills caught up. The food in the fridge was going even faster with Andra here, and the power bill was coming due next week. Even if he caved and applied for something permanent, they couldn't last the two weeks for his first paycheck to come through without having to lean on the neighbors. He'd go hungry before he'd go to his friends with his hand held out.

His stomach grumbled, but he didn't want to stay inside long enough to fix a plate. Instead, he yanked a big plastic cup out of the dish drainer and filled it with water until the tap overflowed onto his fingers.

"Mama okay?" he asked. *Please let her be asleep.* If she saw him in this mood, they'd get into it, and she didn't have the energy right now. He chugged the water, taking swallows so big they hurt going down. Andra was his guest. She shouldn't have to be stuck here waiting on his mother. But without her, he couldn't leave Mama alone long enough to pay the bills for both of them.

"She's been sleeping, mostly. I had to wake her up to take her pills and get her to the bathroom, but she didn't throw up today. I think she might be getting over that flu." There was a hesitation. "Are you okay?"

"Yup. Going outside to work out. See you in a few." He filled the cup again and strode across the room. His gaze seared the floor, the walls, the fucking front door that always stuck because he'd hung it crooked. Anything but Andra.

The air outside smothered him after the brief respite inside with the air-conditioning. He shot past his truck parked in the grass at the side of the house, then Andra's big Dodge Ram. Anywhere else in the country, they'd have a driveway, maybe even a garage. But here, he couldn't even afford a load of gravel to park on. He slugged back half the cup's worth of water, and it did nothing to soothe the burn in his gut.

The streetlights cast only the barest glow into the backyard, and he spun the combination lock on the metal shed so hard he had to do it twice before he hit the numbers right. Heat slapped him in the face when the door rattled open. He reached down blind and swapped his cup of water for the roll of extension cord inside the front door.

How had he ended up back here? This was everything he'd been running from when he'd left for college, and again when he'd swapped his uncle's ranch for a fresh chance in Montana. He didn't want to be one more guy trading a strong back for barely enough money to keep the lights on. Pissed off at a world that didn't think he had any more in him than that. And angrier every day because he couldn't get far enough ahead to prove them wrong.

He could have, once. He had a business degree, and he could have gotten a cubicle with that and worked up to an office. It'd pay better than drywall, but it would itch just as much on his skin when what he wanted was open air and the smell of hay. But even in Montana, Bill had believed the worst and hadn't been interested in giving him a chance to prove differently.

If nothing was ever going to change, why did he keep trying so hard? He should just become the criminal they all seemed to think he was. At least then he'd have some fucking money in his pocket.

"LJ?"

He stopped, squeezing the extension cord in his hands. If he stretched it out to the plug at the back of the house, Andra would see the utility light that was all the electricity he could afford for this shed. She'd see the foam spilling out of the weight bench he'd taken from underneath a "Free" sign on a Marigny sidewalk. Most of all, she'd see the rage roiling under every muscle in his body, and if she looked at him with fear in her eyes right now, he'd fall apart.

"Did I do something wrong?" She sounded curious, confused, but not nervous. It was the only thing that allowed him to keep the lid on his temper.

"No. Long day."

"Did something happen? Do you want to talk about it?"

He glared down at the grass at his feet. Even in the dark, he could tell he needed to mow it again. One more goddamn thing he didn't have time for. "Just need to blow off some steam. Give me half an hour, okay?"

"LJ, why don't you ever let me use the Saints cup?"

"What?" He glanced back at the plastic cup he'd left by the shed. She wanted to argue about dishes? Screw it—she'd have to put up with the light and his crappy shed. If he didn't throw his energy against some iron, it was going to explode out somehow, probably in words he'd regret later. He threw down a loop of cord, stomping toward the house as he fed it out. "Use whatever cup you want. I don't care."

"Don't you? Because you always push it to the back of the cupboard when you're getting a glass out for me." She hesitated. "When we were in Montana, even when you were mad, you could talk to me about it. What changed?" Her voice wavered on the last word.

He threw a look her way, but the yard was too dark to make out more than her shape. Fumbling, he plugged in the light.

She blinked against the sudden glare, putting a hand up to shield her eyes.

He should figure out why she was suddenly worried about cups, but he couldn't deal with that right now. "I just need to work out— that's all. Thank you for everything you did for Mama today." He moved a cardboard box closer to the rest of the stack at the left of the shed and started piling weight plates onto his bench press bar.

The thin metal of the shed creaked as Andra leaned against it.

Why the hell wouldn't she leave him be? He had to stop to throw rounds on the other side so the bar wouldn't tip off its stand. The forty-five-pound weights felt like paper plates, as if he could crumple them in his hands. Yeah, right now he was definitely not the kind of guy Andra needed to teach her how to trust again.

As he finished loading the bar, the raw handcuff marks around his wrists glared at him. Would she recognize them? She had little pink marks around her wrists, too. Blood roared through his head as the marks on his wrists overlaid his memory of hers. And they matched.

He hit the bar with the flat of both palms, sending it jumping out of the stand and crashing to the floor, metal plates bouncing off.

"LJ!"

He grabbed the weight bench and squeezed until it creaked, telling himself if he punched the shed wall, it'd fold and he'd need a new shed. "Please go inside," he whispered.

He knew that asshole had tied her up. She'd told him that. Funny how that did nothing to quench the fire in his brain at the fresh thought of her yanking against handcuffs until she started to bleed.

Fuck, they made you so powerless. He'd pulled so hard today, and the handcuffs had barely scuffed the skin. His marks wouldn't even scar.

Her hands spread over his back, gentle and so small. "LJ, what happened to you?" she whispered. And then she was hugging him, her cheek over his spine; his wet, filthy shirt against her skin.

He pulled away, pacing out of the shed. "I'll be back." If she wouldn't go, he would.

She must have sprinted to catch up with him, because in an instant she was in front of him, her eyes flashing. "You don't have to hide from me every time you're angry. You don't scare me, LJ Delisle."

As he stared down at her, something shifted in him. She was telling the truth.

He hated the way those cops had eyed him today, one hand on their Tasers and the other creeping toward their guns. But that wasn't the way Andra was looking at him now.

"Why not?" he asked, his voice scraping raw out of his throat.

She shook her head. "You're the last person alive who would hurt me. The only thing I'm scared of is what you'd do if somebody else did."

She took his hand, and he folded his fingers gently around hers, letting her lead him back toward the shed. She sat down on the weight bench and pulled him down next to her.

"Now tell me what happened to you today, because whatever news could piss you off this much actually does freak me out."

"Not news." He let go of her hand and bent forward to lean his elbows on his knees, rubbing his eyes. "It sure ain't anything new, Andie-girl."

"Okay."

He sighed. "Took a two-day job as extra bodies for an overbooked moving company. We filled up the moving van. Instead of making two trips, Ty put the last few things in my truck. Cops came driving by and saw a couple of black guys loading antique furniture out the back door of a Garden District mansion into a Datsun. They decided we were stealing it. We weren't wearing uniforms, the moving company's van had already gone ahead, and—"

He shoved to his feet, picked up the bench press bar, and resettled it in the stand with a grunt of effort. She moved off the bench to make space for him.

"It's always like this. I'm doing my job, trying to take care of my family, and they think they know who I am just by looking at me. But I don't want to get shot, so I've got to be all goddamn meek and polite, even though they're the ones in the wrong."

"Shot just for loading a truck? Of course they wouldn't—"

He glared at her. "Don't start. You don't know how the cops are down here. They're dancing on their toes, waiting for us to forget to pay for a pack of gum so they can work us like a punching bag. Meanwhile, if we call them because we're getting robbed or something bad's going down, they take their sweet time coming across the canal because they figure we deserve what's coming to us."

"I'm sure they don't do it on purpose. It's a big city. They probably have a lot of calls to deal with."

"Oh, no? During the storm, cops saw a black guy walking around *near* a store and they shot him for a looter." His eyes flared. "That's not the kind of thing that happens to white people, Andra. When a stranger picked him up and took him to another police station to try to get help, the cops beat up the Good Samaritan and then burned the first guy's body to try and hide the evidence."

She sucked in a breath. "You can't be serious."

"Just a day in the life, sweet girl."

He lay down, rolling out his neck before he lifted the bar, dropped it toward his chest, and caught it at the last minute so he could feel the hard snap of muscle.

"I tried to tell the cops today that we were hired to move the furniture, and I barely got the words out of my mouth before I was facedown beside my own truck, with cuffs on. Ty told them we were paid to be there, but they didn't care. They were trying to stuff us into the back of the squad car when the owners came home and gave them holy hell for messing with us."

That was just lucky. Most people would have fired his ass for stirring up trouble. These guys gave him a bonus and said if he came back tomorrow, they'd double his wage to make up for the incident. Of course, to do that, he'd have to beg Andra's help with his mother again.

He racked up five reps over his previous record, trying to burn away the thought of that.

"That's . . ." She exhaled. He set down the bar, shaking out his arms. "What's wrong with the world, LJ? How can they—"

He didn't answer. Just picked up the bar and pushed all his strength up through the weight of it over and over again. All that effort changed nothing. But maybe it would make him tired enough that he could bear it for another night.

She sat down against the wall of the shed, her legs crossed carelessly in front of her as she stared at the floor. The bar started to tilt in his hands, and he snapped his gaze straight again.

"I thought I understood," she said. "Back in Montana, when you'd get upset because people were looking at you. After a couple of days here, I thought I *really* got it, you know? How self-conscious it makes you feel. But everything you're talking about, it doesn't make sense to me. Even when you told me you got pulled over taking the ranch truck to get an oil change, I thought, they must have had another reason. I mean, inside their heads, do they *know* they're treating you different because you're . . . black?"

The bar wobbled, and he had to set it back in the supports, even though he wasn't anywhere near ready to stop. He ground his teeth, trying to rein himself in enough to speak. "That little hesitation before you said 'black,' like it's a dirty word? That's what it is, Andra. That's the whole damned thing."

"What do you mean? I wasn't—I didn't mean to . . ." In his peripheral vision, he saw her curl a little tighter. "I just don't know if it's okay to say. If I say it, am I the same as they are, boiling everything down to a color?"

He rolled up to sitting. "It is a color, but it's a hell of a lot more than that. Black is what I *am*, Andra."

"But it's not everything you are!" She sat up straighter. "There are a million things about you that have nothing to do with that, and—"

"Of course there are. But they don't change what people see when they look at me." He grabbed her hand. She tensed at the speed of the movement but didn't pull away. "Look." He held their hands up in front of her face, her fingers starkly pale against his. "Just *look*, for once. They're never going to look the same. And when white people claim they're color-blind, they don't notice the difference, it's a lie. My history is not your history; my culture is not your culture. I don't want them to be. I'm proud of who I am and where I come from. All I want is to not be the last one rescued in a flood but the first one to wind up in handcuffs."

Her fingers stiffened in his. "I never—"

"I know *you* didn't." His voice softened. "But when you make excuses, like maybe the people at the store were staring at you, not me, or maybe the cops were just too busy to come our way . . . that's bullshit, Andra. People claim a million damned reasons for treating you and me differently except the real one. They won't say it's our color, so they can act like it's deeper than that."

He cradled her hand between both of his, because even in the steamy heat of the night, it was chilled, trembling.

"I'm sorry." Her voice caught.

"Me too." He let his head drop and rested his forehead on their hands. "Me too, Andie-girl. But I need you to listen instead of trying to explain things away. Okay? That's what I need." He pressed a kiss to her hand, breathing in her scent for a minute before he let her go. He picked up one of the weights, bracing his elbow against his knee for bicep curls.

"So am I imagining you pushing the Saints cup to the back of the cupboard?" Andra's hands fidgeted in her lap. "Because okay, yes, we're different, but when we were back home and the other employees didn't invite you to watch baseball games at Curt's, you hated it." Andra tilted her head. "You said it was stupid they thought you wouldn't like baseball because you're black. So what? Do you think I wouldn't like the Saints because I'm white?"

He swapped hands for the weight, moving through reps faster than he should as shame fisted in the base of his neck. "Not because of the Saints."

He didn't want to say this, and he knew there was no way to avoid it now. Still, he could tell how much courage it had taken her to confront him, so he matched it, pulling his eyes back up to hers.

"Because it's plastic." Her long lashes flickered with hurt. He hurried to add, "No man wants to bring a woman home to plastic go cups and a mattress with no frame." He dropped the weight and tried to smile, though his lips felt too tight. "If I had my way, I'd have welcomed you with chandeliers and vaulted ceilings and cut crystal."

"You should know me better than to think that's what I want."

He hung his head, rubbing a hand over the back of his sweaty neck. "I know it. Don't make it any easier."

"It's not just you, though. It can't be. Because when Mona came over today, she did the same thing. Took the Saints cup for herself and gave me a different one."

His eyes snapped up. "Mona came over? Did she say anything to you?" Reggie's mama was old fashioned. The kind who would see him dating a white girl as a betrayal of his family and the whole neighborhood.

Andra glanced away, pushing a stray strand of hair back over her ear. "I just thought the cup thing was weird. That's all."

That wasn't an answer at all, which meant whatever Mona had said, it probably hadn't been kind.

"Come over here." LJ scooted back to straddle the bench, crooking a finger to beckon her closer. His chest swelled a little bit when she didn't hesitate, kicking a leg over and sitting down so their knees touched. "You're my girl," he whispered, and touched the end of her nose. "You can have any cup in my house. You got that?"

Her eyes warmed, and she poked him in the side. "If I'm your girl, then stop running away from me every time you get mad."

"I'm trying. I just don't quite get it."

"Get what? Communication?"

He picked up her wrists, cupping them in his hands. "I guess I don't get how I keep triggering those attacks if you're not afraid of me."

"I told you, I don't control those. It's just a second of anything that's like the kidnapping, and then I'm just gone."

She was right. She'd said it before. But maybe he just hadn't been in the right frame of mind to listen. Thinking about it now, he realized there were a lot of things about himself he couldn't control, either.

He skimmed his thumbs over her wrists. "You know, when it rains, I can't sleep. If the wind is blowing, I get twitchy, anxious. There have been times during hurricane season when I got so drunk I couldn't even stand up, so I didn't have to hear the wind."

The way she'd hit the floor during that very first panic attack . . . it reminded him of something he hadn't thought about in years.

"When I was about nineteen," he said slowly, "there was a car crash."

Andra's breath hitched, but he shook his head, not looking up from their hands.

"I wasn't in it. I was just walking along the street, and the crash was so loud. Just like the levee breaking. I fell down, and for a second I was drowning on dry ground."

She rubbed her thumb softly over his hand and didn't interrupt. He had planned on stopping there, but now he heard the embarrassing words spilling out, stuff he'd never told a girl before.

"I was balled up on the sidewalk, hands over my head. This lady half my size helped me up. Dusted me off, didn't say a word. She must have been in Katrina, too. She knew."

Andra lifted his hand, leaving a kiss just above a raw place where he'd scraped off the skin on the pavement today. "I can deal with the attacks, you know. Have been for years now. But what I hate is that even now, when I'm here in your home, you won't let me in. That you're suddenly afraid to touch me."

He stole his hand back from her and tipped her chin up with one knuckle, smiling the way only she made him smile: with his whole chest and all his heart. "I'm not afraid of you, Cassandra Lawler."

"Prove it." She reached down and pulled her shirt up and over her head.

Twenty-nine

◇◇◇◇

LJ got up and closed the shed door before any of his neighbors could see inside. "Taking off your shirt in public is not the way to keep me from getting in fights, Rodeo Queen."

Even as he teased her, he couldn't help the smile tugging up the corners of his mouth, because he loved the brave, unequivocal way she'd chosen to show him that she trusted him. That she welcomed his touch even on a day like today, when all his rough edges were showing.

By the time he turned around, she had her bra off, too. Her breasts were small and stood out pertly, capped with pale-pink nipples that reminded him of every dirty thought he'd had in the last ten years. He went hard so fast it almost hurt.

She reached into his shorts.

His eyes widened as she gripped the base of his cock in one hand and shoved the elastic waistband down out of her way with the other. It had been way too hot today to wear anything under his shorts, and he was so, so glad.

"Uh, oh God . . ." He blinked.

Andra smiled, her face lightening. She explored all the way up to his tip before she trickled her fingertips back to the base. "So that's what it takes to finally knock you speechless. I'd wondered."

She gave him a tentative squeeze. The pleasure expanded into the base of his spine with an itching pressure that wanted to *thrust*.

"I gotta sit down," he muttered, feeling behind him for the weight bench and then sitting down with one leg on each side. Her eyes were warm and soft when she looked at him, and that was half of what was making it hard to stay on his feet.

He'd always hated people being afraid of him, but no one's trust had ever meant as much as hers. She looked at him like she saw something better than everyone else was seeing. Like *he* was something better.

She came with him as he sank down, finding a spot on her knees right in front of the bench. That position alone was enough to make his head melt into wordless, devious fantasy. A drop of moisture beaded at his tip, a reminder of the control that was already slipping away from him. All he could do was stare at her breasts, those gorgeous, perfect—holy shit, he was being such a selfish idiot right now.

He took Andra by the arms and lifted her. The elastic of his shorts dug into his balls, but as soon as he had her straddling his lap, he didn't give a shit about that anymore. She was centered right over him with heat bleeding through the seam of her shorts and all over his bare cock.

Before he could think better of it, his hips surged upward in a thoughtless movement. Andra gasped, rocking herself against his dick in tiny, jerky movements like she wasn't paying attention to anything except how much she liked it. His eyes rolled back beneath his lids, and he clamped his teeth together to keep from shouting. The denim of her shorts chafed his skin, but he would have died twice before he'd have complained.

She hung on to his neck, breathing in shallow little pants as she rode him. Judging by the sound of it, she was getting close on that alone. Thank Christ, because he was about to come all over his own stomach just watching her. He'd been so afraid to do more than kiss her since that first time in her bedroom, and all along, she must have been wanting this as badly as he was.

All he'd thought of in the beginning was that he didn't want her to be lonely. Then he'd hoped he could just make her smile. He could hardly conceive of the idea that she'd followed him halfway across the country, into this dingy little shed, and after seeing all that, still she craved more of him.

This time when she touched him, he did groan, way down deep in his chest. Andra whimpered as if she liked the sound.

He opened his eyes, and her breasts were right there. He ducked his head to her. Her skin tasted faintly of salt, and her nipple was a hard nub rubbing against the texture of his tongue. He curled the tip of his tongue to tickle her with it, his ears drinking the tiny, broken sounds she made.

"LJ," she whimpered.

He liked the sound of that, really a lot. She arched her back, and he ducked his head to her other nipple, exploring its sensitivity until he dragged a full, throaty moan from her. She rode him so hard the muscles in her bottom clenched against his thighs with every thrust, and his dick was starting to hurt from the scrape of fabric. It did something beautiful inside his chest to see her worked up like this over him.

He kissed her, wanting to share that feeling as he worked his hand up between them. The increase of heat as he got closer to his goal drove him half-mad.

Her hips rose against his hand as she tried to wriggle closer to his touch. "LJ, please."

He grinned. "You know I love a woman who says please."

Her shorts were frustratingly tight. He worked a finger up through the leg opening anyway, wiggling it until he found the crotch of her panties and then slipping inside. Wet. Hot. *Yes.*

He dropped his forehead against hers and let out a long breath at the same time she gulped one down.

"Kiss me," he whispered as he explored under her panties. Up and down, a little bit inside and then out again. God, she was wet. How long had it been since anybody had taken care of her like this?

Andra took his mouth so fiercely he forgot to pause for air. His finger slipped inside of her, and she responded with a silky rush. He wriggled his hand, finally managing to get enough space in her shorts to fit two fingers inside her, and oh sweet Lord, he could feel her stretch just to take that. He went light-headed as all the blood in his brain headed south. She bucked, asking for more. He pressed deep, curling his fingers toward her front wall.

She flinched and squeaked, and he pulled back. "Bad or good?"

She gripped his shoulders, half rising off his lap with the tension in her legs. "Good. Good good good. Can you do that again?"

"Like this?"

He curled his fingers, very slow this time, petting that one little sensitive spot he'd just found. Making friends with it. Moisture slicked down his fingers.

LJ muttered a curse, his vision going blurry for a second. Which was terrible, because her thighs were spread wide by his legs and his weight bench, his hand disappearing under the crotch of her shorts, with her breasts jiggling every time her hips jerked. If the visual alone wasn't enough to drive him out of his mind, her inner muscles eagerly throttling his fingers would have done the trick.

Andra gasped. "Please. *Please.*"

He twisted, but he couldn't get his thumb to the right place inside her cutoffs. Fuck his giant hand, and fuck her gloriously tiny shorts.

"Can I take your shorts off?" He kissed her neck, her hair, her forehead. *Say yes. Please say yes.*

The fabric twisted around his hand, and he looked down to see her unzipping her fly. He started to withdraw, and she gripped him even tighter inside. "No," she gasped. "Don't—I'll take them off around your hand. Don't stop. Please don't stop."

That was definitely not going to work, but he didn't have the heart to tell her. She stood up and tried to work her shorts and panties off, getting them all tangled in his hand. He slowly plunged his fingers into her, curling them the whole way back out as he watched her struggle with her panties, her hands getting weaker and more ineffectual the closer he brought her to the edge.

Finally, he couldn't take it anymore. "One second, okay? Just one second." He pulled his fingers out of her, yanked her panties down, and was back inside her before she had a chance to take a full breath.

She stood in front of him, naked with her shorts and panties crumpled above her knees, the weight bench keeping him from pulling them all the way down. Not even his many fantasies touched the reality of how insanely sexy she looked right now. He touched his thumb to his own soaked palm to wet it, then stroked it up through the layers of her until he found her swollen, neglected clit. She yelped and grabbed his wrist.

Yeah, the neighbors definitely heard that one. But that didn't matter half so much as pleasing her did.

"It's okay," he murmured. "I know it's sensitive. I'll be real careful—I promise. You trust me?"

She let go of his wrist, her hands trembling, and he skimmed the pad of his thumb around the edges of her clit. Not rubbing, just teasing her enough so that she could feel exactly how much she was going to love it. Andra shifted, trying to spread her legs to let him farther inside but caged by her shorts at her knees. He calibrated the rhythm to exactly what kept her trembling, and increased the pressure on her clit with every inward stroke. When her knees started to wobble, too, he leaned forward and finally let himself taste her.

Just a little, his tongue tracing around the edges of his thumb, but it was enough to make her scream.

He grinned, even though she cut herself off halfway through, swallowing the rest of the cry. He curled his fingers into her sweet spot, keeping his thumb steady over her clit as he teased his tongue around its edges. With his free hand, he reached around and cupped the bare curve of her bottom. Her legs clenched as she arched into his mouth, quivering . . . and then she broke. With an exhale so hard it was almost a yelp, she started to come.

"God, yes, I want to feel you. Get me wet," he urged. "Come all over my hand."

He couldn't resist. He took his thumb away, nuzzling his tongue into its place so he could enjoy her clit pulsing in perfect time to the squeezing of her muscles around his fingers. His hips jumped, the vinyl of the bench squeaking against his ass because his shorts had crept down more while he was playing with her.

She started to fall forward and knocked him off-balance. He had to pull out to catch her, and even then he cracked his head on the bench press bar on the way down. Though he managed to keep her head away from it, at least.

"You okay?"

Andra was curled a little into herself, lying on his chest as she gulped down air. "Mmm. Uh. Uh-huh." She twitched as an after-shock ran through her. A second later she arched, reaching back to try to push her shorts the rest of the way off.

Man, this shed was hot. Especially with her lying on top of him. But her breasts against his chest as she squirmed . . .

LJ's fingers twitched, and he realized they were still slicked with her response. Nothing had ever turned him on like that—to know that she hadn't wanted sex in years, but now she was shaking with the pleasure he'd brought her. He reached between their bodies and wrapped a hand around himself, rubbing her wetness all over the stiff shaft. He groaned through his teeth, giving the head an extra squeeze.

Andra pushed up on his chest, peeking down to see what he was doing. He couldn't stop, didn't want to give up the feeling of his dick glistening wet with her pleasure. This would have to tide him over until the day when she finally wanted him inside her.

She exhaled a small, broken sound while she watched him stroke himself. Her thighs clenched over his as she curled her hips forward again. When she glanced up, her green eyes practically steamed the air between them. "I like that," she whispered.

He was going to die. His brain was going to explode right along with his hard-on, and that was going to be the end of him. Also, he did not care.

"I want you," she said, scooting up until slick skin bumped his knuckles where they were fisted around his erection. "Please?"

"I don't have a condom." It hurt even to say it, so he pushed up and stole a kiss as a consolation prize. Why was this shed full of all these useless boxes and not condoms?

Her face fell. "Do you have one inside? I could get dressed and go get it. Wait!" She reared back. "I have an implant. Birth control implant. I only got it to help control my—" She stopped, blushing. "But it's birth control. That works, right?"

He had to chuckle. She was naked in his backyard shed, practically pushing herself onto his cock, and she couldn't say the word "period"?

"Yeah, Andie-girl. That will work just fine." If his dick would shrink about two sizes, it would work even better, but he was definitely not going to tell her that. He'd just get her wet enough she wouldn't notice she was tight as any virgin.

Except the last time he'd been inside her, it had gone badly. Even if she wasn't afraid of him, he wanted to make sure he didn't trigger any bad memories. His brain whirred into action. He'd gone too fast last time, definitely. This time, it would be all slow. Also, she had been on the bottom, which was probably—he didn't want to think about that. Top. She could be on top. That would be perfect. The bench press bar had to go, though, or one of them would certainly end up with a concussion.

He reached past her and gripped the bar, lifting it out of its cradle. Bending his elbows, he let it drift back past his head. As soon as it cleared his forehead, he dropped the bar with a crash. "Andra, could you . . . ?" He reached down and snapped the elastic waistband of his shorts, currently caught around his thighs and beneath hers.

"Right, of course." She stood up and tugged his shorts down his legs, toeing off her cowboy boots.

She bent down, pulling off his shoes, then starting on his socks. He sat up, shucking off his shirt as he went. "Hey, I'll get those."

"Too late." She flipped her hair back, and uncertainty flashed through her green eyes. "So should I—I mean, where do you want me?"

He rubbed his hands down her arms and lifted her hands so he

could kiss one and then the other. Why didn't he have anywhere ro-
mantic to take her? Someplace with candles and an air conditioner
and a big bed about a million miles away from his mama's room. He
wanted Andra to be comfortable.

"How about my lap?" He gave her a smile—the teasing one that
usually cheered her up. "You seemed like you liked it earlier."

Her eyes warmed, and she let him draw her back to her feet and
tug her forward until she had to part her thighs to allow room for
him and the weight bench. This time, she blushed as she spread her
legs. He didn't want her to be self-conscious about any part of this,
so he searched for a way to distract her.

"Here, run your nails through my hair. Feels good when you do
that." He placed her hands for her, then nuzzled his face against her
belly, saying hello with soft kisses and then warming her up with a
little bit of tongue. Her fingers clenched against the back of his head,
and he brought one hand up between her legs, tracing a single finger-
tip along her slit.

Ah yes. Still so wet for him. She gasped but only leaned closer.
Perfect. Next step, getting her to decide his cock was a good thing,
so she'd let him use it to rub that sweet spot inside of her.

Touching her shoulders, he eased her down onto his lap. She
tightened her thighs, trying to hold herself up. "It's okay. Relax." He
gave her a crooked smile and slapped his scarred thigh. "I'm tough.
I can take a little bitty thing like you sitting on me."

She laughed and sat down, teetering as she balanced on his thighs
until she got a toe on the floor to steady herself. Her legs were stretched
wide open for him in this position. Why had he wanted a bed again?

He kissed her, running a hand through her hair. Then he nuzzled
his way over to her ear, touching his tongue to her earlobe before he
whispered, "I like it when you get me all wet. Did you see how much
I liked it?"

Her breathing stuttered and she nodded.

"Good." He let his voice drop to a lower rumble, and her nipples
hardened against his chest. "Does that mean I can do it again?"

"Yes." The word came out breathless, but very certain. He reached down and gripped his aching cock, tipping it against her. Gently at first, then more aggressively as he found where she was slippery, her flesh the tiniest bit swollen with arousal.

Andra hugged him, pressing her breasts into his chest and burying her face in his neck. He could feel every heave of her filling lungs and every tattered edge of her exhale against his throat. He took his time, his throat clutching as he waited for the first hint of her stiffening up, for the gasp that signaled the start of an attack. But this time, there was nothing. LJ's heart beat hugely in his chest. She was finally relaxing with him. Maybe all they needed was to build a whole new set of memories around sex, until not so many things were linked to the old ones.

He kissed her temple and closed his eyes as she melted her pleasure all over the head of his cock. He nudged it up through the layers of her, circling her clit. Now he had to grit his teeth, because he was almost too far gone for this kind of playing.

"I'm going to lie back," he murmured, kissing her hair again. "You can come down with me, or you can stay up here. Whatever you want, you hear me?"

She whimpered into his neck, kissed his skin, and then bit him. It was the tiniest of nips, but it exploded white stars all through his head. Tension gathered in the base of his spine again, growling at him to thrust and pound and bury himself so deep inside her that she'd never be able to wash away his scent.

"That felt good," he managed. "You do that as much as you want, Andie-girl."

He tightened his abs and lay back. To his surprise, she stayed sitting up high, not hiding in his arms anymore. Instead, she looked down to where he held his dick, the dark skin tracing her slit beneath midnight curls.

He dipped his shaft low, letting her see the moisture glistening on his head when he pushed it up toward her clit again. She moaned, falling forward and catching her weight with a hand against his chest. Her thighs flexed and clamped against his. And then one of her small hands joined his on his cock.

He mumbled something that might have been a prayer or something far less holy, and he let her have him. As soon as his hand moved, she rolled her hips, rubbing his erection exactly where she wanted it and holding him far less gingerly than he would have expected. But at this point, her hand wasn't enough friction. He needed her all over, squeezing him deep in her body and soaking the base of him.

She hitched herself higher, letting his arousal taste her entrance. He was lined up perfectly, and he had to lock down every muscle he owned not to thrust.

"Andra. Open your eyes, sweetheart." He reached up and cupped her jaw, letting his thumb rest over her slightly parted lips.

When her lashes lifted, her green eyes were dilated as all hell. He was pretty sure his were, too, as she sank down, taking the first inch of him. Her mouth fell open on a gasp, and then she nipped his thumb. His hips leaped, driving him another inch into her.

"Sorry, sorry." He retreated, lowering his ass back to the bench. "We can go as slow as you need to, darlin'."

Her eyelashes fluttered at the friction of him sliding back out of her, and she closed her lips around his thumb.

Oh sweet Jesus. His lids drooped closed as he got lost in everything she was making him feel.

Andra lowered herself, taking more of him. Three inches now, four. Not enough. Then she made a tiny noise.

His eyes flew open. *No. Please, no.*

She smiled. "I'm okay. You take some getting used to, is all." Her legs tightened and she lifted up again, the slide all silky grip that had him panting and her sighing. "Worth it. So worth it." She pumped herself a couple of times on only the head of him.

His neck went loose. "Please. Oh God." Then he realized what he'd said and swallowed, his fists gripping the bench at his sides. "No. Slow is perfect, sweet girl. You take all the time you need."

"You want it faster?" Her eyes flared, all green challenge. This time, when she sank back down, she took him all. He couldn't even think through the crazy tight grip of her. All around his cock, molding to his every ripple even as he pulsed and swelled impossibly harder.

He dug all ten fingers into the bench. Before he had a chance to get himself under control, Andra lifted up and slid back down, each pass wetter, hotter than the last.

He was going to come. *No.* No, that could not happen. Not yet. He gritted his teeth, but then she bounced on his dick, three fast little jerks, and he almost lost it again.

"LJ?"

A pang twisted in his chest when he found frustration straining her face.

"I can't—I want . . . I don't think I'm doing it right."

"You're doing it way too right," he muttered, but he pried his hands off the bench with a creak of overused knuckles and took her hands. "Hold on up here, okay?" He brought them up to the supports where the bench press bar used to rest. This stretched her out, her breasts teasing just above him, her arms spread sensually wide. He took her by her tiny waist and lifted her, sliding his dick ever so slowly out until only two inches were left inside. "Lock your arms and brace yourself right there, okay? You doing all right?"

She stared down at him, her eyes running over his body and catching on his face. "You're beautiful," she said. "God, you're so beautiful." Her inner muscles clenched along with her words, tugging at the head of his cock.

Yes and yes and more yes. He loved the way she was looking at him, that they were sharing this moment and she looked every bit as happy about it as he was.

He rolled his abs torturously slow. Starting all the way at the top and running all the way down to the bottom as he stroked the full length of himself into her. Slow at first, so he could blur the edges of both their thoughts with the sweet slide of it. She was starting to relax, her walls stretching to let him farther inside even as she gripped him, begging for more with tiny little squeezes that tormented his swollen dick.

LJ held his breath as he watched her face, giving her the first hard thrust with a curl of his hips at the end.

She squeaked and almost lost her grip on the weight bench, her little nipples pebbling even tighter.

He reached up and cupped her ass, driving into her with short bursts that hooked hard at the bottom. Her jaw clenched tight, and she let go of the weight bench and leaned back, angling instinctively to try to prolong the burst of pleasure at the end of each pass. "Yes. Please, yes, LJ, oh my—"

Something wordless and intense roared through his ears, dangerous tingles already gathering at the base of his arousal.

"I can make it feel better, but I have to have you on your knees," he gasped. "Can I put you on your knees, sweet girl?"

Even the words turned him on.

Her eyes came open but were only hazy green slits. "Yes, any—I need—oh God. Yes."

He surged upward, wrapping his arms around her waist, and stood while still buried inside her. That got her eyes wide open, and he started pumping into her while standing. One arm under her ass, one around her waist, his thigh muscles clenching. He wanted her up against a wall, her back against something firm so he could push deep and—

He pulled out the second before it was too late, gasping as he held her up in shaking arms and tried to fight the orgasm already roaring through his head, begging to burst out through his tip. The air in the shed clung molten hot to his skin. A thousand and three degrees, and still it felt cold on his erection after the warmth of her body.

LJ lowered her to her feet and she staggered a little, reaching for the weight bench and climbing up onto it on hands and knees. She fumbled for a second and then dropped one leg to the ground so she could open a little more.

Before she could get self-conscious, he joined her. His hands were so hot her skin seemed cool against his palms when he smoothed them up her back, leaving kisses along her spine. "I'm here. I'm right here. You hear my voice, Andie-girl? I love you. You know how god-damn much I love you."

She turned her head, shaking the tumble of her black hair out of her face as she reached one hand around to draw his mouth to hers. "It's okay," she murmured through the smile that crept into their kiss. "I'm okay."

He laid his cheek between her shoulder blades and closed his eyes. He was not okay. He wanted this so bad, wanted to take her deep from behind in a way he couldn't explain in words, or as a mere fetish. It was more like part of his DNA, the need to claim her as his.

"You hear me, love? You hear my voice?" He kissed the back of her neck, wrapping one arm around her and holding himself up on the weight bench with the other. "It's going to go deep from this angle."

She curled her ass back into his lap, pushing the head of him into her. "I love your voice. I want you to do it hard. It doesn't hurt, LJ." She rocked back a little more, her muscles fluttering around him. "It feels so good."

He curled his abs and eased into her with a long, exhaling groan.

She squeaked, squirmed a little, and started begging in tiny broken sounds that drove him out of his mind. He was pumping into her before he'd made the choice to do it, slamming so far in that the swollen head of his dick locked into some perfect, secret clasp that made her moan every time.

He had to hit that spot again. Again.

He dropped his hand farther down, where everything would be more sensitive.

She clamped her teeth against a scream, and she fisted around his dick as she crashed into orgasm again. He thrust even harder, his legs screaming as the head of his cock dragged through the convulsively tight clasp of her. He exploded, hot waves of liquid bursting from his tip, spreading deep within her body. Just when he thought there couldn't be any more, pleasure flashed brightly behind his eyes, pulsed once up his shaft, and then slowly ebbed away.

He held her with his one free arm, sweat slick between their bodies as he buried his face in her hair, breathing her scent with every ragged breath.

They needed to lie down. That one thought beat inside his head with every too-big beat of his heart, but it took him a second before he could pull out. Once he did, he maneuvered them until they were sitting, lifting Andra into his lap so he could hold her better.

"Oh my God," she said, her head sagging against his shoulder. "I didn't know. I just didn't know."

He grinned. "Did *Cosmo* magazine tell you that's what a man likes to hear? Or am I just that good?"

She blew a hair out of her face and gave him a narrow-eyed look belied by the smile tugging at her lips. "You know, smugness is not attractive."

"That's not what you said a minute ago," he teased. "I do believe you called me beautiful, Rodeo Queen."

"I was under the influence at the time," she mumbled, letting her head sag against his shoulder again.

He tugged her hip a little closer into his lap, dropping a kiss on her hair. She said something very soft, and he lifted his head. "What was that?"

"Do you think it's because this place is so different from home? Why my attacks stopped, I mean?"

He wasn't so sure they *had* stopped. It had been only a few days, after all. He didn't want to jinx it, though, in case she was right. "Nothing to trigger bad memories, maybe?" He turned his head enough to kiss her cheek. "And hey, if you happen to like making love in a backyard shed, that's all right with me."

As soon as he said it, it hit him that she'd never said it back. She had only said she loved his *voice*. He'd told her he loved her so many times now—with his saxophone, with his body, with words, and she'd never said it back. Sometimes, she looked at him in a certain way, and he thought maybe . . . But he wanted more than maybe. His heart was so tied up in this girl that he knew damned well he was never getting it back.

Then again, maybe she was the smarter of the pair of them. He was starting to doubt he was ever going to be able to leave his mama or New Orleans for long, but he could already feel the itch of going a whole week without riding a horse. He loved his life in Montana, living his days to the rhythm of the wind and the animals beneath his saddle.

And location was even less of a choice for Andra than it was for him. She owned part of that ranch, and the better part of the Lawler reputation was built on trophies won by horses she'd trained. Plus, she was welded by the heartstrings to that palomino mare of hers.

Andra lifted her head from his shoulder. "You okay? Or is the heat killing you, too?"

He grabbed his shirt off the floor and handed it to her so she could get cleaned up. "Missing my cowboy hat, that's all."

She got up out of his lap, her face lighting up.

"What?"

She grinned, and blushed the tiniest bit. "Next time we do that, will you wear your cowboy hat?"

Her smile soothed some of the ache in his chest even as it stabbed a little deeper, because he never wanted her to turn that smile toward any other man.

"Darlin', if you let me do that again, I'll wear anything you want," he said. "Except pants."

Thirty

◇◇◇◇

"Faster!"

Andra picked up the pace of her whisking, frowning down at the uninspiring tan goo in the skillet.

"Faster, girl, or the roux's going to burn." Rose clucked her tongue.

"Why don't we turn down the heat if it's going to burn?"

"Wouldn't taste right. You've got to brown it right at the edge of burning to get it nice and dark, but if you let up whisking, you might as well throw it in the trash." Rose tucked the blanket higher up on her legs, glancing over at the Cubs game playing on the tiny TV in the corner of the kitchen. The sweatshirt she wore puffed around her whole upper half, the words on it so faded that all Andra could make out were the words "Middle School." She couldn't decide what was more adorable: that LJ had been so tall by middle school, or that his mom still wore his sweatshirt.

Adorable or not, Andra had no idea how Rose could be wearing a sweatshirt in August. The AC was on the highest setting, and she was still sweating in cutoff shorts and a tank top. The only nice thing about the heat was that LJ always wore shirts that exposed the thick muscles of his arms. Or no shirt at all.

"Quit your daydreaming, girl. Whisk!"

LJ chuckled, swiping diced bell peppers to the side of the cutting board with his knife. "Dang, it's kind of fun to watch her yell at somebody else in the kitchen."

Rose gave him a half-fond, half-aggrieved look. "LJ was seven before I could get him to come out with a decent roux. But it took Mona's girls until they were twelve."

Andra laughed. She never got tired of Rose's stories about LJ, though the older woman rarely bragged about her son in front of him. "You had him cooking when he was seven?"

"Well, I had to! I didn't figure any woman was going to put up with that attitude of his, and I didn't want him to starve. Besides, he didn't grow that tall on only three meals a day. Took more like six or seven when he was in high school."

He turned halfway around, grinning. "If you'd known I was going to turn out so pretty, you wouldn't have had to bother."

"See?" Rose said to Andra. "Manners like that, of course I thought he'd starve."

"Y'all just don't want to admit my cake got snatched up before yours at the last barbecue 'fore I moved."

"Why do you insist on talking like you just slogged out of the swamp?" Rose demanded. "You have a four-year degree, LJ Delisle, and I'll thank you to do it justice."

Andra's whisk jerked to a stop. "Having an accent doesn't mean you're uneducated." As soon as the words were out of her mouth, she wanted to cringe, because she'd just picked a fight with LJ's beloved mom. But she hated everything about the entire argument. "It's ridiculous. Nobody ever says British people sound uneducated, even though they tack an *r* on the end of all kinds of words that don't have one. The idea that a southern accent makes you sound dumb has a whole lot more to do with prejudice than IQ points." She lifted her chin. "I happen to like the way he talks."

Rose blinked, and Andra braced herself for a fight. "Well, then," the other woman said, the corner of her mouth twitching upward.

The door rattled under a too-enthusiastic knock.

Rose turned toward the sound, brushing off the tense moment.

"LJ, take that whisk and see if you can salvage the roux before you have to run off to work. Andra, honey, go see who's at the door and tell them the gumbo won't be ready until this afternoon no matter how many times they ask."

LJ hooted with laughter, stealing Andra's whisk. "After she ate your red beans with a straight face, I thought for sure Mama loved you too much to teach you a thing. Turns out even love has limits, and those limits start with messing up gumbo."

"I wasn't messing it up." She gestured at the pan. "It's goo! It was goo five minutes ago, too." She crossed the kitchen and pulled the door open, yanking hard to get it past the sticking point. "The gumbo's not ready, Ty, and I promise you don't want to come in here. These two are both crazy."

LJ's best friend grinned at her from the porch. "Maybe I came to see you."

She snorted. "After what I did to your guitar? Not likely." She turned and gave Rose a pained look. "He said the sounds I made were like the babbling of an infant." She narrowed her eyes at Ty. "They were chords. I am almost sure they were chords."

"Girl, you're pretty and all, but if music is a language, you're illiterate." He laughed.

"Not fluent," LJ corrected from the stove, whisking with quick, exact strokes. "Illiterate would be if she couldn't read, not speak."

"Oh, she can't read music, either, fool." Ty shook his head. "It's sad."

"Did you come here to make fun of me?" Andra opened the door a little farther, leaning on the edge. "Because I have to tell you, these two pretty much had that covered."

He brightened. "Nope. I got something for y'all."

She couldn't help a smile to match his. It was so easy to see why he and LJ were friends: they both started at a thousand watts and only dialed up from there.

"Remember that family we helped move last week? They called me to haul off a load to the thrift store, because they knew I'd do it cheaper than the moving company. They had a bed that wouldn't fit in their new spare bedroom, and it happens to be the size of frame you've been looking for." He reached over to the wall and hauled a headboard over in front of the door. "See? California-king-sized."

Black metal headboard. The scrape of handcuffs jerking against the post.

Andra jolted backward, the sight a battering ram straight to her chest. Her bare foot skidded on the linoleum, her ass smacked the floor with a bruising thud, and she skittered backward.

"Andra?" Rose asked. "What's the matter?"

She tried to go faster, get farther away from that bed frame. Her legs stopped working. At the same time, her arms went weak and she was helpless. Stuck there for whatever came next.

"Shit." LJ hit his knees beside her, turning her face toward him. "Look at me, sweet girl. You're safe. You're okay."

Blood, dried on her fingertips as she crept off the bed, digging at the screws with cracked nails as she tried to gauge how long she had to try to get loose before he came back.

LJ exploded up. "Get that thing out of here."

Ty's voice sounded closer now. "What? What'd I do? Is she okay?"

The cotton of the gag expanded, stuck in her throat so she couldn't pull air around it or even get enough to cough it out.

"Go." LJ stuffed him outside and slammed the door to hide the bed frame. He was back with her in a second. "Breathe, Andra. It's gone. You're safe." His voice shook, and his eyes were fastened on her lips. They felt the numb kind of cold they got when they started to turn blue. LJ must be scared, too, because he knew she was dying. He knew her body was broken and it would turn on her, kill her before it would let her be stuck in that place again.

"LJ, you leave her be," Rose said. "See to dinner."

He threw a wild glance over his shoulder. "No, she—"

"Mind your mama, now."

He stood up, slowly, and Andra couldn't even get her eyes to move to follow him. Tears blurred everything, and she couldn't blink. The burn started in her chest, sending urgent fingers upward. Cells dying, begging for oxygen she couldn't give them.

"Turn off the burner and see if you can scrape that roux off my good pan. Did you buy onions? They're good for your immune system, you know. And they fight inflammation. When you're old, LJ, you'll thank me for feeding you so many onions." She clucked her tongue at the scrape of a spatula on cast iron. "Oh, it burned on good this time, didn't it? Well, simmer a little water in it, see if you can cut the black part loose."

The edges of Andra's vision started to go. Black to gray to a blur of color still left at the center. Her whole body collapsed in on itself, a balloon sucked empty of air.

"In Montana," LJ said, "they get these fat yellow onions, sweet enough you could eat them like an apple. From over in Washington. Next time, I'll bring you a bag."

They sounded so calm, normal.

"How long has that lattice been loose under the porch?" LJ asked. "You know if I'm not here, Ty will nail it back down for you before the possums move in."

"Tyrone has his own mama to do chores for. He doesn't need to be doing mine. I was just waiting for a good day so I could swing my own hammer."

Their conversation was utter normalcy, while her heart raced like she was fighting for her life. But then, she wasn't, was she? She was in a kitchen, they'd been cooking, and there was nothing binding her hands. She blinked, and oxygen rushed into her lungs. Clean linoleum stretched in front of her, a couple of black smudges on the bottom of the door where shoes had brushed against the paint. Her muscles ached, and she stretched them gingerly before she pushed back to her feet.

"Sorry." She kept her eyes on the floor, not wanting to see how Rose looked at her after that little episode. The counter was only a few steps away, and she meant to start helping so she would look normal again, but she was too shaky to risk picking up the knife.

Instead, she held on to the edge of the counter. She hadn't had a single attack since she'd followed LJ to New Orleans, not even when they'd made love in the shed: the first time she'd been with a man since her kidnapping. Everything here was so different from home, and she felt bolder, lighter here. She thought all that was over. But she was the same person.

The heat of LJ's chest steadied her back, his arms coming around so one crossed her chest, the other winding around her waist. He ducked his head, his cheek pressed to her hair. She wasn't sure if the quivering was coming from her body or his. Maybe both.

"Don't apologize," Rose said. "There's some things a person can't help. Better they happen at home than out in the rest of this hard world." Andra didn't realize the older woman had gotten up until a hand smoothed over her hair and brushed away the marks of the tears that had streaked down her cheeks. "There now," she murmured, and Andra leaned into her touch, her throat clenching.

"That one was over faster, didn't you think?" LJ asked.

Andra gritted her teeth. She didn't want shorter panic attacks. She wanted to not *have* panic attacks. But she didn't want them to see how much it hurt to start all over again, so she just freed a hand to squeeze LJ's forearm. "How did you know to just go about your business?" she asked his mom. "It actually did help."

LJ let her go, coming around and ducking his head to see her face. "Really? Because it made me feel like a jerk."

Rose turned, made her slow way back to the table, and sank into her chair.

"When it happens, it feels like I'm dying." It felt odd to say it out loud, but Andra focused on LJ's brown eyes, willing him to understand. "Not like I'm injured or something but that my body goes haywire and stops working. Every single time I *know* I'm going to suffocate, and I can't move or do anything about it. This time, though, you guys were so calm I knew it couldn't be real." She touched the back of LJ's wrist. "I knew if I were actually dying, you'd be freaking out."

"You can't suffocate yourself," Rose said. Her arms sagged in her lap now, as if even the trip across the kitchen had used up all the energy she needed to sit upright. "I read all about it at the library, years ago. You can get so mad or so scared you quit breathing, but as soon as you faint, you start right up again."

Andra frowned. "Why would you research that? Do you get panic attacks?" It was hard to imagine anything that might frighten LJ's crowbar-tough mom.

"When LJ was a little boy, he had fits. Not really temper tantrums. He was the sweetest child, so helpful, and you could see he wasn't doing it on purpose. But sometimes it'd come over him, like his fa—" Rose cut herself off and kept going without a pause. "He'd get so mad he couldn't control himself. Sometimes he'd hold his breath until he turned blue and slumped right over to sleep. Didn't matter if I cuddled him or scolded him or anything. Only thing that helped was to leave him be until he came around on his own." She smiled, her eyes falling to her lap. "It sure did upset some folks in the grocery store, though."

LJ went back to the counter and started washing the dirty pan, his shoulders hunched tightly.

"Well, I guess it came in handy," Andra said, wanting to draw the attention back away from him. She kept her voice light, testing the waters. "I guess New Orleans wasn't the magical cure after all. So much for all the voodoo magic you told me you were putting in your food." She tickled LJ's side, and his abs clenched under her fingers.

"It's no big thing." His lips tipped up toward a smile, and a little bit of hope crept in under her disappointment.

Even after all that, they weren't treating her as if she were crazy. But then, they wouldn't, would they? LJ had told her how nervous it made him when it rained, and last week Rose had pointed out with a shaking hand where her grandmother's piano used to sit, before the floodwaters washed it away. These people weren't untouched by their past, and they didn't expect her to be, either. Her father had always been so upset by her attacks that she'd never considered that in a certain way . . . they were normal.

LJ's smile grew. "Besides, I'm going to have a great time telling Ty it was his ugly old face that sent you into fits."

"Please don't." She cringed. "He's been so sweet. When you were on that landscaping job the other day, he and Tash came over to teach me guitar chords. Even after Tash gave me up as a lost cause, he was so sure I'd get better and my fingers would stop getting twisted all up and hitting the wrong things." She paused. "Wait, weren't you two supposed to be doing a drywall job together today?"

LJ glanced at the clock and said a word that had his mother frowning at him. "I gotta run. Will you be okay?"

"Depends on if I mess up the roux, I think, and how fast your mom can find a weapon."

He dropped a kiss on her cheek. "I'll hide the knives."

She went to the sink and stared down at the pan he'd been working on. Now that he was gone, she needed to wrap her mind around the idea that she might be crippled by these panic attacks forever.

She swallowed. They had gotten better, and that would have to be enough. It was a little easier with LJ and his mom, because they understood having an ugly past, and all the messy ways it butted into the present. But not even that would do Andra much good, considering they lived thousands of miles away from her.

She picked up the scouring pad. Tonight. She needed to confront LJ as soon as he got home. After last night, she couldn't stand not having some kind of plan for how they could stay together. Whether Rose could move to Montana, or if they'd have to move down here for good. Her throat clamped shut at the idea of leaving her ranch, her horses, and she scrubbed harder as she tried to think of a third choice.

"You're fretting so hard I can hear it all the way over here." The floor creaked, and then Rose patted her arm. "What's the matter, girl?" She sounded so much like her son that tears stung Andra's eyes, but her phone rang before she could figure out how to respond. "Go on and get that," Rose said, handing her a dish towel to dry her hands. "I'll be three weeks in the grave before I'm old enough I need help to make a roux."

Andra flashed her a strained smile and went for the phone. Rose had been out of bed more the past couple of days, though Andra wasn't familiar enough with lupus to know whether that meant the worst was over for now.

She picked up her cell, and as soon as she saw the name on the screen, her heart jumped like she was headed for a second attack. It was her father.

Thirty-one

◇◇◇◇

Andra stepped outside into the ruthless sunlight, trying to push away her unease. It wasn't like she hadn't talked to her father since she'd left. He tended to avoid the subject of LJ, but other than that, they were okay. It was just that usually he waited for her to call him.

"Hi, Dad, what's up?" She worked to keep her voice light. "Did you like the pictures I sent? I still haven't figured out the whole fire-swallowing guy, and LJ refuses to explain the trick to me."

"Well, I'm glad you had fun, Andra, but it's time to come home."

She turned her back to the sun, sweat already trickling down her spine. "What's wrong? What happened?"

"Your brother broke his leg last night. He was trying to get Taz used to the lariat, but it was nearly sunset and the light was funny. He thinks that's why she spooked. She busted through a fence and went down on top of Jason's leg." Dad cleared his throat. "He came out of surgery okay, but he's not feeling his oats too much right now."

"Oh my God." Andra shifted her weight off her right ankle, the one she'd broken barrel racing when she was ten. It throbbed when she thought about how much more it would hurt to break a leg. "What about Taz? Is she okay?"

"Just cuts, but she'd better get her head straight about lariats, because she's a lot more likely to be working the range rather than the show ring with the kind of scars she's going to have now."

Andra paced across the porch, the shock making her thoughts come slower even as her feet sped up. "Jason always starts right at six. What was he doing still riding at sunset? That's nearly fourteen hours."

"We've got a ranch that takes three trainers to eke by, and we have one, Cassandra. Why do you think he was riding at sunset?"

She flinched. "I'm sorry, Dad."

"It's not your fault. These things happen," he said. "But I can't spare you any longer. Right now, we've got a whole crop of horses looking to hit the circuit a year later than we can afford, unless we hire some help."

She glanced back toward the house. "I can't come home yet, Dad. LJ's mom barely has the energy to make it to the bathroom on her own most days. She can't cook, much less go back to work, and with LJ working to support them both, there's no one to take care of her."

"Well, I'm sorry to hear that, but you have your own family to look after, Andra. You think your brother's having an easy time getting to the bathroom with six pins in his leg?" His voice rose.

"No, but—" She needed a few more days. Weeks.

Unfortunately, she knew the finances of the ranch even better than her father did. The feed bills, the new fence for the western pasture, the tractor they'd replaced last summer, their tab with the vet. They needed to sell this batch of horses to feed the ones who'd be born in the spring. There was a saying among ranchers: land rich, cash poor. She couldn't justify selling off Lawler acres to stay here with LJ.

"Look, how soon can you get here? I've got interviews for new trainers lined up all day Wednesday. Now that you're not minding having men on the place, we should be able to fill two or three spots without a problem, but I'd rather have you vet the candidates yourself."

"Are any of them local? People aren't going to want to move for a job that's temporary. Jason will get better, and we have to hold LJ's position open for him. In case he . . ." She glanced down the street, too embarrassed to admit she didn't know if he was still planning on coming back. His mom's health wasn't the only thing calling him back here.

"He had a job up here, and he ran out on it. I'm not inclined to rely on someone like that."

She gripped the metal of the porch railing, and it nearly burned her palm. "You don't know him like I do."

"Then why don't you know if he's coming back?" His question hung there until Dad sighed, his voice softening. "Listen, sweetie, if he's the man you say he is, he'll be back once his mother's better, and you'll have nothing to worry about. And if he wouldn't do that for you, you need to stop hanging around there waiting on him."

"It's not that simple." She picked at a peeling bit of paint on the railing. His mom would eventually pull out of this lupus flare-up, but it wouldn't be the last. Every time, LJ would face the same choice: his job or his family. *Her* or his family.

"It is that simple, sweetheart. When you love somebody, you want them to be happy, no matter what it costs you. If this is the man for you, he'll do the right thing."

She squeezed her eyes shut against the sudden threat of tears. LJ would do the right thing. For her, for his mom. Whatever he *could* do, no matter what it cost him. But would she?

If she were a good person, she wouldn't ask him to come back to a place where people snuck sideways glances at him every time he went to town. She wouldn't expect him to leave his mother alone and forget about his friends to move someplace where he had to play his music to the dead space of a tiny apartment. No band. No audience.

"We need you, Andra. Come home." Quietly, her father disconnected.

She glanced at the front door, then hit the number for her brother's cell. It rang through to voicemail. He was probably sleeping, which meant she was out of excuses to delay what had to be done.

She walked back inside on numb feet. A pot bubbled merrily on the stove, and Rose rested at the kitchen table, watching the small

TV. She flipped it off as soon as she saw Andra's expression. "Come here, honey. Tell me what happened now."

Andra shook her head. "I have to go home, that's all, and—" She gulped down a breath, the other woman's face coming into sharp focus as Andra realized she might not see her again. She went over and knelt next to her. "Rose, it's been . . ." She fumbled for the right words. "I'm just glad I got the chance to be here. I don't think I knew how much I missed my own mom until I met you."

Tears started to sparkle in Rose's eyes, and she reached out and gripped Andra's hands. "I love you, too, honey, and I'm so grateful to the good Lord for bringing you here. But don't go saying all your goodbyes. I think I might have a few years left in me yet."

Andra straightened her shoulders. "Listen. Whatever happens, wherever he decides to go—" Her voice wavered, and she forced back the lump in her throat. "I know you don't want to tell him when you're sick because you think it might hold him back. But you didn't see his face when he found out you needed him and he wasn't there."

Rose's expression stiffened, and her lips pressed thin.

"If he can't trust you to tell him when you need help, he'll never leave again," she said all in a rush. "I don't even know if he wants to leave, but if you want him to have the option, you need to be honest with him. He's your *son*, Rose. Let him be there for you."

Rose's chin lifted, the skin tightening over her cheekbones. High, like her son's. One tear broke free from her eye when she nodded.

"Thank you," Andra whispered. Her stomach twisted greasily. That whole speech had probably been unnecessary.

The truth was in LJ's smile the other night when he introduced her all down the line of mule-carriage drivers. In the difference in the distant way her father said his name compared to all his friends they'd run into around town, who said it like an exclamation, usually right before they wrapped him in a hug.

"I have to pack," Andra whispered, and she fled into LJ's room. It had felt perfect to sleep in there last night, in LJ's arms. But this place was his, not hers. No matter what he said, it would never be theirs.

LJ took off his shirt on the porch, flapping it until a cloud of drywall dust puffed up into the scathing midday sun. Damned Sheetrock always made him itchy, but it paid good when Leo got behind enough to call for extra help. He flipped his shirt over his shoulder and shoved the front door open with a grin. "Hey, y'all had better not have had lunch without me. The crew's not going back on until tonight when it gets a little cooler, and Leo sent me back with a mess of shrimp. Thinking I might make some grits to go with them."

He dropped the bag of shrimp in the fridge, hesitating before he closed the door. The sounds weren't right. Andra hadn't come out to meet him, but hangers clashed inside their bedroom. He stepped into his mama's room, and she was sitting up in bed but not doing a thing.

His frown deepened. "What?"

Mama jerked her chin toward the back of the house in response, her lips compressed.

He took two long strides toward the next room. "Andra?"

He saw the suitcase first, and he had to grab the doorframe to keep from stumbling. The shirt slipped off his shoulder and puddled on the carpet.

She looked up at him, her eyes a little red, and tried for a smile that failed miserably. "Hi."

"Where you going?" His voice came out weak and he cleared his throat. If she was packing up with no notice, he must have said something to upset her, but he couldn't think of what.

"Jason broke his leg."

Air whooshed out of his lungs with relief, immediately chased by guilt. They weren't exactly close, because Jason didn't talk much, and he got cagey about his sister, but he was a good guy. A busted leg meant a lot of slow months of recovery, and that was hard on a working man. "Which horse?"

"Taz."

LJ flinched. It was the first colt he'd worked with on the Lawler Ranch. "Shit. I told you she was still squirrelly and I needed some more time with her."

"I know, but I left in such a hurry, I forgot to tell Jason. It's my fault." She threw a pair of jeans into the suitcase. "I need to get back. The ranch is shorthanded." She straightened and turned his way, but her eyes avoided the touch of his.

She'd opened up a lot in the last few months, but Andra still did most of her talking with her back instead of her words. And right now her spine was stretched tighter than any guitar string he'd ever tuned.

"It's time to face my responsibilities," she said.

LJ's nerves started jangling, and he gripped the doorframe tighter, the cheap wood creaking. "What does that mean?"

Her eyes skittered even farther from his. "Let's go outside."

His heart punched out a single beat that rattled his ribs. "Uh, okay."

She edged around him. Mama's eyes followed them as they passed through her room, not one of the three of them breaking the silence.

He took Andra around the back of the house, where they'd have more privacy. The hair on the back of his neck bristled, and LJ had an idea he wasn't going to like a single thing she had to say.

When she turned around again, tears glistened on her face, and the sight all but broke him.

"Why are you crying?" he whispered.

"I'm not ready," she said shakily. "Damn it, I'm not ready."

"For what?" He shook his head. "You'll go back to Montana and ride about a million hours a day to catch up. Mama will get on her feet again, and then I'll be back to help you. What's the problem?"

She looked at him, and he itched all over like he hadn't gotten rid of enough drywall dust. "You know you're not coming back to Montana."

He gritted his teeth and hunched his shoulders. It was like she could sense the arguments he'd been having with himself. Every mile on the way down here and nearly every hour since then. "I'll figure it out."

It tasted like a lie. How could he figure his way out of the family of his blood needing him in one place and the family of his heart needing him in another?

"You can't change who you are," Andra said. "I know you want to be there for your mom, for me and the horses and everybody in the world who's hurting, but you can't, LJ. You belong here. This place is your heart, built up into a city, and it needs you." She wrapped her arms over her chest, and it was the old, brittle way she used to move. "I've been so selfish. I wanted you to teach me to cook and laugh, and help me remember what safe felt like. I needed you so bad I pretended I didn't know what you needed."

Energy pulsed up through his legs, into the thick muscles of his stomach and chest. People had been telling him his whole life that what he wanted was unrealistic, and he'd managed to pull off most of it anyway. He didn't want his life dictated to him by anyone, not even the woman he loved. "So what, now you're going to tell me what *I* need?"

"Yes," she said. "Because you won't. You'd endure anything if it helped someone else, but you don't deserve that, LJ. I know you want to help me, and you did." Her voice caught, and she said it again. "You *did*. But I'm not going to let you walk away from your home and your family for me."

"I wanted you to be my family." His hands were too big, his voice too rough. He knew she was about to tell him no, and he wanted to break his own bones just to feel the pain of it.

Fresh tears welled in her eyes, blurring the brilliant green. "I came down here because I wanted to find a way to make things work between us. I had no idea how wrong I was for you, because I never really knew all of you until I came here." She gestured out toward the street. "This place is what it is because everybody knows each other's story. How could you ever have a family who didn't know everybody here? Who didn't speak the language? I don't play, LJ. I can't even sing. And if I came here, looking like I do, being who I am, and being with you . . . they'd hate me for it."

Her words warped and blistered inside his mind, peeling away in layers like the flimsy excuse they were.

"No shit." His voice came out low and dark, and when he scoffed, it did nothing to ease the tightness of his throat. "What did you think was going to happen, Andra? Life is never going to give you a montage where black kids start playing in the sprinklers with white ones and the curtain goes down on racism. You want to pretend the reason you're uncomfortable here is because you don't play the guitar, fine. The truth is you came down south, had your eyes pried open, and decided you didn't want to deal. Plain and simple."

"This has nothing to do with what I want." Her face twisted with anguish. "What I want doesn't change that I don't fit here, and it's not any easier for you up there. There's no place for us to *be*, LJ."

"So what, I'm supposed to accept that this is some kind of star-crossed thing because I'm from the city and you wear cowboy boots?" He took a step closer, eating up all the ground between them. "Well, I wear boots, too, not that you probably remember that right about now. Don't bother with another excuse, because I hear what you're saying loud and clear. My home and yours ain't the same. My people and yours ain't the same. And dealing with that is too damn hard for you." Heat seared up through his every vein, and he had to grind his teeth to keep his voice from building to a shout. "Fine. Hard ain't new for me and mine, Cassandra Lawler. When the floods come, we stay." He slapped his hand against his bare chest. "And you wash right on down the river." He threw out an arm. "So go. Go back to where it's easy, because that ain't ever going to be here."

Thirty-two

◇◇◇◇

Water.

It was all around Andra: gray concrete and silver water. The sharp flash of sunlight off windshields. She'd taken a wrong turn leaving New Orleans and ended up on a bridge over a lake so big it might as well have been the ocean. Miles of divided highway on two separate bridges left nowhere to pull over, no place to duck off the road and catch her breath. The traffic was all shoving her too fast along the road.

She could barely steer her truck, because all she could see were LJ's eyes when she'd left, dark with hurt.

Her hands tightened on the steering wheel, the light-pink hand-cuff scars around her wrists glaring in the brutal sunlight.

He'd started out as just a handsome man with gentle hands, holding a cake. He made her feel safe, and beautiful. He made her feel like it was safe to *be* beautiful.

She'd come down here for so many reasons, but mostly because she'd missed LJ, pure and pitiful. She wanted to be more to him than another person to save, but the ache of disappointment in her throat told her that part of her had still wanted to be rescued.

She wasn't fixed.

Cuddled onto his lap in the backyard shed with that lovely

after-sex lassitude, she'd thought she was done with panic attacks. And then she'd ended up on the floor all over again, frozen and helpless. Love hadn't healed her, and neither had this trip. Time passing had done nothing but torment her. All her hope had died in Gavin's dusty room. She might as well still be shackled to that same damned bed.

Andra closed her eyes, fighting tears, and then jerked them open again to track the bumper of the Chevy in front of her. She had to drive, goddamn it. Her family and her ranch were waiting. She didn't have time to pull over for a pity party.

Within a couple of days, she'd be back in her house. Back to her lonely kitchen and days of wrangling horse after horse into obedience. The hills, the pine trees. The utter emptiness of her life, the way it'd been for five long years.

Her hands started to shake, panic lancing into her chest. She couldn't go back there. Air turned to brick in her throat, and the muscles of her shoulders locked.

Shit. Not now. Not while she was driving.

She clamped her sluggish fingers harder against the wheel. As she slowed, a car passed her, a couple of kids fighting over a tablet in the back seat. She gritted her teeth, trying to move her hands just enough to steer her truck away from them. She couldn't focus on the road with her heart hammering so hard in her ears that it felt like her eardrums would burst.

The edges of her vision started to blacken from lack of oxygen. Her tires crossed the yellow line, and a horn blared as a car swerved out of her way.

Thanks to Rose, she knew the panic attacks couldn't really kill her. But right now, this wasn't a psychological trick or an illusion of suffocation. This was paralysis and thousands of pounds of steel hurtling along a narrow highway with no one here to help her regain control of her body or the truck. She was going to crash, along with any other car in her path, and that would be it. Cold water swallowing cold metal.

The bridge curved, but her hands on the steering wheel stayed locked into place. Her truck sailed through the second lane and toward the concrete barrier on the far side.

The cuffs felt hard as steel around her wrists, the cotton gag filling her whole throat. The road in front of her went vague, because she was still locked in that room. Had never left, could never escape.

Frantically, she focused all her energy on trying to move. Anything, any part of her she could control. One toe twitched in response. She curled her toes hard, even when that pressed the gas pedal harder.

No matter how tightly you tied someone, no matter how hard you choked them, they could still move their toes.

Her bumper shot sparks as it edged close enough to kiss the concrete barrier.

Fresh adrenaline ripped through her, and she remembered that moment in her room when she'd touched her body and realized it was still her own. Right now, nothing held her in place but her mind. *Her* mind.

Her hands clamped tight on the wheel, and she took the curve.

Andra inhaled air down deep in her lungs. Sweet and light and utterly under her control. She adjusted the path of the truck, as steady now as if she were holding reins.

She'd done it. Pulled herself out of a full-blown attack twice in one day, despite being stressed to the max. She grinned and pounded the dash with one fist, wishing she could call LJ. He'd just laugh and say—her stomach dropped. He wouldn't say anything to her, probably ever again.

Leaving had been the right thing to do, the best thing for him and everyone in his life. And no matter how much it hurt, she knew she was strong enough to give him that one final gift.

Andra sat back in her seat, exhausted and proud and sick to her stomach all at once. If she could wiggle her toes, she could pull herself out of the attacks, now that she knew it was possible. Even without LJ, things would be different now.

Every time she had taken more control over her life, her attacks had gotten a little weaker, a little less frequent. She'd never get back to being the carefree girl she'd been in high school. But today, she could tell she was moving ever closer to the woman she would become, and somewhere deep in her gut, that felt better. More solid.

And yet every mile she drove away from New Orleans felt like it carried her further from the future she wanted.

Thirty-three

◇◇◇◇

The Ford truck barely pulled off the highway, two tires still sitting on the white lines marking the shoulder. LJ hopped out of the bed of the pickup and grabbed his duffel, giving a little wave of thanks through the side window to the young couple who'd finally picked him up a few miles back. They smiled but didn't roll down the window to say goodbye before they took off, dust and gravel scattering in their wake.

The Lawler Ranch sign creaked in the relentless Montana wind as he passed beneath the massive log gate and started down the driveway. The big spread was deserted, just like the first day he'd ever seen the place.

Three days had passed since she'd left New Orleans, so best he could figure, Andra would have been home last night or this morning. She'd want to visit her brother, of course, but by now, she was probably riding. He turned toward the arena where he'd first seen her. As he got closer, the red walls of the barn blocked his view, but he could hear hoofbeats, the drum of them matching the thunder of his own pulse.

He'd lasted two hours after she'd left. He'd gone out back to lift weights and ended up smashing the flimsy little shed into a crooked ruin. Ty had come running up the street and hauled LJ out of the torn wreckage of sheet metal, thrown his shirt over LJ's bleeding fist. And then LJ had started to cry.

He hadn't cried in front of anyone since the first time he'd seen his house after Katrina: tipped half off its foundation, with the walls ripped open and the roof broken like an old toy. But now his life felt as unfixable as that old house. Andra wasn't coming back, and her absence sucked all the oxygen out of his chest until he couldn't breathe except in huge, shuddering gasps, tears blocking up his throat even worse.

At the sight of him, his friend had stuttered for a second and then gone coward—turned tail and run to get LJ's mother. LJ had knuckled his eyes dry before Mama came out, which was maybe why he hadn't gotten an ounce of sympathy from her. She'd raked him over the coals for letting Andra go, ordered Ty to get a tarp to cover the boxes that had been in the shed, and gone back inside. He'd been on a plane to Montana before sunset.

LJ passed into the shade of the barn, the cessation of heat nothing so dramatic as what he was used to. The air here was sharper, drier than in New Orleans. The sunlight cleaner but somehow less powerful. One of the horses whickered in greeting, and he stroked a hand down its nose without noticing which one it was. He didn't slow down as he strode out the door on the other side of the building.

She was there. Riding a horse that was all uncollected, its hindquarters sloppy and its shoulders tight and fighting her cues. Her hands on the reins looked tense, but her balance was solid, and sweet Lord was she beautiful.

The slenderest nip of waist was visible through her baggy shirt, the rays of the sun beating through old, thin fabric. A wisp of black hair fell forward from beneath her hat. He dropped his duffel and leaned his arms on the fence to watch. Maybe one of the rails creaked, maybe the air just shifted, but she turned to look at him. Even from across the arena, he could see her entire posture brighten as she recognized him.

"LJ!"

He grinned and everything got lighter: the worry, the ache in his shoulder from sleeping on concrete, and the ticktock of the charity clock, counting down the time until he had to get back. "Hey, hey, Rodeo Queen. Long time no see. Looking good out there."

But then her smile cracked and ebbed away, her hands tightening on the reins until the horse began to back up. She let go of the reins and dismounted, not looking at him.

Something dark shook LJ's gut, and he grabbed the top rail, vaulting over with a yank and pull that did nothing to dissipate the energy coursing through his whole body. He'd come all this way, and she looked the same as the last time he saw her: like it was going to make her cry, but she was going to leave him anyway.

"I should have asked," he said. "When you left New Orleans, I should have realized someone must have said something stupid to you between when I went to work and when I came home. Was it Reggie?"

She tied the horse's reins up short, letting it loose to wander in the arena.

"Mona?"

Andra pulled her back straight and walked to meet him. "It doesn't matter, LJ. Nobody could say anything to change the fact that there's no way for us to be together. Not without you sacrificing everything that means anything to you. Not without me becoming a different person."

He took it like a punch, trying not to flinch. When she'd told him all that the first time, she'd been in tears, and she hadn't sounded so certain. He'd planned an apology and a long speech refuting every possible point that might have motivated her to break up with him. In person, she was so steady and beautiful that everything he'd meant to say fell away into one bare plea.

"Tell me you don't love me," he said.

She wrapped her arms around herself. "Don't," she said raggedly. "LJ, we can't."

He swallowed. "There's only one reason for me to leave here," he said. "One reason for us not to build a herd of horses and a life together. And that's if you don't love me. Because I love you so much I'm crazy with it."

She squeezed her eyes shut, tears bleeding out from beneath her eyelashes. LJ took a long step forward and cupped her cheek in one hand, barely daring to touch her.

"Say yes," he whispered, his heartbeats counting out every second that passed as he waited for her answer.

"I can't believe you had the balls to come back here after the way you left," a male voice growled into the silence. "Now get your hands off my daughter."

Thirty-four

◇◇◇◇

LJ didn't look away from Andra's face, so pale and pretty beneath the shadow of her cowboy hat. Reality had rarely been kind to him, and yet he still found himself hoping she might answer. Instead, a tear slipped down her cheek, catching in the corner of her trembling lips. She didn't even seem to register her father's voice.

"Hey!" Bill half growled the word. "Did you hear me?"

LJ let his hand drop. Andra's silence left him empty, the earth too big and wild beneath his feet. He turned around. "I heard you. And I didn't give a damn."

Bill Lawler's face tinged red with rage. He ducked through the rails and stalked into the arena. LJ's muscles tightened, and Andra's head lifted.

"You had your chance," Bill snarled. "And you couldn't even look me in the eye."

LJ's cheek twitched as he remembered staring at the floor in the other man's office, listening to everything he wanted being snatched out of reach. "And what chance was that?" LJ cocked his head. "Was that when you yelled at me for making her laugh, or when you threatened to fire me for loving her?" He figured it hardly mattered if Andra heard it now. She'd made her choice and it hadn't been him.

At his side, she jolted. "Dad, what is he talking about?"

Bill's jaw flexed under half a beard's worth of unshaven stubble. "You can paint it any way you like. The fact is, you chose a paycheck over the girl you claim to love, just like I knew you would. Did you tell her that when she followed you halfway across the country?"

Retorts screamed through LJ's head, but that was the kind of accusation so ridiculous the only answer was a broken jaw. Except this was Andra's *father*, and of the two of them, Bill was the one she was going to listen to.

"He didn't choose anything, Dad." Andra's feet stayed planted. "I was the one who left."

"That's not what I'm talking about, Andra." Bill looked at LJ and jerked his chin toward the highway. "I grew up in a trailer park just down the road from here. I know the only people who don't care about money are the ones who have enough, like my kids."

LJ gritted his teeth, because on that small point alone, they agreed. The difference was, Bill thought because he'd gotten his hands on a little money, he had the right to dictate other people's lives.

"I saw the ambition eating at you," Bill said. "People who are just working for the weekend don't come out after sunset to fix a loose rail or check on a fidgety horse. You don't want to work on a spread like this. You want to own it, just like I did." He turned to Andra. "You've been through enough, sweetheart. I didn't want you to get your heart broken the first time you tried to date again. So I told him if he wanted you rather than a foothold in this ranch, he'd find a different job. He didn't. And after that, I never saw you two together until he took off and you told me you were going after him. Apparently, rather than showing me straight that he wasn't angling for this ranch, he started lying and sneaking around, trying to pull one over on me."

"Is that true?" Andra looked at LJ. "Did he give you some kind of ultimatum? Why didn't you just tell me? I never would have let him fire you over that. It's not like you were trying to get a ring on my finger and steal all the horses. You were just teaching me to cook, and things happened from there. We were just . . ." She trailed off, her face paling beneath her hat. "LJ?"

He swallowed. Because he hadn't just been teaching her to cook. He'd been fascinated from the first moment he'd seen her, and if he were any kind of real man, he'd have stood up for that no matter how many jobs it cost him. He could have found another way to support Mama, somehow.

Bill's face went somber. "I married your mother when we could barely afford diapers for Jason. I would have fought the flow of gravity for that woman, and that's what I wanted for you, Cassie. A man who loved you above everything. More than horses or his pride or his ambition."

"Bullshit." It was the single word LJ let escape, shaking with the power of all the things he was holding back. If this man didn't have Andra's blood running through his veins, he'd already be on the ground.

But there was no reason to keep silent anymore. Andra knew he'd lied to her dad and refused to give up his career for a chance to openly date her. Not that he thought her father would have approved no matter what he did, but what mattered was how bad it looked to Andra. If he had the chance now, he would choose her a thousand times over, but it was too late.

He had nothing left to lose, and he wasn't going to stand here and let Bill twist reality to make himself look good. LJ remembered Stacia's story too well to believe that crap. She used to live in the same trailer park down the highway. She'd pointed it out to LJ once when they'd driven to town together, told him all about Bill giving her a chance before she knew a spatula from a spark plug.

"If I were white and poor," LJ said hoarsely, "you'd have admired my guts and given me a job even if I burned every grilled cheese for a month. Even if I could barely change the oil in a truck, much less a tractor. But somehow my kind of poor means my ambition scares you instead of impressing you."

He took a long step forward.

"You think you know me? I *begged* my neighbors to take care of my mama so I could come after Andra. My uncle's been driving on bald tires for six months, and I asked him for every cent he could spare so I could get a plane ticket and not risk my truck breaking down on the way. I landed with eight bucks in my pocket, and when that wasn't enough for a bus ticket to the ranch, I hung my thumb out to strangers."

He couldn't look at Andra. It'd taken him two days of mostly walking to get through what would have been a few hours' drive, because not too many people were keen to pick up a hitchhiker who looked like him. He'd washed the smell of those days off himself with cupped handfuls of sink water in a gas station, and he'd damned well never planned to tell Andra what he'd had to do to get back to her.

"Why didn't you call me?" she said, her voice so soft it ached in his ears.

He still couldn't meet her eyes, didn't want to remind her of the angry words he'd thrown at her before she left New Orleans. Of what she'd said as soon as he got here. He knew if he'd called, she'd have told him to go home, but he'd dared to hope if she saw him in person, he might be able to change her mind.

Andra reached out and took his hand. Her fingers hesitated when she felt the fresh scabs over his knuckles, and then settled even more gently over the top of them.

LJ stopped breathing for a long moment, afraid of everything that might mean. Or might not mean. Without letting go of her, he stared down her father, because this was the truth. If that wasn't enough to win her over, he had nothing else.

"I put her before my pride, before my job, before my family—" His voice cracked, thinking of his mama recovering at home for the last three days without him. Andra clutched his hand, and he wondered if this would all backfire, if she'd hate him for leaving Mama in the care of their friends and neighbors. He swallowed and kept going, refusing to blink. "When you lied to Andra, where did you put her on your priority list, huh? Because it wasn't in front of your pride."

Bill's chin quivered slightly, his skin paling like he could feel the argument slipping away from him. "So you're going to drop your

sick mother and move here for my daughter, is that what you're telling me?"

LJ opened his mouth, and nothing came out. What could he say
to that? Because no. The answer was no. He had to go back for a
while whether or not Andra forgave him, and Bill was right. Mama
wouldn't move, and every time she ever called, he'd have to go.

"Jesus, Dad! What are you saying? It's his *mother*."

"I told you once that relationships weren't as simple as you young
people like to make them out to be," Bill said, his tone as tired as his
posture. "I told you being from different places would bring you
nothing but hurt, but you didn't care to listen. I don't want him leaving you behind crying for him. Not once, not ever again. Where are
you going to *live*, Andra?"

That was the question LJ hadn't dared to ask, but his stomach
curdled as he waited for her answer, her hand in his so far from a
promise it felt like it might vanish if he squeezed too hard.

"I don't know, but I'm not staying here. Not after everything you
did behind my back." Her voice was scathing. "Call a lawyer and
have him draw up the papers. You're buying out my share in the
ranch, and I'm taking Gracie. I'll be gone by morning."

Her father flinched like she'd hit him, but LJ forgot to watch the
rest of the other man's reaction when Andra turned to him instead.
He stared, reeling from her pronouncement. How could she say that?
The ranch was her family, her future. She'd trained or bred nearly
every horse on the place. If she left, she might as well shave off her
fingerprints and rewrite her DNA.

Her eyes only met his for a second before they fell again. "I'm
sorry," she said. "I can't tell you how sorry I am, for all of this." She
let go of his hand, caught her horse, and left.

His skin was still warm where she'd touched it. She'd reached for
him, in the middle of all that. He'd dared to hope that meant she
forgave him, that she wanted to try. But then she just let go again.

He glanced at Bill, only to see the older man's face crumple. Bill
turned his back, but not before LJ saw the glint of tears, heard the

quick throat clear he'd used himself once or twice in an attempt to salvage his dignity in a particularly low moment. He was desperate to go after Andra, but there was no chance they could figure out a future together if he left things like this. This man was her blood.

LJ pulled off his hat and stared up at the big Montana sky as he ran a hand over his hair, too thick because he hadn't taken the time to run the clippers over it before he left New Orleans. He glared at the puffy summer clouds, wishing he couldn't hear his mama's disapproval loud and clear in his head. Once, just once, he'd like to do exactly as he damn well pleased, without her opinion playing any part of it.

LJ crammed his cowboy hat back on his head and said to Bill, "I'll talk to her. She's mad, but she'll come around. Family's too important to throw away." He had no idea what else he could offer to get Andra to take a chance on a future with him, but he knew he could talk her into forgiving her father, eventually.

Bill coughed and turned so he was staring out across the acres of his own land. Not looking at LJ, but not ignoring him, either. "I appreciate the gesture, but there's no point. If she says she's signing over her part of the ranch, it's as good as done."

LJ smiled thinly. "I meant she'd talk to you again someday. Not that she'd be on this continent when she did it."

Bill choked on a sound that might have been a laugh or something more miserable.

LJ started toward the barn, then turned back. "When you gave me that choice, I should have told you where to shove it."

The corner of Bill's mouth twitched upward just for a second. "Yeah. Or maybe I should have known I never needed to ask at all."

Boot heels rapped against the concrete of the barn aisle, and the horse Andra had left tied there nickered in greeting. The strides were too far apart, too quiet to belong to her father. Andra retreated farther into the tack room, dropping onto the old plaid couch between saddle racks and flinging her hat toward the microwave and fridge that marked this as the employees' unofficial break room.

She ripped off the corner of a feed sack to blow her nose on. Quickly, so hopefully no one would hear. The footsteps paused outside the doorway. She tried to use the waxy piece of sack to wipe her nose, but the tears just kept coming. LJ came inside and closed the door.

He knelt down next to her, but for the first time since she'd known him, he didn't seem to know what to say. He just watched her with an anguish in his eyes that brought a fresh wave of tears brimming to the surface.

"I'm white, LJ." It felt like a dam breaking to finally say it out loud. "I never felt white until I was the only one who was, and it took me longer than it should have to admit I can't change all the things that means for us."

A shadow flickered across his face, but he didn't move away. "That's nothing new, Andie-girl. I been thinking about that since the first day I stepped foot in your kitchen." He shook his head. "It'll be some kind of the same everyplace I go. If I cared about that, I never would have kissed you that first time."

"I kissed *you*. It's not like you had a choice in the matter."

He smiled sadly. "You just keep on thinking that, Rodeo Queen." His hand lifted toward a stray piece of hair that had fallen across her cheek, but then fell again, the space between them remaining unbridged. "Tell me what I have to do, Andra. I'll do it. You know I will."

Her breath caught hard and she shot to her feet. "That's the problem! I'm not letting you move to Montana just so you can take all of this on your shoulders, with my idiot dad and the stupid people in town, all so I don't have to face—"

"That's not why." He rose to his full height. His interruption was quiet, but she broke off anyway, to let him speak. "I should have explained it better when you were telling me all the reasons you didn't think I would come back to Montana. It's just . . . I was mad and I made a mess of things." His eyes were dark and intent on hers. "New Orleans is me—you were right about that. But it's not all of me. There's shit there I don't want to deal with all the time, like hurricane season, or those reporters filming the Graviers' old house, or cops hassling me for nothing. Sometimes I need to get out of the city and smell the pine trees, have nothing on the schedule but horses to ride." He stroked the edge of his thumb down her cheek. "I can't be here all the time, but I want to be."

She bit her lip. Everything he was saying sounded so perfect she could hardly stand to hear it.

"You said back in New Orleans that none of this was about what you wanted," he said, his voice that low, rumbly tone it got whenever she was upset. "What if it was?"

She froze, her gaze locked on his chest because she was afraid to look at him.

"You keep talking about everybody else. About the places we live, the jobs we do. I'm here because you haven't said once that you don't want me." He shook his head, his voice so light, so gentle even now. "All you have to do is say it, Andra. I'll go."

Her hands knotted into fists. After everything her father had just thrown at him and everything he'd gone through to get here, she couldn't lie about her feelings. But if she told him the truth, it would only hurt him more when the world tore them apart.

The silence stretched, every second clawing at her like the ragged edges at the beginning of a panic attack. Then LJ turned toward the door. She grabbed his wrist, hanging on with all her strength.

"I love you." The confession burst out of her in pure, ugly fear, because she couldn't bear seeing him leave. It was the only reason she had left first. But once the words were out, her whole body sagged. There was no reason to try to lie now, no way to hide it. "I love you so much," she whispered, the words catching in her throat like a prayer that was almost too sacred to voice.

LJ took one rough breath and kissed her. His hands trembled where they cradled her face, and she covered them with her own, her heart pounding so hard it was like it wanted to break out of her chest and beat within his.

"God," he gasped against her mouth. "That scared half the life out of me. I thought you were going to tell me no."

She wrapped her arms around him and shook her head against his chest. "Never. It's everything else that I'm not sure about. You've never been the problem."

He kissed her forehead, her hair, laughing like it was the only way to handle the same relief that was making her giddy. "You just disowned your daddy over me, sweet girl. I think I might be the problem."

"Because he's a jackass." She scowled, burying her face back in his chest to soothe herself with the scent of him. "Not your fault."

"Well, it's still something we're going to have to deal with if we live here. And I think we should."

She squeezed her eyes shut and groaned, but she was smiling, too, because she was back in his arms again and everything felt better there. "So you're a gold digger after all. I should have known. The prettiest ones always are."

LJ didn't laugh. He pulled back and ducked his head to catch her gaze. "If we leave now, it'll fester. You'll start to miss your dad, but when you call, it'll be awkward. All this'll be sitting under the table every Thanksgiving, every Christmas, and he'll hate me a thousand times more than he did before." The corner of his mouth kicked up. "But if we stay right now, when he's feeling sorry and small, he'll end up kissing my ass for the next decade to make up for it."

She blinked as she tried to determine if he'd just said what she thought he had. He winked, and she burst out laughing. "LJ Delisle, you ought to be outlawed."

He shrugged one thick shoulder. "Your daddy ain't cruel. He's just ignorant. One's no better than the other, but the second can be fixed."

"But what about New Orleans? I mean, not just your mom, but your home." She caught his hand, her eyes dropping. "I wish we could have had more time there. Seemed like with the people who didn't approve of me, I never made a dent in changing their minds, but when it was just me and you or Tash and Ty, I loved that place. As much as I love the ranch, though for different reasons."

"Yeah," he said slowly, "I been thinking about that." He straightened to his full height. "My mama's never going to kick lupus for good, Andra, and she won't even talk about moving up here with me. Claims she doesn't need any help." He shook his head. "But it seems like neither me or you fits just right in one place, so maybe we ought to live in two."

Her brow creased, even as hope fluttered in her throat. "How? We're horse trainers, LJ. It's not exactly a mobile profession."

"Right. So when Mama needs us, maybe we trailer a big load of horses down to my uncle's ranch outside New Orleans. Do our training there for part of the year and take turns looking out for Mama." He tried out a smile. "Horses may be heavy, but they are portable."

She hesitated. "I mean, of course we could work them just as well there, but that's a lot of moving stock around."

"Sure, if you look at it that way." He played with her fingers. "But most horses get all their training in one place, and then they go bug-eyed when you try to stuff them in a trailer and go to a show. Lawler horses are bred to show, and that means travel. What if we raised them that way from the start? Get them used to trailers and being ridden in new places."

The idea tugged at her. From a training standpoint, it was a unique idea, one so effective and bizarre that only LJ would propose it. It felt unexpected and right, just like the first time he walked into her kitchen.

"Do you think we really could?"

"I think I'd train horses on the moon if that's where you wanted to live," LJ said. "Though that whole gravity thing might turn out to be a problem."

She started to laugh, and he kissed her right in the middle of it, so her smile got all tangled up with his, the warmth in her chest rising until she wasn't sure if it was his body heat or the flood of her own relief. She wrapped her arms around him and gripped the back of his shirt, knuckles throbbing with the ferocity of her hold. She didn't have to let go. Thank God, she didn't have to let go.

"I was just trying to do the right thing when I left," she whispered. "I never meant to hurt you."

"I know, sweet girl. I know it." He kissed her again, and she stopped worrying that it was all about to be over, and melted into him.

When they eventually parted for air, she let him go just long enough to lock the door. Not that it would help much, since all the employees had a key. LJ must have been thinking the same thing, because he took a tack trunk and shoved it in front of the door. She grabbed his wrist and tugged him backward until they hit the plaid couch. A button popped off his shirt when she pulled it off his head, and he threw it aside as she went after his jeans. LJ kicked off his boots and lay down, Andra snuggling into his chest.

She couldn't believe he was really here, that LJ had followed her thousands of miles north, even knowing that when her father found out, it would cost him his job.

She laid a kiss on his shoulder, his collarbone, his strong throat. Taking her time and enjoying him the way she hadn't gotten a chance to in his backyard shed. The feel of his body was so much more than she would have known to wish for. Thick muscle with just the right amount of cushion to make it comfortable to curl against him, yet firm enough he always felt steady. Powerful, but in a casual way that was so quintessentially *LJ*.

Her hands roved down his body, slowing to stroke more gently when she reached his erection. She loved this part of him. The gorgeously smooth skin, the way it filled her hand. The way his desire translated so honestly through it that she could *see* how much he wanted her. All that time when she'd been yearning for him, wanting more and afraid to take it, she'd been certain that was the one part of LJ that would always scare her. But there was no part of him that didn't love her, and that made fear impossible.

LJ slipped his hands under the back of her shirt. "I want to feel you against me," he whispered. "I don't think anybody's going to come in here, but I won't do it if you don't want me to."

"I want you." It was the most truth she could pack into three words, because love could be a knife that never stopped twisting, but she'd chosen him over her father because she didn't just love him. She was going to do something about it.

He undressed her.

She relaxed more with every layer gone, with every time his hands came back to her skin. This was exactly what he'd been doing since the day their eyes had first met. Stripping away her reserve, her fear, and her doubts with every one of his smiles and winks and laughs. She melted into his hands and knew that for all the years of her life, this was the place she'd been heading toward.

His breath came out on a groan that sounded like her name, and she inhaled the scent of leather and horses that surrounded them, perfectly at ease.

Andra curled her hips against him, pleasuring herself even as she enjoyed him lengthening for her, his desire rising to meet hers. She slipped a hand between them and wrapped her fingers around the thick base of him, loving the way his head fell back on a quiet moan. She braced a knee on the couch and lifted herself up until the swollen head of his cock was poised right at her entrance, teasing the hollowness inside her that squeezed and begged, waiting for him.

"Slow down," LJ gasped, cupping the back of her neck. His biceps bunched and trembled, belying his words when he said, "We don't have to rush. I don't want to risk setting off an attack, okay? You listen to my voice and take it as slow and easy as you need, sweetheart." His dick flexed, sending a trill of pleasure bolting up inside of her.

She sank down, her scalp tingling at how smoothly they came together, because she knew how much it turned him on to make her wet. She took two inches of him, the stretch of his cock a beautiful kind of pain. Four inches.

She leaned down and whispered over his lips, "I don't have to go

slow. I know you, LJ Delisle. My body knows you." She took all of
him with one confident jerk of her hips, and he gasped at the jolt of
sensation.

She relaxed, easing around his cock and holding him inside her
body until they were both comfortable. Once he exhaled, she squeezed
her muscles around his erection in a small, secret caress. His eyelids
fluttered, and his mouth opened on an airless sound. Andra bent closer
so her nipples would tickle across his chest, laying kisses on both of his
high, gorgeous cheekbones. On his temple, where his pulse beat so
gratifyingly fast.

She cupped his cheek in her hand. "I need you deeper. And I need
you to hold me."

He kissed her, gasping his answer into her mouth. "Yes."

He pulled out and turned her onto her side, both of them barely
fitting on the narrow couch. She trusted him with her weight as he
pulled her back into his chest, pillowing her head on his arm. Her
bottom fit neatly into the curve of his hips, and his hand stroked
down her bare breasts and over her stomach. He flirted around the
edges of where she wanted him, but then moved to clasp her thigh
instead.

"Lift up a little, sweet girl." When she did, he fit his knee between
hers and lifted it up, the hair on his leg teasing her inner thigh. "Ah,
God," he growled. "You got no idea what it does to me when you let
me do that." His cock thrust out between both their legs, and he
fisted it in one hand. "I want you to get me all wet." He teased his
erection over her entrance, all her muscles tight to bowing as he
moved higher.

Then his slick cock touched her clit, and she clamped her teeth
together.

"You're close, aren't you?" He put the hint of a rock into his hips,
rubbing her in tiny little pushes, and she couldn't . . . she couldn't—

She moaned, her body curling forward as waves of sensation
bolted through her. LJ's knee kept her legs pinned open, and he thrust
into her, the clasp of her orgasm clamping down on his dick. His hips

snapped forward, his erection hitting that deep, secret place that burst white stars behind her eyelids.

She cried out, and LJ's hand came over her mouth, muffling the sound.

"You moan all you want, gorgeous," his slow drawl said in her ear. "You scream all over my hand. Tell me what I do to you."

His hand over her mouth had scared her once before, but now it felt erotic, keeping her ragged breaths a sexy little secret just between them. She kissed his palm.

When his next thrust hit home, a cry ripped out of her like a begging shout. Tingles raked down the naked front of her body, and his warmth enveloped her back. His arms held her safe, and his cock jolted pleasure through her over and over again until she couldn't decide if she was coming or he was, if she'd peaked twice or never stopped. Her tongue went dry and her throat raw, and his hand still drank her moans.

Liquid heat melted through her, and he twitched, the last burst of his release lost in her body. She sank against him, her muscles unclenching into limpness one by one, in perfect contentment.

Kisses smoothed over her tangled hair, and LJ's hand moved away from her mouth. His knuckles stroked her cheek. "How do you feel about baking cakes, Andie-girl?"

She blinked and tried to crank that question through her rusty brain. "Um, why?"

He nibbled on the back of her neck, rich laughter riding underneath his voice when he said, "Because we owe your employees ten or twelve to make up for the little sound show we gave them."

She squeezed her eyes shut. "Oh shit. I meant to be quiet. You don't think my dad heard, do you?"

"Nah, doubt he stuck around. Besides, big dick like mine, no way you could have helped yourself."

"You're terrible." She laughed. "Never change, okay?"

"No worries, darlin'. They don't shrink with age, far as I can tell." Carefully, he pulled out. "You okay?"

She scooted up to sitting, glancing around. "I cannot believe we just did it in the tack room. There's no way to get out of here without everybody knowing what we've been doing, and Stacia will be giving us crap for the next twenty years. I really didn't think this through."

"You're crazy kinky, girl. It's all I can do to keep up." LJ reached down and plucked his fallen cowboy hat from the floor, dropping it onto his head with a grin and a languorous stretch of his naked body. "I think you said you wanted me to wear this next time, but you got a little too vigorous for it to stay on." He linked his hands behind his head and grinned.

She couldn't stop giggling, even as she drank in the sight of him. "If you're going to wear that hat, I'm going to need a bigger couch for our second round."

LJ bent his knee so his ankle wasn't hanging over the end of the couch. "I wouldn't argue with that for a hot second. Speaking of, why is it they design planes in miniature? Don't adult-sized people ever fly anyplace?"

She winced, feeling guilty he'd put himself through that just for her. "I never thought of that. I bet you don't fit that great in airplane seats, do you?"

"Still got the imprint of the seat in front of me in my kneecaps. Plus my shoulders were taking up half the spot next to me that was supposed to belong to a nice old lady named Marge. Cost me my mama's second-best cupcake recipe to get her to stop glaring, and if Mama ever finds out I gave it away, she'll whup my ass for sure."

Andra burst into laughter, starting up all over again every time she pictured him charming a hostile elderly woman with a cupcake recipe.

When she eventually quieted, there were just the soft sounds of horses in the stalls outside, the scent of hay and sex, and one big, beautiful man—a whole lifetime of unlived years quivering between them like a question.

"Are you sure we can do this?" she whispered. "Louisiana and

Montana, my family and yours, all the . . . everything that comes with that?"

"I know it's not perfect, Andra. But nothing is, not even me." He smiled, so brightly it almost covered the uncertainty in his dark eyes. "What do *you* think?"

She lay down next to him and pulled him close so in this moment of all moments, he couldn't feel alone. She knew the road they had ahead of them. It was bumpy, but it wasn't impossible. They'd been through so much worse, back before they'd found each other.

"I think some things are better than perfect." She smiled back. "And you make me believe in all of them."

Epilogue

◇◇◇◇

Two years later

LJ kicked the dust off his boots and nodded to his mama, who was sitting on her porch with her purse in her lap. "Going someplace?"

Mama pursed her lips, like she did when she was trying to hide a smile. "As a matter of fact, I'm headed down to Mona's."

"Want me to walk with you?"

"I'm perfectly fine and you know it." She pushed to her feet. "You could have been back in Montana three weeks ago if you didn't hate the snow so much."

It was probably true. Since his paychecks had gotten bigger, she'd been able to cut back her hours at the restaurant, and her lupus was responding well to the extra rest. She didn't have too many flare-ups these days, but Andra and LJ had gotten spoiled on spending winters in New Orleans even when she was well. The horses they brought with them seemed happier in the warmer temperatures, too.

"Can I help it if I wanted three more weeks with my beautiful mama?" He slung an arm around her shoulders and grinned. "And yeah, snow in Montana's up to your belt buckle this time of year. I don't mind skipping that."

She hugged him and then stepped back to adjust the collar of his shirt, even though it was both dusty and sweaty from a day of working Lawler horses at his uncle's ranch.

"I'm not headed to church, Mama," he protested, squirming a little.

"You might want to look nice. Andra's in there with a surprise," Mama said in an undertone.

What kind of surprise required his mother to wait out on the porch?

He glanced at the house, his pulse perking up. Last year in Montana, Andra had decided she wanted to be more comfortable naked, so they'd cranked the heat and she'd stopped wearing clothes in their cottage for a month.

It was pretty well his favorite thing that had ever happened.

"I'd, ah, better go see what it is," he said, edging away from his mother's fingers.

She gave him a stern look. "Don't you laugh at her now, Lyndon Johnson. What seems funny to one person doesn't necessarily seem funny to another."

"I promise I won't laugh." He'd promise most anything right now if it'd get her to turn loose of his collar so he could see about his surprise.

She patted his shoulder. "Good. Now I'm going to go have a nice, long visit with Mona. And she might want me to stay for dinner."

"Okay, have a good time." He was already halfway up the porch steps, loving his mama more by the second, but his phone rang in his pocket before he made it to the door. He checked the screen and gritted his teeth against a groan when he saw Bill Lawler's name. What was his luck with getting cock-blocked by parents today?

But he knew he'd answer, because Bill called him mostly for business matters, and he liked that he'd earned that respect from the older man.

When he'd first come back to Montana, Bill had swapped hostility for chilly politeness. As they fixed a few miles of fence, that politeness had eased to a working rapport. The first time they'd shod a horse together, Bill had actually cracked a joke—and admitted that LJ could shape a shoe faster than he ever could. He hadn't thought,

years ago when he sat sweating in the guest chair of Bill's office, that
he'd ever be comfortable sharing a beer with the other man. A lot of
things had changed since then.

"Hey, Bill. How're things back at the ranch?"

"Fine, good. Except Stacia won't lay off about that terrible blood
pressure diet my idiot doctor told her about. How's Rose? Did that
cough of hers turn into anything more?"

"No, the doctor said it was nothing. Thanks for asking, though."

Ever since Mama had visited Montana last summer, Bill was always checking up on her. She hadn't been fond of Lawler Ranch. She
thought it was a howling wilderness rather than a simple ten-minute
drive to town. However, she and Bill got along like they'd been raised
in side-by-side cribs.

"Well, I'm glad to hear she's doing well, because I've got a colt
who hates trailers."

"Uh-huh." LJ tried to sound neutral. As much as it gave him a nice,
warm feeling to have Andra's father calling him for help, it wasn't exactly unusual for a colt to hate a horse trailer.

"Don't use that politician voice with me, Delisle. This colt would
drive you through two rosaries and halfway to drink, and if I'm
wrong, I owe you a bottle of Bushmills."

LJ grinned. "Hates 'em a little more than normal, does he? Make
it a bottle of Maker's Mark, and you've got yourself a deal."

"Well, I'd ship him down to you and call that a thirty-dollar bottle well spent, but I can't exactly get him in a trailer, now can I?"

Ah, so he didn't just need help; he was starting to miss his daughter and was ready for the two of them to start making their way back
west. LJ let him off the hook easy, mostly because he wanted to hang
up the phone and practice looking surprised for Andra.

"I think we were planning on heading north for the season soon
anyway. Save that colt and that bottle of bourbon for me, and we'll
see you next weekend or so."

"Sounds good. Give my daughter a hug for me."

LJ glanced at his phone. "I, uh . . . I definitely will." Man to man, he and Bill got along decently, but it still caught him off guard on the rare occasions when Bill said something approving like that about LJ's relationship.

LJ stuck his phone back in his pocket and brushed off thoughts of his boss before he went inside.

In the back of the house, a door slammed. "Shit! Crap, crap, crap, I'm not ready!"

He stopped in the midst of toeing off his boots. "Want me to go out and come back in?"

Andra poked her head out of the front bedroom and scowled at him. "Rose gave it away, didn't she?"

"No!" LJ said. Andra raised a skeptical eyebrow. She was wearing eyeliner, which both made her eyes even more beautiful and seemed to indicate that something about tonight was special. LJ decided he liked eyeliner. "Well, she did say very loudly that she was going to Mona's. Why, was there something to give away?"

She came out of his mother's room, one hand still hidden behind the doorframe. She wasn't naked, but she was wearing a short denim skirt and tooled cowboy boots with turquoise flames up the sides, plus a silky little tank top. That outfit was definitely the next best thing to nothing at all.

LJ gave her his best smile, trying to coax her a little farther away from the door so he could see what she was hiding. "I really will go out and come back in, and I'll look real surprised when I do it, too."

She shook her head and laughed. "No, it's okay. I was going to— but it's fine. Just sit down. And close your eyes."

He pulled one of the chairs away from the table and sat, clasping his hands over his belt, then changing his mind and propping them on his armrests. Just in case this was the kind of surprise she might need to sit on his lap for.

Andra's surprises had become a constant in the last two years, one of the things that stayed the same no matter whether they were in Louisiana or Montana. She said she liked surprising him because he gave the most satisfying reactions. Other than the time with the live lobster, he supposed that was probably true.

The piano bench scraped, and he worked to keep from looking disappointed that she was still so far away. "Any chance I can get a kiss before my surprise?"

"I—just let me do this, LJ, okay? I didn't think I'd be this nervous."

His eyebrows ticked up a bit. Nervous? When it was just the two of them in the house? He listened sharply for any kind of clue, a little tempted to sneak a peek. But he didn't have to listen long before he heard the first four chords of "The House of the Rising Sun."

His eyes popped open, and Andra grinned at him, her long black hair brushing the curved body of Ty's acoustic guitar. Her fingers stuttered, but she looked down and picked up the chord progression again, only a little halting.

"Hot damn." He draped his wrists over his knees, unable to stop grinning. "I didn't think there was a thing in the world that could make you any sexier, Andie-girl, but that guitar . . ."

"Don't go getting hard over the guitar. It's Ty's, and I don't think he'd appreciate that."

She slowed down a touch but managed to keep up the chords even when she was talking, and his chest swelled with pride.

She beamed at him. "Do you recognize the song?" She sang, "*There is a house in New Orleans . . .*"

"I get you," he said, his voice a little hoarse. How long must it have taken her to practice this, all for him?

He tried to wait for her to finish, but he was out of his seat two chords before the end. He brushed the long strands of her hair back away from the guitar and kissed her. Slow and languid, because too often these days they ended up with quick pecks on their way past each other. He should take more time to sink into the taste of her like this, their tongues playing together, comfortable and teasing all at once.

When the guitar started biting into his ribs, he pulled away and kissed the tip of her pert little nose. "I love you, sweet girl. And just so we're clear, I loved you even before you learned just enough music to make me look good."

She exploded with laughter and shoved him away. "Oh, you caught me. This was all about making you feel better about how you play. Especially since Ty has you beat on a guitar even on your best day."

He clapped a hand over his heart. "You're killing me, girl. A man's ego is a delicate thing, you know."

She snorted. "Maybe some men's, but certainly not yours. Thing's as big as Texas and twice as tough."

He laughed and turned toward the refrigerator. "We ought to have a celebration dinner after that. What are you in the mood for?"

She caught his hand. "Hold on. There's more, and . . ." She wet her lips and tugged at his hand. "Maybe just sit here with me for it?"

Her voice was too small to tease her, so he dropped cross-legged on the floor in front of her. "Sure I will."

He pretended to look up her skirt, and she slapped halfheartedly at him, laughing. When he settled down, she carefully placed her fingers on the frets like she'd practiced this song a lot.

This one was slower. He listened to several chords, nodding along, and when she peeked up at him, he smiled. "It's nice. Keep playing."

Uncertainty flickered in her eyes, and she stopped midsong and started again, watching his face this time. He broadened his grin, hoping that would suffice until he figured out what the hell she was playing.

The song finished, and he smiled even harder as he reached for her. "Dang, girl. It's a good thing my mama's gone, because that was gorgeous. I mean—"

Relief suddenly washed all the tension out of her expression. "You don't have any idea what I'm playing, do you?"

"Not one tiny clue."

She groaned and pushed at his shoulder. "Come on, LJ, the wedding march?"

"The—" He froze, his eyes flying up to hers.

She slid off the bench, the guitar bumping the floor as she knelt before him, taking both his hands. "Lyndon Johnson Delisle, I want you to be my husband."

He swallowed, but his voice still came out scratchy, just barely above a whisper. "Now, why'd you have to say something so pretty and mess it up with my big ugly name?"

She squeezed his hands. "LJ, you don't have to make a joke. If you don't want to get married, you just say so, and we'll figure something else out, okay?"

He shook his head and swallowed, but this time it didn't do a bit of good. He just had to nod. Fast, two or three times so she couldn't mistake how much he wanted to be married to her.

He ducked his head and pressed her hands to the back of his suddenly hot neck, holding his hands hard over hers to hide their shaking.

He wanted to pull every dollar out of his bank account and lay them at her feet so she'd know the secret he'd been keeping. He'd been saving for months, but he didn't have half enough for a ring worthy of her. He wasn't about to ask until he did.

Her thumbs made a slow, soothing sweep over the back of his neck. "If you're this upset about the proposal, you're going to be flat on your back after the next surprise. It's . . . a little weird."

He swiped his face against the shoulder of his shirt before he lifted his head and mustered a shaky grin. "Sweetheart, if you want to be on top after saying something like that to me, you surely can be."

"There he is," she whispered, and leaned in for a kiss. "Thought I scared you into a heart attack." She set aside the guitar. "Don't be mad, okay?"

"Way I feel now, I'm not sure I could work up to a good mad before next Christmas." His whole body was surging with waves of heat and electricity. Andra Lawler was going to be his wife. She hadn't been scared off by all the hardships of blending two very separate lives together, and now she wanted to make it permanent. Hell, she wanted it enough she couldn't even wait for him to save up for her ring.

"Okay, well, brace yourself." She opened the hinged top of the piano bench. "Ty would only loan me the guitar on one condition. That if you said yes, you'd wear this when you returned the instrument."

Out of the piano bench, she pulled a filmy little veil, its tiara studded all the way around with tiny plastic penises, punching triumphantly toward the sky.

LJ stared at it. "You drive a hard bargain, Andie-girl."

She bit her lip. "I could maybe tell him I lost it . . ."

"Not a chance in hell." He stuffed the penis tiara onto his head, the veil tickling his neck, and pulled her up to standing. "Everybody in the neighborhood is about to know you're marrying me. And wearing this thing, nobody is ever going to forget it."

ACKNOWLEDGMENTS

This book took a lot of help from a lot of people. All my thanks to the following folks:

To Naomi Davis, for being a stellar agent and fighting fiercely for all my books. This book is only on shelves today because you believed in it and put all your energy behind it at a time when many people would have hung it up for something safer. Thank you for helping me come up with the new ending, and giving me a necessary nudge to extend that one scene that shall remain unnamed. You make a killer muse.

To Kristine Swartz, for giving my book a home and the absolutely perfect title, and for knowing its complicated soul right away—you already knew how it should be presented without me having to say a word. You've been a dream to work with.

To Becca Wolf, for letting me borrow your wealth of horse knowledge, which outstrips my own severalfold, and for choosing the perfect location for Wild Falls, Montana.

To James McNorton III, for speaking so honestly, kindly, and openly to me about your experience with desegregation and race issues in Florida, California, and Idaho. You helped so much to inform the experience of my own fictional characters, and all remaining mistakes are my own.

To Nic Stone, for helping me get deeper into the experience of my characters than I was capable of doing on my own, and for articulating the issues with kindness and humor and an immense amount of compassion. This book is vastly better for your influence, but again, I'm certain I've still made mistakes and they're all my own.

To Keyanna Butler, for all your help and insight on early drafts of this book.

To Layla Reyne, Andrea Contos, Suja Sukumar, and C. L. Polk for reading and adding invaluable comments to early versions of this book.

To Sandra Lombardo, for being my longtime favorite beta reader.

To Heather Van Fleet, for your endless enthusiasm for these characters, and for prompting the penis tiara epilogue. You were so right.

To Claire Zion, for all your excitement and hard work on this project.

To the Lower Ninth Ward Living Museum, for keeping record of the firsthand accounts of Hurricane Katrina that informed much of the detail work in this book.

To my amazing writing community on Twitter and in Pitch Wars, who keep me from feeling alone in the crazy world of publishing.

To my husband, who always knows exactly the right thing to say. Maybe someday you'll write a book on the proper care and feeding of Writer Wives!

And last and very most, thanks to Katie Golding (aka Goldnox), my partner in this whole writing journey. For helping with every sentence and every hard day and being excited about every tiny milestone with me. For having to build an autocorrect shortcut into your phone to save your thumbs because we were celebrating about this book deal for so many days in a row. From A Modest Proposal to fanfic to signing multi-book deals in the same year, we've done all of this together, and we've pulled off every long-shot dream we dared to have. We did it, girl. We really, really did it.

AUTHOR'S NOTE

All the details I used for LJ and his friends' experiences after Hurricane Katrina are taken from true stories. I wish I could say they weren't true, and that those things had never happened.

The grocery store in the Lower Ninth is real, as is the date that it opened: November 2014. The man who opened it has paid for it with his life savings, which he saved up from a lot of working-class jobs. Frequently running it at a loss, he's done an incredible job of trying to provide this neighborhood with the goods that it needs. The portrayal of it in this book is fictional, and meant to highlight the desperation of the circumstances in the Lower Ninth even many years after the flood, but Burnell Cotlon should be commended for everything he's done to stock the shelves of that store.

The episode with the police shooting a supposed "looter" is based on the death of Henry Glover. The officers in question were convicted of various charges for the incident and jailed, though the appeals and retrial process for each of them continue to be contentious and politically charged even now, thirteen years later. Many believe the white officers have escaped consequences for their actions due to the racially charged nature of the crime.

During the hurricane, several white people in Algiers Point started shooting black people on sight. The "shooting anything darker than a paper bag" was taken from a direct quote of a man who was charged with the unprovoked shooting of three people. His trial was delayed over a dozen times before he finally pled guilty in 2018.

After Katrina, I read accounts of people unable to locate family members for up to eighteen months. Some friends never saw each other again and never knew if the other had lived or died. Around seven hundred people are still unaccounted for to this day.

Photograph of the author by Chris Holcomb

Michelle Hazen is a nomad with a writing problem. Years ago, she and her husband swapped office jobs for seasonal gigs and moved out on the road. As a result, she wrote most of her books with solar power in odd places, including a bus in Thailand, a golf cart in a sandstorm, and a beach in Honduras. Currently, she's addicted to *The Walking Dead*, hiking, and Tillamook cheese.

CONNECT ONLINE

michellehazenbooks.com
facebook.com/michellehazenauthor
twitter.com/michellehazen

Ready to find
your next great read?

Let us help.

Visit prh.com/nextread